FOREVER BOY

THE FOREVER SAGA
BOOK 1

MICHAEL J BOWLER

1

THE MYSTERIOUS BOY

Isaac spotted a boy he'd never seen watching him as he wrangled a flying disc from high up in a maple tree. He gripped the flying disc and squinted against the setting sun, his gaze drawn to the new boy, who sported brown hair that fell in waves down his back. His old-fashioned ankle-length coat had a cloak attached, and it fluttered in the breeze. The boy looked back at Isaac, his eyes seemingly fixed on him to the exclusion of all else.

Slightly disconcerted, Isaac slid the ring-shaped disc over one arm and clambered down branch by branch. As soon as he dropped to the ground, two eager young boys grabbed the disc and scampered away toward town without a word of thanks.

"That was most inconsiderate of those youngsters," said the strange boy as he approached, "to not express gratitude for your assistance, especially after you volunteered to retrieve their disc." He stopped in front of Isaac and set down his leather bag, a valise—at least that's what Isaac thought it was called. It looked like an antique gym bag.

"That's how it is." Isaac shrugged, then after a moment added, "Wait, you saw what happened?"

"Yes," the boy replied. "I've been observing you." He wasn't tall, about Isaac's height of five six. His voice, much like Isaac's own, sounded on the verge of adolescence, having perhaps just begun the change, but still boyish, and he had an accent of some sort Isaac couldn't place. It had traces of British, but something else was mixed in.

"Why were you watching me?" Isaac shifted uncomfortably. The other boy's light brown eyes seemed to peer right through him.

"I was quite impressed when you assisted those young children. Most boys our age would dismiss them with a curt word or two." He extended his right hand. "I am Drágan Albescu."

"Your name is Dragon? That's epic."

"Sorry to disappoint, but it is spelled D-R-A-G-A-N, with an accent over the first A."

"Still, it's the coolest name in Millwood," Isaac gushed. "I'm Isaac Foster."

They shook hands and Isaac felt the boy's strong grip, but he couldn't take his eyes off Drágan's hair. He tilted his head and almost gasped at how long it was—nearly to the boy's waist.

"Your hair is amazing," he gushed.

"Thank you. It has not been cut in some years."

"No kidding." Isaac chuckled. "I never had my hair real long. I don't think I'd want to spend so much time washing it."

"It can be a burden, but there are reasons I keep it the way I do."

Isaac could tell Drágan would provide no more details on that subject.

"I like your accent," Drágan said in a conversational tone.

Isaac pulled a face. "I didn't know I had one."

"Oh, yes," Drágan replied. "You pronounce the letter R at the end of a word as an *ah* sound. For example, instead of Foster, it sounded like Fostah. I like it."

Isaac smiled. Drágan was unlike anyone he'd ever met. "Did you just move here? Where's your parents?"

"I'm new to Maine, but, alas, I am an orphan."

"Oh, I'm sorry, man. Who you here with?"

"I'm traveling alone."

"Yeah? You look my age."

"I am fourteen as of my last birthday."

Isaac grinned. "Cool. I just turned fourteen last week."

"Congratulations on your birthday."

"Thanks."

"Perhaps you know of a boarding house in town where I may lodge during my stay?"

Everything about Drágan confused Isaac, and yet everything also intrigued him.

"Um, yeah, I do, but, uh, if you, you know, want company, I have an extra bed in my room. My mom used to have foster kids, for which I got made fun of at school cause my last name is Foster, but, um, anyway, I bet my mom would love to have you stay, and I know I'd like the company. You wanna have dinner at my house and we can ask?"

Drágan's perfectly trimmed eyebrows rose in surprise. "We have only just become acquainted, and yet you would have me in your home?"

Isaac shrugged. "My mom says I'm a good judge of people."

"I am, as well," Drágan replied, "and I shall be honored to dine with you." He picked up his large valise from the ground. "Truth be told, I'm rather hungry."

"Follow me."

The boys left behind the expanse of tall, deciduous trees and strolled across a bridge overlooking the placid Abenaki River, named, Isaac explained, after one of the five Native American tribes to still live in Maine. After passing over the river, they headed up a street fronting a row of houses, most in the Victorian style and quite old. The narrow street, which had no room for parking in front of the houses, wound around into the downtown area.

"There's my house," Isaac said, pointing to a white, two-story Victorian without fancy adornments or cupolas. In back sat a large barn, which was painted a dark red color and rose to the height of the house. With the onset of dusk, tall trees cast long shadows across the roof.

"That barn is a garage on the bottom, and on the top floor is a rec room. My mom holds parties there sometimes, but mostly it's for me to play games in."

Drágan's eyes surveyed the house and barn appraisingly as a car drove past. The driver waved to Isaac, and he waved back.

"A friend of yours?"

"Naw. He works at the drugstore. In this town, everyone pretty much knows everyone."

"Much like the village where I was born."

Isaac was about to ask where, but they'd arrived at his house. He steered Drágan up the cracked driveway to a side door and they entered.

"Mom? I'm home."

"In the kitchen, honey" came his mom's voice.

Just inside the door, there was a hallway leading around past an adjacent sitting room to the kitchen. Directly in front as they entered were numerous coat hooks on the wall, very useful during snowy winters. Isaac shrugged off his parka and slipped it onto a hook with ease.

"You can leave your coat here."

Drágan slipped out of his overcoat and hung it on a hook.

Isaac felt the material. It was thick and rough, and he liked the ankle-length style.

"I have owned this coat for many years."

Isaac stopped admiring the coat to gaze questioningly at Drágan. How many years could he have had it since it fit him perfectly?

"I hear voices, Isaac," his mother called from the kitchen. "Who's with you?"

"A friend, Mom."

He gestured for Drágan to follow. They rounded a corner and passed through the sitting room with an old wood burning stove. Beside it was Isaac's favorite reclining chair. On cold, snowy days, he'd curl up within its comforting softness and devour book after book.

He led Drágan into the kitchen, where his mom stood at the

counter chopping vegetables. She wore an apron and had her shoulder-length brunette hair tied back off her pleasant face. She broke into a warm smile.

"Mom, this is Drágan Albescu."

Drágan stepped forward and bowed gallantly. "It is my great pleasure to meet you, Mrs. Foster."

She was taken aback by his greeting, but her smile grew ever broader. "Why thank you, Drágan. What an exotic name and your clothes are amazing. Your whole appearance, really."

"Thank you," Drágan replied.

"I invited Drágan for dinner," Isaac interjected. "Is that okay?"

"Of course it is," Penelope replied. "Your friends are always welcome."

"Except I don't have any," mumbled Isaac.

Drágan eyed him but focused on his mom. "I am an accomplished chef if you'd like some assistance."

Penelope's eyebrows rose in astonishment, and Isaac gazed at Drágan with wonder.

"No thank you, Drágan," Penelope replied. "But I appreciate the offer. Why don't you boys hang out in Isaac's room, and I'll call when dinner's ready."

"Thank you." Drágan bowed once more.

Isaac tugged his arm. "C'mon, I wanna show you my room." Flush with excitement, he hurried from the kitchen, Drágan in tow.

They passed through the sitting room and out into the main hall. The floors were hardwood, but the stairs leading up to the second floor were covered in thick sky-blue carpet.

Isaac showed Drágan the two hallways on the second floor. One led to his mom's bedroom and the study, which she used as her home office. The other passed the guest bedroom and a large bathroom before ending in Isaac's room at the rear of the house. It was the largest bedroom and had always been perfect for Isaac to share when a foster child was a boy. Bunk beds rested against Isaac's back wall with chests of drawers along the adjoining wall overlooking the driveway; a large wooden desk sat across the room beside a window looking out at tall, majestic maple trees.

Drágan's eyes swept the room, settling on the bookshelves above the twin chests of drawers. Lining the shelves were meticulously detailed hand-painted models of famous movie monsters, which Isaac had spent countless hours crafting. With long slender fingers, Drágan picked up a model of the original Wolfman from the 1940 Universal film. The monster bared its fangs at a lovely young woman cowering before him.

Normally unsettled if anyone touched his models, Isaac instinctively sensed that Drágan revered them as much as he did.

Drágan turned with the model in hand. "Do you believe Larry would've killed Gwen when he grabbed her in the woods?"

Isaac was shocked that this boy would ask such a movie-geek question, but figured Drágan must also love *The Wolfman,* so he dove right in with his answer. "No. He loved her too much."

"At long last, someone who agrees with me." Drágan lovingly replaced the figure on the shelf and studied the others.

Isaac gazed at him in surprise. "You're a geek?"

"A what?"

"A geek. You know, someone who's into pop culture stuff like horror movies."

A look of understanding enlightened Drágan's face. "Ah, I understand. I love the horror genre. In fact, Larry Talbot is my favorite character. His struggles as the wolfman brought me near to tears on several occasions."

Isaac's heart pounded with excitement. "Me too! Especially when he was finally cured. But those were tears of joy."

Drágan regarded him as though doing a complete reevaluation. "You are the first I've met to feel as I do. How fortuitous that we've made each other's acquaintance."

Isaac felt stupid listening to the other boy speak and, if he were honest—which he had no intention of being at that moment—he didn't understand half of what Drágan said to him. The boy was a walking dictionary!

"Uh, wanna sit down?" Isaac pointed to a beige-colored couch against one wall.

Drágan nodded and lowered himself onto the couch, looking stiff and formal while Isaac sat in his desk chair.

"Is the couch uncomfortable?" Isaac asked, worried he might have offended the other boy.

"No," replied Drágan, but his face looked tight and strained. "It's merely that I've never been in the bedroom of a youth my age. I'm accustomed to the company of adults."

Isaac's mouth dropped open. He was appalled, but suddenly the other boy's high vocabulary made more sense. "Never? What about your friends?"

Still sitting up as though in a straight-backed chair, Drágan placed both hands in his lap. "I've never had a real friend my age, at least not for any significant period of time."

Isaac was speechless. "I'm sorry, man. I mean, I have no friends either, mainly cause I'm a geek and they all like sports and stuff. Plus, I wear hearing aids, which makes playing sports suck big time." He reached behind one ear and slipped off a small hearing aid, holding it out to Drágan.

"I've heard of these small devices but have never known anyone who wore them." He turned the aid over in his hand. The unit was small with a tiny tube leading to an earmold. "Are they effective at improving your hearing?"

He handed the aid back to Isaac, who deftly slipped it back onto his ear. "First of all, thank you for not shouting. Every time I tell someone I'm hard of hearing, they start yelling. Drives me crazy. Anyway, these work pretty well. I control 'em with an app on my phone. But in noisy places or big sports fields they aren't so good. I can always hear the PE coach yelling at me, but I don't understand what he's saying. Then he gets mad afterward and says I didn't listen."

"My hearing is excellent, so I have no notion of how your life has been."

Isaac shrugged. "I was born this way and have no idea what it's like to have perfect hearing, so I guess we're even."

Drágan nodded.

Now that they weren't moving, he studied Drágan's features and clothing with greater scrutiny.

Drágan's long, wavy hair was a light brown color and framed his soft features, draped over his small ears, parted in the middle, and brushed across both sides of his smooth forehead. His skin reminded Isaac of some dolls his mother used to collect. What were those made of? Oh, yeah, porcelain. Drágan's skin was like perfect, unblemished porcelain, white to the point of being pale, without the slightest indication that he'd ever had acne, which thankfully Isaac hadn't experienced yet either. Drágan's eyebrows, the same color as his hair, were slender and looked professionally trimmed. His lips were full, with a slight reddish tint, really the only visible coloration on his face.

But it was Drágan's eyes that held Isaac's attention. The color of hazelnuts, they seemed to dance with power. As they fixed on him, Isaac felt himself sliding into oblivion. The sensation lasted only a split second, but he would not soon forget it.

"Your clothes are cool, Drágan. Get 'em at a vintage clothes place?"

The boy's long-sleeve shirt was baggy, almost like a pirate shirt, with a small collar encircled by an old-fashioned tie that looked to be made of leather. Over the shirt he wore a dark brown vest that looked quite old. Over that was a suit jacket with the styling of an era long past. His pants were navy blue, and his brown leather boots looked antique.

"With no disrespect to your own clothing, I prefer attire from past eras."

Isaac wore jeans, a long-sleeve hoodie shirt and sneakers.

"I think you look great."

Looking slightly more relaxed, Drágan asked about the film camera on Isaac's desk that rested beside a twenty-seven-inch iMac computer.

Happy to talk about something to break the awkwardness, Isaac picked up the camera, a high-end model with a powerful lens.

"I plan to make my own movie. A horror film, of course." Isaac realized he'd begun rambling but couldn't stop. "There's this film festival in Bangor at the end of next month, Halloween weekend, in fact, and there's a category for student filmmakers under eighteen. Big prize money too. But the best part is, one of the judges of the horror films will be Stephen King. He lives in Bangor and he's my favorite horror writer. Ever read any of his books?" Out of breath, he finally stopped and laughed. "Sorry, I get carried away."

Drágan replied, "I've read many of Mr. King's works. My favorite is *Salem's Lot*. I have an affinity for vampires, I suppose, in addition to werewolves."

Isaac broke into a huge grin. "That's my favorite too. It really must be fortui … what you said before that we met."

"Fortuitous," Drágan repeated without any condescension. "It means fortunate. How many performers will be in your film?"

Isaac frowned. "Well, that's the tricky part. There's two leads and a few smaller parts, but I don't have any friends at school, so I'm thinking of going to the next town over to audition strangers."

"I have performing experience in my past," Drágan commented without boasting. "Alas, all on the stage, but I'd enjoy being of assistance."

Isaac's heart nearly burst. "That would be fantastic."

"What does your story entail?"

"Well, you'd be playing a guy like Larry Talbot, except a kid, who's a werewolf."

"And how would you create the transformations?"

Isaac indicated his computer. "I got some cool AI programs that can do amazing stuff. Let me show—"

"Boys, dinner's ready!" came his mother's voice from downstairs.

"I'll show you after dinner."

2

DISTURBING DISCOVERIES

Isaac and Drágan set the table and carried out the food. Penelope had made a heaping bowl of spaghetti with meatballs, green salad with vegetables, and fresh garlic bread. Isaac sat immediately, but Drágan waited for Penelope to sit before he slid into his own chair. She smiled at him.

"How gallant of you, Drágan."

"I was taught to sit only after the ladies have seated themselves."

Penelope and Isaac exchanged a look. He shrugged and grabbed for the overflowing bowl of spaghetti. Drágan folded his hands in his lap and bowed his head.

"May I ask for blessings on our meal?"

Isaac froze, glancing once more at his mother. She nodded at their guest, and Isaac pulled back his hand.

"Of course, Drágan," she said.

"Dear Lord, thank you for this lovely meal before us and for guiding me to such kind benefactors. Amen."

"Amen," echoed Isaac and his mother.

Isaac once more grabbed for the bowl, but noting Drágan's look, offered it to his mother first.

"Thank you, Isaac," she said with a smile.

She used a serving fork and spoon to hoist some spaghetti out of the bowl onto her plate. She passed the bowl to Drágan, who did the same before passing it to Isaac, who loaded his plate. Drágan eyed the huge portion while Isaac met his gaze across the table.

"What? I'm a growing boy, right, Mom?"

"That you are."

Penelope laughed, but Drágan looked almost sad as he added a little salad and garlic bread to his plate and began eating in silence.

"So, Drágan," Penelope began after swallowing a mouthful of spaghetti, "did you just move to town? Where do your parents live?"

Drágan looked up without expression. "I'm an orphan traveling alone."

Her face fell with concern. "How old are you?"

"Fourteen as of my last birthday."

Isaac wanted to intervene, but he decided to let Drágan fend for himself. He seemed more than capable.

"So, how do you get around?" Penelope asked, brows furrowed with motherly concern. "What do you do for money?"

"I am what is known as a fashion model," Drágan replied with ease, causing Isaac's mouth to drop open in shock.

Penelope nodded, offering her trademark warm smile. "I can certainly understand that, can't you, Isaac?"

"Uh, yeah, I mean, he's beautiful. I mean, like, really photogenic. I mean, you know what I mean." Flustered, he shoveled spaghetti into his mouth.

"I have always been told I'm beautiful," Drágan commented, as though to ease Isaac of his embarrassment. "Unlike most American boys, I treat that word as a compliment, not an insult against my masculinity. Modeling is, if I may say so, a heartless profession, but if people want to pay me money to wear clothing that doesn't belong to me, who am I so say no? Trust me, Isaac, were you in the modeling world, you would be defined as *cute*."

Penelope chuckled at Isaac's red face. "That's what I call him."

"Bruh..." Isaac mumbled, not enjoying being in the spotlight.

"Did I offend you, Isaac?"

Isaac gazed into Drágan's handsome face and saw no sign of mockery. "No. Thanks for the compliment." Then it occurred to him to ask, "Is that why your hair is so long?"

Drágan nodded. "My agent prefers it long because she feels it makes me look more beautiful. Her words, not mine. And because it can be styled in a variety of ways."

"Who takes care of your money, Drágan?" Penelope asked.

"I'm an emancipated minor, Mrs. Foster, and my agent is in charge of contracts and money."

"What about school?"

"Yeah," piped up Isaac, hope in his voice. "Will you be going to school here?"

Drágan eyed him a moment, his expression unreadable like always. "As a model, I am often required to travel. Therefore, I have tested out of high school." He faced Penelope. "I possess documentation to verify what I've told you. And you may contact my agent as well."

Isaac had never seen his mother so flustered. "Oh, I believe you, of course. It's just, well don't you get lonely without a family?"

Isaac watched the other boy's face and saw a flicker of such intense sadness he nearly gasped.

Drágan quickly regained his composure. "I've learned how to be alone. Solitude has its virtues, if utilized properly."

"Okay, but where will you live while you're in town?"

Isaac saw his chance and took it. "Why not here, Mom? I've got that other bed, or we have the spare room, and I haven't had a roommate for a long time. Please? He has money, he can pay."

Clearly appalled, Penelope replied, "I would never take money from a boy."

"I can assure you, Mrs. Foster," Drágan interjected, "I am quite comfortable when it comes to money."

She shook her head.

"Please, Mom?"

She eyed him a moment, then offered Drágan a smile. "Of course, you can stay. But you're not paying."

Drágan looked troubled, as though he didn't like accepting favors. "I agree, so long as you allow me to cook from time to time."

Penelope grinned and raised her glass of water. "Now *that's* a deal." She clinked Drágan's raised glass and then Isaac's.

"Are you in town for a modeling assignment?

Drágan glanced away from her ever so slightly. "No, my business here is of a personal nature."

Isaac watched Drágan, who suddenly seemed uncomfortable. "I wish you could go to school with me. I got no friends over there and the jerkwads mess with me for wearing hearing aids and stuff."

Penelope frowned. "I thought that ended in middle school."

Isaac rolled his eyes. "It's a small town, remember? Everyone in eighth grade is in my ninth."

"Is Jack still being..." She trailed off, as though not quite sure how to phrase her question.

"A little bitch?" Isaac spat. "Yeah."

Penelope frowned at his choice of words. "I still don't understand how he could change so much."

"He has new friends now" was all Isaac said as he gulped some water, anxious to move on from the "Jack" subject.

Drágan watched their exchange curiously. "You know, I've spent most of my life surrounded by adults. I wonder what it would be like with youth of my own age."

"They're dirtbags," Isaac muttered, crunching into his garlic bread. "You haven't missed anything."

"Still and all, I believe attending school with you would be quite educational."

Isaac nearly choked on his bread. "You mean that?"

"I never say anything I don't mean. You're my benefactor. If you're experiencing difficulty, perhaps I can help you."

"That'd be awesome!" Isaac could barely contain his excitement. Maybe, at long last, school wouldn't be unbearable.

Penelope sighed. "Well, I guess you've both decided." She laughed. "Do you have immunization records, Drágan? I'll need them to enroll you."

"Yes. They're also required for modeling, though I'm never ill."

"Okay. I'll enroll you on Monday."

"Make sure he's in all my classes," Isaac insisted.

His mom smirked. "Might not be a bad idea. He can help you with your algebra homework."

"Bruh."

After dinner, the boys entered the hall near the side door where Drágan had left his valise.

"I'll take your bag up to *our* room," Isaac offered with a grin.

Before Drágan could respond, Isaac gripped the bag handles with his right hand and attempted to lift it off the floor. The bag barely moved, practically yanking him downward. Grimacing with shame, he gripped it with both hands, but still barely got it more than a few inches off the floor.

Releasing the bag, he faced Drágan, exasperated. "What have you got in there, gold bars?"

Smiling, Drágan easily picked up his bag with one hand.

"How did you do that?"

"I'm quite strong."

"That's for sure."

In their bedroom, Isaac showed Drágan a closet and chest of drawers he could use for his clothing. He stared intently at the valise as Drágan slid it into his assigned closet and closed the door. He had to know what was so heavy he couldn't lift it, but any investigation would have to wait until Drágan was in the shower.

He also directed Drágan where to find towels and other items, including clean toothbrushes, in case he needed one. He was disappointed when Drágan said he'd shower in the morning. Drágan pulled a cell phone from out of his top drawer and checked it quickly before replacing it in the drawer.

"You don't carry your phone in your pocket?" Isaac asked, slipping his own out and connecting it to its charge cord.

"Only my agent calls me, and I've told her I don't wish to accept any jobs while I'm in Millwood."

"I only keep mine on me in case Mom calls," Isaac said with a shrug.

By the time Penelope told them good night, Isaac wore full pajamas—which he did in fall and winter due to the drop in temperature at night—and Drágan wore what he called a sleeping gown. To Isaac, it looked like a long white dress that nearly reached Drágan's ankles. When Isaac asked him if he'd be cold in that, Drágan confessed that he never felt cold. Isaac thought that was peculiar, but said no more.

Isaac woke the following morning and found that Drágan wasn't in the upper bunk. He sat up, snatched his hearing aids out of their charger on a small table beside his bed, slipped them on, and powered them up. He rose and peeked into the bathroom, but it was empty. He didn't know where Drágan had gone, but curiosity was killing him, so he decided to go for it.

He hurried back to his room and eased open Drágan's closet door. Spotting the large valise in one shadowy corner, he paused. He felt guilty, like he was invading Drágan's privacy, but he just *had* to know why that bag was so heavy.

Dropping to his hands and knees, he crawled into the closet and examined the bag. There was no zipper, but rather leather ties that bound the mouth of the valise together. He listened for any sound of returning footfalls, then deftly undid the four ties and pulled open the stiff leather mouth. The closet had no light, so he reached in with one hand, feeling around for something heavy. His fingers brushed against metal. Gripping it, he pulled.

What emerged were the thickest links of chain he'd ever seen! He squinted into the interior and couldn't make out how long the chain might be, but based on the weight of the valise, he suspected it was quite lengthy.

What the hell? Isaac felt a chill envelop him. Was he so desperate for a friend that maybe he'd accepted Drágan on face value just because he wanted to? Who carries around heavy chains in their travel bag? What could they be used for? He wanted to believe Drágan was what he said he was, but maybe caution was a good idea moving forward.

Fearing that Drágan might return, he lowered the chain back inside the bag and retied the leather strips.

Drágan stood at the stove preparing breakfast for the Fosters. He thought he'd made a good impression the night before, but he hoped being helpful around the house would improve his chances of staying. He knew he'd made Isaac suspicious with the valise incident and cursed himself for not picking it up faster. Would that event prove to be his undoing?

He liked Isaac a lot, and Penelope, too. During all his travels, he'd wished more than anything for a real family. Despite what he'd said the previous night, being alone wasn't preferable to being with other people. But most people, based on his experience, wanted something from him and didn't really care much about him as a person. Isaac and his mom seemed to genuinely like him. Would that change if they knew the full truth, like it had with most everyone else he'd ever known?

He heard footsteps and focused on his cooking.

Isaac bounded into the kitchen, startled to see him at the stove.

"I believe I said that I enjoy cooking," Drágan offered with a warm smile. He indicated the stove. In one skillet was scrambled eggs in the making and in the other pan-fried potatoes, while a third held the bacon. He gently coddled the eggs with a spatula while flipping the bacon with his other hand.

Penelope entered, fully dressed, and stopped in shock. "I could smell your cooking all the way upstairs, Drágan. It looks delicious."

"Thank you, Mrs. Foster. I hope you and Isaac enjoy my work."

Penelope smiled at Isaac in his pajamas and bare feet. "Could you set the table, Isaac?"

Drágan said, "I took the liberty of doing that. It was the least I could do in exchange for your generosity."

"At least let me help you serve the food," Isaac said. "Mom, you go into the dining room, and we'll bring it in."

She grinned, lighting up her lovely face in a way he hadn't seen in some time. "I could get used to this kind of treatment." She tousled Isaac's hair and left the kitchen.

Isaac stepped up beside Drágan and said, "I hope I didn't keep you awake too late by talking so much. It's just been a long time since anyone's stayed over."

Drágan tossed off a smile, hoping it was the appropriate response. "Not at all. We have many interests in common and I especially enjoyed discussing the different film versions of *'Salem's Lot* and how they differed from the book."

Isaac looked relieved. "Me too." He studied the food. "So, how can I help?"

Drágan felt foolish for not looking earlier and said, "What can we serve the food in?"

Isaac chuckled and hurried to a cabinet to one side of the stove. Drágan eyed him as Isaac pulled out some serving bowls. Between the two of them, they scooped the food into separate bowls and set them on the counter.

"This smells amazing!" Isaac gushed as Drágan placed the cooking utensils into the sink. "Where'd you learn how to cook?"

"During my travels I met many accomplished chefs who enjoyed teaching me their secrets." Drágan replied, choosing his words with care. "We should serve the food now, while it's hot."

Isaac didn't want to insult his mom, so he didn't admit aloud that Drágan's cooking was the best he'd ever eaten. Even his mom was impressed. Their compliments, not to mention the quick work they made of the food, clearly pleased Drágan. Isaac thought it odd that

Drágan ate much less of his wonderful food than they did, claiming he wasn't hungry.

Penelope chuckled. "That's a switch. I thought growing boys never stopped eating."

She winked at Isaac, and he mumbled, "Bruh."

Drágan stood to bus their plates, but Penelope said, "Oh, no. You cooked. I'll wash the dishes."

He nodded. "I shall leave my plate on the counter."

He left the dining room and Isaac glanced at his mom. "I think we should keep him."

She laughed. "I agree."

He stood with his own plate, picked up hers, and headed for the kitchen. As he was about to enter, he spotted something that stopped him cold. Drágan had the fridge door open and was swallowing a piece of raw bacon!

Isaac stepped back, not wanting the other boy to think he was spying.

Raw bacon? Can't you get diseases from it? And why would someone eat that? It had to taste disgusting, right?

Between the chains and the raw bacon, Isaac knew there was much more to Drágan than met the eye.

He purposely rattled the dishes before entering and when he did, the fridge was closed and Drágan was heading his way.

"Here, let me help," he said genially, as though he hadn't just been doing something weird.

He took one plate and set it atop his, and Isaac added the other to the pile just as Penelope entered with their juice glasses.

"Why don't you show Drágan around Millwood, honey, since he'll be living here."

He was about to protest that the other boy would be bored doing that when Drágan piped up. "That's a splendid idea. Give me the lay of the land, so to speak."

Isaac would rather have shown him the rec room above the garage, but he'd save that for later. "Okay. I'll run up and change."

He padded out of the kitchen and through the main hall, turning when he heard footsteps behind him. Drágan was following.

"Aren't you already dressed?"

"Of course. I merely thought to organize my belongings while you change into your outdoor clothing."

Isaac sensed he was lying, but Drágan gave not the slightest indication he told anything but the truth.

Does he think I'll check out the valise in his closet?

Fearful his expression might give away that he'd already done that, Isaac hurried up the stairs.

Drágan rifled through his drawers while Isaac slipped into jeans, a thick, long-sleeve shirt, a hoodie, and sneakers, but whenever Isaac peeked at his new roommate, he saw no attempt to reorganize anything.

Isaac had so many questions for this strange boy, but he felt bad about peeking into the valise, so he decided not to pry. For the moment. There must be a reasonable explanation for the chains. And the bacon. At least, he hoped so.

"Millwood is really old," Isaac told Drágan as they strolled down Main Street. "Most of the people work at the paper mill outside of town. The rest own shops or work as teachers, police or fire fighters, stuff like that."

Cars drove back and forth, many of them pickup trucks or SUVs. The cool breeze felt good against Isaac's cheeks. He loved fall best of all the seasons, especially Halloween when every storefront had brightly lit jack-o-lanterns in their windows.

"That is a lovely old cinema," Drágan said, pointing at the Millwood Playhouse with its attractive crown molding and towering marquee announcing its current offerings. It also had a separate ornate box office in front of the entrance, something Isaac often saw in old movies.

"It's pretty good," Isaac said with a shrug. "The better theaters are in Bangor. This one has only one screen, but you can see it's showing two movies. They alternate nights."

Drágan appreciated the small-town facades and architecture of the businesses they walked past. Isaac knew the stores by heart, but somehow, as the other boy pointed out the origin of this or that architectural styling, Isaac saw them in a new light. Everything about Drágan seemed to fill him with a wonder he'd never known.

"Tell me about where you grew up," he asked, keenly interested. "You have such a cool accent."

"Thank you." Then Drágan's tone became wistful as he brushed strands of hair off his face. "I was born in a farming village within Romania near the Carpathian Mountains, made famous by Bram Stoker and Dracula, as I'm sure you know. From the time I could walk my father bade me work the fields, till the ground, carry animals nearly as large as myself. It was a hard life by the standards of today."

Isaac jokingly flexed his arm. "That how you got so strong?"

"In part. My life revolved around work from dawn to dusk. I never played with the other boys in the village."

Isaac felt a lump of sadness fill his stomach. "That's sad."

Drágan eyed him inscrutably. "I suppose from your perspective, but that was the only life I knew."

Isaac was about to ask what happened to his parents when Drágan said, "May I ask *you* a question?"

"Sure."

"Does your father live with you?"

Isaac pulled a disgusted face. "No. He left when I was four."

"You have not seen him since that time?"

Isaac shook his head. "Not even a birthday card."

"In some ways, such a situation may be more painful than being an orphan," Drágan said with a sigh, his tone wistful once more.

Isaac was about to ask about Drágan's parents when the sound of a man yelling drew their attention to a house up the street. Even if he hadn't been wearing his hearing aids, he'd have known that voice anywhere.

The downtown shops had given way to rows of homes, mostly

two-story Victorians like Isaac's. A girl he knew from school burst from the second house on the left and ran up the street as a pinched-faced middle-aged man with unkempt hair and what looked like three-day's worth of beard stubble shouted, "You come back here, you little slut! You hear me!"

The girl ignored him, looking down as she slowed to a walk, her long brown hair in front so her face wasn't visible.

"What is this?" Drágan asked, concerned.

"That's Stephanie, a girl from my class. Her stepdad's a drunk. He's always screaming at her."

"Wait'll you get home, you bitch!" the man shouted. "You'll pay big time!" He re-entered the house and slammed the door so hard Isaac almost felt the vibrations.

Head down, Stephanie didn't even notice them. Drágan started toward her. Isaac almost called him back, then sighed and hurried after.

"May I be of assistance?" Drágan asked as he neared the girl.

Startled, she stopped up short and looked at him through her hair. Quickly wiping away tears, she pushed her brown hair, which fell well past her shoulders, off her face and stared in amazement at Drágan.

"What are you?" She eyed his clothes with distaste. "You dress like my grandfather, who's dead."

"I suspect your grandfather had lovely taste in clothing," Drágan replied, not the least bit offended.

She stared in amazement, then eyed Isaac. "He for real?"

Isaac nodded.

"I am Drágan Albescu at your service." Drágan bowed with great deference.

"Look, guys, I'm not in the mood."

"Sorry," Isaac said. "I think he's just worried after seeing your stepdad and all."

Stephanie looked about to respond, then gave Drágan a more thorough once-over. "Well, you're hot and your accent is cool." To Isaac she added, "Relative?"

Isaac didn't want to get into Drágan's history, at least what he knew, so he said, "No, he's an orphan, you know, staying with us." He figured everyone knew about his mom taking in foster kids, so he hoped she'd buy his story.

Stephanie eyed him with squinting brows. "That sucks. For him, I mean."

"Yeah."

"It's cool you and your mom took him in." She gazed at him as though they hadn't gone to school together since first grade. "You know, you're a lot cuter than you used to be."

Isaac was startled, but even as she said that she made eye contact with Drágan and seemed unable to look away. Isaac didn't like that look, nor the focused look Drágan gave her in return. Isaac decided it was because Stephanie was so beautiful, with her soft features and full lips.

Not sure what to say, he blurted, "Drágan's a model."

That split apart the connection. "I get that. I hope you model something more modern."

"I do."

Stephanie's ringtone blasted from her pocket. She slipped out the phone and put it to her ear. "Mom, I'm not going back with that creep —what? Okay, I'll be right there."

She ended the call and her soft face bore a look of distress. Even though they never spoke at school, Isaac had always felt sorry for her living with that jerk.

"My mom needs help with something." She held up her phone. "Can I take your picture?"

"Of course," Drágan replied in the tone of one who posed for a living.

She snapped off a few. "Well, guess I'll see you at school."

"You will."

Isaac felt like he wasn't there. He wasn't ready to lose Drágan before they could cement a friendship, but what could he do?"

She smiled and walked slowly back toward her house, head slumped.

Drágan watched her until she entered and closed her door.

"Hello, I'm still here," Isaac said with an edge to his voice he wished hadn't been there.

Drágan turned, brows furrowed in surprise. "Perhaps we should return to your home, and you can give me a tour of your recreation room."

Isaac nodded stiffly and they resumed walking.

"How long have you known her?" Drágan asked.

Isaac sighed. "All my life. She's one of the popular kids at school, cheerleader and all that. She doesn't talk to me."

"She said you were cute."

Isaac shrugged. She had, hadn't she?

They walked a moment in silence.

"May I pursue a more personal topic?" Drágan asked.

"Like what?"

"You mother mentioned someone named Jack and you took offense."

Isaac felt his stomach tighten. "It's painful."

"I don't wish to pry."

Isaac was going to accept that response and drop the subject, but suddenly he felt the need to talk about Jack, in more detail than even to his mother.

"Jack and me were best friends all through elementary school. I mean, we did everything together, watched horror movies, played video games, went camping, snowboarding. He even helped with my models, but mostly he watched me work cause he said I was an artist."

He paused as the memories flooded in. Drágan walked alongside in silence.

"Anyway," Isaac resumed after taking a deep breath and expelling it, "everything was cool til I guess, end of seventh grade when Jack seemed...different. I mean, it was like he wanted me to do something, and I didn't know what it was. That summer was okay, but he kinda drifted away, like always being busy when I wanted to hang out."

Isaac stopped again because the worst was yet to come. He

glanced at Drágan. The other boy gazed at him as though he could wait forever.

"When eighth grade started, Jack and me still had lunch together and we goofed around like we always did. One day, we had each other in a sort of headlock when some of the jock boys saw us. One of 'em said, 'Aren't they a cute couple.' Stephanie was watching, I remember that. I just scowled 'cause they were jerks anyway, but Jack kind of went crazy. He pushed me away and..."

Isaac's heart began pounding and he wasn't sure he could continue, but Drágan's calm, patient expression, and the look of concern in his soft eyes, gave Isaac the courage to continue.

"He told everyone I tried to kiss him. They all laughed, and I wanted to die. From then on, Jack's been hanging out with those jerks and messing with me. I don't even try to talk to him anymore, but he won't leave me alone!"

Blinking back tears, Isaac sucked in breath after breath to calm himself. He felt a hand on his shoulder and looked up into Drágan's sympathetic face.

"I don't know what I did wrong, Drágan," he gulped, wiping the tears away. "I don't know why he hates me."

"Perhaps the person he hates is himself."

"That doesn't make sense."

"The human psyche is complex and often illogical," Drágan replied in his calm, boyish voice. "Thank you for sharing with me. I feel your suffering."

Isaac gazed into those hazelnut eyes and knew the other boy wasn't just saying something to make him feel better, but truly empathized, as though he'd experienced similar pain firsthand. He also wondered why a fourteen-year-old sounded like a therapist.

"Thanks for listening. I been too embarrassed to even tell my mom exactly what happened."

They continued walking in silence.

"Jack shall trouble you no more." Drágan's tone was...dangerous.

A chill ran up Isaac's back. "What do you mean?"

"You're my benefactor," Drágan replied coolly. "No harm will befall you."

Isaac wasn't sure what to say so he remained silent. What would Drágan do to Jack? Sure, Jack had treated him like crap for a long time, but...

"You're...you're not gonna hurt him, are you?"

Without breaking stride, Drágan replied, "I try never to cause injury."

Isaac shivered at that response, but understood it was all he was going to get.

3

SECRETS UNCOVERED

Isaac was surprised that Drágan had never played video games once they'd both settled on the couch in the recreation room to use his PlayStation. The rec room had a bar and stools, both made of lovely maple, a small refrigerator for soft drinks, several comfy soft chairs, and a combo pool/air hockey table.

As Drágan gazed at the controller in his hands, Isaac asked, "You never played video games? Ever?"

He shook his head. "As I believe I've mentioned, all of my life has been spent in the company of people who wanted something from me, beginning with my father."

Isaac just shook his head, sadness forming a lump near his heart.

The other boy caught on quickly to the controller, and the purpose of each game they played, easily besting Isaac after only a short time. Isaac hadn't played much since Jack turned against him, but his pride wouldn't let him just roll over. Still, Drágan mastered each game with ease and played aggressively, trouncing Isaac in match after match.

Practically sweating from exertion, Isaac finally put down his controller and sighed. "Okay, I give up. You're amazing. How do you learn stuff so fast?"

Drágan set his controller on the couch. "I have exceptional hand-eye coordination."

"No kidding." Isaac rose to grab a soda from the fridge. He brought one for Drágan, who'd risen from the couch to examine the pool table.

"You ever play pool?" Isaac asked, handing the can to Drágan.

"It looks like billiards, which I've seen, but never played."

Isaac explained the rules of the game and demonstrated by attempting a shot into the corner pocket. He missed.

Drágan's face lit up. "It's like geometry."

"Huh?"

"Much of geometry is triangles. For example, look at the red striped ball in relation to the cue ball and the center pocket. Picture a line drawn on the fabric from the red ball to the pocket, then from the red ball to the cue ball. That is known as an isosceles triangle, meaning two sides are equal, the third is not. If you direct the cue ball precisely along the triangle line, it will bounce off according to its natural trajectory. May I try?"

Fascinated, Isaac handed him the cue stick. Drágan lined up his shot. He sent the cue ball along the invisible line he'd described. It struck the red striped ball and directed it right at the center pocket. The ball struck the pocket so hard it bounced back, rather than in.

Drágan stood and regarded Isaac sheepishly. "Of course, one must determine the correct amount of force, which I suppose requires practice."

Isaac grinned and they played several games. As with the video games, Drágan rapidly improved and easily beat Isaac on their third game. After that, Isaac flipped the table and taught Drágan air hockey. Again, he learned fast, but Isaac was quite good, and they split their games.

The bottom line was, they had fun. Isaac could almost forget the chains and the raw bacon.

Almost.

∽

Isaac sat alone at the kitchen table eating some chocolate chip cookies when his mom entered.

"Where's Drágan? I thought you boys were in the rec room."

Isaac shrugged, feeling glum. "We were, but he said he wanted to take a walk. Alone."

Penelope sat across from him and picked up a cookie from the plate, nibbling as they talked. "Did you guys have an argument?"

"No, Mom. We were having a great time. But then, like he had an appointment or something, he said he had to go out. Alone."

"Well, honey, he is his own person and he said he came to Millwood for a reason."

"What reason? He never told us."

"True. Since he's living here, we should probably ask."

"What if it's something illegal?"

She frowned. "You don't believe that."

He sighed. "No. I'm just mad he wouldn't let me go with him. Just when I thought we were we're bonding...."

She reached across and squeezed his hand. "I have the feeling he's spent so much of his life with adults that he has no idea how to be a boy."

Isaac munched on a cookie, digesting her words. They made sense.

"When you get a chance, ask him why he's in Millwood."

"Okay." He paused. "Mom, can I ask you something?"

"Anything."

"Do you ever hear anything from Dad, you know, maybe even stuff you don't want me to know?"

Her lovely face clouded over with sadness. "Just the monthly child support. I so wish he'd kept in contact with you. I wanted him to, and I was even fine with visits here, if that's what he wanted, but..."

"Why didn't he? Did I do something wrong?"

"No, honey, of course not. He left me for someone else. I was hurt, sure, but never enough to keep you away from him. He just...started a new life, I guess, and didn't want any part of the old one." She smiled lovingly. "He doesn't know what he's missing." She squeezed his hand again.

"Thanks, Mom."

~

Isaac was tinkering with the special effects programs on his computer when Drágan entered.

"Everything go okay?"

"What do you mean?" Drágan asked.

Isaac felt awkward, but this was his house and Drágan was a stranger, after all. "I just meant, were you doing whatever you came to Millwood for?"

Drágan seemed to understand. "You're worried that I might be up to no good?"

Isaac blustered, "No, it's just, well, we, I mean I was wondering."

"You've taken me into your home, so you have a right to know. I came to Millwood for health reasons."

Isaac suddenly felt afraid. "Are you okay?"

Drágan nodded. "Yes. But...it is a personal matter."

"It's okay," Isaac said, worrying that Drágan might be ill and not telling him, but he didn't want to push harder because Drágan looked embarrassed. "Check this out." He indicated his computer screen. On it was the frozen image of someone who looked half human, half wolf. "I'm trying out transformations for the movie."

Drágan slid into the chair beside Isaac's and gazed at the screen.

"Now, in the script, we'll see your character as a werewolf several times. The first time is near the beginning when he kills what we call an extra. Near the end, he'll change back into the boy after the girl he loves shoots him with a silver bullet."

"I see." Drágan fixed his eyes on the wolfish looking teen boy on the screen but made no other comment for a long moment. "Does this program allow your creations to move about?"

Isaac nodded. "But that's the tricky part. You have to put in just the right directions or the program'll get it wrong."

"I'm not proficient with computers," Drágan said, sitting back from the screen. "Perhaps I should read through the script."

"Sure." Isaac fished around under books and other loose items on his messy desk before pulling out a small sheaf of papers, stapled together. He handed it to Drágan.

The other boy gazed at the title. "Wolfboy."

"Yeah, it's kind of my teen version of *The Wolfman*," Isaac said with a shrug.

"Perhaps you should ask Stephanie to play the female lead."

Isaac frowned. "Why her?"

Drágan's face was expressionless. "You know her. And she did say you were cute."

Isaac wondered if Stephanie would take direction from him. "Maybe."

Drágan rose from his chair and moved to the couch, where he sat back and began reading as though Isaac wasn't even there.

Deciding he'd likely never understand his new roommate, Isaac returned to work.

THE FOLLOWING DAY, Sunday, was always a quiet day in Isaac's home. Often, he and his mom would go hiking or hang out down by the river, but today Isaac wanted to work more on his script. Drágan had left early for his solitary walk and Isaac wanted to show him the revisions when he returned. Drágan had made some excellent suggestions that might improve the plot.

Isaac was excitedly typing away when his mom called from downstairs. "Isaac, could you come down, please?"

Annoyed, he tromped down the stairs, expecting some unpleasant chore or other, but stopped dead upon seeing his mom standing just inside the front door next to...Stephanie!

He quickly smoothed back his unkempt hair and approached. "Uh, hi, Stephanie. What are you doing here?"

"Isaac!" His mom looked embarrassed.

"It's okay, Mrs. Foster. I mean, I haven't been here since..."

"My birthday party in first grade," Isaac finished, scowling.

Stephanie shifted uncomfortably. "Yeah. You're a lot cuter now."

"I'm not so sure," his mom said, nudging him playfully.

"Bruh."

Penelope faced Stephanie. "I went from mommy to mom to bruh."

Stephanie laughed. "I need to talk to you, Isaac." She glanced at Penelope. "Alone."

More nervous than he could remember, Isaac waved her in. "We can talk in my room."

"Leave the door open three inches," Penelope said as they headed for the stairs.

"Mom..." Isaac grumbled and followed Stephanie up the stairs.

"Make that five," his mother called after.

By now they were on the second floor out of sight of his mom. "I apologize for my mother."

"My family's the worst," she replied with disgust, waiting for him to show the way. "The whole town knows that."

The deep resignation in her voice touched Isaac deeply, but unsure what to say, he led the way to his room, noticing that she carried a messenger bag over one shoulder. As he entered his bedroom, he heard a gasp behind him and turned to find Stephanie staring in awe at the various horror film posters blanketing his walls. He'd been afraid she'd laugh, but instead she was grinning.

"This is the most amazing room I've ever been in!" she gushed, her head swiveling from one wall to the next. "I've seen every one of these movies."

"Wait... what? You like horror movies?"

"Who doesn't?" Her gaze settled on the shelves filled with his models, and she practically leaped forward, sweeping over each with her eyes as though soaking up water in a desert. "Did you make these? Sorry, stupid question, of course you did. May I?"

He nodded and she reverently picked up the figure of Dracula in a graveyard, encircling himself with his cape, blood dripping from his fangs.

"The detail work," she muttered, scrutinizing it, "the craftsmanship. You're the geek of all geeks."

"Thanks," he mumbled, sarcasm saturating his voice.

She spun around, grinning. "Oh, I meant that in a good way."

Honestly, even at school with her friends, Isaac had never seen her look so animated, so...happy.

As though handling the crown jewels, she set the figure back onto its shelf and stepped back. "I have a thing for vampires. They seem so sexy."

"If you say so."

She spotted his book collection, all horror titles. "Whoa, you like Stephen King too?"

"Course. He's the greatest horror writer in the last hundred years. In fact, I'm making a short horror film to enter a competition in Bangor over Halloween weekend. King will be one of the judges."

Her face lit up. "That's awesome. Who's acting in it?"

"Only Drágan so far. I need a female lead and a few others."

"I could do it," she blurted. "I was in the school play last year."

He squinted at her with suspicion. "Sure you don't just wanna be around Drágan? There's no kissing scenes."

She flinched, clearly offended. "You sound like my lousy, stinking pig of a stepfather."

He bowed his head. "Sorry. Would you really be in my film?"

"And get a chance to meet Stephen King? Of course!"

"Um, well, great. I'm just revising the script, but I can get it to you this week."

"I can't wait." She paused, gazing at him so intently he squirmed. "You and I have so much in common, I never knew."

He attempted a flippant tone. "Since we never talk, I guess it's hard to find these things out."

Her grin fell away, replaced by a look of shame. "I'm sorry. You know how it is at school. The popular kids and the..."

She trailed off, but he finished for her. "The losers, like me."

"Except you're not, but..."

"But you still can't talk to me at school. I get it. I can email you the script."

"Awesome!" She recited her email address and Isaac put it into his phone.

"So, what'd you wanna talk to me about? If it's Drágan you came for, he's gone."

"I know. I've been watching your house all morning, hoping he might leave."

He furrowed his brows. "Why?"

"To show you these." She crossed the room on her long, athletic legs and set her messenger bag on his desk. Flipping it open, she extracted what looked like a bundle of large photos. "Remember I took those pics of Drágan yesterday?"

"Yeah, so?"

"Since you said he was a model, I uploaded one of them and did an internet search."

Isaac was growing impatient. "And you found out he's not a model?"

She shook her head, shoving the length of her hair back over one shoulder. "He's a model, all right, but check out these pictures. I wrote the dates at the bottom, like when each one first showed up in print."

She handed him the stack of photos. The top image nearly took his breath away. Drágan stood on a beach wearing only board shorts and sunglasses. The makeup people must've put suntan oil on him because the perfection of his flat, elegantly defined muscles glistened in the sunlight. His long hair seemed to be flying to one side, as though in a breeze, and his face glowed.

"Wow."

"Hotter than hot, right?"

He nodded, feeling more inadequate than ever.

"So that one was taken earlier this year, for a summer catalogue," she went on. "Check out the next one I printed."

He slid the beach photo to the back of the stack and found

himself looking at a shot of Drágan wearing what he assumed was supposed to be some modern dressy style for men, but to his eyes it just looked weird.

"Look at the date."

Isaac lowered his eyes to the bottom of the photo and gasped. "2010? The hell…" He met her gaze, the beginnings of fear creeping over him. "It can't be him."

"I know, right? Check out the rest."

Isaac slid that one to the back and barely glanced at what Drágan wore in the next. His eyes found the date scrawled in black sharpie: 2000. His breathing became ragged, and his heart pounded as he flipped through the pictures faster and faster. 1990, 1980, 1970, 1960, 1950, 1940, 1930, and the last, 1920. Lightheaded, he dropped into his chair, gripping the photos as though they held the secrets of the universe. He looked up and found Stephanie's lovely brown eyes regarding him with a similar look.

"They're not Photoshop or AI," she explained before he could ask. "I found lots more like these, but nothing before 1920. He's a popular model. With his looks, that's a 'duh.' "

"It's not possible," Isaac blurted, flipping through the photos again. The one from the 70s showed Drágan wearing long pants with flared bottoms and a flowery shirt. He studied it, and the others. The oldest ones from 1920 and 1930 were in black and white. He scrutinized every detail of the boy's face. It was Drágan, all right. "How?"

"Can you ask him," Stephanie replied casually, as though asking if Drágan would like to go on a date with her.

"Ask him if he's been alive more than a hundred years?" Isaac stared at her in amazement.

Apparently more calm than he felt, she shrugged.

"Why not? I mean, when I saw these pics, trust me, I freaked out. But, I've watched a lot of horror movies and read tons of books like you have and I've also done lots of research on legends and supposed monsters and, well, turns out they might be real. Some of them, anyway. And they don't have to be bad, right? I mean, Drágan hasn't hurt you or your mom yet, has he?"

"Yet?" Isaac considered the fears he'd already built up regarding Drágan and wondered if maybe he and his mom were wrong, that maybe Drágan was dangerous after all.

Stephanie's lovely face lit up. "Hey, maybe he's a vampire."

"You've seen him outside during the day," Isaac said, his mind suddenly whirling with possibilities, rather than fears. "Maybe it's more like *The Picture of Dorian Gray,* you know, that book that's been made into a bunch of movies."

"Drágan's gorgeous enough for someone to make a painting that would keep him young forever."

Isaac put the photos on his desk. "Can I keep these to show him?"

"Sure."

"You won't tell anyone else, will you? Not even Mary Anne?"

Fellow cheerleader Mary Anne was Stephanie's best friend and they stuck to each other like glue.

"No, but you can fill me in tomorrow. He'll be there, right?"

"Yeah."

She glanced at a smart watch on her slim wrist. "I gotta go. My stepdad isn't at work today and he'd already started drinking before I left. I'm gonna kick it with Mary Anne. See you tomorrow." She started for the open door.

He was about to speak when she turned back. "I wasn't kidding, by the way. I'm really excited about your movie. I want to be a professional actress, so this is perfect."

She bounced from the room.

He wasn't sure what was more surprising—Drágan's Dorian Gray photos or Stephanie's change in attitude toward him after all the years of noninteraction. He rifled through the photos once more, taking in more details than before. Drágan looked amazing in all of them, and exactly the same, excluding his hair length. That had changed over the years. He paused on the beach pose, then lifted his shirt to examine his soft belly. In Maine, there wasn't a lot of opportunity for him to go shirtless except swimming in one of the nearby lakes during the summer, but he couldn't help feeling insecure, nonetheless. He shoved that photo to the back of the pile and stood up.

Stepping into the hall, he entered the bathroom and gazed at himself in the mirror. His brown hair just brushed past his ears, and it wasn't parted in the middle like Drágan's but to one side so it swept across his forehead just missing one slim eyebrow. He had a smooth baby face, what his mom called a button nose, and dimples when he smiled.

Am I cute? he wondered.

Stephanie said he was, so maybe?

He was more concerned, though, about those photos. He'd returned to his desk and was rifling through them once more when Drágan entered the room.

He probably looked like a deer in the headlights because Drágan asked, "Are you okay, Isaac?"

"Uh, yeah, I'm good. Look, um, I need to show you something Stephanie found on the internet."

Looking curious, Drágan crossed the room and sat in Isaac's secondary chair, probably thinking Isaac wanted to show him something on the computer. Instead, Isaac handed him the stack of photos without a word. Drágan flipped through them, his face displaying no visible emotion. When he finished, he handed them back to Isaac.

"I have never seen any of my modeling photos before" was all he said, clearly dodging the obvious.

Isaac stared at him. "Yeah, you look great in all of 'em. Even the one from 1920."

Drágan's eyes squinted with concern. "Has Stephanie showed these to anyone else?"

"I convinced her not to til tomorrow. She wants you to explain them. I'm pretty curious myself."

Drágan shook his head in dismay. "I foolishly forget that everything is available on the internet these days. We shall not mention my modeling again."

It didn't sound like a suggestion. It sounded like an order.

"I won't tell," Isaac said. "I promise. Is it like, well, like the painting of Dorian Gray from Oscar Wilde's book?"

Drágan looked surprised. "No, but Mr. Wilde did base that character on me."

Isaac's mouth fell open. "You knew him?"

Drágan nodded. "He took quite a fancy to me."

"I guess so."

Isaac was trying to recall when Wilde's book was released when Drágan asked, "Do you know much about your neighbor in the back, Dr. Wilson?"

The change of subject threw Isaac for a loop. "Uh no, never met him. Mom says he's a recluse."

"That may well be so, but he's also one of the preeminent hematologists in the world."

Isaac screwed up his face. "A what?"

"A blood specialist," Drágan clarified.

Recalling what Drágan had said before about his health, Isaac froze. "Are you sick?"

"Not in the sense that I will die," Drágan answered, a distinct note of sadness punctuating his words. "On the contrary, I will live forever unless a cure is discovered."

"I'm confused."

"There is something like a virus in my blood that prevents me from aging," Drágan explained. "I'm hopeful Dr. Wilson can generate a cure."

"Wow," Isaac exclaimed, sitting back in his chair, momentarily stunned. "I mean, your blood is like the fountain of youth."

Drágan scowled. "Eternal youth is not a gift; it's a curse."

Isaac opened his mouth to ask more questions, but Drágan raised one hand. "I'd rather not say more at this time, if you please."

Disappointed, Isaac realized he was prying. "I'm sorry."

Drágan squinted, his expression severe. "Something must be done about Stephanie."

Isaac shuddered at the ominous tone in Drágan's voice. "If we tell her not to blab, I'm sure she won't."

Drágan was staring across the room at Isaac's models on the shelf. "*You* might be sure, but I'm not."

He hurried from the room before Isaac could ask what he meant.

4

SCHOOL BECOMES TOLERABLE

Isaac wore a thick, long sleeve shirt and jeans for school the following morning, while Drágan dressed in his vintage style, including a tie with an extra-large knot and his long coat. Drágan told Isaac this style of tie was worn in the 1850s. Unlike during the weekend, he wore a hair tie, so his voluminous length of hair rested against his back in a ponytail.

Isaac wondered what the other kids would make of his new roommate. He figured the girls would swoon, but the boys? He knew some who'd laugh, but he didn't think Drágan would tolerate any harassment.

After finishing breakfast, he dug out of his closet an old backpack for Drágan to use for his books. Drágan had already gotten permission from his agent for Penelope to enroll him in school, so there should be no problems.

"You boys ready?" Penelope looked sharp in a long-sleeve turtleneck and jeans.

The boys stood before her, ready to depart.

"When we get there, you hang out in the quad, Isaac, while I get Drágan registered," she instructed, fishing in her purse for the van keys. "You have your paperwork, Drágan?"

Drágan held up a manila envelope. "Yes, ma'am."

"Make sure he gets put in all my classes," Isaac insisted.

His mom smiled. "I'll try."

ISAAC SAT on a concrete planter in the quad area watching students milling about with their friends.

Millwood High was over a hundred years old and mostly built out of bricks and stone. The classroom buildings were two-story with an adjacent gym and sports fields tucked in back surrounded by tall trees, branches partially stripped bare by the onset of autumn.

Chilled, Isaac stood to walk around so he might warm up, anxious for Drágan to join him. Most of the other kids ignored him, as usual, at least until he turned around and Jack Drake stood before him. Of course, his hearing had failed him once again, even with the aids. He couldn't even count all the times kids had snuck up behind to embarrass him in some way.

Jack was taller and more filled out in the shoulders. Being biracial, he seemed to have captured the best features of both parents, especially his hair that he wore in tight cornrows, courtesy of his African American mom.

It was his mouth that used to delight Isaac when they were younger, for Jack could twist it outrageously like it was rubber and always make him laugh.

As they faced off, Jack looked as though he might not say anything rude, but when a group of kids began gathering, Isaac knew he was in for it. He also decided in that moment that whatever Jack dished out he'd get back in full measure.

Clearly aware of his audience, Jack smirked. "So, Foster, who'd you suck off this weekend?"

Isaac said the first thing that popped into his head. "You."

The assembled kids laughed and *oohhed*, causing Jack to redden in the face. "Think you're funny, huh?"

Isaac shrugged. "Why tell me to keep it a secret if you're gonna blab it to everyone?"

More laughter aimed at Jack pumped up Isaac's courage, at least until Jack raised a meaty fist. Isaac tensed and prepared to try and block it, when out of nowhere Drágan stood behind Jack and grabbed his fist in one hand. Isaac blinked in confusion. Where had he come from so fast?

Drágan spun the startled Jack around and, before the boy could even react, grabbed his jacket lapel with his left hand and lifted him off the ground! The watching kids gasped in astonishment and Isaac stared open-mouthed as Drágan's arm straightened out completely, leaving the terrified Jack almost two feet off the pavement.

"Let me down, man," whimpered Jack, his voice rife with fear.

Drágan's eyes became those of a bloodthirsty animal, and he hissed, "You will harass Isaac no more!"

The squirming Jack looked so helpless Isaac almost felt sorry for him.

Drágan lowered Jack so their faces were close. "I know your secret," he said quietly, but with an undertone of menace. Then he leaned closer to Jack's ear and whispered something Isaac couldn't hear.

Jack whimpered even more, as though fearful Drágan might rip his head off. The second Drágan allowed Jack's feet to touch the ground and released his hold on the boy's jacket, Jack mumbled, "Sorry, Foster," and bolted from the quad as if running for his very life.

The stunned assemblage gazed in astonishment at Drágan, who once more looked calm and at peace. The bell ripped through the quad, causing one girl to scream in startled fright.

Drágan took the speechless Isaac by the arm and led him toward the classroom buildings. "Time for class."

That was all he said.

~

Drágan needed no introduction in first period ELA, but Mr. Sommers, the thirty-something teacher who doubled as track coach, didn't know what had happened outside. Most of the students in class had witnessed Drágan's manhandling, for want of a more suitable word, of Jack in the quad, and just stared with a mix of fascination and fear.

Jack sat in back with his jock buddies, who had not witnessed his humiliation, and kept his head down during the introduction. Beside him, Serg Quintanilla and Ron Johnson chortled at Drágan's clothing and Mr. Sommers glared them into silence.

After the introduction, Mr. Sommers told them all to get out their copies of William Golding's *Lord of the Flies*, which Isaac had devoured in two sittings, equating it to a psychological horror film. Rustling and shuffling accompanied the students retrieving the book from their backpacks and then Mr. Sommers began dissecting the themes of the story.

Isaac could barely concentrate. His mind replayed over and over the confrontation with Jack. How had Drágan moved so fast to suddenly appear like he did and how in the hell had he the strength to lift Jack off the ground? He also wanted to know what he said to Jack that scared him so, but on their way to class, Drágan had ignored all his questions.

Serg, a big, overweight linebacker for the freshman football team, began mocking Golding's characters, describing Piggy as fat and weak. Then Ron chimed in that another character, Simon, must be gay because of the way he clung to Ralph, the book's protagonist, and loved to touch leaves and plants. He also threw in how Jack, Ralph's rival, was the best character in the book because he took no crap from anyone.

Serg sneered. "Piggy and Simon deserved to die 'cause they were weak. Like Foster."

"That will be enough, or you're suspended!" barked Mr. Sommers, glaring at the unrepentant Serg.

Isaac squirmed with humiliation as everyone stared at him.

During all this, Jack Drake kept his head down and didn't join in with his buddies, which was unusual.

Mr. Sommers, looking only slightly calmer, focused on Drágan. "Have you read the book, Drágan?" When Drágan nodded, the teacher went on, "Would you like to share your thoughts on what our class clowns had to say?"

Drágan stood up, clearly confident. Isaac noticed the girls seemed fixated on him, especially Stephanie who looked like she'd never seen him before, which was weird.

"May I approach and address the class, Mr. Sommers?"

Eyes widening with surprise, Mr. Sommers nodded and waved him forward. Drágan strode up the aisle as though he owned the room and then spoke confidently to the class.

"In addition to depicting the dual nature of man, the author brilliantly describes the psychology of projection." Drágan spoke to the class as though he'd been a teacher for years. "Jack hates Piggy because he is Piggy's intellectual inferior and feels threatened by the other boy, therefore he mocks Piggy's weight to appear superior. He also knows he's inferior to Ralph, who is the more democratic leader, but pretends he's superior by insisting only those who hunt should lead, a rather trite authoritarian argument. It can be further argued that Jack feels he must threaten the smaller boys before they conclude that, as a choirboy, he is quite possibly homosexual."

Isaac gazed at his roommate with wonder. Somehow Drágan's fancy European accent made what he said sound even *more* interesting than it already was.

Drágan fixed his intense gaze on Serg and Ron in the back, practically pinning them in place. "You mock Piggy and Simon in much the same way as Jack in the novel, indicating similar insecurities. Those who comment on the appearance of others usually feel disdain for themselves, and those who accuse others of being homosexual often do so to deflect attention from their own orientation."

Stiff with anger, Serg and Ron slouched down and stared at their desks. The other students gazed in stunned amazement at Drágan, much as they had in the quad, and were silent as he returned to his seat.

Flustered, Mr. Sommers recovered his aplomb and stepped forward. "Thank you for that analysis, Drágan. Any comments on what he said?"

To Isaac's surprise, an unusually spirited discussion ensued regarding the book and Drágan's comments on projecting our insecurities onto others. It was the most stimulating class Isaac had experienced since high school began in August.

BEING A SMALL TOWN, all the freshmen had the same teachers during rotating periods throughout the week, so Isaac didn't see Jack, Serg, or Ron the rest of the morning, and Stephanie only for Art, one of Isaac's favorites.

Stephanie sat beside Mary Anne, her attractive friend, who had short, curly hair, light freckles, and a huge smile. Like the other girls, Mary Anne gazed dreamily at Drágan as the hip young teacher, Ms. Worthington, got him set up with art materials for the day.

Why doesn't Stephanie recognize Drágan?

Isaac had been sure she'd be on him first thing that morning about the modeling photos, but it was as if she'd forgotten the whole matter.

Isaac had been using art class to sketch storyboards for his movie, thereby creating the film shot by shot on paper with as much detail as he could muster.

Drágan set to work sketching in charcoal a drawing of Isaac himself. Isaac watched with fascination as he came to remarkable life on Drágan's thick art paper. By the time class ended, Drágan had created an image of Isaac that looked almost photographic, earning heaps of praise from Ms. Worthington.

Drágan asked Isaac what he thought, and Isaac could barely speak he was so amazed. "Do I...really look like that?"

"And more," Drágan replied. "I created it for your mother. Do you think she'll like it?"

Isaac shrugged. "Maybe, if she isn't too tired of looking at the *real* me." He grinned and they headed to the cafeteria for lunch.

The school cafeteria had been recently renovated and it looked much more modern than the rest of the buildings. The floor had been laid in a shiny tile that reflected the light from a huge, raised skylight spreading across most of the ceiling. He couldn't wait to see what that skylight would look like covered with snow. The tables were on wheels and could be rolled together for larger groups or kept separate for losers like him, and the attached seats were round metal that rolled with each table.

Drágan pulled out money from deep within one pocket, while Isaac used what his mother had given him that morning. They bought some burritos with chips and milk before searching for a table. There was one in the back, but Jack sat there alone, head bowed, barely touching his food.

"You really did a number on Jack," he said, studying the boy who used to be his friend.

"Did he not deserve rebuke?"

"I guess."

Isaac led the way to an empty table and sat on the seat beside Drágan, deciding not to pursue the matter any farther. Stephanie and Mary Anne entered laughing about something. When they saw Drágan, they huddled up and whispered to each other.

Isaac tried to get their attention, but they'd gotten in line to buy food. "I'll be right back."

He hurried to where Stephanie stood in line and tapped her on the shoulder. She turned and frowned, lowering her voice to a whisper. "I thought we agreed not to talk in school."

"Yeah, but I thought you'd want to know about the pictures."

Her face drew a blank. "What pictures?" She was placing items on her plate and sliding her tray along toward the cashier.

Isaac whispered, "The modeling pictures."

She turned back, glancing around to see if anyone was looking.

"Look, Isaac, I said I'd be in your film, but I don't know anything about modeling pictures."

She turned back to Mary Anne, who was gazing at her quizzically and then both ignored Isaac completely. Mystified, he returned to his table and sat down.

"Will she still be in your film?" Drágan asked as he sipped his milk.

Isaac nodded, then leaned closer so no one nearby could overhear. "She didn't remember the pictures she gave me, the ones of you."

Drágan kept a poker face. "Perhaps she has other matters on her mind."

"How could she forget something like that?"

"It is a mystery." He resumed eating.

Isaac stared a moment longer before picking up his burrito and taking a bite. Could Drágan have somehow made her forget? Isaac recalled the look on his face when he mentioned Stephanie, not to mention all the other oddities about his new roommate, and decided he might not want to know.

Instead of asking more questions, he watched Serg and Ron try to sit with Jack, who waved them away. Isaac couldn't make out their conversation, but the two bullies looked annoyed as they moved to another table and sat with some girls.

Just then Isaac saw Nathaniel, a fellow ninth grader, leave the lunch line and look around for a place to sit. Though they hardly ever spoke due to Nathaniel's shyness, Isaac liked him and was about to wave him over when Nathaniel headed toward Jack's table in the corner.

Isaac expected Jack to wave him off or say something nasty, but when Nathaniel seated himself across from him, Jack looked up, stared at Nathaniel for a long moment, then resumed picking at his food.

After lunch, Isaac ducked into the boys' bathroom to wash his hands. Drágan followed and did the same. The door opened and Ron and Serg barged in, both looking as pissed as Isaac had ever seen them. He stepped away from the sink, Drágan behind him, and started for the door. Serg, at least twice Isaac's weight, swatted him aside.

"Out of the way, pussy. We got business with your new boyfriend."

They stepped forward.

"We heard you messed up Jack this morning, asshole," Ron growled. "And you made us look like fools. You're gonna regret that."

Once more, almost faster than his eye could follow, Drágan darted forward, grabbed both boys by the throat, and shoved them so hard against the wall they looked dazed. Drágan's eyes became feral once again.

"Leave us, Isaac."

Again, not a request. A command.

Isaac complied, hurrying from the bathroom almost breathless, and falling back against the wall outside. Passing students eyed him suspiciously, but no one approached. He expected to hear screaming from within, but there wasn't a sound.

After several minutes, Drágan emerged looking like he always did, calm and peaceful. "Let us proceed to our next class."

He started down the hall and Isaac stumbled after, still shook up from the encounter.

Their next class was one of Isaac's least favorite, Algebra 1. He'd complained more than once to his mom that he'd never use any of this class in real life.

They sat together as the other students bustled in noisily. Isaac held his breath because Serg and Ron had this class, along with Jack. The latter entered and sat in the back, never even glancing his way. But the other two did not appear.

Did Drágan kill them?

Would he hurt me if I turned against him?

Mr. Bandini, the portly, balding math teacher, was calling the class to order when the two jocks entered. Unlike their usual swagger, they looked weary as they moved to their seats beside Jack, who gave them a head raise in greeting. They did not respond.

As had happened with teachers in every other class, Mr. Bandini began class by introducing Drágan, though by now *everyone* knew him.

Class proceeded as it always did, with Isaac completely lost. Maybe his mom was right and Drágan could help him with the homework. He glanced back several times to check on the jocks, worrying they might be plotting revenge on him and Drágan. But they sat listlessly at their desks and made not one smart remark during the entire class.

Even Mr. Bandini noticed. He stopped after completing a problem on the board and watched the boys in back languidly copy it down. "Nothing from the peanut gallery today? Not that I'm complaining, but are you guys all right?"

He waddled down one aisle and stopped before them. The boys would not raise their heads to make eye contact.

"We're fine, Mr. Bandini," Serg said with no spirit to his voice.

"Just tired," Ron added, also not looking up.

Mr. Bandini resumed the class, but Isaac was more interested in the two boys. Even Jack noticed the change in behavior. He looked up and caught Isaac staring. Isaac faced forward once more.

What had Drágan done to them?

5

ISAAC ACQUIRES A FILM CREW

After school, Drágan did his usual disappearing act for two hours, but when he returned, he proved tremendously helpful with Isaac's homework. He completed his own in under thirty minutes and then proceeded to explain algebra in a way Isaac almost understood. At least Drágan's examples were clearer than Mr. Bandini's.

"You should share this stuff in class tomorrow," Isaac suggested. "Maybe it'll help other kids too."

Drágan shrugged. "Perhaps."

Isaac broached something he'd been wondering about all day. "Do you really think that character Jack in *Lord of the Flies* is trying to hide that he's gay?"

"If you mean by gay, *homosexual*, and not *happy*, I do not. I merely used that as an example of how Serg and Ron were projecting their own insecurities onto others."

Isaac nodded. "Thought so. Golding didn't give us much about the boys' personal lives. I think Jack chose to be a bully just because he had the opportunity."

"The desire to control others through fear is not uncommon in human nature," Drágan commented. "I've seen it often throughout my life. As individuals, we must learn to control such urges."

"You've been alive a lot longer than me. Have you learned to control them?" He was thinking of how Drágan had dealt with Jack and the others through fear.

"Not fully. I take it one day at a time."

Isaac digested that notion. It made sense to him, given how often he wanted to bash some kid's head in who mocked his hearing loss.

During dinner, Isaac's mom asked lots of questions about school, which the boys answered without ever mentioning the confrontations with Jack, Serg, and Ron. Thankfully, she didn't mention Jack. She expressed joy that Drágan was helping Isaac understand algebra, especially because she didn't understand it herself, and she nearly cried when Drágan presented her with the drawing he'd done in art class.

"It's even more beautiful than the real Isaac," she gushed, admiring his handiwork.

"Bruh," Isaac said.

She laughed and pulled him into a hug.

Drágan watched them with a wistful expression.

THE NEXT DAY, when Isaac and Drágan entered the quad before classes started, the girls stared, but the boys steered clear. Jack wasn't anywhere to be seen, nor were Serg and Ron. Stephanie and Mary Anne entered the quad and spotted them sitting on a concrete wall that fronted the grass and made a beeline for them. Both wore their cheer jackets over warm shirts and long sweatpants.

The bell rang just as they arrived.

Stephanie whispered to Isaac, "I printed out your script. Gonna read it today."

Then she took off toward the classroom buildings with Mary Anne.

Serg and Ron still seemed listless all day, and Jack clearly noticed but as far as Isaac could see, made no move to ask why. It was algebra class that proved the most entertaining that morning. Mr. Bandini kept using odd examples like pretending to empty a wastebasket as a method of gaining the students' understanding of variables. It wasn't working.

Drágan raised his hand.

"Yes, Drágan?"

"Could you perhaps demonstrate how algebra is used in the real world? That might help all of us in better understanding the concepts."

Mr. Bandini scratched his bald head, drawing a blank. "Can't think of any, off the top of my head."

Students laughed because his hand was on his head as he said that.

"May I approach and demonstrate a few to the class?" Drágan asked.

"Oh, yes, yes, come forward by all means."

Drágan rose and a rustle of excitement went through the class. Most had been present during the *Lord of the Flies* discussion the previous day. He took the dry erase marker and launched into the various uses of unknown variables, which much of algebra revolves around.

He began by using grocery bills as an example and explained how a monthly budget is the absolute value while the various foods we want to buy are the unknown variables. Likewise, he demonstrated the use of algebra in finance, construction, borrowing money, and even in warfare, wherein there might be several unknowns for generals to consider, and working out those unknowns is a form of algebra.

"Most of the time, people don't consciously use the algebraic expressions we see in class, but if those expressions are presented in real-life contexts such as those I've demonstrated, the subject may feel more useful. Do any of you agree?"

Every girl raised her hand and Isaac rolled his eyes. But even many boys put up a hand and Isaac had to admit, Drágan made sense.

Drágan handed the marker back to the flabbergasted Mr. Bandini and took his seat. The math teacher paused a moment to examine the examples Drágan had put on the board, turned, and said, "Thank you, young man. That was most instructive."

He conducted the remainder of class as usual, but for homework assigned everyone the task of working out some real-world problem using algebraic equations from class.

Lunch provided Isaac with more surprises. He and Drágan purchased their food and sat at the same empty table as yesterday. Nathaniel sat alone at the back table. There was no sign of Jack or the two football players.

Just as Isaac bit into his grilled cheese sandwich, Stephanie and Mary Anne plopped down their trays and sat across from them. Stunned, Isaac glanced over at the table where the other cheerleaders stared at them, mouths agape.

"Aren't you at the wrong table?" He indicated the glowering cheer squad across the cafeteria.

Stephanie shrugged, sipping her orange juice. "They'll survive. Your movie'll be much more fun."

"Stephanie told me about the film," Mary Anne gushed, "and I wanna help in some way, maybe even play a small part."

Isaac wasn't sure what to say, but Drágan came to his rescue. "She could play the lead character's best friend, the one killed by the were-wolf. And you will likely need a crew."

"I'd love being killed by a werewolf, and I'm practically a professional makeup artist," Mary Anne burbled. "Haven't you ever been to one of my Halloween parties?"

Isaac looked down, embarrassed.

Realizing her blunder, Mary Anne mumbled, "Oh, yeah, I never invited you."

Isaac felt like disappearing into the floor, but Stephanie wouldn't allow that. "So what? Her parties suck anyway."

Mary Anne pulled a face, and Stephanie elbowed her with a grin.

"So," Stephanie went on, "I read the script this morning—"

Startled, Isaac cut her off. "When?"

"During Health. Trust me, that class was a snooze. Anyway, I love the story, but your dialogue between the boy and girl is beyond cringe. Seriously, you don't know many girls, do you?"

Isaac's face felt hot with embarrassment. "Isn't that obvious?"

She waved that off as of no importance. And she still hadn't mentioned the Drágan photos, which really bothered him.

"Look, I'll work on the dialogue before we start shooting. Trust me, it'll sound real."

"No cussing," Isaac insisted.

She tilted her head and raised her eyebrows. "Have you heard some of these kids?"

She indicated the cafeteria at large.

"Hollywood overdoes the swearing," Isaac said. "I want this movie to feel like the old classics, like *The Wolfman.*"

"Fair point. But I do think the young lovers should kiss at some point."

"No kissing." That came from Drágan in a tone of finality.

The girls exchanged a confused look.

"I'm not talking about a sleazy sex scene here," Stephanie went on, "just a simple kiss."

Drágan's body stiffened. "No."

The hard look in his eyes must have convinced Stephanie. "You're gorgeous, but weird. Okay, no kiss."

They went on to discuss the shooting schedule, which Isaac said he'd have ready the following day.

Drágan noticed Nathaniel sitting alone. "We should include him."

Stephanie followed his gaze. "Are you kidding? That kid hasn't said three words since first grade."

"His name's Nathaniel," Isaac explained, annoyed by her tone. "He's just super shy."

"All the more reason to include him," Drágan insisted. "Shall I ask?"

"Go ahead," Isaac replied. "But I bet he'll say no."

Drágan rose and threaded his way through the tables. Isaac watched him closely. Nathaniel looked up, clearly startled to find Drágan sitting beside him. Isaac couldn't hear their conversation, but he soon realized that almost everyone in the cafeteria was watching the exchange. It seemed Drágan couldn't do anything without drawing attention.

Nathaniel turned as Drágan pointed out Isaac's table, then faced forward again. Isaac was dying to know what his roommate was saying. After another few moments, Drágan stood, and Isaac figured he'd failed. But Nathaniel stood with him, and the two boys approached the table. Drágan indicated the empty seat to one side of Isaac while he resumed his seat on the other.

"Thanks for asking me to help," Nathaniel said to Isaac so quietly it was almost inaudible.

"If you're gonna help, you need to speak up," Stephanie said in her typical blunt manner.

Nathaniel, a thin, mousy boy with short brown hair and large ears, cowered back into his hoodie.

"Don't mind her," Isaac said. "She's like that with everyone. I'm happy to have you on my crew."

"You're really going to meet Stephen King?" Nathaniel asked, peeking back out like a turtle.

"Once we make it into the festival, yeah." Now he knew how Drágan had convinced the shy boy.

They all agreed to meet the following day at lunch to discuss the shooting schedule. Isaac said he'd bring his storyboards.

"And I'll bring the revised script," Stephanie added just as the bell rang.

They tossed out their trash and headed to class.

After lunch on Tuesdays and Thursdays was PE, the only class Isaac hated more than math. The teacher was Coach Lancaster, an almost stereotypical burly football coach, thick-chested, booming voice, with thinning hair beneath a Pittsburgh Steelers snapback, and the patience of a four-year-old.

Ever since school began in August, Isaac had told the coach about his hearing problem and how difficult it was for him to make out instructions if he was far away. This only resulted in the coach screaming in his ear when they were face to face and then reaming him in front of everyone for not following directions during a game.

They'd been playing flag football since school began and, even though the goal was to grab the other team's flags, the jerkwads on the freshman football team loved "accidentally" slamming into Isaac as they grabbed his flag, sending him crashing to the ground. After a hearing aid was dislodged several times, Isaac took to storing them in his locker for safe keeping. The result was he still got slammed into and yelled at, but at least his expensive hearing aids were safe.

This day began much like the others, changing in the locker room. They wore gold shorts and a blue tee—the school colors. Usually, Serg and Ron started in on Isaac before they even got out onto the field. But today, they ignored him completely. Their languid demeanor drew the attention of the other guys, and Isaac was forgotten.

The Millwood combination football and soccer field was green year-round due to the abundance of rain. Set behind the school buildings, it was surrounded by trees on three sides, with bleachers rising on both sides of the field.

Walking out into the field, Isaac felt vulnerable, as he always did without his hearing aids, because all sound was muted, including voices, and he hated the overwhelming feeling of insecurity, but that day, he felt safer. Drágan would protect him.

Coach Lancaster took roll in his usual foghorn voice, then selected the teams for flag football. As always, his freshman football players made up the bulk of one team, and the weaker kids the other. Isaac, naturally, was with the weaker kids so the football guys could "accidentally" trip him. But Coach Lancaster made a big mistake that day. Noting Drágan's slim form, he shouted, "You, new kid!" and pointed to the weaker team with one thick finger.

Flags were passed out and the two teams walked onto the field. At Drágan's urging, Isaac pointed out the boys who regularly tripped him. Drágan leaned close to Isaac's ear. "I shall teach your tormentors a lesson they'll not soon forget."

Isaac nodded, relaxed for once and ready to play.

As Isaac's team huddled to discuss strategy, Drágan admitted he'd never played flag football. Blond and tall, Jason was the team captain mainly because he was the fastest runner. He explained about scoring touchdowns and how taking an opponent's flag meant a first or second or third down. Isaac could see that Drágan understood, especially as he eyed the goal posts at either end of the field.

"They will not capture my flag," Drágan announced to the team, his voice dead serious. "If I possess the ball, I'll score."

Normally, Isaac knew, if any other kid said that they'd all accuse him of bragging and laugh. But everyone present had some experience with Drágan over the past two days, so no one even argued.

"Okay," Jason agreed. "I'm quarterback. You're wide receiver. I'll pass to you, and you run it in."

Isaac took up a position as the other wide receiver, but Jason would always throw to Drágan so Isaac should be safe. The other team placed their girls outside their line and the football players were the linemen. The freshman quarterback, a smug pipsqueak of a kid who had the good fortune of an excellent throwing arm, stepped into place.

Jason and Braedon, his best friend who hiked the ball, took their places. Off on the sidelines, no doubt hoping for another shellacking by his football players, Coach blew the whistle to start. As a consolation prize for having the weaker team, Isaac's squad had the ball first.

Braedon hiked the ball to Jason. The opposing team plowed through Jason's line to grab his flag (and knock him down "by accident," if all went as usual.) It didn't go as usual. Jason threw the ball to Drágan, who plucked it out of the air with ease. The football players, except Serg and Ron who brought up the rear, plowed across the grass toward Drágan.

But Drágan was no longer there. He'd darted through their line and sailed into the endzone for an easy touchdown.

Isaac's team stared in shock, then jumped up and down with elation. Their first touchdown of the year!

Drágan trotted past the other team, all of whom stared at him with fury, except the girls, who grinned. He handed the ball to Jason, who looked amazed.

"I've never seen anyone so fast. You gotta join the track team."

The game resumed.

Now the other team had the ball. The smug little quarterback looked like he had a plan to outsmart Jason. The ball was snapped, and the pipsqueak sent a nice smooth spiral right to one of Isaac's tormentors, except it never arrived. Somehow, Drágan was there, in the air, grabbing the ball before Mr. Tormentor could touch it and then he ran the ball past the other team for a second touchdown.

Jason, Isaac, and their team were ecstatic with joy, jumping up and down and clapping Drágan on the back. The other team didn't look so happy. Even so, their next play failed when Drágan plowed through their linemen, knocked them sprawling, and snatched the quarterback's flag before he could make a pass.

Isaac had never seen such happy kids as his teammates, while the opposing team looked ready to commit murder.

Jason and Braedon stepped into position for their next hike. The ball was snapped. Jason trotted back as two of the larger football players charged through his line. The rest of the team charged at Drágan. Jason threw the ball into a high wobbly arc. Two players plowed forward, but Drágan leaped high into the air over their heads, grabbed the ball, landed on his feet, and ran it in for third touchdown.

Left to guard the goal, Serg and Ron barely moved as they watched Drágan score. Isaac's teammates jumped for joy, while Coach Lancaster screamed at his "preferred" team to "Get your asses in gear!"

The other team had the ball again, still angling for a first down. This time Pipsqueak handed the ball off to Tormentor Number Two, who charged through the line only to have Drágan snatch his flag before he was even at the fifty-yard line. To Isaac's delight, Drágan also managed to trip Tormentor Two so adeptly that no one was sure how he did it.

The other team tried again and again with Pipsqueak passing the ball to someone, but Drágan was always there to shut the play down and finally, the ball returned to Jason's team.

On their next play, Drágan grabbed the ball from Jason's handoff and darted toward two of Isaac's worst tormentors, somehow tripping them both—again making it look imperceptible—and scored again. The indignant players, disliking a taste of their own medicine, complained to the coach. But Lancaster's eyes had never been wider as he watched Drágan saunter back to Jason. Isaac felt certain the football coach was seeing his next star player.

"Looked clean to me," Lancaster barked. "You two are clumsy, that's all." He blew his whistle. "Next play."

Snap after snap, Jason got the ball to Drágan, sometimes via another player, but every time, Drágan evaded the other team and scored. He also managed to unobtrusively trip the bullies several more times.

The other team never managed even a single first down.

With each touchdown worth six points, and the opposing team never scoring once, by the time the ninety-minute period ended, Isaac's team had creamed them 60-0.

None of the kids were strong enough to lift Drágan into the air, but if they had been, they would have. Jason and the team clapped him on the back and babbled nonstop about his talents. Isaac trailed behind in his muted bubble, fearing he might lose his friend, but Drágan, as if reading his mind again, let the other kids pass so he could walk side by side with him.

"I've never seen anything like that," Isaac gushed, happy he wasn't being ignored. He leaned closer. "And thanks for giving those jerks a taste of their own medicine."

Coach Lancaster suddenly blocked their way. He eyed Isaac with contempt. "Beat it, kid."

Before Isaac could leave, Drágan grabbed his arm. "If you have something to say, Coach, you may say it."

Lancaster was too flustered to argue. "I've never seen anything like you before. You gotta play ball for me! With you on the team, we'll be state champs for the first time ever!"

Drágan eyed the much bigger man coldly. "I have no wish to play for you."

"What! Why on earth not? Kid, you can get a scholarship anywhere in the country."

Drágan didn't break eye contact but tilted his head toward Isaac. "What is his name?"

Confused, Lancaster glanced at Isaac like he would a bug. "I don't know. The kid who's deaf, I think. What's that have to do—"

"His name is Isaac Foster," Drágan interrupted, "and he's hearing impaired, not deaf. He's also the boy you have belittled since school began. You cannot even correctly recall his disability, yet you humiliate him for making mistakes typical for one with hearing loss. Further, you ignore, or more likely encourage, your brutish football players to trip him and other smaller students because, I suppose, you find such behavior amusing. These are but a few of the reasons I would never help you win anything."

The coach's face turned so red during Drágan's speech that Isaac thought he was having a heart attack.

"How dare you talk to me like that, you insolent punk! Go to the office now! You are suspended!"

Drágan didn't budge. He just offered a nasty smile that sent a chill up Isaac's spine. "You may wish to reconsider your actions, sir, lest the remainder of your beloved football team end up like those two."

He indicated Serg and Ron, slowly trudging off the field as though in a daze. The coach stared at his two players in bewilderment, but when he turned back to address Drágan, the boys were already at the locker room door. Isaac observed a look on the big man's face he never expected to see—fear.

The boy's locker room was in an uproar when Isaac entered, with the football players arguing with Jason and his team. Drágan entered and stood in their midst, and the clamor died down.

One of the bigger boys, a freshman linebacker, asked, "So, you gonna join the team? I know the coach asked."

Drágan turned his head slowly to address the much taller boy, who fidgeted with his shoelaces. "I would never be persuaded to do anything that would advance the fortunes of a bully, nor should you."

He crossed the room to his locker, a shocked Isaac on his tail. No one said much after that as all the boys dressed and left for their next class.

Drágan was not suspended.

6

A MAJOR SECRET REVEALED

The remainder of the week went much the same at school, except in PE everyone wanted Drágan on their team. When he decided to stay on the "weak" team, all the football players crossed over to join him. That seriously pissed off Coach Lancaster who, Isaac was sure, wanted to suspend the entire class. But one look from Drágan seemed to shut him down cold, which pleased everyone, even his team members. Finally, with no one wanting to oppose Drágan on the field, Coach decided everyone should walk the track for the time being.

While they were walking, Jason and a few others kept after Drágan to join the track team. Isaac hoped he would say no, but Drágan only said, "I'll think about it."

Isaac bit his lip, fretting. *If Drágan gets seriously into sports, when will he have time to hang out with me?*

Isaac did find it interesting that some of his teachers seemed to have taken Drágan's impromptu lessons to heart. Mr. Bandini, as much as he could, reframed his algebra course to reflect real world applications. Mr. Sommers engaged with the class in more of a discussion format, throwing out challenging ideas and asking for feedback, which was readily given.

After school that Thursday, Drágan said he was going to see Dr. Wilson.

Not sure how Drágan might respond, Isaac said, "Could I come along, maybe? Dr. Wilson is my neighbor and I've never even met him."

"I'm sorry, but I prefer going alone."

Drágan's tone was not to be argued with, so Isaac stayed home and put the finishing touches on his storyboards and shot sheets.

Later that night, after they'd finished homework, Isaac finally asked the question for which he might not like the answer. "Did you decide about the track team?"

Drágan eyed him uncertainly. "I confess I've never seen a track team, so I don't know exactly what they do.

"It's running, mostly—you against boys from other schools. They throw stuff too, I think, like a heavy frisbee."

Drágan's eyes lit up. "Ah, akin to the Greek Olympics."

Isaac nodded. "Yeah. Wait, you weren't in those, were you?"

Drágan raised his eyebrows. "I'm not *that* old."

"So, what will you tell Jason? Will you join the track team?"

Drágan frowned. "That would be a form of cheating."

"How?"

"I explained to you that my unique blood has also quickened my reflexes and given me greater strength than other youth my age. To challenge ordinary boys would be unfair. I'd win every time."

Isaac sighed with relief. "I'm glad you don't want to do track anyway. I'd never see you much if you did."

"And that would trouble you?"

"Hell, yeah. I mean, you're the best thing that's ever happened to me."

Drágan fell silent and Isaac feared he'd said something wrong. Then Drágan made eye contact. "I confess that, in all my long life, at least among youth I've met, I've enjoyed your company most of all."

Isaac beamed. "Seriously?"

"Seriously."

"Thanks, man."

FRIDAY NIGHT WAS varsity football night at Millwood High, and most of the town attended the games. Isaac and his mom always stayed home and watched horror films instead. But this week was different. Stephanie and Mary Anne had been bugging Isaac and Drágan all week about going to the game with them, insisting it was "tons of fun" hanging out in the stands. Since the varsity team had its own cheer squad, they were free to just watch the game.

Drágan shot down the idea each time it was mentioned and, while Isaac thought it might be fun to do something with girls for a change, he felt torn about going without his friend. When Friday dawned, Drágan seemed restless, which was unusual.

"I can't go out tonight with the girls. There's a matter of great urgency I must deal with, and I'd like you to be there. But I fully understand if the girls are more important."

Isaac didn't hesitate. "Course they aren't. If you want me, I'm there."

Drágan nodded and they resumed dressing for school. Stephanie was angry the boys wouldn't join them, but Drágan reminded her that they'd be spending the entire weekend together filming Isaac's movie, and that mollified her a bit.

After school that day, Drágan informed Isaac that they'd be out quite late, so Isaac asked his mom if he and Drágan could camp in the nearby woods.

"Camp?" Penelope looked incredulous. "It's September, Isaac. That can mean temps in the forties."

He shrugged. "I know. But I got tons of warm clothes, and we have a tent. Please, Mom? Drágan really wants to."

She gazed at the two of them. "Boys," she said, shaking her head. "Okay, just take your phone and don't go far."

Isaac gave her a look. "Seriously, Mom? I grew up in these woods."

"I know." She tousled his messy hair. "Be careful. Both of you."

Isaac dressed in his warmest shirt, hoodie, heavy coat, and a beanie while Drágan dressed the same as always.

"Bring your camera and perhaps one of your lights that is powered by batteries."

"What for?"

"To film what occurs. Oh, and I shall not be needing a sleeping bag."

Mystified, Isaac pulled out the smaller of their tents, one that could fit two people snugly, and packed up his camera, an extra battery, and one of his battery-powered lights. He slung the camera and light bags over one shoulder, then gripped the tent bag in one hand and a powerful flashlight in the other. Drágan carried only his valise and Isaac's sleeping bag.

"Don't you want a flashlight?"

"I see well in the dark."

That seemed strange to Isaac, but then everything about this boy was strange. His mom fretted over Drágan not dressing warmer, but he assured her he would be fine. Isaac noted the valise as they left the house at dusk and wondered if Drágan had removed the chains before leaving. And if he hadn't, what did *that* mean?

Drágan led the way through the woods, even though Isaac carried the flashlight.

"What are you, a cat?" he asked at one point. Sure, the full moon would be up soon, but the density of the trees would mostly block it out.

"I have excellent vision" was all Drágan said. "Don't worry. I preselected a spot during my solo walking excursions."

They didn't speak for a time as Drágan threaded his way through thick maple and white pine trees. Balsam fir, the softer wood used to make paper, wasn't prevalent in these woods, only in forests north of the mill, so loggers never came to these woods.

Scenes from Friday the 13th movies, not to mention many other horror films, flitted through Isaac's mind, something that never happened to him in these woods. It was only happening now because of Drágan—his weird behavior, his cat eyes, and the chains he might be carrying.

Shivering, he mouthed to himself, "I trust him, I trust him" over and over as they headed deeper into the woods than he typically ventured.

Drágan stopped beside a hugely thick pine tree that towered upward into the encroaching night.

Not a sound could be heard, at least to Isaac's imperfect ears.

"This is the tree I preselected," Drágan said, setting his valise on the needle-covered ground. He pointed to a spot about ten yards from the tree. "That should be a safe spot for the tent."

Isaac eyed him in the growing shadows. "Safe?"

Drágan ignored him, instead taking the tent and sleeping bag over to the indicated spot. "If you place your camera there"—he pointed to a flat area just in front of where the tent would sit—"you'll have a clear view of the tree. Do you require help preparing your equipment?"

Isaac shook his head, fear twisting its way around his heart. Sure, he'd accepted that Drágan's blood gave him eternal life. But all of this other stuff was unsettling, and he wished the other boy would explain himself.

What was Drágan up to?

Isaac realized his hands were shaking as he unzipped the tent carrier. As he set about erecting the tent, he noticed Drágan pull a long piece of rope from the valise.

"I'll return shortly," Drágan said, vanishing into the woods without waiting for a response.

Trepidation filled Isaac as he finished popping open the tent and unrolling his sleeping bag. Nothing about this night made sense to Isaac, and he became even more perturbed when Drágan emerged from between the thick trees leading a young deer by the rope tied around its slender neck.

He started forward, but Drágan held up his free hand. Isaac stopped and watched as Drágan tied the rope once around the trunk and into a knot. The docile animal grazed placidly.

Drágan walked to his valise.

Isaac pointed to the deer. "Why is it here?" He felt oddly afraid of the answer.

Drágan didn't reply. Instead, he pulled the heavy chains from his valise.

So, he did bring them!

Drágan wrapped one section of the chain around the trunk twice and then locked it in place with a thick padlock. Isaac just watched, fascinated. The remainder of the chain lay piled on the ground in front of the tree. Drágan picked up the valise and moved it to a spot about twelve feet from the tree.

"How is the tent construction?"

Startled by Drágan's voice, Isaac spluttered, "It's...it's done."

Drágan removed his heavy coat and laid it carefully inside the valise. As instructed, Isaac unpacked his camera and tripod, setting everything up where Drágan had indicated. Pulling out his portable light stand, he placed it off to one side so the tree would photograph better in the dark.

By this time, Drágan had removed his tie and vest, folding both and placing them within the valise. He now wore only boots, pants, and the billowy shirt he favored.

Isaac approached, confused. "What're you doing?"

Matter-of-factly, Drágan asked, "Have you ever beheld another boy naked?"

Isaac lurched back in shock. "Wait, what...?"

Drágan just stared, awaiting an answer.

"Well, no, actually," Isaac blustered. "I mean, we don't shower for PE. You know that."

"Perhaps you should avert your eyes, for I must remove all of my clothing."

Isaac's mouth hung open. Was Drágan into some kinky stuff and wanted him to join in? Or was it something worse, something more insidious?

Drágan apparently took Isaac's not turning away as an answer and removed his shirt and boots. Isaac found himself staring at the other boy's torso. Even in the encroaching darkness it looked shaped to perfection. Before he could turn, Drágan's pants were off. He wore no underwear.

Isaac turned as quickly as he could, but still caught a glimpse of Drágan's privates. Embarrassment set his heart pounding, but when he heard the chain clanking, he risked a peek over one shoulder.

Drágan was squatting beside the pile of chains. It was then Isaac spotted something he hadn't seen before – manacles. As though it were the most normal thing in the world, Drágan clamped manacles around both of his own ankles and both wrists.

Isaac couldn't look away now. Fear made his throat dry and his breath raspy. What was happening here?

Drágan stood up, smooth and well-muscled, but shackled like a wild beast. "It's nearly time. You may wish to start your camera."

Pulling his gaze away from Drágan, Isaac stumbled back to his camera and uncapped the lens. Looking though the viewfinder, he framed a shot of Drágan and the tree. Thinking now as a director, he stepped over to the light and adjusted its angle to cast his mysterious friend with an almost mystical glow.

Darkness had fallen, and Isaac searched the treetops for the moon he knew to be there.

"Hurry, Isaac, and stay back no matter what happens."

Isaac darted back to his camera and pressed the record button.

Drágan stood before him, fully exposed, yet almost apologetic. "I fear you'll no longer welcome me in your home after tonight. But I owe you the truth."

He gazed upward as sharp rays of moonlight pierced the treetops and bathed him in their ethereal light. For a moment, he looked angelic.

But only for a moment.

Isaac gasped as Drágan lurched spasmodically, as though in the throes of a bout of epilepsy. His body twisted and contorted in ways Isaac couldn't even have imagined. And then Drágan became something else. In Isaac's mind, what happened took hours, but in truth, it was less than a minute.

Drágan's legs thinned, his feet elongated, his fingers and toes became sharp claws. Gray fur sprouted everywhere on his normally hairless body. As Drágan morphed into something completely inhuman, Isaac focused on his face. His picture-perfect features became harsh and covered with fur as his chin and mouth elongated, revealing razor-sharp teeth. His ears became pointed and large, while his hazelnut eyes turned savage.

It was those eyes that convinced Isaac that his friend was still inside this creature he never thought he would see in real life. Those eyes looked angry, as they had at Jack and Coach Lancaster, only now they gazed outward, not from a boy, but from the face of a werewolf!

When the creature focused those squinting eyes directly on him, Isaac nearly peed in his pants. He took a step back, almost stumbling over the tent. The formerly placid deer now fought with a frenzy to escape the werewolf, who noticed its struggles and pounced. With one snap of its slavering jaws, the creature tore out the throat of the deer, splashing blood on the ground and bathing its own muzzle in shiny crimson. As it gutted the animal and began feeding, Isaac gagged on the smell of death, a powerful combination of mothballs and rotting fish. He staggered back into the woods and vomited up his dinner, retching repeatedly until there was nothing left.

Weak and afraid, he wiped his mouth with the back of one hand and crept toward his tent. The werewolf's head was bent over the remains of the deer and Isaac clearly heard the chomping and slurping sounds as it fed, wishing for once that his hearing aids weren't functioning.

He couldn't believe this was happening.

Either through smell or sound, the werewolf knew Isaac had returned. It raised its bloody face and growled at him. It leapt and Isaac stumbled back, landing on his butt beside the tent. But the chains held as the creature struggled and fought, carving a deep groove into the trunk of the tree.

Isaac realized something as he cowered from the snarling werewolf that would, if it could, likely eviscerate him as it had the deer.

Drágan had those chains for just this purpose and he'd known there was no danger to Isaac, or he'd never have risked bringing him.

As Isaac stared at the struggling creature, standing before him on two legs in the very spot Drágan had stood moments before, he thought back on his conversation with Stephanie, about the supernatural being real. He considered all the legends of werewolves that went back centuries across many cultures, and now understood they weren't just legends. The proof stood before him.

Deep sorrow welled up from within him. Tears rolled down his cheeks; his whole being was suffused with compassion for this boy so displaced in time and suffering such a terrible curse. His first instinct had been to run away like a frightened rabbit, but he pushed that thought from his mind. No, he would stay the night and be there when the boy who'd changed his life in so many positive ways became himself again.

After he calmed himself, Isaac filmed a while longer, getting closeups of the creature's face and parts of its body, especially as it once more dug into the slaughtered deer, then turned off his camera to preserve the battery. The werewolf looked up and its eyes followed his every movement, but it didn't try to leap at him again.

"You've helped *me*, Drágan, so it's my turn to help you."

A howl from somewhere in the distance pierced the cold night air, chilling Isaac to his bones. Drágan howled in reply and Isaac nearly dropped his flashlight.

After howling, the werewolf sat in a pool of moonlight and watched as Isaac returned to his tent. Rather than enter, he unzipped his sleeping bag and wrapped it around his shoulders as he sat hunched on the ground behind his camera.

That other howl worried him because there'd been no wolves in this area for decades. If they'd returned, that could be bad for the town. After a long time watching the struggling, snuffling animal, Isaac felt sleepy. He turned the camera back on and powered down his hearing aids for the night, huddling in his sleeping bag.

As sleep seeped into his body, a terrifying thought came with it – what if that howl had come from another werewolf?

7

A BOY WHO IS PURE IN HEART

Isaac woke with a start. The forest was silent, and he could see without the flashlight. It was morning. He barely recalled falling asleep, but he found himself on the ground wrapped up in his sleeping bag.

He sat up quickly and, out of habit, powered on his hearing aids. Then he gazed at the huge tree. The chains had gouged out what looked like an inch of bark, but they were still wrapped securely around its massive girth. And lying on the ground before it, still shackled, was a naked boy with long hair splayed outward in a semi-circle around his head.

Isaac threw off the sleeping bag and hurried to Drágan's side. He was facing away, so Isaac rolled him onto his back. Embarrassed by Drágan's nudity, Isaac shucked off his heavy jacket and draped it across the other boy's waist.

He studied Drágan's face. Smeared blood had dried around his mouth and cheeks, and large splashes of blood covered his torso. He looked peaceful, so different from the violent excesses of the previous night. Isaac touched one cheek. It felt cold, but from the rise and fall of Drágan's chest, he knew his friend lived.

Isaac rose and returned to his supplies. He grabbed the large container of water he'd brought and took it to Drágan's side. Realizing he had no cloth handy, he slipped out of his hoodie and long-sleeve shirt. He wore a plain white tee shirt under everything else and yanked it up over his head.

The biting cold stung his naked flesh, but he ignored it, feeling more in sync with the tortured Drágan this way. He poured water onto his tee shirt and gently wiped the blood from Drágan's face. He began with his cheeks and then his mouth. When his friend's handsome features were once more revealed, he ran the damp shirt over Drágan's torso, wiping away the remnants of his transformation with great tenderness.

"No one has ever cleaned me before."

Isaac jumped as Drágan sat up and gazed at him with gratitude.

"Not even my father when I first transformed at the age of twelve."

Filled with jumbled emotions about everything, Isaac grunted in disgust. "Well, he should have!"

Then he proceeded to wipe blood from Drágan's feet. Isaac felt a hand on his arm and turned to meet Drágan's soulful eyes.

"I'm grateful, Isaac. Even for this." He indicated the jacket affording him a modicum of modesty. "In freak shows of the distant past, proprietors felt no compunction about parading me naked in front of large crowds."

Anger welled up within Isaac and he wanted to shout his frustration. Gritting his teeth, he said, "I'm so sorry. You didn't deserve any of that."

Drágan's eyes swept over Isaac's naked torso.

Isaac's cheeks reddened. "I didn't have a towel or anything."

"I've never met someone who has helped me as you have. Thank you."

Shivering from the cold, Isaac said, "It's okay," and stood up. "Do you, uh, need help with those...shackles?"

"No," Drágan replied, feeling around in the dirt beside the tree and producing a key. With practiced skill, he was free within moments and stood up. Isaac's jacket fell away, and Isaac turned around.

"I'll let you get dressed," Isaac said as he pulled on his long-sleeved shirt and hoodie. He felt a hand touch his shoulder and glanced back, averting his eyes as Drágan handed him his jacket. "Thanks. I uh, I'll pack up."

When Isaac got to the camera, he noticed that it was still recording and shut it off. He packed everything into their respective carry bags while he heard the clanking of chains behind him. Not wanting to rob Drágan of any more dignity, he didn't look back until he heard a throat clear.

Isaac turned to find Drágan wearing his boots, pants, and long coat, unbuttoned, revealing his naked torso.

"I didn't wish for remnants of blood to stain my shirt," Drágan explained. "I feel responsible for yours, however."

"Don't worry about it. I got tons of 'em at home."

They set out through the woods, Isaac leading.

"I heard a wolf howl last night," he said, attempting a casual tone. "You howled back."

Drágan stopped dead, his face twisted with worry. "I do recall. Over the years, I have gained great control over my animal form, but I suppose I could not resist the cry of a fellow werewolf."

Isaac was rooted to the spot. So, he'd been right!

"Another werewolf? In Millwood?"

"Undoubtedly."

That was all Drágan said, as if having two werewolves in a small Maine town was an everyday occurrence. He proceeded to pass Isaac and thread his way through the trees. Thoughts churning with fear about what a second werewolf might mean for Millwood, Isaac hurried after.

BACK AT THE HOUSE, Isaac snuck Drágan upstairs and into the bathroom before checking in with his mom. She was already in her home office working away. She designed websites and did other online jobs and, to Isaac's untrained eyes, was excellent at her work.

"Have fun, honey?" she asked, turning from her computer screen to regard him. "Was it cold?"

He shrugged. "Not so much. I had lots of clothes."

"Where's Drágan?"

"In the shower. I let him go first."

"As a proper host should," she said with a grin. "Hungry? I've been waiting for you boys before starting breakfast." Isaac's stomach growled and she laughed. "I'll take that as a yes. You get cleaned up and put all the camping gear away and I'll get started downstairs."

"Thanks, Mom."

She lovingly tousled his hair as she passed him and hurried down the stairs. Isaac replaced the tent in the hall closet and his camera equipment in his room. Knowing he'd be filming all afternoon, he plugged in both the camera and extra battery to charge, along with the portable light. He also removed his hearing aids and placed them within their portable charging unit. He'd need them fully charged for the day ahead. Then he gathered clean clothes for himself and waited for Drágan, the world once more muted so significantly he could no longer hear the shower water just down the hall.

The upstairs bath was grander than the small one downstairs, with an extra-large shower that Isaac loved. He often spent more time in there than his mom liked, but he'd daydream and get distracted. The bathroom door was half-open, and Isaac glanced in, not sure if the water was running or not. Steam wafted out into the hall, so he figured it was. He crept in to leave his clothes on top of the counter in anticipation of his turn. He'd already hung up his jacket and thrown the long-sleeved shirt in the hamper, so he was, once again, shirtless. The bloody tee shirt he decided to throw out. His mom didn't count his underwear anyway.

Isaac padded back to his room and sat on his bed. He grabbed his revised—thanks to Stephanie—shooting script off his desk and reviewed what he planned to film that day.

Isaac's mouth watered as he and Drágan entered the kitchen. There were pancakes and syrup, a huge pile of sausages, and bowls of fresh fruit. Once again, Drágan prayed over their food and Isaac waited politely until he was finished. Then he dug in.

He was starved, especially since he'd vomited up all his dinner the night before. When Drágan chewed his sausages, images arose in Isaac's mind of the werewolf devouring stringy chunks of deer meat, and he nearly lost what was left of his appetite.

After helping his mom clean the dishes, Isaac dragged Drágan from the kitchen, saying they needed to rehearse before Stephanie and the others arrived at noon.

Back in their room, Isaac asked, "Should we talk about the other werewolf?" He could almost think of nothing else.

Drágan looked pensive, clearly choosing his words with care. "Dr. Wilson, who has been studying me, confessed quite by accident that what he calls the 'werewolf cell' in my blood isn't the first he's seen. He's been studying blood from someone else. I now understand how close that someone else is to us."

"It's crazy that werewolves even exist," Isaac muttered. Catching the hurt look on Drágan's face, he blurted, "But I'm glad you're here." He paused, hoping his slight shudder went unnoticed. "Could that other werewolf be dangerous to the town?"

Drágan looked thoughtful. "I find it odd that the werewolf didn't track me down last night. Our sense of smell is acute, even in human form. I wonder if, like me, that person chains themselves up before transforming."

"I didn't think about that."

"I do believe Dr. Wilson would have warned me if another werewolf was roaming free, so I suspect we're safe."

Isaac nodded, feeling a deep sense of relief, not just for himself, but for his mom and everyone else in town. Then an idea struck him. "Maybe I could be your protector on full moon nights, just in case any crazy hunter tries to shoot you."

"T'would do him no good lest the bullets be made of silver."

"So, the legend is true."

"Yes. Even a boy who is pure of heart and prays at night can become a wolf when the moon is full and bright." His voice reeked of grief.

Isaac nodded, unsure what to say, deciding not to pursue his "protector" idea for the moment.

"Perhaps I should rehearse my lines," Drágan said after a long pause in the conversation. "Then you can offer me direction before we begin filming."

"That's a great idea. I'll read Stephanie's part as best I can. I'm not an actor, though, and definitely not as hot as her." He chuckled.

Drágan gave him a serious look "You underestimate yourself far too often. Shall we begin?" He held his script in hand and offered another copy to Isaac.

"Let's try the scene on the bridge," Isaac said, then began to read, "Cameron and Daphne stand against the railing, watching the placid river beneath. Daphne says, 'Are your parents really thinking of leaving? You just moved here.' "

"I know, but they move around a lot."

"What about us? I know we only met a few months ago, but...I don't wanna lose you."

"Is your dad still getting the town's people to hunt the wolf tonight?"

"I think so. What's that got to do with us?"

"I'm afraid for you. There's gonna be a full moon."

"So? Cameron, I love you and—"

Isaac stopped, his cheeks reddening, squirming with discomfort. "It feels, I don't know, weird reading this romantic stuff with another guy."

"How so? I have played many female roles in the past."

"Really?"

Drágan nodded. "But perhaps you're right. Was my performance believable?" He looked hopeful.

"Very," Isaac affirmed. "Especially the way you looked at me, like you really..." He squirmed with discomfort. "Anyway, let's just get everything ready before the others show up."

"Okay. Oh, and you're a good actor yourself."

Isaac grinned. "Thanks."

Stephanie arrived first, blowing into their room like a hurricane. She practically swooped down on the boys, bursting with excitement. "I can't wait to start. My first film role."

Isaac rolled his eyes. "It's not exactly a blockbuster production."

She looked at him in a way she never had before, as though he really mattered. "I'm confident you'll do a great job."

Isaac felt his cheeks burning. "Uh, thanks."

She looked over all the equipment. "Good thing I got you a crew."

Technically, Isaac knew, it had been Drágan who'd convinced Nathaniel to join the project, but he wasn't about to argue with her.

Her eye suddenly caught sight of something poking out from under a pile of papers on Isaac's desk. Too late, he realized they were Drágan's modeling photos. She pulled them out before he could stop her and gazed at them with great intensity. Her face changed to one of shock when she flipped through them.

"These are the pictures I printed."

"Yes," Isaac confessed.

"I forgot all about them, but...wait a minute." She spun to face Drágan. "These pictures go back to 1920. How is that possible and how could I forget something that crazy?"

Isaac said nothing, knowing this was up to Drágan, who proceeded to tell her the same story about his blood, with no mention of his werewolf aspect.

Stunned, she lowered herself into Isaac's desk chair. Then her expression turned on a dime, from amazement to anger. "What did you do to make me forget?"

Isaac wanted to know, too.

"I possess a gift, if you will, for temporarily mesmerizing the minds of others," Drágan replied, but Isaac knew him well enough by now to sense he wasn't saying everything.

"Mesmerize? You mean like hypnosis?" She looked angrier now.

"Somewhat," Drágan went on, clearly aware of her rising anger. "I had no knowledge of your character and was afraid you might expose my secret."

She sat in a steamy silence for a moment and then turned to Isaac. "Did you know about this?"

"No, really, I didn't," Isaac exclaimed, fearful of her temper, which he'd witnessed a few times at school. "I didn't understand how you could forget, but I only just heard the reason right now."

Drágan dropped to one knee as though to propose. "I understand now that you're trustworthy, Stephanie, and I beg your forgiveness for intruding into your mind."

Fear filled her lovely face for a split second, as though maybe Drágan might have learned some dark secret when he mesmerized her. But his obvious sincerity seemed to win her over and she smiled. "It's okay. I guess if I had your secret, I wouldn't trust anyone either."

"Thank you." He stood and backed up to stand beside Isaac.

"I get it now," she said, almost talking to herself, "how you know so much. How long have you been fourteen?"

A shadow crossed his face. "More than five hundred years."

Isaac gasped. "What? You never told me that."

Looking sad, Stephanie muttered, "It must've been very lonely."

"It has been," Drágan confirmed. "But now I have you and Isaac and other youth in my life and...I enjoy your company."

She guffawed and eyed Isaac. "I guess that was a compliment."

Isaac grinned.

For a few moments, they discussed the script and Stephanie admitted she'd only been in a few school plays.

"I really love acting and, don't laugh, I wanna go to Hollywood and become an actress for movies or TV."

"Why would we laugh?" Isaac asked, glancing at Drágan.

"Because everyone says that, right? Either Hollywood or Broadway." She gave Isaac a long look. "That's why your movie is so important to me, and I know you're gonna make it great."

Isaac laughed, but inside twisted with anxiety. "Gee, no pressure, right?"

"She's right, Isaac," Drágan said. "I believe in your talent."

Isaac felt warmth replace the anxiety. "Thanks, both of you. That means a lot. I mean, I wanna be a filmmaker so Hollywood's the place to go, right? You're the first people other than my mom I've told that to."

Stephanie grinned. "Let's get there together."

"Sounds like a plan."

They did the fist bump.

"And we can bring, Drágan too," she added. "What acting experience have you had?"

"I was a player centuries ago," Drágan replied, "at the Globe Theater in London. Will Shakespeare was my mentor."

Isaac's mouth dropped open, and Stephanie stared in shock.

"Huh?" Isaac asked. "You never told me this either."

"You never asked."

"Well, tell us how it was, working with Shakespeare," Stephanie blurted, almost breathless. "I mean, he's like the most famous writer ever."

"I required an occupation to earn money," Drágan began, "and met a boy a year or two younger than myself. He told me I was quite beautiful and should be a player, so we went to the Globe. Mr. Shakespeare and Mr. Burbage agreed with the boy about my appearance. Then, just as now, I had no facial hair and my voice was not yet that of a man, so they took me in and trained me."

"What parts did you play?" Isaac asked, "and was Shakespeare easy or hard to work with?"

"Will, as I came to know him, guided me with great patience. I suspect, after two years with the company and with me having not aged at all, he surmised something was amiss. But he fretted not, for I had become an accomplished player. At various times I performed Lady Macbeth, Ophelia, Desdemona, Juliet, Hermia, and many others—all with excellence. My favorite role was Puck in A Midsummer Night's Dream. That character's other worldly status as a fairy felt most like my own as a forever boy."

Isaac and Stephanie exchanged a look of astonishment.

"You talk like acting with Shakespeare wasn't a huge deal!" Stephanie exclaimed.

Drágan shrugged. "It was merely employment, and the opportunity to bond with people who genuinely cared for me. At the time, Will was famous, and our company played even for the queen, but he had not yet become the world-renowned figure he is today."

"What was the last play you did with him?" Isaac asked.

"I do not recall," Drágan admitted. "We would perform two plays per day, and I remained with the company somewhat more than two years. It became necessary for me to leave when other players, particularly the boys, gossiped about my eternal youth, as they called it. Will summoned me to the room where he wrote his plays, and I informed him of my imminent departure. He wasn't surprised. Will displayed an acute ability to see deep into the human soul and, I felt, he'd detected the supernatural within me. He showed me a new play in which, he explained, he'd created a character based on me."

"Which play?" asked Isaac. "Though I only know a few."

"The Tempest," Drágan replied. "The sprite, Ariel, Will said, he'd created so as to never forget me."

Stephanie shook her head. "Wow."

A knock at the open door broke the mood as Penelope entered with the rest of the film crew. In marched a beaming Mary Anne, followed by Nathaniel, who smiled shyly at Isaac and Drágan.

"Have a fun day," Penelope said. "I packed up lots of food."

"Thanks, Mom." Isaac smiled because he'd forgotten about food, and he planned on filming the whole afternoon.

8

FILMING WOLFBOY

Filming was proceeding smoothly, which surprised Isaac since this was his first movie. Using his detailed storyboards to frame each shot made for rapid progress, as did the way Stephanie and Drágan took his direction without argument. He was grateful for their cooperation and their acting ability. He'd gotten some great footage already.

They were now gathered on the bridge overlooking the Abenaki River. The windless afternoon ensured that its surface looked like a perfect sheet of glass in either direction. It made the perfect backdrop for the emotional scene between Drágan's and Stephanie's characters —the scene he'd felt uncomfortable rehearsing that morning.

Mary Anne was true to her word in the makeup department, though only foundation and highlights were required for the nonhorror scenes. Isaac found it odd to see Drágan with more color in his face and realized he preferred his friend's porcelain-doll look. It was also strange to see him in modern pants and hoodies. As he'd taken to doing at school, he also had his hair tied back into a ponytail.

Nathaniel handled the boom mic, and Isaac held up a large scrim to soften the sunlight striking the actors' faces. They ran through the dialogue where Stephanie's character confesses her love for Drágan's, who becomes ever more worried for her safety.

Stephanie turned to Isaac. "I think I should kiss him at this point."

Drágan faced her, his eyes squinted with irritation. "I said no."

"Why not?" Stephanie asked. "He's afraid, and she doesn't know why so I feel like she should pull him close and kiss him. It's just acting, Drágan. That's what we're doing, right, what's best for the characters to make the scene real?"

Isaac turned to Drágan. "It could work."

"No," Drágan reiterated in a firm voice. "A hug is acceptable, but no kissing."

Stephanie looked from him to Isaac, clearly bewildered.

"Okay, just the hug," Isaac affirmed. "I think that's more romantic anyway."

She shrugged and they proceeded to film a few takes before Isaac moved the tripod to capture the action from different angles. He was struck by how gorgeous Stephanie looked on camera. Sure, she was a knockout in real life, but the camera seemed to enhance the softness of her cheeks, the shimmer of her long hair, even the fullness of her lips. In his opinion, she was a star in the making.

From the corner of his eye, he spotted Jack Drake down the street watching them. He nearly jumped when he heard Drágan's voice in his ear, "Perhaps we should enlist his aid as a crewmember."

Isaac turned to him. "After all he did to me?"

Drágan gazed deep into his eyes, so strongly that Isaac squirmed. "He seems to have reformed. This movie could give him the opportunity to prove that."

"He'd never do anything around you," Isaac protested. "He knows you could throw him in the river."

"I still think we should give him a chance."

Isaac didn't like the idea.

Stephanie approached. "What's up, guys?"

"Drágan wants to let Drake help with the movie."

She gazed at Drágan in confusion, then said to Isaac. "An extra pair of hands can't hurt. He's not gonna do anything to you or I'll throw him in the river."

Isaac laughed. "Okay." He called out. "Hey Drake. We're making a movie. Wanna help?"

When they'd been best friends, Isaac and Jack had always planned on making a movie together. How times had changed.

Jack stood where he was, as though rooted to the spot. Then he started forward, without the arrogant strut he used to employ at school prior to his encounter with Drágan. He stopped ten feet away.

"Is it okay with him?" He indicated Drágan.

"It was his idea, not mine," Isaac said, his tone cold. He still felt every insult Jack had flung at him since last year.

Jack hesitated a moment longer, then approached and stood between Stephanie and Mary Anne, as though the girls might protect him. "What's there for me to do?"

"You can help with the scrim for now," Isaac said, handing Jack the sheer screen. Jack joined Nathaniel, who smiled shyly as he held the long boom pole upright at his side.

They resumed filming the scene from different angles. Jack's presence unnerved Isaac and he couldn't focus. At one point, he struggled to get the tripod to stay upright, and was surprised when suddenly Jack was there, spreading the legs wider and easily fixing problem.

"Uh, thanks," Isaac said, experiencing a turbulent mix of emotions being so close to this boy who had been both his best friend *and* his worst enemy. Still, when it came time to relocate to the next area of town, Isaac was glad to have Jack's extra hands for carrying equipment, though he was too proud to say it aloud.

At some point in the afternoon, Isaac relaxed enough to realize that, as director, he had something of a bird's eye view of his cast and crew. He could focus on behaviors he'd not likely have noticed had he been an actor absorbed in his role.

Stephanie seemed to focus all her energy chatting with Drágan, while Mary Anne tried to engage with Jack. Jack remained sullen and silent, while Drágan was cordial and polite with Stephanie. Whenever Isaac called for action, Drágan slipped right into character, holding Stephanie's hand, delivering his lines with the appropriate emotion, but when Isaac called, "Cut," Drágan released her hand and displayed nothing but casual interest in her conversation. Nathaniel seemed to follow Jack around like a puppy, hardly ever talking but always available if Jack needed help.

Midafternoon, they took a break in Armstrong Park, named after a town hero who'd fought in World War II. His bronze statue set within a fountain had long become a popular roosting spot for robins and cardinals. The group pulled two picnic tables together and dug into the sandwiches and drinks Isaac's mom had provided. At first, Jack refused to eat, but Nathaniel handed him a bag of chips and Isaac was surprised when Jack accepted it.

"So, when do we film the killings?" Mary Anne asked eagerly. "I can't wait to apply wounds to people, and I'm looking forward to my death scene."

"Uh, well," Isaac explained, "the transformations will be done on my computer with some effects programs I have. Your death scene will be cut into that."

"Won't that look lame?" Stephanie took a swig of Coke and awaited his answer.

"Not if he has good software," Jack said, startling everyone by inserting himself into the conversation. "If Isaac has a good enough program, it'll look much better than some crummy costume."

He called me Isaac, not Foster.

"And what do you know about special effects?" Stephanie pinned him to his bench with that cold stare she'd perfected.

Jack looked away at once and, surprisingly, met Isaac's gaze. "Got me some good programs if you need help, is all."

Isaac was about to refuse the offer, but Drágan spoke for the first time. "We'd be grateful for your help, Jack. If this film is to win at the festival, it must look its absolute best. Right, Isaac?"

Knowing Drágan had trapped him, Isaac nodded, meeting Jack's eyes for a split second. "Sure, man."

"I asked my dad to play the guy who makes the silver bullet," Mary Anne said, which broke the momentary tension. "He said it was strange we're making a werewolf movie when it seemed like a real wolf is roaming the woods." She bore a troubled look on her face, as though she might be in trouble for revealing that information.

Drágan flinched. "Did he express concern about this wolf?"

"Not really." She seemed cagey. "But he said he'd be happy to be in the movie."

"Cool," Isaac said, hoping to deflect attention from Drágan. "We'll shoot his scenes tomorrow."

"Oh, and he gave me this." She handed a silver bullet to Isaac.

"Sweet," Isaac exclaimed, turning the bullet over in his hand. "Is it real?"

Mary Anne nodded. "No gunpowder, though. My dad gave it to me, and I painted it silver last night."

Stephanie eyed the bullet. "Nice work."

Mary Anne swallowed a bite of sandwich. "I haven't seen your asshole stepdad around much, not that I'm complaining."

Stephanie shivered, for a moment looking frightened. "He just comes back from work, eats, and goes to bed. He reminds me of Serg and Ron, you know, how they act like zombies. I'm not complaining, trust me."

Isaac wondered if Drágan had done something to Stephanie's drunken stepdad like he had with the football players. Now that he knew Drágan's secret, he'd tried to figure out what his friend might be doing to those guys but drew a blank every time. Even with the knowledge Isaac possessed, Drágan remained a cypher, which, if he were completely honest, concerned him.

They continued filming until the late afternoon shadows covered the park, saving the night scenes for the following day. Everyone bubbled over with excitement about the film and the possibility of winning an award at the festival.

"There's gonna be a lot of competition," Isaac cautioned, "so don't count your awards before they hatch."

Stephanie groaned, then indicated Drágan and herself. "Look at your stars. We'll be the most gorgeous couple there."

Isaac chuckled, but he knew she was right. He couldn't imagine a better-looking couple in a student film.

Isaac's mom swung by with her van to pick them all up, along with the equipment. After dropping off the others, she drove past Main Street in the direction of home. Isaac and Drágan sat in the middle seat, discussing the day's shooting.

"Sounds like it went well," Penelope commented. "I was surprised to see Jack there. You guys speaking again?"

"Only for the movie," Isaac insisted, trying to hide the antipathy in his voice. "It was Drágan's idea."

"I merely thought a larger crew might make the process smoother," Drágan said in his defense.

"And did it?" Penelope asked, her face visible to Isaac in the rearview mirror.

"I guess," grumbled Isaac, though inside, he knew having Jack involved would help a lot, especially if he was as good with effects as he said. It was just...incredibly hard to be around the friend who'd turned against him.

BACK IN THEIR ROOM, Isaac logged into his effects program and attempted to perfect the movements of his werewolf. Drágan sat and watched.

"Do I resemble that, in my other form?"

Startled, Isaac stared at the image on screen. He'd made the fur grayer, shortened the height, enhanced the teeth. He turned to his friend. "Kind of."

Drágan studied the image dispassionately. "If you want to use the footage of me transforming into the wolf and back again, your film would look more authentic. This program might be better for creating glimpses of the wolf's face or feet."

Isaac gaped. "Are you serious? That could put you in danger."

Drágan eyed him soberly. "Why would someone suspect that

footage is real? You can alter it with your computer to blend the real and the make-believe."

"But you're naked! No way."

"Perhaps you can remove my lower half?"

"I guess I could crop the film, so we only see your chest and head," Isaac mumbled, considering the possibility. "But then the main problem would be the chains around you. I don't know how to erase them without damaging the video."

"Perhaps Jack might be of help."

"Why do you keep pushing Jack on me? We're not friends anymore. He made sure of that!" Isaac raised his voice when he hadn't intended to, body trembling with pent up anger.

"Would you not agree that having him no longer a friend is preferable to having him as an enemy?"

"When I figure out what you just said, I'll say something snarky!" Isaac hated himself for taking his anger at Jack out on Drágan.

"I'll say no more on the subject." Drágan climbed the ladder to his upper bunk, stretching out on the bed.

Isaac hated the awkward silence. This was the first argument he'd gotten into with Drágan when the guy was willing to risk exposure by putting his transformation into the film. He pushed his chair back and climbed the ladder. Drágan turned his head as Isaac poked his remorseful face over the top.

"I'm sorry, man. You're right. It's just, having Jack here again will bring up so many memories."

"Are they good ones?" Drágan asked.

Isaac nodded.

"I'm happy you have such good memories with a friend."

The sadness in his voice made Isaac's heart pull into his throat. He wanted to say something, anything, but his tongue was tied into knots.

"Boys, dinner time!" his mom's voice called from downstairs.

Isaac met Drágan's wistful eyes. "I'll ask him."

～

THE FOLLOWING MORNING, Drágan informed Isaac he was going to Dr. Wilson's house.

"Can I come?" Isaac asked, hoping he might glean some insights into Drágan's health status.

"Not at this time," Drágan replied. "Maybe next week. I have my reasons."

Isaac didn't argue, and Drágan departed right after they ate his marvelous French toast, soft-boiled eggs, and fresh squeezed orange juice. Penelope had no issue admitting to Isaac, "That boy is a better cook than I am."

Isaac laughed but didn't agree for fear of hurting her feelings.

He reviewed his story boards and shot sheets, while also making certain his portable lights and the camera were all charged. They would meet up at Mary Anne's place to film the scenes with her dad. Those scenes would culminate with her dad's character hurrying off to rouse the town for a werewolf hunt. After that, Isaac and crew would head into the forest for the filming that would continue until after nightfall.

Drágan returned before noon and Isaac asked, "Good news on your blood?"

"Alas, no."

The pain in those two words made Isaac want to hug his friend, but he knew Drágan didn't care for closeness. He settled for a pathetic, "Sorry, man," and felt like the loser most people thought he was.

With Drágan watching intently, Isaac uploaded the footage from Friday night into his computer. He proceeded to carefully crop the image, so Drágan's privates were not visible. He did the same at the end, when the wolf became the boy, something he'd slept through.

Drágan said nothing as they watched the snarling, struggling beast begin writhing and twisting as hair sank beneath the skin, the head and jaw became smaller, the limbs returned to human form. Just as Drágan became visible, he collapsed to the ground in a faint in exactly the position in which Isaac found him.

"It looks agonizing," Isaac murmured as he wiped tears from his eyes. "I wish I could help you."

"You have, in more ways than you know."

Isaac studied his friend. Drágan looked calm and formal and so grown up. Eyeing him now, Isaac considered how hard it must be for his friend to act fourteen so he can fit in with him and his classmates. He also realized how much Drágan had already changed since arriving in Millwood. His speech patterns were loosening up and he was smiling more, seemingly relaxed around Isaac and the others.

Facing the computer once more, he edited the transformation just as he would edit his final film, trimming anything that displayed Drágan below the waist, and then smoothed out the transitions so the transformations looked somewhat artistic.

"How's that?"

"You're a genius."

Isaac chuckled. "Yeah, right." But deep down, he relished Drágan's praise.

Mary Anne lived in a big house across town from Isaac, so Penelope drove the boys over along with the film equipment.

Isaac stared up at Mary Anne's dark, gothic-looking house in awe.

She hurried out the front door to greet them. "The house is perfect for a horror film, isn't it, Isaac?" Mary Anne giggled as Isaac nodded. "It was built at the turn of the last century."

Isaac thought that explained it's cupolas and stained-glass windows, more traditionally Victorian than his own house. It seemed empty, though, and Isaac recalled Mary Anne's mom had died of cancer some years back.

He heard metal grinding against metal, the sound coming from a huge barn off to one side of the driveway, its wide doors hanging open. He figured her dad must work out there when he wasn't at the mill.

Stephanie sauntered into the front yard to join them just as Jack's mom stopped her car at the curb to let out Jack and Nathaniel. Isaac was surprised to see them together but was more tempted to approach and say hi to Jack's mom, who'd always liked him. But she drove away before he could make a move.

Mary Anne entered the barn. "Dad? The crew is here."

The grinding stopped and Isaac heard a gruff voice. "Bring 'em on in."

Mary Anne waved everyone forward. Stephanie strutted in as if she owned the place. Considering how often she hung out with Mary Anne, maybe she did. He'd acknowledged Jack with only a nod when he'd arrived; now he gestured for him to go ahead of him into the barn. Jack said nothing, merely followed Nathaniel. Isaac and Drágan brought up the rear.

The barn was all wood, with slivers of light peeking through a few warped slats. Above was a hay loft, but without any hay since they didn't own horses. Mr. Givens stood before metal-working equipment —a lathe and other items Isaac had never used. A rough-hewn man, Mr. Givens had worked all his life with his hands. He looked wiry and strong with thick forearms and a short, trimmed beard. He peered at Isaac through beady brown eyes.

"How's your mother, Isaac? Don't see her around so much as I'd like."

"She works from home now," Isaac explained, a bit intimidated by this man even though he'd always treated Isaac politely when they'd seen each other at school events over the years. "And I mostly walk home from high school, so you wouldn't see her picking me up."

He nodded, taking in the whole group. "You all sure grew up fast." His gaze settled on Drágan, who peered at Mr. Givens with an odd expression. "And who might you be, son?"

Drágan lost his strange look and smiled. "I'm new in town, sir. My name is Drágan Albescu."

"Foreigner, eh?"

"I was born in Eastern Europe but have resided in America for some time."

The man gave Drágan a long, pointed look and then focused on

Isaac. "I looked over your story, Isaac, and I think I got my part down." He paused, squinting. "Any particular reason you chose a werewolf tale?"

Isaac felt on the spot, which he didn't like. "Well, I love werewolf movies and decided to make one. That's all."

The tall man studied Isaac, as though searching for a lie. "What say we get started?"

Isaac set up his camera and some lights. They closed the barn door because in the movie, it was nighttime already. The first master shot was looking down from the hay loft because it was a creepy angle. Mr. Givens was playing the father of Stephanie's character, and he makes her the silver bullet, using the one Mary Anne had already painted, helping her load it into a handgun. He suspects that her boyfriend, Cameron, is the werewolf that killed her friend the previous month and insists she be ready to shoot him, if necessary.

Stephanie is hysterical—Isaac was impressed by her acting— saying she could never shoot Cameron because she loves him. As he watched her tearful performance, he considered that she was almost as mysterious as Drágan. She'd hardly spoken to him since first grade, then is suddenly excited to be in his movie and hangs out with him at lunch.

He recalled those times in middle school when he'd seen her off in a corner by herself crying softly. He'd felt bad for her, but feared even approaching because they moved in different social circles.

He threw off these thoughts to focus on the movie. He filmed the scene where Mr. Givens forces Stephanie to take the pistol and orders her to stay in the house. He's getting the men together to track down the werewolf and kill it, he tells her. He grabs his rifle and hurries out of the shot.

Isaac filmed the sequence again at floor level from several angles and then the close ups and inserts. Mr. Givens turned out to be a decent actor, mostly playing a gruff, stand-offish type like himself, but doing it well. Drágan, not in this scene, hung around in the back of the barn.

"Do you always keep your rifles in the barn, sir?" asked Nathaniel timidly, indicating the hooks on the wall from which Mr. Givens had taken down his rifle.

"Guy Rumson up on Tracy Street found a deer torn up in the woods," the man replied. "Could be the wolf that howled the other night. Gotta be prepared."

Isaac flinched at the mention of the deer. He had helped Drágan remove the remains from the clearing so they wouldn't be found, but apparently, they had been anyway. "Will you guys go hunting for it?"

"Like in your movie? Not less the beast kills some livestock."

Isaac nodded and they resumed shooting. When he finally concluded his scenes, Mr. Givens took the handgun from Stephanie, removed the bullet, and replaced it with another.

"That's a blank I put in. It'll sound like the real thing but don't go pointin' it directly at the boy. Blanks *can* do harm, so aim away. You got that, everyone?"

He looked around, but Drágan wasn't with the crew. He emerged from the shadows at the back of the barn and Mr. Givens's expression turned thunderous.

"What you doing back there, boy?"

"Nothing, sir."

"If you kids're finished, I got my work, so scram."

Isaac was shocked by the man's change in demeanor, but quickly directed his crew in wrapping the equipment and placing it in the driveway, where they'd wait for his mom to pick them up.

Mary Anne was mortified about her dad's exchange with Drágan. "I'm so sorry, everyone. He gets cranky, especially if he thinks people are snooping around."

"Yeah," Stephanie said. "He yelled at me before, remember, when I asked about that locked door one time? Jeez, I was only eleven."

Isaac called his mom and within five minutes her van pulled up to take them to the wooded area. By the time they arrived, the late afternoon sun had drifted behind a cloud bank and dusk began to blanket the woods.

"Spooky," Penelope said, as the crew gathered the equipment from the back of the van.

"Yeah," Isaac agreed. "Exactly the feel I was hoping for. Thanks, Mom. I'll call you when we're finished."

The other kids chorused their thanks, and Penelope waved, smiling as she drove away.

During all the afternoon shooting at Mary Anne's, Isaac hadn't spoken to Jack at all. But as he observed Jack and Nathaniel setting up the lights, he approached them.

"So, um, I got this footage of the werewolf chained to a tree, but now I want it to move without the chains. Got any idea how to erase them?"

Jack looked up after spreading the legs of the light stand and considered Isaac's question. "Erase chains?"

"Yeah, without, you know, erasing any of the werewolf."

Jack stood. "Why'd you add chains if you didn't want 'em?"

Isaac was becoming annoyed. "Cause the story was different when I created that stuff. Can you erase 'em or not?"

"Yes."

Isaac was taken aback by the rapid response. "You sure?"

"Yeah. Gotta bring over my laptop cause the software's on there."

They were standing face to face, which they hadn't done in almost a year without fighting. "Cool. When can you come over?"

"Tonight, if you want," Jack replied. "Or anytime."

"Okay."

Isaac felt the tenseness in his body relax as he walked away to talk with Stephanie and Drágan. Mary Anne had her makeup kit open.

"Hey, Steph, help me with this makeup. I gotta look like I've been killed by a werewolf." She giggled.

Stephanie laughed. "You and your makeup effects. You should definitely go pro."

"That's my plan."

The girls set to work right away because Isaac wanted to film the discovery of her body before darkness fell. Mary Anne had worn her tattered, bloody clothes under her real ones and had done an incredible job making them look like she'd been savagely attacked. She and

Stephanie sat at the small folding table she'd brought for makeup applications and got started.

While the girls turned Mary Anne into a dead body, Isaac set up his camera and lights, hoping to create an early morning feel to the scene. Within thirty minutes, Mary Anne's face looked bloody, with gouges and bite marks seemingly carved into her cheeks. Isaac nearly gasped when he turned and there she was.

"Wow, you *are* good with make up."

She giggled. "So where do you want me?"

He indicated the spot near some trees, and she lay down on the cold ground, shivering. He directed her to twist up her body, like it'd been thrown there, and she complied to perfection. Isaac and his crew got to work and filmed the scene. Stephanie let out a blood-curdling scream that would put Jamie Lee Curtis to shame as she stumbled over the body. Isaac made sure to get lots of closeups of Mary Anne's shredded clothes and bloodied corpse, especially her gory face with the eyes open in death.

By now, it was getting darker, so Isaac filmed Mary Anne just prior to her death. He filmed her flailing at something that wasn't there because Isaac needed to intercut the werewolf footage. After each take, he had her remove a few scratches or gouges until by the end of that sequence, her face was clean and unbloodied to indicate the beginning of the attack. Then he filmed shots of her walking through the woods, hearing something, then running away. He chased after her with the camera as though he was the werewolf while she screamed in terror.

Isaac felt confident he'd gotten plenty of coverage and had shot the right angles during her attack to mix perfectly with the footage of Drágan mauling the deer. He'd need to mix in some of the AI werewolf during these scenes, but he was confident it would look good.

The next scene they filmed was Drágan's character—frantic because the moon was rising—confessing to Stephanie's character that he's the werewolf and begging her to get someplace safe before he changes.

"Otherwise, I'll hunt you down."

Daphne shakes her head. "You'd never hurt me."

Tearfully, Cameron says, "Werewolves always kill the ones they love."

Stephanie had pulled on other pants and a different shirt over what she'd been wearing earlier to indicate this was not the same day as when she discovered Mary Anne's body. She warns Cameron that a bunch of people will be hunting him that night, swears her love, and then he runs off into the forest.

Drágan was an incredible actor, Isaac kept thinking as they filmed several takes, but considering he'd been a player with Shakespeare's Globe, that was understandable. His passion, his obvious love for Stephanie's character, his tearful farewell before he charged off into the woods, evoked so much emotion in Isaac that he nearly cried. His friend was technically fourteen, like him, but since he'd lived so long, Isaac wondered if he'd ever felt this way about a girl sometime in the past and was able to recall those feelings so vividly for the camera.

Isaac blinked back tears as he concluded filming the emotional parting of the two lovers and announced that it was time to shoot the finale.

They picked up all the equipment and moved farther into the woods. He'd gotten plenty of shots of the moon, which was full enough for his film, but not full enough for Drágan to transform. Unlike in the movies, Drágan assured him he only changed one night per month, when the moon was at its fullest.

Isaac explained to Stephanie which direction the werewolf would leap at her as she searches the woods for "Cameron." Mary Anne's dad had given her the extra blank cartridges so she could practice, which Isaac insisted on, even though he knew even a real bullet wouldn't hurt his male star.

Stephanie brilliantly displayed frightened hysterics as she fired the gun past Isaac and the camera. He explained that the "digital" werewolf would collapse and transform back into Drágan.

It was time for Drágan's death scene. He removed his shirt, eliciting a gasp from both Stephanie and Mary Anne, who'd never seen him shirtless. In the shadows of the surrounding trees, moonlight bathing him in its soft glow, Drágan looked more beautiful than usual, making the girls' reaction understandable. He lay down on the ground beside a large tree, which Isaac chose because it resembled the one from Friday night and would cut together with the "real" footage.

Mary Anne knelt beside Drágan and painted his face with realistic blood, to simulate that he'd attacked something that night. She drew the bullet wound on his chest with blood spilling down his torso to the ground.

Stephanie stood watching. "You get all the fun, Mary Anne."

Finished, Mary Anne reluctantly stood and backed away. It was time to film. Isaac lay on the ground with the camera pointing upward as Stephanie ran forward and fell to her knees, crying real tears. She begged Cameron's forgiveness for shooting him and Drágan performed his final lines off camera.

The reverse was shot from above. Stephanie ran forward and dropped to her knees with Drágan's bloody face in the shot. She said her lines and he thanked her for freeing him. He murmured, "I love you," and then died. She sobbed over his body, again impressing Isaac with her acting skills.

Isaac dropped to the ground to get a good shot of Stephanie's face as she sobbed. She and Drágan repeated their final lines and when he "died," she sobbed into his chest. Then she did something not in the script. She raised her head and kissed Drágan on the lips.

Enraged, he threw her off and sat up. His eyes had gone wild and his lips red. "I said no kissing!"

Isaac was stunned. He'd liked that improvised moment, but for now he concentrated on calming his friend. He stood as Drágan leaped up, feet planted, fingers like claws, long hair wild and wafting in the breeze. Stephanie backed away and huddled with the crew. Isaac cautiously approached Drágan, who looked even more scary than in his werewolf form.

"It was a mistake, so chill, man. She forgot, okay?"

Drágan fixed his savage eyes on Isaac and his hard features softened once again. He lowered his arms, relaxing his fingers, and the fury faded from his face, replaced by remorse.

"Forgive my outburst, all of you." His gaze took in the frightened crew behind Isaac. "It was the emotion of the moment."

He lay back down on the ground so Isaac could film the closeups. Nervously, Stephanie approached and knelt beside him.

The dialogue was repeated until Isaac had sufficient coverage. Both Drágan and Stephanie slipped right back into their roles as though the outburst had never happened.

When Isaac called, "Cut!" for the last time, Drágan stood without saying a word, pulled his shirt down from where he'd hung it, and slipped it on.

Isaac proclaimed, "That's a wrap, folks. All we need now are some pickup shots at school. We'll shoot that stuff tomorrow."

Still looking spooked, Stephanie steered clear of Drágan as the crew packed up the equipment. She whispered something to Mary Anne that Isaac couldn't hear, but he knew Drágan could and hoped it wasn't something hurtful. But he couldn't blame them if it was. He still trembled from the ferocity of Drágan's outburst. He was relieved when his mom dropped off his silent cast and crew members and headed home.

Why had Drágan reacted so aggressively?

And more importantly, did he pose a threat to them after all?

9

A BETTER FRIEND THAN AN ENEMY

All the way home, Isaac watched Drágan brood, waiting for him to say something. Penelope had dinner prepared, but except for his prayer at the beginning and a "thank you" at the end, Drágan kept quiet. He held his silence while he and Isaac washed the dishes and didn't speak at all until they were back in their room.

Isaac set his equipment down by the chests of drawers as Drágan took the extra desk chair he normally occupied. Isaac sat beside him. "Do you wanna talk about what happened?"

"A memory," Drágan whispered. "One of my most painful."

When he didn't say more, Isaac wasn't sure what to say. Just thinking about Drágan's meltdown sent shivers down his back.

"So, uh, you were kind of scary, I gotta say. You wouldn't...hurt anyone, would you?"

Drágan didn't react with anger. Rather, he looked shamefaced. "I know I can be scary, Isaac. I've done things in the past that...well, that I deeply regret. Despite how I acted, I do have my monstrous nature under control, and you have my word that I will never hurt you or your friends."

The remorse and sincerity in his voice calmed Isaac's fears. "I know. Let's check out some of the footage."

Drágan nodded.

Isaac plugged the camera into his computer and transferred all the footage. He and Drágan were reviewing it when he heard the doorbell downstairs.

Who could it be on a Sunday night, he wondered.

He heard his mother's voice, but not the visitor. In a few moments his mom stood in the open door to his room, Jack Drake beside her.

"Look who's here," she said, her voice sounding like it hid a smile, her expression uncertain.

Jack, wearing a backpack, eyed Isaac sheepishly. "You said to come over."

With all the Drágan drama, Isaac had forgotten. "Uh, sure, yeah. It's cool, Mom. He's helping with the special effects."

"It's nice to see you again, Jack," she said.

"Nice to see you too," Jack replied, and Isaac heard the honesty in his voice.

Drágan stood and offered Jack his chair, sitting instead on Isaac's bed.

"You okay?" Jack asked Drágan.

Drágan nodded, tossing his long hair behind him.

After Isaac cleared a space on his desk, Jack sat in the chair and pulled his laptop out of his army surplus backpack. "I'll need to transfer the footage to my computer."

Isaac put all the werewolf footage on a flash drive and then Jack loaded it into his machine. He opened the videos and they leaned forward, gazing at the screen.

"There," Isaac said, pointing to the chains. "We need to erase the chains and shackles, from all these shots. Can you do it?"

"Is Coach Lancaster a bitch?" Jack said, snark in full force.

Isaac laughed despite himself and watched Jack's fingers fly nimbly over the keyboard. His program worked like the layer and eraser functions in Photoshop, but for video. With deft, careful strokes, he gradually erased first the chain, then the shackles until there was no indication they'd ever been there. He did this for every shot Isaac intended to use, but Isaac made sure Jack didn't see Drágan at all in any of the footage.

"Man, that's cool," Isaac exclaimed, impressed. "I gotta get that program."

"I can give it to you, if you want," Jack said as he transferred the new footage onto Isaac's flash drive. "I can have it on two computers."

"That'd be awesome."

They played back the altered footage as the werewolf growled, attacked the deer, and lunged toward the camera a few times, then morphed back into Drágan, which is where Isaac had cut it off.

"It looks so real," Jack said, captivated. "How'd you do this?"

"It's an AI Visual FX program I found," he lied. "You gotta figure out exactly how to write what you want, but I finally got it to do this."

"You're gonna win for sure with a werewolf like this." Jack was still staring at the wolf, now on freeze-frame, and his tone was genuine. "Those eyes...they look familiar."

Isaac reflexively glanced at Drágan, then faced Jack. "Listen, uh, you know, thanks for your help."

Jack sat back and glanced around at the walls. "I see you added some new posters. Cool."

"Yeah. You know, change it up."

They sat together in silence for a moment, then Jack closed his laptop and stood. "I better get home. Still got that algebra homework I don't understand."

"Maybe Drágan could help you like he did me." Isaac looked over at Drágan, still sitting on the bed watching them. "Could you?"

Drágan rose from the bed. "Did you bring your work?"

"Uh, yeah, it's in my backpack." Jack eyed Drágan with caution, obviously recalling the earlier outburst. "You sure it's okay? I really don't give a shit about my math grade."

"I'm sure," Drágan replied, his voice even and calm.

Jack pulled out a folder and opened it on the desk. A series of algebra equations dropped down the page from one to fifteen. He hadn't done any of them.

Isaac stood up from his chair so Drágan could sit, happy that his friend seemed back to his nonviolent self and, if he was honest, happy that Jack wasn't leaving yet. It felt kind of good to have Jack back in his room.

Isaac lay on his bed.

Drágan patiently explained the first few problems. Jack asked some questions, and then suddenly blurted, "I get it!"

Isaac sat up.

"Thanks, man," Jack said, more comfortable than he'd been in the beginning. He tossed his notebook into his backpack and slid the laptop in after. He and Isaac gazed at one another awkwardly.

"Guess I'll see you tomorrow," Jack said, sounding shy instead of his usual bluster.

"Yeah," Isaac replied, unsure of everything at this moment.

Jack started to leave, then turned back to Drágan. "I get why you went off on her. I wouldn't let Stephanie kiss me if it was the end of the world."

Drágan's eyes bulged with surprise and Isaac burst out laughing.

Jack offered a lopsided grin and was gone.

"He makes a better friend than an enemy," Drágan said before waving Isaac to sit on his bed.

Confused, Isaac did as directed.

Drágan stood before him. "You're the first youth in all my long history with whom I will share my story. I cannot hide the truth from you any longer. You've done too much to aid me."

"Me? You're the one who's like, I don't know, Mary Poppins or something, swooping in here and getting all our lives on track."

"You possess a kind heart and a trusting soul. You deserve the truth."

Drágan crossed the room to his closet and slid out the valise. He rifled around within and pulled out a small book, carrying it back and sitting on the bed beside Isaac.

"Here is one of my diaries."

"You mean journal, right? Only girls use diaries."

Drágan sighed. "And only in America is such gender foolishness practiced. I wrote this *diary* once I'd finally learned how to read and write."

"You didn't have a school in your village?"

"Everyone worked, as I previously mentioned."

"Yeah, I remember," Isaac said.

Drágan opened his diary and handed it to Isaac. "Perhaps you should read it yourself."

Isaac glanced at the pages. The hand-written cursive—which Isaac had learned in elementary school—was lovely and graceful. Some of the words looked like Spanish, which he was taking in school, but it was *definitely* not English.

"I can't read this."

Surprised, Drágan took back the book. "Latin is no longer taught in America?"

"I guess not."

"Then I shall have to read it to you."

Isaac rested his head on his pillow as Drágan began to read.

INTERLUDE

Drágan's Diary

I am called Drágan Albescu. My birth occurred sometime around the year of Our Lord AD 1500, so far as I've been able to determine. I lived on a farm within a tiny village beneath the shadow of the Carpathian Mountains. As a young boy, my life consisted of farm work from dawn to dusk. Never did I experience the joys of play with other boys in the village. My father believed play made boys weak.

One chilly autumn night during my twelfth year, Father and I were late leaving the field because the moon above blazed with a brightness that fully illuminated our meager plot of land and allowed for the opportunity to work longer than was customary. I paused to gaze up at its majestic beauty while Father trudged on toward our hut.

I felt the hairs on the back of my neck prickle with fear. A wild animal was surely near, likely another wolf down from the mountains seeking our livestock. I raised my spade just as something gigantic leaped from behind a tree and drove me to the ground. Teeth like daggers tore into my shoulder before I heard a shout from my father and then a struggle. Somehow, he drove the beast away and carried me into our hut.

My mother, a small, gentle soul, was frantic with worry, seeing to my ragged wound as best she could. The blood pouring forth made me light-headed, and I swooned.

When I next awoke, it was daylight, and I found my mother sitting beside my bed. I sat up, but no pain assailed me from the shoulder.

"Oh, mother, it was a wolf," I explained as the memories flooded in. "A wolf that walked like a man! Father...is Father hurt?"

She shook her head, eyes wet as with dew. "He fought it off with this." She reached down and lifted a heavy club I'd seen often as a boy, a club that had been dipped in silver. "Silver is the only defense."

Father entered the hut just then and strode to Mother's side. "Let me see the wound." His tone was harsh and cold.

Gently, my mother peeled back the layers of cloth from my shoulder. I gasped. It had healed! There was nary a sign that I'd been injured.

Father squinted beneath heavy brows. "You're good to work. We're behind thanks to your carelessness." He stomped out of the hut.

Mother offered a smile and stepped back so that I might rise. My arm seemed as strong as before, but I was soon to learn it had become much stronger, as had my whole body.

Life returned to what it had been prior to the attack, except Father sold most of our farm animals. I asked why, of course, since I tended to their needs, but he refused to speak on the matter, and my parents never ever again spoke of the attack on me. However, I spotted my mother on subsequent nights gazing up into the darkness in fear.

The moon waned and waxed again, proceeding toward fullness some thirty days after my attack. My Father, who had worked the farm all his life, seemed to know precisely when that great orb in the heavens would be at its brightest.

On that day, I heard him tell my mother, "It's tonight," and we ate our supper earlier than was customary. It was barely dusk. He rose from the table and said to me, "You're coming with me." He retreated to our pantry and returned with a thick burlap sack. I knew the contents must have been heavy, for he carried it with both hands.

I followed him past our plantings and into the woods. We stopped before a majestically tall tree displaying a thick trunk. My father set down his sack and extracted heavy links of chain. With these, he circumvented the trunk, then secured them with a large metal padlock no doubt forged along with the chains by the village blacksmith in exchange for our farm animals.

For the first time my body trembled with fear, for I beheld four shackles secured to the chains.

My father turned to me. "Strip off your clothes."

"Sir?"

"You heard me. Everything!"

That fear tightened around my pounding heart like a vise. "But why, sir?"

"They are the best you have. Now off!"

Bewildered and terrified, I also felt embarrassment course through me. As a small boy, being naked in front of others was commonplace. As a youth of twelve, it felt unseemly of me to strip in front of even my parents. But my father was possessed of a terrible wrath, so I did as I was bid.

I soon stood beneath the trees naked as the day I came into this world. Fearful though I was, I noticed that I felt no chill to my body, despite the cool autumn night. These thoughts vanished in an instant when I felt the shackles clamped over my thin wrists, first the right then the left.

"Father..."

He said nothing, just dropped to a squat and shackled my bare ankles as though I was nothing but a wild beast. He stepped back to examine his work.

"Why, Father? Have I offended you in some way? Am I being punished?"

Father gazed at me through hard, brown eyes for a long moment. Then he looked upward through the trees as though searching for

Heaven itself. Stooping, he scooped up my clothing and hurried away through the trees.

"Father! Come back!"

He did not. But I heard his footsteps in the underbrush for, it seemed, far longer than should have been possible. I studied the ground beneath my feet. It felt rough and rocky yet did not pierce my flesh.

For the life of me, I could think of no crime I'd committed save for being unable to work as a result of the wolf attack.

My mind reflected on the moment of that attack. It had been a wolf, yes, but one that seemed to walk on two legs. I'd heard whispers of such creatures, but my father had defeated it with a mere club. I recalled my mother's words: "Silver is the only defense."

I noticed a wild goat trapped within thorns quite close to me. It bleated in distress and struggled against the thorns that raked its thin fur with every movement, drawing blood. I strode toward it and my arm stretched out to stroke its head, but the tightness of the chains prevented me from freeing it.

It was then an extreme warmth overcame my body, a fire beneath my skin. Agony tore through every muscle and every fiber that made up the whole of me. I cried out in pain as my body began to twist and contort in ways seemingly impossible. I managed to call out, "Father!" only once before my voice fell silent. I could no longer articulate words. I felt my face expand and my ears grow larger.

And then I knew nothing more.

When I awoke, sunlight peeked through the treetops, and I found myself lying on the rocky ground. The shackles remained in place, only now my hands were red with dried blood. I sat up at once, the rocky terrain not causing my bare buttocks the slightest injury. I stared in horror at my hands and felt a stickiness on my face and chest. I searched my naked body for damage but found none. Yet splattered blood covered me. I turned to glance behind and saw the bloodied remains of that trapped goat. It had been torn from the thicket and ripped asunder. Disemboweled, it had also been partially consumed.

Was I responsible? How? Why?

I began to weep in my despair.

Footsteps approached from far away, yet I recognized my father's distinctive gait. I feared to stand, feeling even more exposed and ashamed than I had the previous night. Soon, my father entered the clearing. He stopped, eyeing the shredded goat with disgust. He knelt, extracted a thick key from his jacket pocket, and freed me from my prison.

Our eyes met. He gently wiped away my tears with one calloused thumb and pulled me into the first and only hug he ever gave me. He held me close for some time before helping me up and unclasping the chain from the tree.

"Father, what am I?"

"A vârcolac," he answered solemnly.

I had heard fearful whisperings of that word. It was of my people's folklore.

Werewolf.

"Come," said my father. "This is how it'll be from here on."

He replaced the chains in the sack and started in the direction of our hut. Bloody, naked, and fearful, I followed.

Life proceeded in its inexorable path, the primary difference being the monthly shackling to the tree for my transformation. My howling attracted no undue attention due to the abundance of wolves in the area. My father would, at times, tie a pig to the tree beside me and I would awaken the following day splattered with its blood. Always I returned home naked and gory, using frigid well water to wash the horror from my body.

But could my soul ever be cleansed of this terrible evil?

By the attainment of my fourteenth year, I found myself assailed daily by sensations of such intensity I often feared for my sanity. My ears had become so finely tuned that I could hear with clarity the heartbeats of those around me as the village gathered each week for religious services. I found my glances drifting to girls and boys of my age and knowing, by scent alone, when they had last bathed, or what sort of work they had been engaged in the day before. And my thoughts drifted to places I suspected the priest would consider improper.

Ours was an Eastern Orthodox denomination and the elderly white-haired priest would often cast his baleful eye upon me or another of my age and rail against "impure thoughts," without ever clarifying their nature. My body, too, reacted to my impure thoughts, but my father would not speak of such matters, so I ceased to ask.

One evening—a night before the next full moon—I wandered about after supper to clear my thoughts and prepare for sleep. I stood gazing at the forest trees, dreading the next night of horror and pain, until I heard footsteps approaching. I turned, but no one had yet materialized. I waited. After several minutes, a man appeared out of the shadows and stopped before me. He smiled.

"You must have excellent hearing, boy, for my tread is near silent."

"I do." I'd never seen the like of this man before. His clothing was of soft-looking material and his ankle-length cloak spoke of richness beyond our poor village. "Who are you?"

"Jourdain Aubrey, at your service." He bowed as though I were royalty and then fixed his gaze upon me.

I took in the man's face. He bore not a blemish, not even a scratch, and minimal facial hair. His lips were full and red, his skin pale, his hair black as pitch. His hands looked soft, like those of a pianist. This man was not accustomed to work. But the eyes were what held me. Black as coal, they seemed to bore into me, and I grew weak in the knees.

"Shall we walk together?"

I could not protest, though I knew I should. I was mesmerized by his soothing voice and those magnetic eyes. He turned toward the forest, and I followed. We stopped deep among the trees, farther than I had ever roamed. The night was still and silent, yet for me, the gentle rustling of leaves in the breeze sounded like a symphony.

I attempted to guess his age. Perhaps twenty-one or two. It mattered not. He leaned closer as though to plant his lips upon mine. This felt wrong. And yet I could not look away. His lips brushed mine like butterfly wings then dropped to the soft skin of my throat. I shivered as they touched my flesh. A sharp stab of pain brought me to my senses for but a moment. Liquid streamed down my chest.

And then I felt nothing.

I stirred to wakefulness to find the forest as it had been when I'd lost consciousness. Darkness had fallen, but barely. I sat up to clear my thoughts. Remembering the strange man, I clapped a hand to my throat, but it felt clean.

And yet dried blood coated the front of my rough-hewn tunic and pants.

I rose to my feet, bewildered as to what had happened. I recalled the man and remembered his name—Jourdain Aubrey. My body recalled the sensations of being in his presence, of losing control of myself and feeling enthralled to this stranger. But my thoughts were vague as to what had transpired between us.

Feeling certain of punishment for being out later than was mandated, I hurried toward home. My body felt oddly light and yet powerfully strong. I surmised it was because the full moon would show its face the following night. I bounded from the forest onto my family's land and halted in horror at what I saw. High in the night sky, glaring down at me, was the moon at its fullest!

I barely had a moment to realize I'd been in that forest a night and a day when the change began, and I was lost.

I awoke to such carnage I never again hope to witness. I lay on the floor of my hut, drenched in sticky blood. The stench assailed my nostrils and sent a wave of intense hunger throughout my body. I pulled myself to a sitting position and gazed at what remained of my parents. The wolf had eviscerated their bodies, leaving little resembling the people who'd raised me. The silver-headed club lay smashed into pieces near my father's corpse.

Tears formed in my eyes, but that new craving from deep within grew ever more powerful. Unable to stop myself, I crawled to their mangled corpses and lapped up the blood that had not yet congealed. I fought to control my urges but could not.

Finally, I rose to my feet, the hunger rampaging through every inch of me. Naked and bloody, I left the hut and hurried around back where pigs and goats were penned. With a growl from deep within, I leaped over the fence and fell on them. Unlike as the wolf, I did not tear and rend but rather sank unnaturally long fangs into their throats and drank with gusto the blood which poured forth. I'd slain them all before my thirst was slated. Then I sat in their slop, surrounded by death, and wept.

Later, I cleaned myself and dressed in my father's church clothes, which fit better than my own, all the while reflecting on my circumstances. That blood had satisfied my thirst for the moment, but I knew deep within that human blood was now necessary to my existence. I must flee the village, for in no way could I account for the slaughter of my family and livestock. Nor could I feed on the people of the village without being discovered. I located my father's savings, packed the heavy chains and keys into an old carry bag, and stepped outside into the bright, cold day. Something fluttering in the breeze caught my eye. A long, heavy cloak hung from a tree branch beside our fields.

His cloak.

I snatched it off the tree, fully intending to tear it piece by piece for what that man had wrought upon me. But I brought my bout of fury under control and considered that I'd need to appear respectable to make my way in the world. To that end, I wore the cloak to appear higher than my station in life. I'd return it to its owner after I had tracked him down and killed him.

I understood that, despite his beauty and charm, Jourdain Aubrey was *moroi*, later known in the common tongue as *vampire*. Somehow, he'd made me *moroi*, as well, and yet there I stood in broad daylight, a fact the legends did not support.

Perhaps, I considered, my werewolf aspect comingled with the vampire had turned me into something so horrifying it was only spoken of within the darkest folklore of my people – *pricolici* – a fusion of vampire *and* werewolf.

I had become an eternal fourteen-year-old boy, a monster twice over, who set out into the world hoping to discover a way to become human once again.

10

A CURE FOR ETERNITY?

Drágan stopped reading and looked up. Deeply moved and saddened by the story, Isaac sat up, feeling the need to hug his friend, to assure him he'd find a cure, to say something that might reflect his feelings. Instead, he held himself in check, awash in sorrow.

"I'm so sorry" was all he managed to blurt out as he fought to control his emotions.

Drágan set the diary aside. "I didn't share my story with you to get sympathy, but to be honest. Now you understand what sort of monster shares your room. I know I've already given you numerous reasons to fear me, so if you want me to leave, I will."

Isaac brought himself under control. "No way in hell! You're staying right here."

"You're not afraid I'll drink your blood in the night?"

"You haven't yet, have you?"

"No."

An idea came to Isaac at that moment. "Those guys at school, Serg and Ron. You drank from them, didn't you?"

"Yes. It seemed the easiest way to satisfy my needs and protect you at the same time."

"What about Jack?"

"No. I only shared that I knew a secret he harbored."

"What secret?"

"That's his business."

Isaac considered everything that had happened since Drágan came to town. "Some of the other rowdy guys are quieter too. Your doing?"

"Yes."

"Did you, you know, drink from Stephanie?"

"No. Only the boys."

Isaac considered this information. While he would be repulsed to watch Drágan drink blood from someone, he recognized that his friend fulfilled his needs discreetly and in such a way that life at Millwood High had improved for everyone except, he supposed, the bullies he drank from.

"The chains you carry. Are they the ones your father had made for you?"

"Oh, no," Drágan replied. "Those rusted away ages ago. The ones I carry now are forged of solid steel."

"What about Jourdain? Did you ever destroy him?"

"No. And he pursues me to this day."

"Why?"

Drágan considered a moment. "For many, children are mere property. I suspect, at first, he considered me *his* property because he had turned me. But his tenacity indicates a darker design that I haven't figured out. I've successfully eluded him for many years now, probably because I've been accepting fewer modeling assignments."

"I hope he doesn't show up here," Isaac said, shivering. Then another thought came to him. "You told me your blood makes you immortal. Was that a lie?"

"No. Doctors have discovered over the years that two foreign cells exist within my bloodstream. Dr. Wilson believes that one controls my werewolf aspect and the other the vampire. He can explain better than I. Shall we go over together?"

"But it's after dinner."

"He'll be working."

Dr. Wilson's house looked like it was buried in trees, but they merely surrounded it like a high wall and gave him the privacy Drágan said the doctor craved. Isaac was surprised that Drágan had his own key but made no comment as they entered through the front door. Drágan locked the door and proceeded down a long hallway to another door on the left. Isaac followed in silence. Drágan pulled open the door and light spilled out from below.

The wooden steps creaked and groaned as they descended into a much larger basement than the one beneath Isaac's house. This one was finished and set up as a high-tech laboratory.

Isaac had only seen glimpses of Dr. Wilson a few times before, so this was his first chance to get a good look. The first thing he noticed was how serious the doctor seemed—probably because of his glasses. Judging from the gray sprinkled through his short, dark hair, Isaac guessed his age at forty-something. And when Wilson stood up from where he sat to greet them, Isaac realized that "recluse" didn't mean "unfriendly."

"Drágan, how good of you to drop in. I see you brought the friend you've talked about."

"He talked about me?"

"About nothing else," Wilson replied. "Come closer so I can look you over, Isaac. We're neighbors, are we not?"

"Yes, sir."

Isaac stood before the tall man and shook his hand. Wilson eyed Drágan across his table filled with test tubes, microscopes, and Bunsen burners. "I take it you've told him everything?"

"I have, Doctor," Drágan replied. "I thought you could explain my blood situation better than I can."

"Absolutely. Come, Isaac. Look into that microscope."

He indicated the closest microscope, and Isaac closed one eye to peer through the ocular lens. What he saw made no sense to him. It looked like two micro monsters fighting, with one grabbing hold of the other. He stood up, mystified.

"What you just saw is the werewolf cell I isolated from Drágan's blood sample. What behavior did you observe?"

"It looked like one grabbed the other."

"Excellent, Isaac. It appears that the werewolf cell grabs on to healthy white cells and prevents them from doing their job, which is to purge the bloodstream of foreign invaders." He reached over to a beaker with an eyedropper poking out. He sucked a bit of the murky liquid into the eyedropper. "Place your eye there again and watch what happens."

Isaac did as he was instructed. The two cells still battled, but one clearly had the other in a headlock, of sorts. A drop of murky liquid mixed in with the sample. Almost at once, it seemed like both cells exploded. Isaac lifted his head, brows furrowed.

"What happened?"

"I separated and distilled the two isotopes that make up silver, reputed to be the only substance that can kill a werewolf, and created the serum you saw. As you witnessed, it not only destroyed the werewolf cell, but the healthy white cell, as well."

Science wasn't Isaac's strong suit. "Which means what?"

"If I were to inject this serum into Drágan, death would likely be the result, not a cure. However, he is unique in that his blood is also tainted by the vampire cell. Look here."

Isaac glanced at Drágan, who stood patiently as the doctor brought Isaac up to speed. Wilson indicated a second microscope. Isaac bent and focused the image. This time, he clearly saw red blood cells. But another, gray in color and larger, swallowed them up as he watched in horror.

"What you saw there," Wilson explained as Isaac lifted his head, "is the vampire cell devouring Drágan's hemoglobin. Now this has the effect of rendering him bloodless, so to speak, after a period of time. Thus, he must replenish his blood supply by drinking from others."

"Dr. Wilson keeps some blood here for those times when using the boys at school might be dangerous," Drágan explained, pointing to a large refrigerator in one corner.

"There's something about Drágan's metabolic system that requires he drink blood and absorb it into his body through the stomach, just like he does his regular food."

"Which is why," Drágan added, "I can't just receive regular blood transfusions.

"Now," Wilson went on, "legend tells us that only two things kill a vampire, a wooden stake through the heart and sunlight," Wilson went on as though giving a lecture. "Now Drágan experiences sunlight with ease, so that option is of no value. I suspect the symbiotic relationship between the vampire and werewolf cells has made him more of a half vampire, but it's not like there are scientific journals on the subject. I'm considering that some distillation of wood might counter the power of that virulent vampire cell, but I'm still experimenting."

"It sounds like you're no closer to a cure than when you started," Isaac said, feeling a deep sense of hopelessness sweep over him.

Wilson looked genuinely sad. "Unfortunately, you're correct. But, as I'm sure Drágan told you, I have samples from another werewolf, pure blood this time."

Drágan reacted with surprise.

"I'm one of five brothers, Drágan, and I know how boys cannot keep such things secret, even a boy who is over five hundred years old."

Isaac and Drágan glanced at each other and shrugged.

"Sadly, even with the purebred blood, all my cures would result in the death of the host. But I'll not give up."

"Thank you, Doctor," Isaac said, "for helping him. He deserves it."

"On that we agree," Wilson said. "But so do you, if your friendship is to continue."

Isaac frowned and Drágan uttered an exclamation of annoyance.

"What do you mean?"

Wilson must've caught Drágan's look and said no more.

Isaac focused on his friend. "Drágan? What does he mean?"

Drágan sighed. "If a cure isn't discovered in the near future, you'll leave me behind."

"Never!" Isaac's response was more passionate than he'd intended, but the thought of losing Drágan was...unthinkable.

"You'll turn fifteen, sixteen, seventeen and so on," Drágan said in a wistful tone, "while I remain a boy of fourteen. Then you'll become an adult, and once again I'll be alone."

Isaac opened his mouth to protest but closed it because he knew his friend spoke the truth. He couldn't stop time, much as he wished to, and time would, indeed, take Drágan away from him.

He faced Dr. Wilson. "Please, you must cure him. He's the best friend I've ever had."

Drágan gasped, and Isaac turned to see him gazing back at him with what looked like surprise.

"I'm doing my best," Wilson said. Then, as if an idea occurred to him, he added, "I have a friend, a fellow blood specialist, in South Dakota. She's studied rare blood diseases for many years. Do I have your permission, Drágan, to consult with her on your case?"

"Of course," Drágan replied.

"Excellent. Now, you boys best head home. I'm going to consider other directions to pursue before I turn in. Nice to finally meet you, Isaac. You're exactly as Drágan described you."

Eyeing his friend, Isaac asked, "And how did he describe me?"

"Loyal, compassionate, and..." Wilson glanced at Drágan, who lowered his eyes in embarrassment.

"And what?" Isaac asked.

"Cute enough to be a model," Wilson replied, sounding amused.

Isaac laughed and punched Drágan lightly on one shoulder. "You're nuts. Let's go home."

ISAAC SAT ON HIS BED, his mind awhirl with all he'd learned in the past two hours. Drágan entered wearing his sleeping gown, placing his folded clothes atop his bureau for school the next day.

"I won't be able to sleep, Drágan, after today. Tell me another story. You lived so many years and in so many places, you must have hundreds."

"That's true," Drágan agreed. "I've collected many in my various diaries."

"Read one to me, please? I want to know everything about your life."

"Everything about my life would take a long time." He considered a moment. "I do have a story that takes place shortly after arriving in the New World from the old. Will that work?"

Isaac nodded with great fervor.

Drágan retreated to his closet, rummaged a bit, and then returned with another old diary, bound together with a thin strip of leather. "May I?" He indicated the spot beside Isaac on the bed.

Isaac scooted over, making sure there was enough space between them for Drágan's comfort zone.

"You know, I presume, of your esteemed president, Abraham Lincoln?"

"Lincoln? Course. Wait, you *met* him?"

"Yes." Drágan opened the diary and began to read.

INTERLUDE

Drágan's Diary

In the year of Our Lord, 1862, I arrived in the New World hoping advances in medicine might lead to a cure. A war raged between the states of the North and those of the South. Having participated in numerous wars on the continent as drummer boy, fifer, and bugler, I chose to enlist in what was called the Union Army. It was there I met President Abraham Lincoln.

My regiment was stationed in the nation's capital, and the good Lord saw fit to bring the president to inspect my company. As the only boy present, Mr. Lincoln singled me out for questioning.

"What's your name, son?"

"Drágan Albescu, sir."

"And how old might you be?"

"Fourteen as of my last birthday, sir."

"Is your father also an enlisted man?"

"No, sir, I'm an orphan. I reside in the barracks."

Mr. Lincoln seemed perturbed by this news and studied me from beneath his tall, stovepipe hat. "I'd like to hear you play."

He ordered me to play various messages intended for the

directing of troop movements. I had learned them all with ease upon enlistment and performed on my drum with flawless perfection. The president smiled, clearly impressed. He then asked me to play on the bugle slung over my shoulder. I did so, playing various battle tunes, including reveille.

He gazed long and hard at me after I'd completed his instructions, then wandered, hands behind his back, toward my platoon leader. They spoke quietly, but with my werewolf enhanced ears I easily heard Mr. Lincoln inform the platoon leader that I was now to be his personal drummer boy and would travel with him.

The platoon sergeant saluted as Mr. Lincoln, accompanied by two men I presumed to be bodyguards, returned to his carriage. My sergeant whistled for me to approach and explained what I already knew, then walked me to the president's carriage. I was ushered into the backseat with one of the bodyguards.

This event occurred in August of 1862.

I was brought into the servants' quarters within the stately home of the president, aptly named the White House due, no doubt, to the color of its exterior. I was provided my own room—a rare experience in my long life—with a bed and wash basin. Fresh linens and clothing were given me as I only possessed the one uniform, which the butler insisted *must* be laundered. My valise had already been sent over from the barracks. Such good fortune had never befallen me, and I felt the hand of Providence at work.

I only saw the president when I was commanded to accompany him, which happened often. He frequently visited his troops, telling jokes to boost morale. For such a stern-looking man, he possessed a powerful sense of humor that elicited laughter even from me, which had seldom ever occurred with anyone but Will Shakespeare.

When not on duty, I had permission to explore the White House gardens. I met the president's son, Tad, then nine years of age, and he showed me around as though I were a guest, rather than a soldier. He seemed quite taken by my military attire and said I was the first uniformed boy near his age whom he'd met.

One evening, I sat alone on a bench within the lush gardens

gazing up at the night sky. The moon would soon be full and I required a plan as to where to go and how to explain my absence should anyone ask.

I heard the president's distinctive step long before he came to stand beside me, gazing up at the stars. I rose to my feet at once, stood at attention, and saluted.

"Sit, Drágan, and enjoy the peace of this night."

"Yes, sir." I reseated myself.

"So, tell me, where did you learn such fine drumming skills?"

"I took part in many wars on the continent, sir. Of course, upon enlistment, I rapidly learned what was required for this one."

He squinted in the darkness. "Seems to me you're too young to have had such experience."

"As an orphan, sir, I must earn my keep how I can, and people seem to like war."

He sat beside me, his long legs stretched out before him. "There's a lot of wisdom in what you say, Drágan. War seems to be in our blood."

"What is the purpose of this one, sir?"

He looked surprised. "You enlisted without that knowledge?"

"As I mentioned, Mr. President, I must earn my keep."

He nodded sadly. "War is the purview of men, but more often than not it's the children who suffer most. Do you know how this country came to be?"

"The colonists rebelled against the English crown."

"That's correct. But this country is different than any in the world because it was founded on ideals, not on culture or race. And those ideals are worth fighting for, which is why the union must endure."

"I understand, sir. I hear the men speak of slavery."

"Yes. Keeping humans as property is a profound evil."

I'd witnessed much slavery over my long life, everywhere I'd traveled, and had resisted many an attempt to enslave me, so I well understood his sentiment.

"You're not like other boys your age," Mr. Lincoln said, fixing his piercing gaze on me. "You have wisdom, as though you've lived decades rather than years."

Fearful he might deduce my secret, I smiled. "I listen more than I speak, sir."

He laughed heartily and clapped me on the back before heading into the house.

The war seemed to drag on, and I had already been with Mr. Lincoln for a year without any of my secrets being revealed. My monthly transformation often proved difficult to hide and other times, while camped on a battlefield, proved relatively easy. Washington D.C. bustled with activity day and night, but the forests of Maryland provided sufficient cover. Often I walked or ran carrying my valise, and my enhanced abilities made that task easy.

But after a year, I felt certain Mr. Lincoln would notice I had not grown and would comment. He did not. I felt other eyes on me, commanders in the field, for example, but did my best to perform my duty and then move to the rear, beyond the sight of the curious.

I had witnessed many bloody battles during my long lifetime, but at a field called Gettysburg the bloodied dead seemed to stretch to the horizon as crumpled bodies fanned outward in all directions. I felt the agony of the president as he toured the site and later spoke on that very spot so eloquently about the need to keep the union together.

I had never met a man like him and found myself growing attached, as though he were the father I lacked. I learned that one of his sons, Willie, had died several months prior to my arrival. Perhaps my presence, young as I was, offered the president some slight solace.

Two more years passed, and I was still the beardless boy I'd been at the start. Since I spent most of my time at the White House, it was primarily the household staff who stared at me as though I were bewitched. Tad, of course, was now twelve and growing with great rapidity, already taller than me. He had come to look up to me as something of an older sibling, and I found much happiness in that role, having never had a younger brother of my own.

In April of 1865, the president ordered me to accompany him and

Tad on a tour of the defeated city of Richmond. Tad had asked me prior to our departure why he was younger, but taller, and I suggested he took after his father, while my people had been small. He thought my response to be a sound explanation.

As we embarked on foot throughout the city, former slaves crowded around the president, cheering him with great passion. Mr. Lincoln seldom traveled under heavy guard, which troubled me, so I made use of my supernatural hearing and eyesight to keep threats at bay.

A carriage was brought for the president and Tad, while I strode alongside through the ruined city. Mr. Lincoln, I knew, wanted peace, and had been prepared to negotiate, but the confederate leadership had fled in fear prior to his arrival.

One starry night a year prior, during our frequent visits in the serenity of the White House gardens, he'd inquired of me, based on my experience with war, what I thought was the best strategy for success.

"Encircle the enemy from all sides and crush them without mercy."

He'd given me a curious look for my bloodthirsty assessment, but merely nodded with sadness. I suspect he already knew the strategy I mentioned but was loathe to use it against fellow Americans.

I satiated my true thirst for blood through people on the streets late at night, or from confederate soldiers while out on the battlefield. I had often thought over my nearly three years that I might easily enter any confederate stronghold to kill or subdue the combatants, and their leaders. The war might have ended with minimal bloodshed and death. But, in so doing, I'd be committing outright murder, which I'd sworn to myself never to do. I'd also have given away all my secrets, and I couldn't know whether Mr. Lincoln would have accepted my monstrous self. I could not face rejection from this man. Anyone but him.

Four days after our trip to Richmond, the war ended when Confederate General Robert E. Lee surrendered to Union General Ulysses S. Grant. The president was ecstatic at the news, more pleased than I'd yet seen him, but he'd aged terribly during the war due to the burden of command. His naturally sallow face had become sunken, his tall, lanky frame stooped. He sent for me the day following Lee's surrender, and I entered the Oval Office for the first time. Its opulence overwhelmed me, but I'd come in uniform so I saluted.

"Sit down, Drágan," the president said.

I sat as instructed and looked at this man whom I so greatly admired.

"Now that the war is over, your services as drummer boy will soon end," he began solemnly. "Do you have plans?"

His question caught me unawares. "No, sir."

He leaned forward on the large wooden desk and clasped his hands together. "I've grown quite fond of you, Drágan, and I should like nothing better than for you to remain. Tad considers you as a brother and I...well, I feel great affection for you. However, remaining here might prove difficult when you do not age."

I'm seldom startled, but at that moment I gasped.

"Tad has noticed, as have I and many others. Do you feel confident enough with me to explain how such a thing could be?"

I knew I could not share my monstrous nature, so I concocted a partially true story that something in my blood prevented me from aging and I'd been seeking a cure.

He seemed quite intrigued, invigorated even, "Indeed, I've never heard of such a thing. What is your true age?"

"I'm fourteen, sir, that was truth, but...I've been fourteen for more than three hundred years."

Now *he* gasped in surprise and sat back in his chair, contemplating this new information. "How long has it been since you've had a proper home?"

"The last was with Will Shakespeare and the Globe Theater players in London, long ago."

"Indeed?" The president's eyebrows lifted in surprise. "I do enjoy a good Shakespeare play. I would have loved watching you perform."

"Thank you, sir."

"This is quite a conundrum," Lincoln went on, his brilliant mind clearly searching for an answer. "I suppose, much as I wish for you to remain, I shall have to release you, or share your secret with the family, which I suspect you may not want."

"No, sir. I shall vanish from sight upon leaving here. After such a long and bloody war, I may return to England for a time. I've not yet decided."

"Such a bleak existence for such a remarkable boy." His voice trembled with emotion. "I shall truly miss you, Drágan."

He stood and rounded his desk. I stood as well. He engulfed me in a loving hug, which I gratefully accepted.

"Thank you, sir, for giving me a home."

He stood tall above me and smiled, a twinkle in his eye. "You are always welcome in my home, wherever that may be. Perhaps we'll meet again."

"I'd like that." I paused, then said, "Mr. President, permission to speak?"

"Of course."

"As long I remain in your employ, I wish to be your bodyguard. I feel you are soft in this area, and I've heard much grumbling against you in the city."

Lincoln eyed me with curiosity. "Would you require a gun?"

"No need, sir. I'm faster than any assassin. And I have...other abilities, as well."

The president eyed me with even greater interest. "You indeed are a cipher, Drágan Albescu. Naturally, I agree. I relish your presence. And I'll make certain you're paid extra prior to your departure. Travel expenses, you understand."

He winked and I smiled.

The fourteenth day of April 1865 is a day forever etched upon my heart. I had little to do most of that day, for the president was engaged with meetings and had no need of my services. Late in the afternoon, I accompanied Mr. Lincoln and his wife as they toured the battleship, Montauk. Mrs. Lincoln, never one to speak to me, secretly (or so she thought) asked him to explain my presence.

"He is my loyal bodyguard," the president whispered in return.

Upon returning to the White House, I took my meal in the servant's quarters as was customary. I overheard talk of the Lincoln's attending the theater that night. I took it upon myself to observe as the president's most loyal bodyguard, Mr. Cook, was relieved and replaced by Mr. Parker, a man prone to drink and one whom I did not trust. I had often smelled alcohol on him and felt anxious that he would be the president's only protection.

As the Lincoln's entered their carriage for the theater, I approached, receiving a scowl from Mrs. Lincoln.

"Please, sir, I'd like to stand guard outside the theater."

The president placed a gentle hand on my shoulder and offered the last smile I'd ever see from him. "I wouldn't have anyone else."

I walked to the theater on foot, dressed in my uniform. The streets teemed with people as I planted myself outside the entrance to Ford's Theater. The president had already arrived, and the play had begun.

At some point in the evening, Mr. Parker exited the theater, crossed the street, and entered a drinking establishment. I leapt up in concern. I'd neither seen nor heard anything that might threaten the president, but I would not have him left alone by that scoundrel.

I attempted to enter via the front door but I had no ticket and was told to leave, despite my military attire. I trotted around to an alley behind the theater where I spotted a boy similar in age to myself standing beside a horse, holding its reins.

He saw my uniform and saluted. I enquired as to his business, and he informed me that a famous actor had paid him to hold the horse ready for immediate departure.

A chill ran through me. "Is this actor in tonight's performance?"

"I think not, sir. He entered well after the performance began."

I bolted up the back stairs and in through the rear door. The audience was engaged in raucous laughter from somewhere I saw not, but then the clear sound of a pistol shot reached my ears. I ran in that direction. Pandemonium erupted within the theater, and I heard a man exclaim in Latin, but I'd found the stairs leading to the location of the shot and bounded up them.

Upon entering the president's state box, I found him slumped in his chair. Mrs. Lincoln was in a frightful state. A young man, also in uniform, bled profusely from one arm, but my concern was with the president. Screaming continued from below, and no one paid much mind to me as I hurried to the president's side. A man rushed in claiming to be a doctor. He and the wounded man lowered Mr. Lincoln to the floor and the doctor examined him. I knelt beside the president and observed the examination with keen eyes.

Even before the doctor declared, "His wound is mortal," I knew it to be true. I heard Mr. Lincoln's weakening heartbeat and uneven breathing, and I discerned when the doctor lifted his eyelids that the man whom I'd come to love was no longer present. I'd promised to protect him, and I'd failed. I took his large hand in mine and sobbed.

The following morning, I encountered Tad upon returning to the White House, whereupon he threw his arms about me, and we cried like brothers who'd lost a beloved father.

I marched at the head of the drum corps, just behind the drum major, leading the president's funeral procession as it wound its way throughout the city, fighting back tears as thousands along the streets cried in earnest.

I was paid a large sum of money, per instructions left by the president, for my services. I requested of the new president, Mr. Johnson, that I accompany Mr. Lincoln to his final resting place in Illinois. He agreed and waved me away as he might a fly.

Tad grieved at my departure, but, like his father, he seemed intuitively to comprehend that I was something outside the norm of other boys and bade me best wishes.

Mr. Cook, whom I liked, offered me a hug as I left. Without even speaking, we both knew we'd failed Mr. Lincoln that fateful night. I never saw Parker again.

The train ride to Illinois would have fascinated me as I'd seldom traveled by train. But my heart had been shattered, so I merely sat at the back of the car containing his casket and endeavored not to shed tears.

Of all the times I'd played *Taps* throughout the war, this moment was the most agonizing. I gripped the bugle, fighting to keep my trembling hands steady as I performed that mournful refrain. The soldiers saluted as Mr. Lincoln's casket was laid in its final resting place within his tomb. I completed my tribute to the greatest man I'd ever known, and lowered the bugle to my side. Then I bowed my head and wept.

11

THE ESSENCE OF POPULARITY

Isaac wiped tears from his eyes, unable to speak for a long moment as Drágan crossed the room and replaced his diary inside the valise.

When he returned, Isaac said, "I think I understand now, what you meant about how eternal life sucks. I don't think I could lose people like you have."

"Perhaps now you understand why I'm reluctant to seek attachments."

Isaac nodded, but he still hoped one day Drágan would think of him as a friend and not just a benefactor.

THE FOLLOWING DAY AT SCHOOL, the entire film group gathered for lunch. They drew many a curious look from other students, but Isaac felt accepted for the first time. He attempted to follow the girls' animated conversations about the weekend's filming, but the background noise inhibited his hearing, and he missed a lot of it. He decided he'd best let them know the important information about upcoming work on the film before lunch was over.

"Listen up, please," he began, shocked when the girls fell silent.

"Quiet everyone," Stephanie ordered in a stern tone. "The director speaks. Hail, oh director." She made bowing motions with her arms.

Isaac sat frozen in place, wondering what to say when she burst out laughing and Mary Anne joined in.

"Gotcha," she said, and Isaac smiled with relief.

He described the pickup shots he needed, especially around school, asking everyone to stay after to shoot them. The girls had cheer practice, they said, but not until four thirty, so they could help until then.

Isaac eyed the others. Nathaniel looked at Jack, who'd said nothing as he ate his lunch. "You gonna stay, Jack?"

Jack made eye contact with Isaac.

"I could use you," Isaac said.

Jack nodded, and Nathaniel added, "I'll be there too."

Isaac went on, explaining about the festival. "I have to submit the film this week, so I'll be editing like a madman." They all wanted to be on hand for the editing, and Isaac suspected, the girls might want to be near Drágan. But the more he noticed Mary Anne staring at Jack when the boy wasn't aware, he wondered if she had a crush on him, instead. Ultimately, Isaac agreed to let them watch some of the editing, but not the werewolf footage.

"You have to see the whole movie for that."

They all threw crumpled napkins at him, except Drágan who observed the youthful exuberance with a sober eye.

THE FILMING after school went smoothly, with Isaac capturing shots of Stephanie and Drágan walking around, holding hands in the quad. Some shots included Mary Anne as the couple entered and exited buildings. Jack and Nathaniel were extras—students passing the main actors as they went about their business. No scenes took place in classrooms, and Isaac was satisfied with the footage he obtained.

Back home, he dove full on into editing, while Drágan took his "walk." Isaac now understood that the "walk" was a euphemism for him sating his thirst for blood. With Drágan gone, Isaac edited some of the werewolf scenes to his satisfaction, saving dialogue stuff for when the crew arrived.

He liked his footage, especially the variety of camera angles he'd chosen. His story boards had helped him create scenes that cut together seamlessly. He felt pride in himself for once, no longer feeling like an outcast. He froze the film on Drágan's face and reflected on how much this cursed boy from so far away had changed his life for the better—despite his dark side—and all without asking anything in return.

He'd need music in the film, of course, but he'd already found tracks of stock music he could use that fit the mood and didn't sound intrusive. He had less than a week till the final deadline for student films, but he'd be ready.

Drágan returned before the others arrived.

Isaac turned from the computer. "The usual knuckleheads'll be quiet in class tomorrow, I'm guessing?"

Drágan grinned, his lips redder than usual. "Indeed."

At seven thirty, the doorbell rang.

Isaac eyed Drágan. "You ready for the girls?"

Drágan climbed to the upper bunk and sat cross-legged. "Please remove the ladder, Isaac."

Isaac laughed. "Pretty slick." He hid the ladder inside his closet just before the gang arrived.

Naturally, Stephanie blustered her way in ahead of the others and dragged Mary Anne over to look at the models. "These are amazing," she gushed.

Jack noticed Drágan on the top bunk and looked relieved. He sat next to Isaac at the computer. Before Nathaniel could sit beside Jack's chair on the bottom bunk, Mary Anne hurried over and scooted in first. Nathaniel sighed and slumped onto the bed beside her. Stephanie eyed Drágan mischievously.

"Want me to come up there and keep you company?"

"No, thank you," Drágan replied in a no-nonsense tone.

Jack stifled a laugh and Stephanie lost her smile. Instead, she stood behind Isaac, hands on the back of his chair and leaning in so closely he squirmed with discomfort. Afraid of offending her, he ignored the closeness as best he could.

"So," he began, irritated with Stephanie's hair tickling his neck, "here's the stuff I edited so far."

He played the dramatic scenes he'd cut together, and they all applauded with gusto.

"Thank you, thank you," Stephanie said, bowing to everyone.

Jack asked Isaac, "How'd the werewolf footage cut?"

"So far, so good. The part you helped with looks great."

"What'd you do, Jack?" Mary Anne asked, sounding interested.

"That's between me and Isaac."

She lost her inviting smile and sat back. Isaac noticed Nathaniel trying to hide his grin. Having never had friends except Jack, he began to realize that maybe the over-the-top high school relationship stuff on TV might *not* be so over the top, after all.

They watched him cut in some of the school footage he'd shot that afternoon and for a while no one said anything, which he preferred. By eight-thirty, the girls and Nathaniel said they had to leave.

"You coming, Jack?" Mary Anne asked hopefully.

"Naw, I'm gonna kick it here for a while."

Disappointed, she slunk from the room.

"I'll wait, if you want, Jack," Nathaniel said in that mousy tone he had.

Jack focused on the computer screen. "No need. See you tomorrow, Nat."

Isaac noticed that Nathaniel seemed to like Jack calling him Nat, for some reason.

"Thanks, man, for all your help," Isaac said as the skinny boy ambled from the room.

Drágan, who'd been silent, dropped lightly from the upper bunk to the floor with hardly a sound. Jack jumped slightly as Drágan approached.

"Uh, can I, you know, see the werewolf stuff we worked on?" Jack asked in a timid voice.

"Sure," Isaac said, "but no details to anyone."

"I won't." Jack laid his arms on the edge of the desk and waited while Isaac located that footage.

"Now, there's no music yet, but I pretty much cut together the finale."

He pressed the play button. The film began with Stephanie wandering the woods, gun in hand.

"I still have to cut in the sounds of the hunters getting closer."

Jack nodded, his eyes riveted to the screen.

Stephanie stops suddenly.

"That's when she hears the howl," Isaac explained.

Stephanie comes upon the werewolf devouring the deer. She gasps in horror and the creature looks up at her. The werewolf steps forward, the large tree in the background. It snarls, its mouth bloody, its eyes glittering with malice.

She tries talking to it, calling it Cameron, but as the scene cuts back and forth, the werewolf just stares balefully at her, ready to pounce. Because the werewolf footage was real, Isaac couldn't include a two-shot of them, which he lamented.

The werewolf lunges at the camera. Stephanie raises the gun and fires, looking away as she does.

The werewolf yelps in pain, then twists and writhes as it transforms back into Drágan. This footage had been intercut with shots of the crying Stephanie watching in horror. Isaac had carefully cut away just as the first glimpse of Drágan's naked body appeared. After that, she drops the gun and runs to him on the ground, and they have their tearful goodbyes.

Isaac froze the image.

"It looks amazing," Jack muttered, clearly impressed, "almost like a real werewolf."

Isaac resisted the urge to look at Drágan.

"No sign of the chains," Isaac said.

Jack met his gaze. "Yeah. Maybe I'll go into special effects and work on your movies when you're famous."

"Yeah, maybe."

Jack faced the screen once more, frozen on Stephanie's tearful face. "I can't stand her, but she's a good actress."

"May I enquire," Drágan interjected, "the nature of your antipathy toward her?"

"Huh?"

Having grown accustomed to Drágan's speech patterns, Isaac asked, "Why do you hate her so much?"

Jack eyed him with incredulity. "You really don't remember?"

Isaac furrowed his brows. "I don't think so."

"She was with those jocks when they called us queer last year," Jack spat, anger bubbling to the surface. "She made kissy faces at me. Man, I hated her after that."

Isaac bowed his head. He did remember now. "Not as much as you hated me."

Jack looked startled, then composed himself. "I never hated you." He stood abruptly. "I gotta go."

He hurried from the room before Isaac could respond.

"The essence of peace is finding reasons not to fight," Drágan said. He left the room, and seconds later the bathroom door closed.

Isaac stared after him for a moment, then shook his head. *What the hell did he mean by that?*

ISAAC NEGLECTED school assignments to focus on finishing his film, including the credits, sound effects, and music. His deadline was the twenty-ninth and he finished on the twenty-eighth. He screened the film for his mom and Drágan to get their responses in case anything needed tweaking.

His mom was brushing a tear away as Isaac turned on the lights. "Well?"

"Honey, it was beautiful. So sad."

His face fell. "Not scary?"

She smiled. "Very much, but I've watched so many of these movies with you, it takes a lot to scare me."

He laughed and she hugged him. "How ever you do in the festival, you're always a winner to me."

She left the boys alone.

Drágan said, "And to me."

"Huh?"

"A winner," Drágan affirmed.

Isaac felt his cheeks redden.

He sent a link to his film on Vimeo to the festival that night. If the film qualified, he'd have to send in a DVD or, better still, a Blu-ray. His equipment could make both.

"Does it feel weird," Isaac asked as they lay in their bunks later that night, "to see yourself in that other form in a movie?"

"I'm just happy this curse of mine can finally help someone."

Isaac heard the sadness once again and wished he could do something for his friend.

AT LUNCH THE FOLLOWING DAY, Isaac told the group that he'd submitted the film, and they bubbled over with excitement. Even Jack was animated with Nathaniel about their chances to win, while the girls chattered excitedly about the premiere.

Isaac said, "I guess we have to dress fancy, right?"

"That's no problem for Drágan," Stephanie said with a laugh. "He always dresses to impress."

Drágan replied, "I wear these clothes because they suit me, not to impress anyone."

"Chill out," Stephanie admonished him, sounding annoyed. "It's just an expression."

"Oh."

"When will you know our movie is in the festival?" Mary Anne asked, her voice effervescent with excitement.

"Hopefully, by next weekend," Isaac replied.

Mary Anne turned to Jack. "Isn't it exciting, Jack? What will you wear to the festival? Maybe we could match."

"Like never will that happen." Jack looked down at his food and scarfed some fries.

Mary Anne looked hurt, but Stephanie's ebullience kept her afloat. "Forget him, he's a grinch. You and me'll have a blast."

Isaac listened to them plan out their wardrobe without reminding them that the film hadn't been selected yet.

"And don't forget, Homecoming is the week after the festival," Mary Anne squealed, as though just remembering it. "We all have to go to the dance."

"We don't hafta do anything," Jack grumbled.

Stephanie jumped into the potential fray. "It'll be fun, especially after we win the film competition. I bet you can dance, Drágan, coming from Europe."

"What does Homecoming refer to, aside from the obvious meaning?" Drágan asked the table at large.

"It's the first football game at home after the team has played away for a while," Mary Anne gushed. "But the game is a whatever. The dance is what will be fun. Our first high school homecoming dance. We gotta go!" She focused on Isaac, since, due to his status as director of the film, he was nominally in charge. "Come on, Isaac, if you go, I bet the others will."

"Like how?" Isaac exclaimed. "I'm a nobody."

Mary Anne's mouth dropped open. "Seriously, after the movie you just made?" He gave her a "look" and she got the message. "Okay, I guess we have treated you like you didn't exist, but that was before we knew how cool you were."

"Thanks." Isaac hoped his tone displayed the sarcasm he intended.

Just then two girls from the cheerleading squad stopped at the table and glared at Stephanie and Mary Anne with anger.

"Why do you keep hanging out with them?" one girl snapped, eyeing the boys. "They're all losers except the hot guy, but he's spooky."

"Yeah," said the second girl, "you're supposed to stick with us at lunch."

Stephanie eyed them, then looked back at Isaac and the other boys before shucking off her cheer jacket and handing it to the first girl. "I'm done with cheer. Gonna concentrate on acting. You know there's three runners-up who'd die to be on the squad."

Watching her, Mary Anne pulled off her jacket too, handing it to the second girl. "Me too. I'll be a makeup artist for stage and film."

"And for your information," Stephanie added, "these guys are more real than your football jerks."

The girls looked stunned, especially with everyone in the cafeteria watching the confrontation.

The first girl glared at Stephanie with venom in her blue eyes. "You just gave up all your popularity."

Stephanie shook her head. "I have all the popularity I need right here." She indicated those seated at the table.

In a huff, both girls stormed back to the other cheerleaders and slammed the jackets onto the table hard enough to knock cups to the floor.

Stephanie turned to face Isaac, whose mouth hung open in shock. "Why'd you do that?" he asked.

She met his gaze straight on. "That kind of popular means we have to make other kids unpopular, like I used to do with you. I'm sorry."

Mary Anne looked contrite. "Me too."

"You know," Stephanie went on, still focused on Isaac, "the dance might really be fun, all of us together?"

Isaac glanced around. Jack was looking at him wearing an unreadable expression. Nathaniel appeared to be waiting for Jack to decide. Isaac turned to Drágan beside him.

"I'll only go if you do, Isaac," he said.

Isaac grimaced. He hated being on the spot. "It'll be so loud I won't hear anybody talking to me," he said. "And my ears can't handle that pounding music."

"You used to turn your hearing aids down when things got loud," Jack said, as though recalling a good memory. "I always said you should do that in every class so you didn't have to listen to the boring-ass teachers."

Isaac smiled, recalling those conversations.

"Please, Isaac," Stephanie begged. "It won't be fun without you."

"I can't dance," Isaac said, still reluctant to agree.

"I can instruct you," Dragan commented, "though the dances I teach you might not be apropos."

"Thanks, man," Isaac said, not completely sure what "apropos" meant. He looked across the table at Jack. "You gonna go?"

"I guess," he replied. "Gotta dance with all the girls, right?" He nudged Nathaniel, who didn't respond.

"Okay," Isaac reluctantly agreed. "I'll go."

The girls squealed with delight and then started planning what to wear.

Do girls talk about anything but clothes? Isaac wondered, rolling his eyes at Jack.

12

FRIENDSHIP

The following week, two incidents of note occurred. One was the October full moon, and the other was an email Isaac received congratulating him on his film earning a spot in the festival. The email arrived on the Monday after he submitted. When he read it, he whooped for joy, leaped up from his desk chair, and grabbed Drágan in an excited hug.

Immediately, he pulled back, a horrified expression on his face. "I'm sorry, man, I forgot you hate hugs."

Drágan did not appear angry. "Under the circumstances, the hug was warranted. I'm happy for you."

"For all of us, man, especially you."

"Why me?"

"I bet anything that footage of you is what got us in," Isaac gushed, then paused. "I'm still not sure it was right to use it, though."

"It was," Drágan assured him. "Friday night the moon will be at its fullest again."

Isaac nodded. "And I'll stay with you all night, standing guard."

"That is unnecessary."

"You heard Mary Anne's dad. What if that other werewolf howls again? Him and his buddies might go hunting you."

"They cannot harm me. Only silver is fatal."

"I'm staying and that's that." Isaac folded his arms across his chest in defiance.

"What if I simply leave without you?"

"Like I don't know these woods and couldn't find you?"

"You could be shot by accident if hunters do approach."

Isaac hesitated. "I'm afraid to leave you alone."

"I've been alone for hundreds of years."

"Well, you're not anymore. I promise I'll be careful, but I'm gonna be there."

Drágan sighed with defeat. "Has anyone ever told you you're incredibly stubborn?"

"Yeah, my mom, all the time."

Drágan laughed. "I concede. Now perhaps you should contact the others with the joyous news about the film."

Isaac sent out a group text about the festival and each of the crew texted back their happiness. Even Jack wrote, "Good job, man."

The following day at lunch, the girls were even more into their discussion of clothing and suggesting they just *had* to go shopping because neither of them had a *thing* to wear. The boys rolled their eyes, but Isaac didn't have any nice clothes himself and might have to ask his mom to go shopping with him.

That Friday night, Isaac accompanied Drágan back into the woods for his full-moon ritual. Penelope couldn't understand why they liked camping in the cold, but Isaac just said, "We're boys."

Worried about hunters after what Mr. Givens had said, they delved deeper into the forest until another behemoth of a tree was located. As before, Drágan captured a deer and brought it to the tree, tying it up.

This time, Isaac helped Drágan wrap the chain around the tree. Still hating the indignity of his friend having to strip naked, Isaac refused to look until Drágan had secured the shackles and planted himself against the tree, legs pulled up to cover himself.

Isaac stood before him, wearing his warmest clothes. The temperature had started dropping into the thirties overnight. "You won't be alone."

"Do I not frighten you in my other form?"

Isaac made eye contact. "Truth? Yeah, you do, even though I know you can't hurt me when you're chained up." He paused, uncertain how to say what he wanted to. "I guess I wonder sometimes if you might hurt me without the chains."

Drágan gazed at him a long moment. "I hope never to find out."

Isaac accepted that answer. It was honest, after all. He walked to his sleeping bag, shivering against the biting wind that had kicked up earlier in the evening. He sat and pulled his sleeping bag around himself. He'd brought a propane lantern this time and kept it on low, its soft glow illuminating him as he gazed at Drágan.

The silence of the forest soothed his heart—until Drágan transformed and ripped apart the terrified deer. Isaac kept his eyes averted and concentrated on focused breathing to calm himself. After that, he watched in silence, listening for approaching danger.

WHEN HE AWOKE the following morning, the lantern had used up all its fuel and Drágan lay on his back, naked and bloody. This time Isaac had brought plenty of rags and extra water. He unshackled his friend with the key and proceeded to wipe Drágan's body clean. He no longer felt as embarrassed cleaning Drágan but, rather saw it as his duty. When Drágan awoke, clean and ready for his clothes, Isaac had already brought them, draping the cloak over him. Drágan stood and dressed, thanking Isaac for his ministrations.

"It's what friends are for, right?"

"But no one has ever done for me what you have." The gratitude in his voice touched Isaac to the core.

This time, they'd brought a large plastic trash bag and scooped the remnants of the deer into it, then covered up the blood with dirt. Isaac tied off the bag, nearly gagging at the stench, and they tossed it into his outside trash can, which would be picked up Monday morning. He just hoped his mom didn't find it before then.

The following Monday, the trash went out as scheduled with Isaac's mom being none the wiser. The girls had used the weekend, they announced at lunch, to find "the perfect outfits for the festival," with Mary Anne adding, "And for Homecoming."

Isaac's mom had agreed to go shopping with him, but he preferred to go with Drágan, since his friend had good taste in clothes. She agreed. "But don't spend too much." After school that day, she handed him her credit card and the boys went into town.

"Where are the clothing stores?" Drágan asked, looking around at the storefronts.

"I think I know the perfect place. C'mon."

He led his friend around the corner of Main and 2nd Street to a shop he'd only seen but had never been inside of—Rachel's Vintage Clothing and Accessories. They entered, and Drágan's eyes lit up with joy.

"Pick me out a nice outfit," Isaac said. "I know nothing about clothes."

Drágan nodded, his gaze flitting everywhere at once. Racks of shirts, jackets, coats long and short, hats, ties of various styles, vests, and a wide variety of footwear took up the men's section of the store. Drágan seemed to know exactly what to choose and, when Isaac tried everything on, it all fit perfectly.

"How'd you know my size?" he asked after emerging from the dressing room.

"By studying you," Drágan answered, gazing deeply at him.

The look in Drágan's eyes sent a chill throughout Isaac's body and he quickly glanced away. He took his place before the full-length mirror and nearly gasped. He looked like something out of an old movie, but he also looked like Drágan with shorter hair. He wore a fancy patterned vest, an ankle-length blue coat, black pants, a white shirt. The blue tie was more of a scarf wrapped around his neck and tucked into the vest.

"What's this?" he asked. "Never seen a tie like this."

"It is a cravat," Drágan explained, "quite popular near the end of the 19th Century."

"Boy knows his clothes" came a female voice to one side.

Isaac turned to find Ms. Rachel standing there, one hand to her hip, sizing him up. She was middle-aged with red hair and had on one of the vintage dresses she always wore around town.

"You look sharp. Big event coming up?"

Isaac told her about the film festival and the homecoming dance. She became animated at the thought of Millwood having a famous filmmaker living there.

"Not famous yet," Isaac laughed.

She grinned. "You'll slay in that outfit, especially at the dance. These high schoolers don't know how to dress anymore."

Isaac laughed, though Drágan looked confused by her choice of words. "I'll explain later." To Ms. Rachel he added, "Let me get this stuff off, and I'll bring it up front."

She winked, and Isaac returned to the dressing room.

As he was paying for his purchases, the little bell over the door tinkled, and in walked the last person Isaac expected to see—Jack. Nathaniel peeked in from behind him.

Jack spotted Isaac and turned to push Nathaniel out the door.

"Don't go, guys," Isaac insisted. "We're leaving anyway."

The silent boys hovered near the door as Ms. Rachel bagged up Isaac's clothes. She thanked them, and they headed for the exit. Jack blocked their way. He indicated Drágan with a nod of his head.

"He find some cool clothes for you?"

Isaac nodded.

Jack shuffled his feet. "Think he could pick out something for us?" He indicated himself and Nathaniel behind him.

Isaac stepped aside so Jack and Drágan faced one another. "Ask him."

"So, uh, how about it?" Jack asked. "I got no dad and I know nothing about fancy clothes."

"Me either," Nathaniel said, his voice timid.

"Come with me," Drágan said, heading back toward the racks. "I think I saw some things that would suit each of you."

Jack made eye contact with Isaac for a split second before he and Nathaniel followed Drágan back toward the men's section. Within fifteen minutes, both boys stood before the full-length mirror looking like the brothers of Isaac and Drágan. Jack sported a similar cravat, but in a silvery fabric that complimented the gray and black of his outfit, including the ankle-length black coat. Nathaniel's similar ensemble featured light blue and gray stylings.

"You guys look amazing," Isaac said, forgetting for a moment the distance between him and Jack. "I mean, what do you think?"

Ms. Rachel sauntered over and gave Jack and Nathaniel the once over. "You guys look good. I couldn't have chosen better."

That seemed to satisfy the boys and they paid for their purchases. When all four of them reached the sidewalk outside, preparing to go their separate ways, Jack offered Drágan a shy look.

"Thanks, man."

Nathaniel added, "Yeah, thanks."

WHEN ISAAC and Drágan entered the house, his mom insisted he model the clothes for her. Embarrassed, he complied. She *had* paid for everything, after all.

She proclaimed him "Stunning," and added, "My boys will be the most handsome and best dressed at both events."

Isaac noticed that she included Drágan as one of her "boys."

Drágan noticed too, and smiled with pure delight.

Isaac, his actors, and film crew all received tickets to the full festival, but they decided to only go on Sunday, which was the day the student entries would screen. In the horror division, they noted on the online schedule, only five films had been accepted.

"That's pretty good odds," Nathaniel commented during lunch the Friday before. Isaac was amazed how much he'd come out of his shell and attributed the change to Jack conversing with him. The two seemed in sync more often than not, which caused Isaac odd pangs of jealousy he had to quell when they were together.

"Did you see that they're gonna give awards for best actor and actress?" Stephanie gushed, bubbling with genuine excitement. "You and me, Drágan."

"If anyone should win, it should be you, Stephanie." Drágan's tone was genuine.

"Thanks. But your performance was so heartfelt, it was easy to act opposite you."

"Best success to all of us," Isaac said, raising his milk for a toast. The others lifted their juice or milk and all the cups touched together.

Isaac found it difficult to concentrate in his classes that afternoon, grateful once again that Serg and Ron and their jock buddies didn't heckle him. Since Drágan had put them in their place the previous month, they'd not been a problem to anyone.

After school, Isaac's crew gathered in the quad, discussing what to do until Sunday. Stephanie said there was a new horror film at the Playhouse and suggested they all go.

"Come on, it'll be fun."

Nathaniel eyed Jack shyly. "I'll go if you do."

"Need someone to hide behind?" Jack said with a grin, then elbowed Nathaniel to let him know he was joking. "Sure, I'll go. You guys in?"

He directed his last question to Isaac and Drágan, who exchanged a look.

"I've not been to the cinema in some time," Drágan commented. "Shall we go with them?"

Isaac shrugged. "Sure, why not. I think this movie has a supernatural storyline. I like those more than slashers."

"It's a date then," Mary Anne exclaimed.

"Let's meet at the theater at 7:30 for the 8 o'clock show," suggested Stephanie.

They all agreed and left for home.

Isaac found his mom in her office working on her laptop. She greeted the boys with a toothy smile. "I guess excited is too mild a word for how you feel about Sunday, huh?"

Isaac grinned. "Ecstatic is more like it. Even if we don't win, it's amazing to be selected for my first film."

"It's quite an honor," Drágan agreed, looking more animated than usual.

"We're gonna go to the movies tonight," Isaac went on. "Stephanie invited us."

Her slim eyebrows rose. "So, is this a date, maybe?"

Isaac's face reddened. "Bruh, Mom, we're all going. The whole crew."

"But she likes you," his mom prodded with a smile. "I can tell."

"She likes Drágan too," Isaac replied, glancing at his friend.

"And why wouldn't she be attracted to two such handsome boys?"

"Mom, stop messing with us."

She looked offended. "I can't call my boys handsome? In what universe?"

Isaac laughed. "Thanks, Mom. We're gonna take a walk before dinner, okay?"

"See you soon."

She turned back to her computer and the boys left her alone.

As they stepped outside the front door, Isaac asked, "We going to see Dr. Wilson?"

Drágan nodded.

"Why not call on the phone?" Isaac asked as they left the side porch and headed off through the trees behind his house.

"He prefers not to discuss delicate matters on the telephone for fear of discovery."

Isaac nodded. "I guess that makes sense."

They found Wilson in his lab, as usual, bent over his microscopes. He seemed pleased for their company but had nothing positive to tell Drágan.

"The problem I keep facing is that with every attempt I make to destroy the parasitic cells, I destroy the healthy blood cells as well, which would mean death to the host."

"Host meaning me," Drágan said, a note of resignation in his voice.

"Yes." Though the doctor tended to look older than his years, his distress at failing Drágan had turned his face into a mask of remorse. "I've been consulting with my colleague in South Dakota, but she can only make guesses at this point."

"I appreciate your hard work," Drágan said. "After five hundred years, I've learned to accept failure. Perhaps there is no cure, and I shall be as I am forever."

"Don't say that, Drágan," Isaac assured him. "There's gotta be an answer!"

"I'll not give up," Wilson affirmed, reseating himself at his workstation and changing the slide in his microscope.

"Can I ask you a question, Doctor?"

"Of course, Isaac. We're neighbors, after all."

"Well, you seem like such an amazing specialist in blood and all," Isaac began, uncertain how to phrase his question, "so, well, why come here to Millwood? There's nothing here except one hospital."

The doctor sat up and removed his glasses. "What you mean to ask is why I'm hiding out here."

Mortified, Isaac blurted, "No, I, uh, well, I just wondered."

"You didn't tell him, I presume?" Wilson asked Drágan.

"No, sir."

"You're a good lad, Drágan." To Isaac he said, "I was, some years ago, a prestigious cancer researcher for a major medical university. I had, I'd thought, found a way to purge leukemia from the blood of infected patients."

"That sounds fantastic," Isaac said, meaning it. "So, what happened?"

"I was not given permission for human trials of my serum, yet my patients, those whose blood I'd experimented with, were dying, and begged for my help. I ignored the edict from those overseeing my research and administered my serum to three individuals with advanced stage leukemia."

"And?"

His face fell. "Alas, the leukemia took them all despite my serum and I was fired from my position, disgraced within the medical establishment."

"But they were going to die anyway," Isaac insisted, anger boiling up inside. "At least you tried to save them."

"There are solid reasons for oversight. On that I concur. But, given the extreme circumstances, I went ahead when I should not have and that is not allowed under any circumstances. So, I settled here and have attempted to help those like Drágan with unusual blood ailments."

"Well, I think that's wrong, what they did," Isaac grumbled. "Why have a brain of your own if you aren't allowed to use it?"

Wilson shrugged and returned his eye to the microscope.

"We'll depart and allow you to work undisturbed," Drágan said to the doctor, leading Isaac to the door. "I'll check in next week."

"Yes, yes," the doctor said, already lost within his blood samples.

As Drágan led the way back to their house, Isaac seethed about what had happened to the doctor.

"That's the problem with everything these days," he grumbled, "no one wants to take any chances, even to save someone's life."

"Human nature has not changed in all my five hundred years," Drágan said with a sigh. "I doubt it ever shall. I have learned that it is the few, not the many, who make the most significant contributions to this world, and those few are often treated with disdain. Like Mr. Lincoln."

He said no more as they entered the house.

THE MOVIE that night turned out to be decent and Isaac enjoyed it. The jostling for seats annoyed him, however. He just wanted to sit next to Drágan, but Stephanie insisted on sitting "between the two cute boys." Isaac recalled his mother's words and tried not to blush.

Mary Anne sat on Isaac's other side while Nathaniel ended up next to Jack on Stephanie's side.

Stephanie clutched Drágan's upper arm during the jump scares, leaving Isaac somewhat disappointed, mainly because he felt left out. Nathaniel, it turned out, closed his eyes through much of the film and grabbed no one.

The temperature had dropped after dark, and the night air felt almost frigid as they left the theater with the sparse crowd of mostly teens. Isaac thought it might snow over the weekend, though Halloween was usually too early for snowfall.

Drágan seemed disturbed by something as they exited the theater, as though he sensed danger. Isaac knew his abilities to detect threats were high, so he leaned in while the others were chattering about the film. "What is it?"

"I'm not sure. Let's walk everyone to their homes before we return to ours."

"Okay."

Isaac suggested they all walk together to each of their homes since his house was farthest up the road from downtown. They agreed. The two girls huddled together and gabbed about the jump scares all the way to Nathaniel's house. Just as he turned up his driveway, Drágan called his name.

Nathaniel turned back.

"Do not allow any strangers in tonight," Drágan said solemnly.

"Why would I?"

"Just don't."

Nathaniel looked mystified. "I won't. Night, you guys."

Drágan issued the same warning to Jack and Mary Anne as each was about to enter their homes.

"You're acting awfully weird, Drágan," Mary Anne said. "Why would a stranger come to my door?"

"Please," Drágan said, and she agreed.

"What do you know?" Jack asked Drágan in front of his two-story house with closed shutters on the windows.

"A feeling."

Jack paused a moment, then entered his house. That left Stephanie. As they neared her home, she saw lights on in the windows, but only downstairs.

"I hope my stepfather went to bed early again." Her voice almost trembled with fear.

"I'm certain he has," Drágan said quietly.

Stephanie stared at him. "You sound so confident."

"Humans are creatures of habit, are they not? Why should your stepfather change his behavior of the past two months?"

She bit her lower lip. "I hope you're right. Night, guys."

As she entered through her front door and closed it, Drágan froze like a panther ready for an attack. He whirled around and Isaac turned too.

A tall, regal-looking man dressed in elegant clothes, all black, with an ankle-length cloak, stood before them. He wore large rings on each hand that glittered beneath the streetlight. His thick black hair was perfectly coiffed, his handsome face white, his lips red. But it was his eyes that held Isaac in their grip—piercing, hard, accessing his very soul.

"Jourdain," Drágan growled menacingly. "What are you doing here?"

13

EVIL COMES TO MILLWOOD

"I am here because you are here," the vampire said, his voice smooth and sensuous. He studied Isaac for a long moment. "His blood smells delicious."

Drágan reached out and pushed Isaac behind him, freeing Isaac's mind from those magnetic eyes. "You'll not touch him or the others," Drágan declared with a snarl.

"And have you shared with your so-called friends your true nature?"

He chuckled at his own challenge, and the sound turned Isaac's blood to ice.

Drágan said nothing.

Jourdain laughed. "I thought not. Just how long do you expect they will stand by you if the truth were revealed?"

Isaac pushed past Drágan to confront the newcomer. "They wouldn't care, just like I don't! The real monster here is you!" His heart pounded with fear, but he didn't back off.

"He didn't think so when we first met." He indicated the silent, seething Drágan.

"Well, aren't you full of yourself!" Isaac spat, anger making him reckless. "He was fourteen! Hell, I'm fourteen and I'm wowed by your clothes, your jewelry, your weird eyes, and I don't come from some poor-ass village in the middle of Romania!"

Jourdain raised a hand and Isaac noticed his long, sharp fingernails. He touched Isaac's cheek, but Isaac stood his ground, despite a rapidly beating heart.

Drágan slapped the vampire's hand away. "What do you want from me?"

Jourdain smiled, revealing two sharp incisors. "Why nothing. Only your unique blood that lies between the world of the living and that of the undead."

"You'd never drink my blood. You're too afraid of the wolf."

"Who said anything about drinking it?"

And then he was gone, just like that, vanished into the darkness.

"We must hurry home," Drágan urged, taking Isaac by the arm, and leading him along.

Spooked by the confrontation, Isaac said nothing until they were securely locked inside his house.

"He can't come in, can he?"

"Not without an invitation," Drágan said, securing the windows on the first floor. "Hence my warning to the others."

"If that part about vampires is true, should we put garlic around, too?"

Drágan turned to him with one raised eyebrow. "You wish to keep me out, as well?"

Abashed, Isaac mumbled, "Sorry."

Drágan offered a tight smile, and they went upstairs to the study.

"I don't understand," Isaac's mom said, clearly confused. "What stranger would come here?"

The boys exchanged a look, then Drágan said, "He is someone from my past who means ill to me and you."

She stood up from her desk, alarmed. "Then I should call the police."

"The police won't do any good, Mom," Isaac said, eyeing Drágan, uncertain what more to say.

"Why not?"

"Because he's a vampire," Drágan intoned, without the slightest hint of humor.

She blinked and her face went blank, as though trying to comprehend what he said.

"You've treated me like family, and you deserve the truth," Drágan continued.

Isaac grabbed his arm. "Are you sure?"

"Yes. Please sit down, Mrs. Foster. My story may take some time."

Her face etched with fear, she sat again at her desk, while Isaac sat on the floor cross-legged. Drágan took in a deep breath and expelled it. Then he began.

Isaac watched his mother as Drágan told his tale and never once did she gasp or look afraid. Sadness was the only emotion she betrayed, and she cried when it was over.

"If you wish me to leave your home, Mrs. Foster, I will," Drágan said, his head bowed.

"No. I love having you here."

Surprised, Drágan raised his head. "But I just confessed that I'm a monster twice over."

"Maybe, but you're also the best thing to ever happen to us."

Isaac nodded vigorously.

"I admit that what you told me is incredible, and yes, scary," she went on, "but the person I've come to know is not a monster. He's a sweet, handsome, talented boy who has more control over the darker parts of himself than most of us. And it's *you* that I care about." She stood and approached him. "I know you hate being hugged, but I'd really like to give you one now."

Clearly moved, Drágan nodded, and she wrapped her arms around him in a loving embrace. At first hesitant, he lifted his arms and encircled her. They remained in that posture for a moment before Isaac stood and enfolded them both within his arms, his eyes welling with tears.

They finally broke apart, and Penelope wiped her eyes. Isaac did the same, gasping when he saw Drágan swipe at his own moist eyes.

"That wasn't so bad, was it?" he asked Drágan. He held out a fist and Drágan stared at it. "You make a fist and bump mine."

Drágan did as instructed, looking relieved.

"Now that we got that part out of the way," Isaac told his mom, who'd sat back down in her chair, "we need to tell you that the vampire who turned Drágan challenged us in front of Stephanie's house."

Penelope's face hardened. "Tell me everything."

ISAAC AND DRÁGAN were heading upstairs after breakfast the following morning when there was a knock at the door.

"You go on," said Drágan, "I'll get it."

"But what if—"

"It's daylight, remember?"

"Oh, yeah." He continued up the stairs, but stopped at the top when he heard voices from the front hall.

"Hi Jack."

"Uh, hi. I need to see Isaac's mom," Jack said, his voice sounding nervous, maybe because he was alone with Drágan.

Isaac crept to the top of the stairs and peeked down at the two boys facing off in the entry hall.

"No one came to my door last night, if that's what you wanna ask," Jack said.

"That's good, but I'm more curious about your relationship with Isaac."

Jack flinched, like he feared Drágan might punch him. "I told you I'd stop, and I did."

"Yes, you have. But the antecedent to your bullying. What was it?"

"Antecedent?"

"What came before, in your childhood?"

Jack paused, looked like he was going to ignore the question, then sighed. "My old man beat the shit outta me as a kid, always said I was pathetic, called me a pussy. I told Isaac about some of it but not most.

Anyway, when I was nine, the jerk finally fell off something at the mill and broke his neck." He paused, as though not sure how to react to that memory.

"I'm listening," Drágan said in his quiet, soothing tone.

"He'd always made me feel so weak, so when those guys at school started calling me and Isaac queer I...I just couldn't take it. I turned into my father. You know the rest."

His head was bowed, but he seemed more relaxed than when he'd entered, as though confessing was what he'd needed more than anything else.

Isaac hadn't known about everything Jack suffered as a child because his friend wouldn't tell him. Drágan glanced upward, but not all the way to the top of the stairs.

He knows I'm here.

"How come you never told Isaac what you know about me?" Jack looked up and met Drágan's eyes.

"Gossip is a great evil and I refuse to partake of it," Drágan replied evenly.

"Thanks." He looked down, composing himself. "Uh, is Isaac here?"

Isaac started down the stairs. "Oh, hey Jack. Thought I heard the bell."

"I'll leave you guys to talk," Drágan said, easing past them and up the stairs.

"So, what's up," Isaac asked, hoping his face didn't reveal he'd overheard their conversation.

"My mother doesn't believe me about the festival and stuff and won't let me go to Bangor with you guys. I wanna ask your mom to talk to her."

"Sure. She's in her office. C'mon up."

Isaac was amazed how comfortable he felt around Jack again after what the other boy had done, and he had Drágan to thank for it, even making sure Isaac had overheard Jack's confession. But he did wonder again what Jack spoke of, the secret he shared with Drágan which added a clandestine aspect to their relationship.

"Hello, Jack," Isaac's mom said when they entered her office. "I swear you get taller every time I see you."

"Jack wants to ask you something, Mom."

"What is it?"

Jack explained his situation.

"I'll call and let her know I'm driving you in my van and bringing you back home, and that I have your ticket to the festival. She *should* trust me after all these years."

Jack bowed his head. "She should, but she keeps expecting me to turn out like my dad and doesn't trust me."

Penelope placed a comforting hand on his shoulder. "I'll handle it. Aren't you excited for the festival? I know I am."

Jack smiled for the first time. "Yeah, I am." He glanced at Isaac before continuing. "I feel like working on this movie is, well, like the first good thing I've done in a long time."

As they left her office, Isaac asked, "Wanna hang out with us?" He pointed toward his room.

"Okay."

The three of them watched funny videos and memes on Isaac's computer. It felt good to hear Jack's laughter again, but Drágan seemed distracted and often missed the joke in the videos, though he did smile some of the time. Isaac thought his mind might be on Jourdain and what the vampire was planning. Then again, he often found Drágan eyeing him rather than the computer screen, so maybe not?

After a few hours, Penelope entered and said, "It's all set, Jack. I cleared it with your mother. Don't forget to dress nicely." She smiled and left the room.

Jack looked sheepish. "I don't know how to work that fancy tie I got at Ms. Rachel's. I don't even know how to tie a regular one."

Isaac shrugged. "Me either. Drágan can tie them for us, right?"

Drágan's soft eyes looked far away.

"Hey, Drágan."

Drágan faced him.

"You can help us with those cravat things tomorrow, right?"

"Of course."

Jack pulled out his phone and glanced at the time. "Better get home. I got chores to do."

They all stood up.

"Remember not to admit anyone after dark unless you know them," Drágan admonished.

Jack studied him curiously, as though he might once again ask why. Instead, he said, "Sure, man," and left the room.

That night, Drágan announced he would patrol the streets after Isaac went to bed. Isaac wanted to come, but Drágan forbade it.

"He is far too strong for you, but not for me," he said. "The strength of the wolf combined with that of the vampire makes me more powerful than him, a reality he loathes."

"Then why wouldn't he want to drink your blood? Wouldn't that make him like you?"

"I was a werewolf before he attacked me. As a result, I'm a half vampire. Going in reverse, starting as a full vampire, frightens Jourdain because the process might destroy him."

"Then why does he want your blood?"

"I don't know."

Isaac lay in bed but could not sleep until after Drágan returned around one o'clock. He reported seeing no evidence of Jourdain. Isaac relaxed some, but not completely.

Jourdain *would* strike at some point. Isaac just wished he knew when.

14

THE THROWBACK CREW

The next day, Isaac managed to push Jourdain into the back of his mind. It was daylight, for one thing, and that afternoon was the youth portion of the Bangor International Film Festival. His blood ran hot with anticipation. After lunch, when he and Drágan were dressing, Isaac watched the other boy tie his cravat. Try as he might, though, he couldn't master the technique.

"Allow me," Drágan said and stepped behind Isaac, so close their bodies touched. Drágan's arms wrapped around Isaac's neck, and he felt long, powerful fingers gently wrapping and looping the cravat. His heart raced at their closeness and he held his breath until Drágan stepped around to view his handiwork.

He made some slight adjustments and then stepped back. "Perfect."

"Thanks," Isaac said, his body still tingling from the touch of those fingers against the soft skin of his throat.

Penelope gushed over "how handsome" they were and snapped lots of photos before they piled into the van to pick up the others. Isaac had to admit that Jack and Nathaniel looked dashing in their vintage clothes, especially Jack who smiled nervously as he stepped up into the van. As the van pulled away, Drágan rapidly tied both of their cravats the proper way.

"You boys'll have to fight off all the girls at today's screening," Penelope said, embarrassing Isaac in front of the others.

"Bruh, Mom."

Isaac and the others were surprised and pleased to see how the girls were dressed when they picked them up at Mary Anne's house. Both wore long, vintage dresses that blended perfectly with the clothes worn by the boys. Stephanie had chosen an ankle-length black dress with fancy filigree along the bottom and a light blue, long-sleeve lacy bodice with a high collar. Over it, she had on a short black bolero trimmed with gold. Her long hair had been wound up and around like a beehive, making her look like a gorgeous Bride of Frankenstein.

Isaac was stunned by her appearance, and Mary Anne's too—she wore a long red dress with white lace up the center and a lacey, white long-sleeve bodice.

The boys quickly made room for the girls to sit. Even Jack seemed impressed, giving Mary Anne the once over. "You look nice today."

"I don't every day?"

Jack blushed, and the girls laughed as Penelope gushed over their choice of dresses.

As they left town for the ninety-minute drive to Bangor, Stephanie chattered away. "I spotted you guys leaving Ms. Rachel's, and when I asked her what you bought, well, Mary Anne and I just had to dress vintage too."

"You both look lovely," Drágan said, admiring their attire.

"We'll be the Throwback Crew," Stephanie chortled, drawing out a laugh from Mary Anne.

Drágan pulled a face. "Throw back?"

Isaac came to his rescue or tried to. "It's just an expression like... back in the day."

Drágan's handsome face twisted with more confusion. "Back in the day?"

"You know, like, back a long time ago."

Understanding brightened Drágan's face. "I understand. Such as when elderly people say, 'back in my day.' "

"Exactly." Isaac grinned and they did a fist bump.

Everyone talked over each other, even Nathaniel, about the festival and what might happen. The drive was uneventful, most of it on Interstate 95 straight into Bangor, and then practically right to the cinemas where the festival was being held.

According to the email Isaac had received, the festival, which was international in scope, had rented the entire complex for screenings. There was even a lounge area with small tables and chairs where attendees could mingle and winners could have photos taken against a festival backdrop.

Not having been to Bangor all that often, Isaac didn't recognize the cinema complex as they piled out of the van. The asphalt was cracked, but the parking lot was nearly full.

The exuberant group of teens approached the entrance and Isaac showed his pass to the check-in staff. The young lady offered a genuine smile.

"Welcome to the festival," she said, noting their attire. "I have to say, I love your clothes. Best dressed of the day, at least from what I've seen. Which of you directed the film?"

Everyone pointed at Isaac and laughed at their synchronicity.

"I guess that would be me."

"I wish you best success."

She handed over name badges to pin to their clothing and Isaac passed them out. As Penelope pinned hers on, she joked, "I feel like Shirley Jones in *The Partridge Family*."

They stopped attaching their pins to gaze at her with confusion.

"Sorry. It's an old show on Tubi."

The massive lobby was crowded with people milling about, most of them teenagers. Brightly lit movie posters adorned the walls and huge concessions stands sat against the back wall, much larger and more colorful than anything at the Playhouse in Millwood.

Some of the teens were staring at the group and pointing, so Isaac consulted the program he'd been handed by the lady in front to avoid looking at them. Maybe the vintage clothing wasn't such a great idea?

Stephanie and Mary Anne tossed the evil eye at anyone who looked at them funny. Drágan was oblivious, his gaze roaming everywhere, studying the crowd. Isaac gathered his group together and showed them the schedule. The student films had been divided by genre, with five finalists in each. First would be romance, which excited the girls but not the boys, then drama, science fiction/fantasy, and finally horror.

"Look," Isaac exclaimed, pointing, "Wolfboy screens last. Isn't that cool?"

Jack scowled. "'Cept we gotta watch the romance junk first."

"You guys are hopeless," Mary Anne said, checking the romance titles with Stephanie.

"Have you been to many cinemas?" Nathaniel asked Drágan.

"Some. I vividly recall seeing the original Wolfman in a cinema."

"Huh?" Jack said. "That movie came out like, a hundred years ago or something."

"1940, to be precise," Drágan said.

"Uh, he means he saw a reissue of it, obviously," blurted Isaac, surprised that Drágan had slipped up as he had.

Jack nodded. "Obviously." But he stared at Drágan nonetheless, as though suspecting a hidden secret.

"You seem nervous," Isaac whispered to Drágan.

"I've never seen myself on a cinema screen," Drágan whispered back.

Isaac patted him on the shoulder. "Your performance is fantastic."

Drágan offered a nervous smile.

Isaac noted two teen boys wearing dress pants, sneakers, and pullover shirts staring at Stephanie and Mary Anne and whispering to each other. Mary Anne noticed and nudged Stephanie. They pretended not to be aware.

A teen girl hurried up to Stephanie, gushing over her dress. "Oh my God, your dress is amazing. Where did you get it?"

Isaac watched the conversation as they waited for the films to begin. Stephanie explained about Ms. Rachel's place, and the girl insisted she just had to visit it. She was attractive, with short, straight hair, rosy cheeks, and thin lips.

Since Isaac was right beside the girls, he asked, "Did you make one of the movies?"

"Oh no, I acted in one of the drama films. What about you?"

"I directed one," Isaac said. "A horror film. Stephanie and Drágan, here, are the stars."

The girl stared at Drágan, who offered a polite smile.

Stephanie asked, "So, what's your name?"

She looked back at Stephanie and smiled. "I'm Alice Marsden."

"Stephanie Carter. I'll look for you in your movie."

"Same here."

An announcement came over the PA system. "Theater Two is now open for the student films. Please take any open seats. The screenings will begin in fifteen minutes."

Alice smiled. "I have to get back to my group. See you all later."

She pushed her way through the crowd of teens and adults making their way toward a long hallway. Isaac and his crew joined them. The two boys who'd been checking out Stephanie and Mary Anne made it a point to crowd in and chat with them as everyone moved toward the open theater doors near the end of the hall. Isaac watched the interaction with interest. The girls seemed just as interested in the tall, handsome boys as the boys were in them.

The festival had been using many of the theaters for screenings over the weekend, but since the student films represented the fewest submissions, they were all to be screened in the same theater.

Isaac and his group entered the dim auditorium. He loved the bright red curtains along both walls.

"Let's sit in back," he urged, indicating the empty back row. "We can better tell how the audience likes our movie."

Reluctantly, the girls said goodbye to the two handsome guys, who joined their own group for the screening. Then they entered the last row along with Isaac and took the seats in the center. Penelope sat to Isaac's right and Drágan to his left. Stephanie sat next to Mary Anne, and the two of them whispered to each other. Isaac found it funny that Jack made sure Nathaniel sat next to Mary Anne.

The seats were huge, made of soft gray leather and had wide armrests and built in cupholders—easily the comfiest cinema seats Isaac had ever experienced.

His mom squeezed his hand gently. "I'm so proud of you."

"Thanks, Mom."

A tall man wearing nice but not fancy clothes stood in front of the first row of seats beside an attractive blonde woman wearing a stylish pantsuit. The man tapped the microphone he held in one hand, and the buzzing crowd settled down.

"It looks like everyone is seated," he began, his voice like a ball game announcer. "Welcome to Youth Day at the Bangor International Film Festival."

The crowd of mostly teens erupted with applause and hooting.

The man with the mic waited for the tumult to die down. "The films you'll see today represent some of the finest work I've yet seen from student filmmakers, and you should all be very proud of yourselves."

More cheering exploded, but the audience settled down quickly.

He handed the mic to the woman, who said, "As you've no doubt seen if you looked at today's program, there are five films in each category, ranging from ten to nearly fifteen minutes in length. At the conclusion of the final group, horror, we will take a twenty-minute break before beginning the awards ceremony." She grinned broadly. "Let the show begin!"

More cheering gushed forth from the effervescent teen audience, and then the lights went down. Isaac glanced at Drágan and found the other boy already eyeing him in the dark.

"I hope you win," Drágan whispered, drawing a smile out of Isaac.

From the sounds he heard from Stephanie and Mary Anne, not to mention throughout the theater, the five romance films went over well. The two handsome guys were in the same movie, playing best friends vying for the affections of an attractive blonde. Stephanie and Mary Anne applauded with gusto when that one ended. Isaac thought the movie was okay but filled with too many cliches. The other ones in the category were fine, too, for romances, but that was a genre he typically avoided.

The drama films captured his interest, however, especially one starring the girl they'd met in the lobby. The story involved a high school student, played by Alice, who was bullied by some mean girls for a birthmark on her face. Since Alice had no such mark, Isaac concluded that it was an excellent makeup job. Alice's character endured the bullying as best she could. In the story, one of the mean girls was burned in the face when her angry mother threw boiling water at her. Alice felt sorry for the girl despite having been bullied and visited her in the hospital. The mean girl, having become disfigured, was grateful for Alice's visit. None of her so-called friends had been to see her.

Alice gave an outstanding performance, in Isaac's opinion, and should be a major contender for best actress. Some of the acting in the other films was weak, but most of them were exceptionally well made. The rest were quite watchable, and Isaac enjoyed them.

Fidgeting in his seat, he barely focused on the science fiction/fantasy category. The films were entertaining, but none leapt out at him as great. After more than an hour and a half, finally the horror films began to screen.

The first was a routine slasher film, well made with some good jump scares and nice camerawork, but a standard plot. The second was a ghost story set in a school. He had to admit, schools looked even more unsettling in the dark than during the day. Isaac found himself enthralled by the film's stunning cinematography.

The next two were of the slasher/masked killer variety, with the second having a nice twist at the end. They were well made and well shot, and Isaac began to have doubts about his own effort, which was yet to come. The audience response to the films had been positive, lots of cries of fright in reaction to the jump scares, followed by nervous laughter.

At last, it was time for *Wolfboy*.

He'd created, in his opinion, some cool and creepy credits with his computer whereby the full moon began dripping downward until it formed the title, and the effect looked awesome on the big screen. He practically held his breath, praying no one would laugh as the film began. The audience was silent, seemingly engaged. Isaac watched his actors on the screen. Stephanie was terrific, as he'd noticed while filming. But he hadn't fully realized the depth of Drágan's performance. The soulful look in his eyes as he gazed at Stephanie, knowing they could not continue their relationship. His tearful goodbye nearly made Isaac cry. He felt like Drágan was channeling all five hundred years of pain and suffering into his performance, and he could tell the audience felt it too.

He'd only provided glimpses of the werewolf once the moon rose in the sky, but he'd edited some of his real footage of the beast attacking the deer, coupled with bits and pieces of his AI werewolf, to make it appear as though Mary Ann's character was the victim. It looked fantastic—gory, and realistic. People throughout the theater gasped audibly during that scene.

His chosen music cues worked perfectly at setting the mood, and he was pleased with his camerawork and his use of lighting.

The finale involved the confrontation between Stephanie's character and the transformed Drágan. He watched, riveted despite having spent so many hours editing the scenes together. For this sequence, he'd had the wolf tear apart the deer on camera, and Stephanie's reaction shots worked perfectly with the real footage. But when the werewolf paused to stare at her as though in recognition, audience members reacted with small cries of fear. Tearfully, she lifted the pistol. The werewolf charged, and she pulled the trigger.

Isaac had used a computer generated closeup of the bullet entering the werewolf in slow motion. Stephanie's character stared in tearful horror as the werewolf writhed and twisted and became Drágan, seen only from the waist up as he collapsed to the ground.

Their final goodbyes, including the kiss—which Isaac had

managed to include with careful editing—elicited sniffles among the audience members, including Isaac's mom, who'd already seen it.

The final shot was Drágan's bloody, but peaceful face, his long hair splayed out in a halo around his head.

When the credits rolled, the audience burst into vigorous applause, maybe for his film or maybe because it was the last one of the day. In any case, Isaac felt proud of his work.

His mom leaned in, dabbing her eyes with a tissue, "That was even more beautiful this time, Isaac."

"Thanks, Mom," though he wasn't sure beautiful was the best word to describe a horror film.

The lights rose and the audience members stood to stretch. Over the speakers came, "There will be a twenty-minute break. Please clear the auditorium so we can set up for the awards."

Isaac stood to find his cast and crew applauding him from their seats. In just two months he'd gone from "class loser" to this. He couldn't believe it. He applauded as well. "For all of us."

Everyone was ushered into the lounge area. He spotted Stephanie and Mary Anne once again conversing animatedly with the two boys they'd met earlier. Watching them, Isaac understood that Stephanie wasn't into *him* in "that" way; she just considered him a good friend. And he was fine with that, glancing at Drágan surrounded by adoring girls chatting him up.

Isaac had barely greeted Nathaniel and Jack at the refreshments table when he was tapped on the shoulder. He turned to find a small boy wearing glasses and a tweed suit.

"You're the director of Wolfboy?"

Isaac nodded.

"Your movie was amazing, man." The boy gushed as others who must've overheard him began crowding around. "Those werewolf scenes were lit!"

Suddenly Isaac, Nathaniel, and Jack were surrounded by other teens praising their film, especially the werewolf footage.

"I cried at the end," one girl confessed.

"I almost did too," admitted the boy beside her.

Once he was able to speak, Isaac learned that most of these kids had been involved in the other horror films, and he enjoyed meeting his fellow directors and writers. They launched into an excited discussion on camera techniques, lighting, and, of course, special effects.

Naturally, Isaac was cagey regarding his werewolf scenes and hoped Drágan wasn't uncomfortable hearing about them. But when he turned to look, Drágan was busy signing programs for his fans, while Stephanie and Mary Ann still had those boys clearly displaying interest in much more than their acting.

So far, Isaac had seen no sign of Stephen King and mentioned that to the other horror filmmakers, all of whom wanted to meet him, too.

"Maybe he'll be at the awards presentation," the bespectacled boy suggested.

Isaac had not gotten a single snack, which was mostly bottled water, chips, and granola bars, before the lights flickered and an usher announced it was time to return to the auditorium. Everyone wished each other good luck and they filed back into the theater. Isaac glanced at his phone. It was six-thirty p.m.

Isaac and his group returned to the back row. This time, Penelope sat in an inside seat, with Stephanie at the other end near the center aisle, then Drágan beside her, and Isaac next. If any of them were fortunate enough to win an award, Isaac wanted no obstructions blocking their way to the aisle.

As the other teens scrambled for their seats amidst a babble of excited young voices, the same man and woman from before reappeared, this time on the stage area in front of the screen displaying the film festival logo. A podium had been erected, and along one side was a table covered by a red tablecloth. Isaac's stomach performed nervous flip flops as he eyed the shiny awards lined up along the tabletop.

"So that we are not accused of keeping students out late on a school night," the man said into the mic, "your segment of the awards begins now."

The teen audience laughed politely.

"Our MC tonight," continued the man, "asked to be a judge and presenter because he loves fostering new talent. He needs no introduction, Bangor's own Stephen King."

The audience exploded with cheers and applause, and Isaac might have been the loudest one as a small, stooped man ambled out onto the stage. He wore jeans and a long-sleeved plaid shirt. Isaac felt a moment of disappointment, having expected a giant that matched his iconic status, but he clapped all the harder when Mr. King took the mic from the man, who walked to the table and stood beside the woman.

"I'm thrilled to be part of this event," King said, offering a craggy smile.

More cheers and clapping forced him to wait until the exuberant audience settled down.

"I was one of the judges of the horror films, but if you don't agree with the winners, complain to them." He indicated the man and woman, who laughed along with the audience.

"I'm not one for speeches, but I look forward to meeting you all after the awards. Let's get started, shall we?"

More thunderous applause as King stepped behind the podium and placed the mic into its holder. "We'll begin with the award for best screenplay." He fumbled with some envelopes.

Isaac didn't expect a win here because his script was not exceptional. He was right. The winner was one of the drama films, though not the one that starred Alice.

There was hearty applause as the young screenwriter hurried up to accept her award.

"Next in line," King continued, "is the award for best costume design." He tore open the envelope and held up a card. "The award goes to *Invasion.*"

The crowd clapped and two kids rose from the audience to claim the award. *Invasion* had been one of the better sci-fi films, and the alien costumes were excellent.

Next was cinematography. Isaac placed his bets on that ghost story, and he turned out to be right. After each winner posed for photos with Mr. King and said a few words, they took their awards back to their seats.

The next two awards were best supporting actor and actress, which were won by two of the rom-coms, though not by either of the boys who'd taken a fancy to Stephanie and Mary Anne. Isaac agreed both the winners were quite good in their respective films.

He wiped his palms on his pants as the bigger awards were next.

King held up an envelope. "And now the award for best actress in a student film." He turned to the couple handing out the awards. "I'm good at this, right, they should put me on the Oscars."

Scattered laughter rose from the audience.

Isaac figured everyone was holding their breath awaiting the announcement. "Let it be Stephanie," he whispered.

"The award for best actress goes to Alice Marsden for *Imperfections*."

Isaac turned to Stephanie sitting on the other side of Drágan, expecting her to look disappointed, but she jumped to her feet, whooping and clapping with gusto. "Yay, Alice!!!!"

Isaac sighed with relief. He had to admit that Alice had been fantastic in her film.

After receiving her award from King, Alice bounded up the aisle back to her seat.

"And now," King's voice boomed through the auditorium, "the award for best actor in a student film." He slit open the envelope and beamed in the bright lights of the theater. "The award goes to Drágan Albescu for Wolfboy." King clapped, as he had for every winner.

The audience went wild with applause and Isaac jumped out of his seat. "You won, Drágan, you won!"

Drágan looked confused. "I've never won anything. What is the protocol?"

Isaac and Stephanie dragged him to his feet.

"You go up and accept the award, silly," Stephanie said, breathless with elation.

"What do I say?"

"Just thank the judges," Isaac said, "and, I don't know, say whatever you feel."

Drágan exited the row and walked down the aisle as the applause continued.

Drágan hurried up the makeshift steps to the stage and Isaac thought he'd never looked as magnificent as he did just then in his ankle-length coat and red cravat, long brown hair shimmering beneath the overhead lights.

King stuck out a hand to shake as the lady handed him a beautiful award that looked like a reel of film atop an old-fashioned movie camera. A photographer snapped some photos of King and Drágan, as she'd done with the other winners, and then Drágan stood before the podium as the applause died away.

"I'm uncertain what to say," he began. "But I'm very grateful to the judges"—he glanced at King—"who selected mine out of so many worthy performances. I wish to thank all the youth with whom I worked, but most especially my very best friend, Isaac Foster."

He smiled and held up his award.

Isaac's breath stopped. Drágan called him his best friend!

The cheering crowd snapped him out of his daze, and he stood along with the audience to applaud as Drágan left the stage and retook his seat. Isaac stared at him open mouthed and Drágan offered his warmest smile yet.

"And now," King resumed when the clapping stopped, "we come to a big one, folks, best director of a student film. I directed a movie once and let me tell you, it's not easy. My hat, if I was wearing one, would be off to every director here tonight. You're all winners in my book."

Lusty applause followed his kind words. Then he held up another white envelope and slit it open. Isaac leaned forward, arms on the back of the seat in front, eyes wide with expectation.

King pulled out the card in dramatic fashion. "And the award for best director goes to...Isaac Foster for Wolfboy!" He set down the card and cheered enthusiastically.

Isaac leapt to his feet in stunned surprise. Stephanie and Drágan excitedly clapped him on the back as the crowd once again offered exuberant applause. Isaac hurried down the aisle amidst all the clapping and whooping feeling like a rock star. He couldn't believe this was really happening.

He made it onto the stage without tripping on the steps and was handed his award. It felt heavy, and the base was engraved in lovely letters, "Bangor International Film Festival, Best Director of a Student Film, Isaac Foster, Wolfboy."

His eyes filled with tears of joy, and he hugged the award against his chest, eliciting laughter and more cheers from the crowd. He felt like a real person for the first time in his life.

King waved him over for a handshake and a pose for the photos. Then the mic was there before him and for a split second, his voice faltered. He cleared his throat, wiped his eyes with his sleeve, and leaned closer to the mic.

"I'm so unbelievably happy and shocked right now, especially after all the amazing movies I watched today."

He waited for the applause to die down.

"Thank you, thank you, thank you to the judges for this award. It means so much I can't...it just means the world." He looked down at the award for a moment, then back up. "I've always been led to think by kids at school that I'm a loser. But then this incredible boy entered my life who seemed to just, well, bring out the best in everyone. I wouldn't be here if it wasn't for my best friend, Drágan Albescu."

More applause followed.

"And I couldn't have done this without my amazing cast and crew, so this is for you."

He grinned and held up his award as more applause followed. Stephanie's cheering voice was the loudest. He stepped down from the stage and hurried up the aisle where Stephanie pulled him into a crushing hug before he sat down.

"And now we come to the final award of the day," King announced, waving the last envelope around. "Best Film. Every film here today is a winner, but not all can take home an award. So, without further ado, the award for best student film goes to..." He pulled out the card and smiled. "Wolfboy, produced by Isaac Foster, Drágan Albescu, Stephanie Carter, Jack Drake, Mary Anne Givens, and Nathaniel Stokes!"

The crowd erupted, rising to its collective feet in thunderous applause, which shocked Isaac. The Throwback Crew was on their feet hugging and high fiving before spilling out into the aisle to rush up onto the stage. Isaac was almost happier with this award than his directing one because it was shared by them all.

King laughed at the joyous group and nodded in appreciation of their attire as the man and woman handed each one of them an award. They all crowded around King for their group photo while the audience remained on their feet for a full minute.

Once the audience reseated themselves, Isaac, clutching both awards like they were pure gold, stepped to the mic.

"I'm lightheaded I'm so happy," he gushed, laughing, and gazing at the two awards as though they were pure gold. "Again, thank you everyone who chose our film. You're the best. Now, I talked already, so I want the others to have a chance, starting with the bossy one, Stephanie."

She laughed and shoved him as she stepped up to the mic, flush from crying and laughing at the same time.

"I am so stoked right now." Cheers rose from the teen audience. "You know, when Isaac said before that kids at school called him a loser, ignored him...well, I was one of those kids." She paused a moment as a surprised murmur wafted over the crowd. "Like he said, Drágan was like, I don't know, glue or something that brought us all together. I wish I could go back and have been friends with Isaac much earlier because, well, we both love horror movies!"

Laughter rose and a few cheers as she stepped away from the mic.

Isaac turned to the others. "Anyone else?"

Jack stepped forward and Isaac made room. Looking serious, rather than joyous, Jack said in a shaky voice, "Isaac was my best friend from first grade to beginning of eighth. We always talked about making a movie one day. 'Cept, I turned on him in eighth grade because I didn't wanna be bullied. I joined the bullies and..." He looked on the verge of tears. "And I treated the best friend a guy could ever have like garbage. But here I am, standing in front of you all getting this award. Because *he* let me work on his movie. Some people are just better than others. Thank you, Isaac, and thank you, judges."

He stepped back, wiping away tears and allowed Isaac to envelop him in a hug. Cameras flashed right and left, commemorating the touching conclusion to an emotional afternoon.

15

DRÁGAN UNMASKED

An official Bangor International Film Festival backdrop hung against one wall in the lounge area, and each of the winners had his or her photos taken there by the festival photographer as well as by parents or supporters.

Drágan and Isaac posed for individual photos, each proudly holding his award. Then the whole cast and crew gathered in for a group shot, proudly holding up their Best Film awards.

With the awards and the unexpected things Stephanie and Jack had said about him in their speeches, Isaac's head was in the clouds. He absently wondered if his dazed expression would show in the photos.

Alongside the official photographers, Penelope snapped oodles of pictures of each pose. She seemed happier than the winners, her boundless enthusiasm practically overflowing while she chatted with other parents.

After the Wolfboy photo session finished, Stephanie hurried over to offer heartfelt congratulations to Alice, who looked grateful and pleased. By the time Stephanie rejoined the group, they were all excitedly talking over each other.

A cleared throat caused them to stop. They turned to find Stephan King standing in their midst.

"Mr. King!" blurted Isaac, in awe.

"Call me Steve, please, Isaac. We're fellow filmmakers. I just wanted to offer my personal congratulations on your well-deserved awards."

"Did you vote for us?" Stephanie asked.

"Stephanie!" Isaac exclaimed.

"Let's just say I cried at the end of your film," King said with a wink, "which gave me some ideas for my next book."

Isaac grinned and so did Jack. Drágan seemed to be paying attention, but at the same time he looked like he caught a whiff of something bad. Given how good his sense of smell was, Isaac thought, perhaps he had.

"Listen, Isaac," King went on conversationally, "got a dollar on you?"

Surprised by the question, Isaac handed his awards to Nathaniel and fished around in his pockets. He had brought money for snacks, right? His fingers wrapped around some bills, and he pulled out three dollars, peeling one off and handing it to King.

To Isaac's surprise, King pocketed the dollar. "You just bought one of my short stories to adapt into a film, assuming it's one that hasn't already been done."

"I, uh, I don't understand."

"I enjoy encouraging promising young filmmakers like you, Isaac," King explained, a twinkle in his eye, "so I charge only a dollar for the rights to film one of my stories."

The group erupted with whoops of excitement.

Isaac's response came out in a breathless rush. "That's amazing, Mr. King. Thanks so much!"

"Steve, please." King slipped a business card from his front shirt pocket and handed it to Isaac. "Contact my agency and let them know what story you want. Oh, and because I loved your film so much, you can each have an autographed book of your choice. Send the titles and inscriptions in the same email, and I'll get 'em out to you."

"That is so cool, Steve," Isaac replied with unabashed joy. "Thank you!"

After Isaac pumped King's hand, the author said, "I think your mom wants a group photo."

They crowded together, awards in hand, while Penelope and others snapped photos.

King turned to Drágan and said, "Son, your performance tore my heart out."

Drágan still appeared distracted, but he reacted with stunned surprise to the compliment and offered a heartfelt, "Thank you."

They shook hands and King announced, "Well, on to the next group. Don't wait too long to choose your story, Isaac, or the best ones might be gone, and it's a pain in the ass to mail your dollar back."

Isaac laughed. "I won't."

King turned and was immediately engulfed by another group of admirers.

One of the festival photographers approached Isaac and Drágan, saying the festival founders had requested photos in front of a large kiosk across the lounge. The boys followed at once.

Isaac and Drágan were greeted by the man and woman who'd introduced the films. Turned out they were the festival founders and liked to have photos with all the winners for publicity purposes. Drágan posed with them first. He smiled, but Isaac sensed something wasn't right with him. Then they swapped places. As the photographer positioned him, Isaac spotted his crew talking with someone in the farthest corner of the lounge.

Despite feeling suddenly uneasy, Isaac smiled as the photographer snapped off some shots, then looked over the crowd at his group. There was something familiar about the man, but he couldn't get a clear look at his face. He turned to ask Drágan when he heard his friend growl. After handing his award to Isaac—who fumbled with all four—Drágan plowed his way through the crowd so fast that in an instant he was gripping the man around the throat and slamming him against a wall.

As Drágan lifted him off the floor, Isaac gasped.

It was Jourdain!

Repeating "excuse me" and "sorry" over and over, Isaac pushed through the crowd pressing King for autographs to get to his stunned cast and crew. Jourdain, despite his predicament, met Isaac's gaze with a brief smirk.

Isaac stepped forward. "Drágan..." His friend looked over one shoulder, eyes blazing, lips blood red, fangs bared. Isaac gasped, startled at how bestial Drágan appeared.

"Didn't I tell you all he was a monster?" Jourdain managed to croak before knocking Drágan's hand free and dropping to the floor, landing on his feet with ease.

The entire incident had taken mere seconds, and since most everyone was focused on King, no one had really noticed. Fangs still bared, Drágan gazed at Isaac and the rest of the Throwback Crew, who stared back in open-mouthed horror. By the time he turned around, Jourdain was gone. Even Isaac had missed his exit.

"Drágan," Isaac began, inching forward, "chill, man."

Drágan looked desolate—as if he'd just lost his best friend—and then he was gone, vanished through the crowd.

Isaac whirled on the others. "What did that guy tell you?"

Stephanie, sounding too calm for the situation, asked, "You knew, didn't you, Isaac?"

"Knew what?"

"That Drágan is...a monster. For real."

Isaac's nostrils flared with anger. "He is not a monster! That man talking to you was the monster. He's the vampire who turned Drágan into what he is!"

The others stared at him, open-mouthed.

Penelope approached. "What's going on? I saw Drágan run out. At least, I think I did."

"Does your mom know?" Jack asked coldly.

"Know what?" Penelope looked from one face to the other.

"That Drágan's a real werewolf," Nathaniel muttered.

"And a vampire," Stephanie added.

"Yes, I do." Penelope turned to Isaac, clearly concerned. "What's going on, Isaac?"

"They're turning against the boy who helped us more than anyone ever has," Isaac hissed, fury ready to boil over. "He can't help what he is, but unlike some of you, he keeps his monstrous side under control!" He turned on his heel to leave.

Penelope grabbed his shoulder. "Where are you going?"

"To find my best friend." Isaac shook her hand loose, handed her the awards, and ran out of the lounge.

He bolted out the theater doors—to the utter shock of the lady who'd hours earlier handed him his ID badge—and sprinted into the parking lot. He cupped his hands to his mouth. "Drágan!"

Other than traffic noise from the nearby intersection, he heard nothing. He jogged around the lot, running through pools of light from the tall lampposts, shivering in the cold. He stopped, his heavy breathing the only sound besides the distant cars.

His gaze swept the darkened lot, and he suddenly became aware of all the deep shadows in which Jourdain might be lurking.

Maybe this wasn't such a good idea....

Afraid to call out again, he stood in place, helpless and frustrated, wondering where his friend had gone. Would the others tell the police about Drágan?

Deciding he'd better go back and confront them, he turned and bumped into Jourdain.

"Oh, shit!" he exclaimed, heart hammering as he stepped back.

"Such impolite language for a delectable young boy," Jourdain cooed, fangs visible between lush red lips. "I find it mystifying how Drágan resisted your mouthwatering blood for so long. The very scent of you is intoxicating."

Isaac wanted to run, even just to back away, but he was frozen in place by the vampire's eyes piercing his soul.

"That's a good boy," Jourdain whispered, his voice hypnotic. "Stand still while I have a drink."

Isaac remained in place, fixated on those eyes and that soft, soothing voice, and realized that, inexplicably, he wanted to satisfy this man. He pressed down on his cravat and high collar to expose the soft flesh of his throat and closed his eyes, as though awaiting a kiss.

He felt Jourdain's cheek brush lightly against his and held his breath, trembling with anticipation.

"Get off him!" growled a harsh voice and the gentle touch was ripped away from his face.

Isaac took a moment to come back to his senses, and then gasped in horror. By then the two enemies were locked in mortal combat. Drágan's hands encircled the man's throat; his eyes bulged with fury and his fangs dripped saliva.

Isaac staggered back as his mother and the rest of his group ran out of the theater.

"Stay back!" Isaac shouted, as Drágan and Jourdain battled each other.

The pair slammed into a light post and fell to the ground, rolling around on the asphalt like rabid animals.

Jourdain managed to break Drágan's hold on his throat and jumped up to flee, but the boy sprang like a wolf onto his back and sent him sprawling to the ground. For a split second, Isaac thought he saw fur and claws appearing on Drágan's face and hands, but then Jourdain flung him off and Drágan staggered back, a mere vampire again.

It seemed Jourdain might escape then, but faster than Isaac's eye could follow, Drágan was around in front of the fleeing vampire. He grabbed Jourdain around the throat, lifted him off the ground, and flung him across the parking lot out of sight.

Fangs still visible, Drágan's eyes settled on Isaac, and the violence receded from his face. "Did he hurt you?"

Isaac shook his head, unable to speak after what he'd witnessed. Penelope rushed forward, still clutching the awards. Timidly, the other kids joined her, all staring in fear at Drágan.

"We must leave now," Drágan said, his face and teeth normal again. "He might return."

That snapped Penelope out of her dazed state. "You heard him, into the van, everyone!"

They hurried to the van, parked two rows over. Isaac and Drágan brought up the rear. Once inside the van with all the doors locked, Penelope peeled out of the parking lot as though her life depended on it.

After what Isaac had just experienced, he knew it did.

No one broke the silence on the ride home, as though they were all afraid to speak after everything that had happened. Isaac clutched his and Drágan's awards in his lap, feeling like the triumph of mere hours before had been nothing but a dream.

Isaac wanted to defend the silent, miserable Drágan, to remind the others how much he'd done for all of them. But the shock of what they'd witnessed and Drágan's inhuman demeanor tied his tongue in knots. One by one, his shellshocked Throwback Crew dispersed to their homes without a word until only he and Drágan remained.

"We need to talk," Penelope said once they'd gone inside.

In the living room, Isaac gently placed their awards on the wooden coffee table. Then he sat on the small couch beside the still-silent Drágan while his mom sat on the larger couch across the room.

She folded her hands together on her lap, her body stiff, collecting her thoughts. "I want to say again how very proud I am of you both for these awards and all your hard work."

Momentarily, Isaac had expected her to start yelling, but when he considered that his mom seldom raised her voice, he wasn't surprised by her praise.

"Thanks, Mom." Fearing she might be too quick to judge and kick Drágan out of the house, he said, "He was just defending us from Jourdain. Drágan would never hurt me or you."

"I know that, honey," his mom replied, shocking him by her calmness. "Drágan, thank you for saving my son." She teared up, as if the reality of how close Isaac had come to death—or worse—had finally hit her.

Drágan faced Isaac for the first time. "When I saw our friends with Jourdain, I...I panicked and that's why I appeared as I did."

Isaac wanted to hug him because the other boy looked so distraught, but he didn't think Drágan would like that. "I know."

"Do you believe the others consider me dangerous now?"

"I don't know." Isaac turned to his mom. "We should stay home from school tomorrow, in case one of them...calls the cops or something."

Her tear-stained face twisted with concern. "But they know him, you're all friends."

"They didn't look like friends when they saw the true me," Drágan murmured, every word reeking of sadness and despair.

Anger welled up in Isaac. "That is *not* the true you! You are not a monster; I don't care what you say!"

Drágan's eyebrows shot up in surprise.

"Isaac is right, Drágan," Penelope affirmed. "I know you bear a terrible curse, and you could easily kill all of us at any moment. But you don't. You do nothing but give. You're kind, like my son is kind. If I could, I'd adopt you. That's how much love I have for you."

Isaac and Drágan exchanged a shocked look.

Then Drágan crossed the room, sat beside Penelope, and pulled her into a gentle hug. "Thank you."

"Oh honey, we'll get through this."

He released her quickly, but Isaac realized how far Drágan had come in just two months.

"So, Mom, what about tomorrow? School, I mean."

She bit her lip as she considered. "You may have a point. Perhaps we should all be ready to leave quickly, just in case."

Isaac's eyes bugged out. "You'd leave, just like that?"

"To protect my son"—she smiled at Drágan—"of course. But let's hope it doesn't come to that." She paused. "I've seen all of you together so much lately, especially today, and I can't believe any of them would turn against Drágan without even talking to him."

"Jack turned against *me*," Isaac said.

"But now he's back," Penelope reminded him.

"Thanks to Drágan."

"Exactly, that's what I mean. You both stay home tomorrow. I'll call in an excused absence."

"Like what?"

She considered. "Maybe a dentist appointment? You needed your teeth sharpened to match Drágan's?"

Isaac couldn't help but laugh. "C'mon, Drágan, that was funny."

Drágan smiled. "I suppose so."

16

REVELATIONS

Feeling somewhat comforted by his mom's definitive defense of Drágan, Isaac moved some models around on his shelves and placed his three awards in the center.

"May I place mine next to yours?" Drágan asked, holding his awkwardly, uncertain what to do. "This is my first residence that has truly felt like a home."

"Course your award goes here. Best actor in the world."

Drágan offered a grateful smile, and the boys arranged the five awards with Best Film in the center.

As they changed for bed, Drágan asked, "Would your mother truly leave all she has merely for my sake?"

"You heard her," Isaac said, pulling on pajama bottoms. "When she makes up her mind about something, that's it." He paused before removing the dress shirt he'd worn to the festival. "Did you mean what you said at the awards, you know...about me being your best friend?"

Drágan pulled his sleeping gown over his head. "I meant every word."

"So did I."

Their eyes locked for a long moment. Then Drágan offered his shy smile and retreated to the bathroom to brush his teeth.

Nightmares of Jourdain's teeth brushing against his throat made Isaac toss and turn, so he slept in later than usual. When he finally dragged himself out of bed, feeling like a wet dishrag, he spotted the awards glittering in the morning sun and felt a fleeting moment of pride.

Then he noticed Drágan's valise on the carpet outside his closet door. He popped in his hearing aids and hurriedly pulled on some clean clothes before heading downstairs. He found Drágan, fully dressed, sitting with his mother at the kitchen table. His mom was drinking coffee, while Drágan sipped tomato juice that looked disturbingly like blood.

"Morning, hon," his mom said around a sip of coffee.

His body stiff with fear, Isaac asked, "Has anyone called or... anything?"

"No. I called the attendance office and excused you both for the day. Since then, nothing."

Recalling Drágan's valise on the floor upstairs, Isaac asked as he slid into a chair beside his mom, "Are we supposed to pack for a quick getaway?"

His mother smiled. "You sound like we're robbing a bank. Drágan is prepared to vanish, if needed. We'll sneak away after."

Isaac tried to distract Drágan with video games in the rec room, but he was too nervous to focus and finally gave up. Drágan said very little, but Isaac noted the tension in his face, the tightness in his posture.

"How long do you think it would take for the police to arrive if they're called?" Drágan asked as they attempted a game of pool.

Isaac's stomach twisted into knots. "Police department is right downtown." He pulled out his phone and checked the time. "It's already noon. If, you know, anyone called them, they should be here by now, right?"

"That's what I just asked you."

Isaac sighed. "I don't know." He tossed his pool cue onto the table. "Let's go back to our room."

When the time on his phone finally displayed 3:30, Isaac relaxed a bit, holding it up so Drágan could see.

"This is a good sign, right?"

Then the doorbell rang.

Isaac froze, then stood up. "Wait here. Go out the window if you hear the police."

Drágan nodded solemnly.

Isaac hurried down the hall and met his mom at the top of the stairs.

The doorbell rang again.

"I'll answer it," his mom said. "You wait in the kitchen."

"Okay."

They descended the stairs. He darted into the kitchen, and she walked down the narrow hall to the side door. Isaac listened as she opened the door.

"The guys weren't at school today," he heard Stephanie say. "We were worried."

"So were we," replied Penelope in a measured tone. "About who you might talk to about what happened."

"We didn't tell anyone, I swear. Can we see them, please?"

"Come out, Isaac," called his mom.

Isaac hurried around into the narrow hallway to find his whole crew gazing at him. "What's up?" he asked, rubbing his palms against his sweatpants.

"Can we talk to you and Drágan?" Stephanie asked, sounding unusually tentative. "About last night?"

Isaac glanced at his mom.

She said, "Take them up to your room. I'll be in my office if you need me."

Isaac said, "Come on."

So far, only Stephanie had spoken. The boys never met Isaac's gaze and Mary Anne focused on Stephanie. They ascended the stairs and Isaac led them down the hall to his room. Drágan stood fully clothed, including his long coat, ready to flee.

"It's just them," Isaac said before sitting on his bed. Drágan hesitantly lowered himself to the bed beside him, head bowed.

The newcomers, despite having been in this room a number of times, seemed on edge.

Jack spotted the awards. "They look good up there."

"Thanks," Isaac said. "So, who wants to start?"

"I will," Stephanie said, sitting on the floor cross-legged. The others dropped beside her, forming a semicircle. "We talked a lot today at school about last night," she began. "The whole event was incredible. But then that guy—"

"Jourdain," Isaac said.

"Yeah, him. He seemed so nice at first. And then, when he told us that stuff about you, Drágan, we were, like, confused. And then you charged in and..."

"And proved to be the monster he described," Drágan put in to fill the awkward silence.

"No, but, well....it caught me by surprise."

"Me too," Mary Anne chimed in. "I mean, you had fangs and the look on your face was...well, you can understand, right?"

Isaac said, "It caught me by surprise when I first found out, too, but since I already knew him, I knew he wasn't a monster."

"We understood that when we saw your fight in the parking lot," Stephanie affirmed. "You were protecting Isaac just like..."

"You were protecting us in the lounge," Jack finished.

"But it was scary, seeing you like that, Drágan," Nathaniel said. "I mean, it was so different from the guy we know, but, well, it's still scary. Even now."

Drágan studied him with understanding. "You wonder if I might turn on you one day, like a tame tiger that suddenly attacks its master."

Nathaniel looked mortified. "No, but, well...yeah, I guess I do."

"We all wonder that," Jack added, a tinge of fear in his voice. "I mean, you grabbed me that day at school and...well, you could've killed me."

Isaac's instinct was to jump in, but he felt Drágan should defend himself.

Drágan faced Jack, looking remorseful. "I'm sorry I did that. You were going to hurt Isaac and I overreacted. But I never would have hurt you. I just wanted to scare you."

"You did scare me," Jack affirmed. "I was a wreck."

"You scared all of us," Stephanie said. "How do we know you won't, you know..."

"Lose control like the tiger?" Drágan met her gaze. "You don't. But I do. I've lived with this curse for five hundred years and I have control over it."

Other than Stephanie, the others gasped in shock.

"Five hundred years?" Mary Anne stared in amazement. "That's crazy."

Drágan's gaze roamed from her to each of the others. "In all my long life, I've never been gifted with such fine comrades of a similar age, people I can call...my friends. I wish to keep no more secrets from you."

And so Drágan told his story once more, at least up to the point when he'd killed his parents and set off on his wanderings. He did mention how Jourdain has pursued him all through the following centuries—first, it seemed, to possess him, but now to possess his unique blood for purposes unknown but most assuredly evil.

The group sat spellbound during his recitation and Isaac saw on their faces that they now understood their friend and all his peculiarities.

"No wonder you know more than our teachers," Nathaniel muttered, shaking his head in amazement.

"And why you're strong enough to lift me off the ground, even though you're shorter than me," Jack said, his tone more admiration now than fear. "Wait a minute. Them guys I hung out with, the jocks. You been drinking their blood, haven't you?"

The girls gasped as Drágan nodded.

"Of course!" Stephanie exclaimed. "That's why they're too tired to bully anyone."

"Wow," Mary Anne said with a grin. "Sucks for the freshman football team, but it's been great for everyone else."

"Oh, my God!" Stephanie's hand was over her mouth, her eyes wide with understanding. "My stepdad?"

Drágan nodded.

"How did you find out?"

"I saw the pain etched into your eyes when we first met. I could not allow such evil to continue."

Mary Anne looked confused. "What's he talking about, Steph?"

Stephanie's face seemed to collapse in on itself and she burst into tears. Jumping to her feet, she ran from the room.

"Steph!" Mary Anne jumped up and followed.

Shocked, Isaac started to stand, but Drágan's strong arm held him back.

"I wanna find out what's wrong," Isaac said, feeling deep empathy for Stephanie's obvious pain.

"She needs your mom more than any of us," Drágan said, his voice filled with sorrow. "Text her."

Confused, Isaac glanced at the stunned faces of Jack and Nathaniel and then pulled out his phone. With shaky fingers, he tapped out a quick text to his mom.

STEPHANIE STUMBLED DOWN THE STAIRS, the horrors of the past three years practically drowning her in grief. Unsure where to go, she bolted for the living room and its offer of solitude.

She'd barely collapsed onto the couch, sobbing, when Mary Anne lurched into the room, terrified. "Steph?"

Stephanie felt the couch shift as Mary Anne sat beside but couldn't bear to face her best friend. Not in her shame and humiliation.

"Steph?" Mary Anne repeated, placing a light hand on Stephanie's trembling shoulder. "What's wrong?"

Penelope hurried into the living room. "Isaac texted me. What's wrong with Stephanie?"

"I don't know."

Stephanie looked up as Penelope approached and sat on her other side. Their eyes met and then Stephanie pressed her head against Penelope's shoulder and wept. She felt Penelope's arms gently encircle her and welcomed the embrace.

ISAAC PACED HIS ROOM, while Drágan remained on the bottom bunk and the other boys on the floor. Isaac stopped and faced Drágan. "Can't you tell us anything?"

Drágan shook his head.

"She said something about her stepdad," Jack spoke from his place on the floor.

Nathaniel's eyes widened in shock. "You don't think..."

Jack gasped.

And Isaac knew.

WITH PENELOPE'S arm wrapped around her shoulders, Stephanie pulled her legs up and wrapped her arms tightly around them, as though hiding from the world.

"Take it slow, sweetie," Penelope said. "I'm here. We have all the time you need."

Stephanie forced the memories into a kind of box so she could pretend it all happened to someone else while having to share the horror she'd endured. When she began to speak, her voice felt stilted and robot-like.

"It started when I was, um, eleven, I guess. My uh...my stepfather would sometimes come into my room during the night and...get in bed with me."

Mary Anne clapped a hand to her mouth, and Penelope uttered a tiny gasp.

"I cried and begged him to stop, but he threatened to kill my mom if I told anyone. Said he'd kill Mary Anne, or anyone I told. So, I kept it to myself." She looked up into Penelope's understanding face, tears streaming down her cheeks. "I was so scared and...humiliated." She wiped away some tears. "But when Drágan came to town it stopped. He stopped it."

"AFTER WHAT I saw in Stephanie's eyes," Drágan told the stunned boys, his voice trembling with revulsion, "I mesmerized her stepfather before he entered his home each night and drank from him, enough that he should sleep soundly. I never planned to tell anyone because...I've known others who've endured this kind of violence, both girls and boys. I can't imagine the sense of violation they felt."

Isaac had listened with rising anger, and a fury rose up within him that was frightening in its intensity. "Why didn't you just kill the asshole?"

Drágan stared at him in surprise. "Commit murder like Jourdain?"

Isaac paused, then forced himself to calm down. "I guess you're right. But scumbags like that..." He didn't finish the thought because he couldn't think of a severe enough punishment.

STILL SECURE in Penelope's arms, Stephanie wiped her eyes with a tissue Mary Anne brought her.

"I used to think it was my fault," Stephanie said as she held the crumpled tissue in one fist, "and I didn't know what I did wrong."

"You did nothing wrong, Stephanie," Penelope said, her voice tight with emotion. "You are a victim. Jacob is the monster here."

"You need to report him to the cops," Mary Anne blurted, her normally soft features twisted with rage. "I feel like getting my dad's shotgun and blasting that asshole!"

"Mary Anne is right about calling the police," Penelope affirmed.

Stephanie leaned forward, suddenly understanding something. "You're right! *He's* the monster here. Not Drágan. My stepfather is worse than Drágan could ever be!"

"You're so right about that," Penelope agreed.

"It sounds like Drágan helped you," Mary Anne said, her tone one of revelation. "All this time, he's been helping you."

Stephanie nodded. "Now I feel even worse being scared of him."

"You have no reason to feel bad about any of this," Penelope assured her in a firm voice. "Drágan's practically my son and I admit he can be scary. But he only means to help. Jacob, on the other hand..." She couldn't seem to continue. "I'm calling the police."

"Wait. What about my mom?" Stephanie shook with fear over what might happen to her mother.

Penelope paused before dialing 911. "She can stay here."

"What if the police can't keep him in jail?" Mary Anne asked, fear in her voice.

"She's right," Stephanie blurted, not willing to risk harm to her mom. "Drágan has it under control. He'll never let anything happen to me."

"But the man belongs in jail," Penelope insisted.

"He does," Stephanie affirmed, her mind clearer than it had been in a long time. "But not til my mom and me figure out where to hide. For now, I trust Drágan."

Penelope set her phone on the coffee table. "It's your decision. But you need to talk to Drágan first. I'll abide by whatever you decide."

Isaac stopped pacing. "I hope she's all right."

"You know your mother will take care of her," Drágan reminded him.

Isaac nodded.

"Can I ask something?" Jack was looking up from the floor at Drágan.

"Anything."

"Did I hear you howling last month?" Jack asked in a wary tone.

"I did howl once," Drágan affirmed, "but only after hearing another howl first."

"I was there," Isaac attested. "It's true. There's another werewolf around here somewhere."

"Yeah?" Nathaniel's face revealed his fear.

"Yes," Drágan affirmed.

"Thanks for telling us everything, Drágan," Jack said. "It means a lot that you trust us, especially me."

"I trust you completely, Jack."

Jack's face reddened slightly at Drágan's affirmation.

Isaac was happy his two friends had made up but worry for Stephanie still dominated his thoughts.

"I guess as long as we're confessing secrets," Nathaniel said timidly, "I have one that I'm tired of keeping. You're all my friends, right?"

"Of course," Isaac asserted while the others nodded.

"Well, when Jack and the others were, you know, calling you names, Isaac, I wanted to stop them, but I knew they'd come after me and I can't fight for shit."

Jack was looking at him, not hard-assed as he would have three months ago, but shamefaced.

Nathaniel met his gaze. "I like you, Jack, more than I'm sure you want me to."

Jack gasped and Isaac stared at Nathaniel, open-mouthed.

"You mean..." Jack didn't finish his thought.

Nathaniel nodded. "I liked you since seventh grade, but you were always with Isaac and I thought, well, maybe you guys were together. But then you..."

"Became the lowest asshole possible," Jack said, voice filled with recrimination. "Man, you need to find a good guy to like, cause that's not me."

Nathaniel eyed him from beneath his long eyelashes. "I like the Jack I see now more than the other one. Are we...still friends or do you hate me for telling you?"

"It's cool, Nat."

Just then Stephanie and Mary Anne entered the room. Stephanie's face was still red from crying, but she looked solid and strong again, like Isaac had always thought her to be.

"Hi guys," she said with a tiny smile. Her gaze landed on Drágan. "Did you tell them?"

"No."

"But we kind of figured it out," Isaac said, fighting down rage just thinking about what was done to her. "What's my mom gonna do?"

The girls sat on the floor next to Jack and Nathaniel, so Isaac resumed his seat beside Drágan on the bed.

"Something permanent has to be done," Stephanie began, "but until I know my mom and me are safely away from him, I'm hoping Drágan can keep him in line until then."

Drágan's face looked gentler and more compassionate than Isaac had ever seen it. "You have my solemn word."

Stephanie breathed a deep sigh of relief. "Thank you, Drágan, for everything. Like I told Isaac's mom, my stepdad's the real monster, not you. I'm sorry for doubting you."

Drágan offered a warm smile. "Does this mean you'll dance with me at Homecoming?"

She broke into a grin. "You know it."

"So, did we miss anything important while we were gone?" Mary Anne asked.

Nathaniel raised his hand, which got a chuckle even from Stephanie.

"So, um," Nathaniel began, "I told Jack I have a crush on him, and he didn't beat me up."

The girls looked surprised but offered Nathaniel genuine affirmations of support.

"Thank you for telling us," Stephanie said. "It means a lot that you trust us."

Nathaniel shrugged. "Who else would I tell?"

"Your parents?" Jack gazed deeply at him, as though the answer was crucial.

"Not yet. Maybe someday."

"As long as we're sharing secrets, it's not much of one that I've had a crush on you, too, Jack," Mary Anne said, drawing all eyes to her. "I mean, ever since eighth grade, I kept imagining us going to a dance together or to the movies. I'm sorry I made you so uncomfortable. I guess I just kept hoping."

Jack's face reddened. "It's um, it's okay. You're awesome, really, but I'm not...you deserve somebody better than me, that's all."

"Can we still be friends?" Mary Anne looked bewildered by his answer.

"Course. I promise to dance with you at Homecoming."

She beamed. "That'll work."

Nathaniel's face clouded over with fear. "What if...*he* shows up at the dance?"

"If you're referring to Jourdain," Drágan said, his mouth twisting downward in distaste, "I'll protect all of you."

"But in the meantime," Isaac said firmly, his thoughts back on the vampire, "don't open the door for anyone after dark."

Jack's face lit up. "This guy, he's a vampire, right? So, he sleeps during the day?"

Drágan nodded.

"Why don't we try to find his hiding place. This town's not that big."

Isaac exchanged a look with Drágan. "What about that? Does he, you know, use a coffin?"

"I don't know," Drágan answered, "I've never located any of his hiding places. But wherever he is, it must allow no sunlight to enter, for that could prove fatal."

"Well, that lets out my basement," Isaac said. "We have small windows. How about the rest of you?"

"Same," they all said.

"Besides, we'd have to invite him in, right," Nathaniel asked, "before he could use the basement?"

"This is true," Drágan confirmed.

"So, he must be somewhere public where he doesn't need an invite," Jack said.

"Good point," Isaac put in.

"Let's all think about possible places in town and go over them tomorrow at lunch," Stephanie suggested as she stood and stretched.

Chattering about the upcoming dance, the group descended the stairs and Isaac let them out the door. Jack hesitated as the others headed down the driveway.

"What's up?" Isaac asked.

Jack looked uncertain, as though he wanted to speak, but something, maybe Drágan's presence, prevented him. "Nothing. See you tomorrow."

As he closed the door, Isaac wondered if Jack fully trusted Drágan after all.

17

DRÁGAN'S BLOOD

The following day at school, Isaac felt like his group, which had been so tight during the awards, was even tighter now. The attempt by Jourdain to drive them apart had only brought them together stronger than before. Isaac did notice that Jack seemed more comfortable around Nathaniel after the other boy's confession, which he found interesting.

What amazed him was how so many kids were carrying around copies of the local Millwood Gazette. They stopped to congratulate Isaac and his crew for their wins at the film festival, which was front page news in their small-town paper.

Isaac snagged a copy of the paper from a kid who had two of them and saw his whole crew—and Stephen King!—smiling back at him from the front page. And the story, well, it made Isaac sound like a big-time celebrity. Even the mayor chimed in, praising him and the film.

With the rest of the Throwback Crew crowding around him, he held up the paper.

"Hey, we're famous!"

Although they all jockeyed for position to get a look, Stephanie was the first to scan the article. She grinned, and when she spoke, her voice came out tiny, like she was too excited to breathe. "This is lit!"

"Look how they describe you, Drágan," Mary Anne added. "Newcomer to Millwood, Drágan Albescu, took home the best actor award. Good job, son!"

"Well, you're not a newcomer anymore," Isaac said to his friend, who looked bewildered by all the praise. "The whole town knows you now."

"It would seem so," Drágan said in a noncommittal tone.

Isaac tried to join in with the crew as they basked in their celebrity status, but he couldn't help but worry about what Jourdain's next move might be. All of them had put garlic and crosses around their homes, to the chagrin of their parents.

"My mom put her foot down," Nathaniel said with a chuckle, "even though I told her it was for a science project, so I had to hang the garlic outside the windows and hide it in bushes by our front door."

Jack laughed. "I tried the science line too, but my mom saw right through it. I 'admitted' it was to help promote *Wolfboy* and had to hang everything outside."

Mary Anne told them her dad believed in vampires because he'd had some strange experiences in life, so he didn't complain about the garlic. She said no more, but a chill ran up Isaac's back, and he sensed there was a lot more to her story.

Classes moved along smoothly, especially thanks to Drágan keeping Ron, Serg, and their bully buddies under control. Coach Lancaster also continued to play fair, clearly unnerved around Drágan, but still pleading with him to join the football team. Drágan politely declined each time.

After school, Isaac and the group wandered around town, searching for dark places the vampire might hide, but came up empty.

"We're gonna wear our vintage dresses to Homecoming," Stephanie informed the boys as they all strolled down Main Street, "and you guys have to wear your outfits."

"Works for me," Jack said. "It's the only fancy stuff I own."

"Me too," Nathaniel said with a shrug. "I've never been into clothes."

WEDNESDAY NIGHT, while Drágan was in the shower, Isaac's phone beeped with an incoming text from an unknown caller. Immediately, he got a bad feeling about it, though he didn't know why. He dropped the textbooks he'd been shoving into his backpack, picked up his phone, and stared at it for a long moment thinking about scammers. Finally, he decided he'd better check it out.

It read: *Isaac, it's Stephanie. I had to use my mom's phone. Something happened. I'm in the woods behind your house. Hurry.*

Isaac jumped up from his desk and grabbed a jacket from his closet. He considered waiting for Drágan, but knew he'd be a while—he still had to dry his long hair and that would take forever. Isaac bolted from his room and down the stairs. He heard the TV in the living room and almost stopped to tell his mom, but Stephanie had sounded urgent and Isaac imagined her scumbag stepdad stalking her, so he hurried outside.

He hurried out the back door and entered the woods. Cursing himself for not bringing a flashlight, he worked his way carefully between the trees.

"Stephanie?" he called out quietly. "Where are you?"

Silence was his only answer. A chill ran up his spine. Something wasn't right. Through the dense foliage, he spotted the lights of Dr. Wilson's house and made his way in that direction.

"Stephanie!" He kept his voice low, but louder than the previous time. "Are you okay? It's Isaac."

"How good of you to drop by, Isaac" came a silky voice behind him.

He whirled to find the vampire practically on top of him. He hadn't heard a sound except his own footsteps. He feigned bravery, despite his pounding heart. "Where's Stephanie? If you hurt her..."

"How chivalrous of you," Jourdain said in a mocking tone. "So very like my dear Drágan." He stepped closer.

Isaac tried to back away, but found himself pinned against a tree.

"You seem especially significant to that wayward boy who, by rights, belongs to me. I did create him, so to speak."

"You did not! You just tried to make him like you but failed!"

The vampire had come close enough, now, to kiss him. "I may have failed with him, but I shall not with you."

He bared his fangs, and Isaac screamed.

DRÁGAN HAD TAKEN LONGER than usual in the shower, and then dried his hair, which had taken another twenty minutes. He'd faintly heard a scream while showering, but when he'd listened more acutely, he realized the television was on downstairs and decided that must be the source.

He'd been thinking about everything that had changed since the film festival. He had friends who knew the truth, yet still accepted him and cared for him. He had a family, thanks to Isaac's mom declaring him her son. His dreams that had spanned centuries had finally come true. His desire for a cure felt more urgent now than ever.

So did his need to destroy Jourdain.

As he entered his bedroom, towel around his waist, he saw that Isaac was gone. Gripped by a sudden dread, he tuned his senses toward locating his friend.

Outside? Why would he be so foolish!

Drágan dropped his towel and dressed. He didn't bother with a coat as he bolted from the room just as Penelope was ascending the stairs.

"Drágan, what's wrong?"

"Isaac has gone out."

"What? He knows it's dangerous."

"I must find him."

"I'm coming too."

"It's too dangerous."

"He's my son. And I have you to protect me."

Drágan nodded, knowing there was no time to argue. "Stay close."

He tore down the stairs and she followed. They left the house by the side door and Drágan sniffed the air. The barn and driveway were quiet.

"The woods."

He sprinted forward, her footfalls slapping the ground in pursuit. He stopped and sniffed the air. His senses were those of an animal and he quickly caught Isaac's unique scent. Another smell assailed his nostrils—blood!

He pelted through the trees, his wolfish eyes picking out every detail.

There! A body lay tossed into the underbrush.

Don't let it be...

He skidded to a halt by the body, lying on its side facing away from him. He recognized the scent before he squatted and turned it over.

Pounding footfalls approached through the underbrush and then a piercing shriek sounded behind him. Penelope dropped to her knees beside him. "Isaac!" She turned Isaac's head and gasped. Two small punctures on his throat bled in little streams onto the wet ground and, even in the dark, Isaac's face was white as a sheet.

Terrified, Drágan listened. He heard a heartbeat, but so faint he didn't believe someone with normal hearing could detect it.

"He's alive, barely."

Penelope cried out in despair.

Drágan glanced around and spotted lights from Dr. Wilson's house. "Dr. Wilson," he announced, and then lifted his friend's body and bolted toward the lights, leaving Penelope behind.

He arrived at the doctor's front door, cursing himself for not having the key with him. He pounded on the wooden door while cradling Isaac against him with one arm. Gasping for air and crying, Penelope arrived as Drágan waited in desperate fear.

"Who's there?" came Wilson's voice from inside.

"Drágan. Isaac's hurt."

"How do I know you're not Jourdain pretending to be Drágan?"

"Because Jourdain never told you Isaac was cute enough to be a model! Please, doctor, he's dying!"

The door swung open, and the older man stood within wearing a robe, deep concern on his craggy face.

"What happened?"

"Jourdain."

Wilson didn't hesitate. "Get him to the lab."

Wilson swept everything off a long table and threw a clean cloth over it before Drágan laid Isaac atop it. Drágan seldom experienced panic because he was practically invulnerable, but now that emotion overwhelmed him. Isaac looked as white as a sheet.

He can't die, he can't! I need him!

Wilson used his stethoscope to search for a heartbeat. "It's so faint." Isaac looked as white as the cloth he lay upon. "He's lost almost every drop of blood."

"You have to save him, Doctor," Penelope tearfully begged. "You have to!"

Wilson ran to his large refrigerator and yanked it open. "What's his blood type?" he asked Penelope.

"I don't know. I don't even know my blood type!"

Wilson hurried back. "It's gotta be you, Drágan. You're a universal donor."

"But my blood...it's tainted," Drágan exclaimed, hearing the little life left in Isaac draining away. "What'll happen to him?"

Penelope grabbed him by the arms. "Please, Drágan, you're his only hope!"

"He could become like me!" Drágan couldn't bear to curse Isaac as he had been.

Wilson was listening with the stethoscope again. "He's in shock. Decide."

"Please, Drágan," Penelope begged, tears streaming down her face. "I don't care if he's like you. I just want my son!"

"But...it's forever!"

"I don't care! Please!"

Drágan yanked his shirt over his head and faced Wilson. "What do I do?"

The doctor rolled a second table beside the first one. "Get on and lie back."

Drágan did as he was told. His heart pounded with fear. He reached out and took Isaac's cold hand in his. "Do not die!"

Wilson rolled a cart near Drágan and wrapped a length of rubber around his biceps, tightening it. The veins in his arm bulged. Within moments, Wilson had blood flowing from Drágan's arm into Isaac's, but to Drágan, it seemed an eternity. He continued to clasp Isaac's cold hand, willing him to live.

Penelope held Isaac's other hand as Wilson monitored the transfusion.

"I can't take too much from you, Drágan, or—"

"Take it all if you must but save him!" Drágan didn't care if he died so long as Isaac lived. All of this was his doing. Had he never come to town, Jourdain would not have followed, and the most important person in his life would not be near death!

"Color's returning to his face," Wilson commented, once again listening to Isaac's heartbeat. "Heartbeat's stronger. Maybe that's enough."

"My ears are better than your device, doctor," Drágan said, as an unaccustomed weakness seeped over him. "He needs more."

The doctor's worn face creased with worry. Penelope watched the exchange fearfully, still clutching Isaac's hand. "His hand is warmer," she exclaimed excitedly.

"I feel it too," Drágan confirmed. "A bit...more." His mind was feeling muddled, and he knew it was from blood loss. But he could drink any blood type for replenishment. Isaac couldn't have just any blood for his transfusion.

After another few minutes, Drágan's thoughts became a mass of confusion he heard, "That's enough," in Wilson's deep voice before blackness overcame him.

He woke to find himself sitting upright, but being supported, a plastic pouch pressed into his hands. "Drink, Drágan, drink!" His senses unclear, he didn't recognize the voice and his vision was blurred, but he clasped the pouch and felt it being lifted to his lips. He opened his mouth and thick slippery liquid dribbled in.

Blood!

Just the first taste brought his senses and strength back enough to grasp the pouch on his own and gulp down the life-restoring liquid. He sucked until every last drop slid down his throat.

"More," he croaked.

The first pouch was taken from him and replaced with a full one. Within moments, he'd drunk its entire contents. His vision was clear now, his mind unclouded, and he knew where he was. He found Wilson standing before him and turned to find Penelope bending over the unmoving Isaac.

He listened to his friend's life signs. Heartbeat strong, breathing regular. He let out a loud sigh as Wilson took the pouch from him and offered a clean cloth. Drágan wiped his mouth and faced the doctor, feeling more gratitude than ever in his long life.

"Thank you, Doctor, for saving him."

"You saved him, Drágan. Without your blood, he'd be dead. Remember that, no matter how different he may be when he awakes."

Drágan nodded and slid off the table on which he sat, still a bit weak. Spotting his shirt hanging over a chair, he slipped it on and moved to Penelope's side. She still held one of Isaac's hands but with her other she clasped Drágan's, squeezing with gratitude.

Drágan gazed at his best friend lying on the table and considered what he'd done. Yes, he'd saved Isaac's life, but at what cost? He'd never shared his blood with anyone throughout his life because he'd never wanted anyone, especially a child, to suffer as he had. That, he supposed, among many other reasons, separated him from Jourdain, who relished making others like himself.

Drágan thought back to his rage when he'd first learned what he'd become. He'd been so tempted to inflict that pain on others, to make them like him. But before that temptation overtook him, he'd recall sitting in the mud surrounded by slaughtered animals, and disgust would rise in his gorge like bile.

No one should go through what I have. And yet, there was Isaac lying unconscious before him, the kindest and most gentle boy he'd ever known.

Will he hate me when he learns the truth?

Penelope interrupted his thoughts. "Thank you, Drágan."

"I'm not sure I did him or you any favors."

Her lovely face was troubled, adding to Drágan's guilt.

"I confess I was looking forward to him growing up, having a family of his own," she said solemnly. "I guess every parent does. But I want him alive more than anything else. Thanks to you, he is."

Drágan nodded, still wracked with guilt.

She met his gaze. "If he is, well, like you, Drágan, can you teach him how to control...everything?"

"You have my word."

Please, Isaac, don't hate me!

WHEN ISAAC AWOKE, he lay in his own bed at home. His mind seemed fuzzy, and he couldn't remember...wait...something happened to him.

Jourdain!

He sat up in bed, only to find his mom asleep in a chair and Drágan stirring beside him.

"Mom, what's going on?"

She lifted her head, realized he was awake and jumped up. Fully clothed, Drágan clambered off the other side of the bed and walked around to stand beside her.

"How do you feel, Isaac?" his mom asked, worry in her voice.

Isaac felt his neck. "Jourdain, he..." His neck was unblemished. "He bit me, I know he did!"

His mom handed him his hearing aids, and, out of habit, he slipped them over his ears and pressed the power button. He heard the familiar tune as they powered up and then nearly screamed in agony as the worst feedback he'd ever experienced pounded through his head.

"My phone!"

Fearful, she snatched it off his desk and handed it over. "What's wrong?"

"Way too loud!" He opened the app and adjusted the volume on his aids, but the feedback continued. He lowered the volume to nothing, and yet he clearly heard a car driving down the street.

"Take them out, Isaac," Drágan said calmly.

Isaac did as he was told, bewildered. "That's weird." He listened. "Dr. Wilson is moving beakers around in his lab. I hear the glass clinking together."

His mom stared at him in amazement, but Drágan seemed to understand. He took the hearing aids from Isaac and handed them to Penelope. "He'll no longer need these."

"Why not?" Isaac's body felt...different. "I was born needing them."

"In a way, your body has been reborn."

Isaac's stomach rumbled so loudly even his mom reacted to it. Drágan dashed from the room.

"Where's he going? And why do I feel so weird, Mom? My whole body is...hungry, but not for food..." Isaac groaned, his body aching for nourishment, practically tearing itself apart from the inside.

Drágan reappeared, carrying a large plastic bag of red liquid. "You may wish to look away while I feed him, Mrs. Foster."

"No. He's my son." She stepped aside so Drágan could approach.

Isaac sat up and planted his bare feet on the carpet. "What do you mean, feed me? I can feed—" He suddenly smelled...everything! Drágan, his mom, the carpet, everything had a strong, distinct odor. But one fragrance overpowered them all.

Blood!

He practically snatched the heavy bag from Drágan and gulped down the blood until the pouch was empty.

"Is that sufficient or do you need more?" Drágan asked as though swallowing a huge bottle of blood was normal.

Isaac stared in horror at the empty bag, then licked the droplets off his lips, savoring the taste as if the blood was mana from Heaven. His mind both rebelled at and accepted this new reality. He handed the bag back to Drágan, the hunger within him sated for the moment. That's when fear took over.

"What happened to me?"

Between Drágan and his mom, they explained what had occurred the previous night, and he told them of the false text claiming to be Stephanie. He stared at them, letting everything he'd heard sink in, trying to understand his new reality, while dread encircled his heart like barbed wire.

"So, what, I'm...a...a vampire now?"

Drágan stepped over to the window and pulled the curtain back just a bit. A shaft of sunlight struck Isaac's hand, but nothing happened. Drágan opened the drapes all the way and sunlight flooded the room, illuminating Isaac's pale face without burning it.

"It appears you are like me, a half vampire," Drágan said, his tone laced with recrimination.

Isaac looked at his hands and felt his face. "I don't look any different, do I, Mom?"

"You're you, honey," she assured him. "Just with Drágan's blood."

Isaac's eyes bulged with shock. "Am I a werewolf too?"

Drágan sighed. "The next full moon will establish that. I'm so sorry, Isaac, for making you like this."

"I can't believe my hearing is so good." Isaac listened, fascinated and discomfited by all the sounds around him that normally he wouldn't hear even with his aids. "I hear Mr. Ruggles next door working in his garage."

Drágan nodded. "Yes. That will take some adjustment. As will acclimating to your potent sense of smell."

"You smell good," Isaac said shyly, embarrassed for having said it.

Drágan bowed. "I take that as a compliment."

"Wait, what about school?"

"It's too late for today, honey," his mom said. "I called in that you were sick and Drágan stayed home to help me with you, which was true."

Isaac met Drágan's gaze. "What about the dance Saturday? Will I be ready for that? The girls'll be real disappointed if we don't go."

Drágan shook his head. "He learns that he's become like me and worries most about what the girls will say if he misses a dance."

Penelope looked relieved, as though this proved Isaac was still the same person as before.

Isaac offered a wry smile. "Yeah, pretty dumb, huh?" He listened to his body. His blood flowed freely through his veins, and his heart beat at an accelerated rate. "So, uh, what else is...gonna happen to me?"

"You may be more disoriented than me because I already bore the werewolf curse when I became a vampire, but the fact that you are not demanding more blood right now is a good sign."

"Is there more in the fridge?" His stomach gave a slight lurch. "I'm gonna need it soon."

"There is," said his mom. "I know this is hard for you, Isaac, but Drágan's blood was all that could save you. It was my idea, not his. I just couldn't...bear the thought of losing you."

Isaac sank into himself a moment. Everything about his body felt different, but was that a necessarily a bad thing? He was alive, after all, despite Jourdain's attempt to kill him. He jumped out of bed and grabbed Drágan by the lapels, lifting him off the floor with ease.

"Isaac!" cried his mom.

Unperturbed, Drágan said, "He's just testing his body."

Isaac laughed as he lowered his friend back to the floor. "I'm strong like you!"

"It would seem so," Drágan replied, calmly. "But I recommend adjusting slowly."

Isaac thought of something, and he shivered with revulsion. "I'm gonna need blood from people, aren't I?"

"Yes. Dr. Wilson used most of his supply to replenish what I lost saving you."

"How do I do it," Isaac asked, "drink blood from someone?" The idea was both repellant and oddly tantalizing.

"It will all come to you when the time arises. What I must help you do is control the urge to drink or you may kill someone without intending to."

"Oh, God, I don't wanna kill anyone!" Suddenly, Isaac's new strength paled next to this reality. "I mean, really, could I do that?"

"If you don't learn self-control, yes," Drágan replied soberly. "We'll practice on animals first."

Isaac thought he'd cringe at the mere thought of drinking blood from animals, but the craving came from so deep within him he could not ignore it.

"Can we start now? I'm getting thirsty again."

Drágan looked at Penelope. "With your permission?"

"Of course. Just, well, I don't need the details."

Drágan said, "Could you get some of the blood from the refrigerator, Mrs. Foster, so he's not frantic while I teach him?"

"Sure." She hurried from the room.

Isaac noticed the dried blood on his shirt and had to force himself not to lick it. "I need a clean shirt."

He hurried to his bureau and pulled out a tee shirt. Yanking off the soiled one, he noticed that his belly felt solid, the skin tighter, and his abs were clearly visible. He turned to find Drágan staring at him in a way that almost made him squirm.

The thirst increased and he had no more time to consider anything but food. He slipped on the shirt and offered Drágan a smile he didn't really feel. His entire body felt like it was eating itself up from the inside, and he wanted to scream from the discomfort.

"How did you get used to this, Drágan?"

"Over time."

His mom rushed in with the blood pouch, and Isaac snatched it from her hands.

"Only a little," Drágan urged, placing a hand on Isaac's arm. "Save some for later."

Isaac opened the cap and took a gulp before resealing the pouch.

That gulp helped, but it wasn't enough. He handed the pouch back to his mom. "Thanks, Mom."

"We'd better go, Isaac," Drágan said.

Isaac took a long look at his mother's worried expression and understood that his transformation might be harder on her than on him.

Once outside, Isaac followed Drágan into the woods, astonished that he could keep pace with his friend. Trees seemed to fly past at faster and faster speeds. Isaac couldn't believe he could run this fast. And stopping was almost instantaneous. He listened, hearing the tiniest sounds of the forest, even the steps of deer grazing a short distance away. He smelled them. There were two. He locked eyes with Drágan. They were in perfect sync. Darting between trees, each of them had hold of a young doe within seconds.

Isaac's mouth twitched as long fangs appeared. He was about to sink those fangs into the animal's throat when he heard Drágan order, "Observe."

He watched his friend gently press his fangs into the flesh of the deer. He did it so delicately the animal didn't even flinch.

Isaac copied Drágan's actions and soon lovely, savory blood spilled forth into his mouth. He sucked and gulped and swallowed, oblivious to everything around him. Only the hunger mattered. He felt a hand on his shoulder, squeezing hard.

"That's sufficient, Isaac."

Isaac looked up at Drágan standing over him, mouth shiny with blood. "But I want more."

No!"

Drágan's harsh voice pounded through Isaac's sensitive ears so loudly that he released the deer and it slowly moved away into the woods.

Drágan pulled a handkerchief from his coat pocket, wiped the blood from his lips and handed it to Isaac, who did the same before handing it back.

Isaac stood and faced his friend. "You were right, I knew just what to do."

"Yes, but you would have drained the deer had I not stopped you."

Isaac felt ashamed. "The hunger, it's so…"

"It's the most powerful hunger in the world, but you'll learn to control it as I did. You must."

"What do I do when I'm, you know, hungry at school?"

Drágan's eyebrows shot up. "There are enough bullies for the two of us."

Isaac grinned. A swell of pure, unadulterated power surged through him. Intoxicating, but sobering. All at once, he realized he'd become something he had never wanted to be—dangerous.

18

STRUGGLES AND ADAPTATIONS

Of course, the crew came to the house right after school to check on him, and Isaac insisted he felt great, that his illness had passed quickly. Inside, however, he roiled with the overwhelming sensations assaulting him from each of them. He hoped his discomfort wasn't too obvious. Every smell made him light-headed, and every sound—especially their combined voices—was like a rock band in his brain. He fought to maintain a calm demeanor, even with Dragan standing protectively at his side.

"So, you two are still going to the dance, right?" Stephanie asked, sounding hopeful.

"Yeah, course," Isaac said, exuding confidence while listening to the blood flowing through her arteries. And her scent...he forced himself to focus on the conversation.

Drágan must've known how he felt because he distracted everyone until they left for home, leaving behind the boys' homework assignments. Isaac plopped into his desk chair, exhausted.

"Is it that way for you, smelling everyone's blood, hearing their breathing, everything?"

Drágan nodded. "The more you focus on everyday activities, the less your keen senses will disturb you."

"If you say so." They sat down to do the homework and, once more, Isaac realized how much he loved the smell of Drágan beside him. It aroused within him sensations that made him feel...uncomfortable.

After feeding once again on deer in the forest, the boys went to visit Dr. Wilson. They found him in his lab, as always.

"Isaac, you look well," Wilson commented. Then to Drágan he asked, "Is he...?"

"Half vampire, at least. We must await the full moon."

"Perhaps not. Isaac, let me take a sample of your blood. I can determine if both cells are active."

Isaac used to look away when he had blood drawn, but this time he gazed at the syringe as his blood filled it, experiencing a deep, prickly craving. Wilson placed a drop on a glass slide, covered it with another glass slide, and slipped it into the microscope. Placing his eye to the ocular lens, he adjusted the focus.

"Uh huh," he mumbled, "both cells are present and active." He stood and motioned Isaac over to take a look.

Isaac saw the variant cells in his blood and understood exactly what they meant. He lifted his head and faced Drágan. "Does it hurt as much as it looks like, the transformation?"

"I am sorry to say it does." Drágan lowered his eyes in shame. "I've made you a monster. I'll never forgive myself."

Isaac placed a hand under the other boy's chin, lifting his head so their eyes could meet. "You saved my life."

"Indeed, he did, Isaac," Wilson said. "You had mere seconds to live by the time Drágan's blood restored you."

Isaac considered how close he'd come to dying. He was glad he hadn't seen the dread that had surely been in his mother's eyes. "Thank you, Doctor."

He shook Wilson's hand, causing him to wince. "Whoa, there!" The doctor yanked his hand back, shaking it. "You need to adjust to your new strength."

Mortified, Isaac blurted, "I'm so sorry."

Drágan glanced away, shame and guilt written all over his face.

Isaac said, "There's one good side to all this?"

"What is that?" Drágan's remorseful tone suggested there couldn't possibly be a silver lining.

"You're not alone in the world anymore."

Drágan nodded, still looking sad. "But you'll never age, while all your friends, our friends, will leave us behind."

Isaac lowered his eyes as Drágan's words sank in. Eternity, he knew, even with Drágan, would bring more sadness than joy. "Doctor, have you come any closer to a cure?"

The stooped man shook his head, his face lined with regret. "But I have shared all my findings with Dr. Breslin in South Dakota, and she asked me to send blood samples."

"Did you?" Drágan asked.

"Not without your permission. Do I have it?"

"Of course."

"Send mine too," Isaac added, feeling a twinge of hope amidst moments of despair. Could he get used to his new existence? Eyeing Drágan beside him, he decided he'd have to. What other choice was there?

"Very well," Wilson was saying. "I'll prepare the samples for shipment."

"Thank you, Doctor," Isaac said. "For everything."

"My pleasure."

The boys left him to his work.

Walking back to his house, Isaac asked, "Should we tell the others about me?"

Drágan seemed to consider the idea. "Perhaps after that dance this weekend. They have only now adjusted to my condition. I cannot predict how they will react when they learn about you."

"I guess you're right, but I don't want to keep any more secrets from them."

"Neither do I."

Something in his tone made Isaac feel Drágan might have other secrets he hadn't yet revealed.

Friday of that week was hit and miss for Isaac. Often the hunger would sweep over him in class, and he squirmed in place, using every ounce of willpower to resist grabbing the kid in front of him and sinking his fangs into the soft flesh of their throat. He felt Drágan beside him, forcing eye contact, helping to sooth his desires somehow, but never eliminating them. Immediately after class, Isaac would rush to the restroom hoping one of the bullies would show up. As though knowing he was there, one would conveniently make an appearance.

Isaac would never forget the first time he grabbed a much-heavier guy, pressed him hard against the bathroom wall, and drank greedily from his throat. The memory both excited and disgusted him.

Drágan pulled him back with great force before the bigger boy passed out, forcing Isaac to meet his piercing gaze. "You possess a terrible power now, Isaac. You *must* control it."

Isaac wiped his mouth with a paper towel, his thirst sated for the moment. "But guys like this..." He recalled every nasty thing this guy had ever said to him, making his blood boil with fury.

"He will get what is coming to him through *his* actions, not yours," Drágan replied after cleaning the boy's throat and raising his hoodie collar to cover the tiny marks.

As he watched the bully languidly exit the bathroom, Isaac released his sudden onrush of anger and considered his new reality. "I think I understand how power went to Jack's head in *Lord of the Flies*. Can you imagine if he'd been like us?"

"Power must never be abused," Drágan replied. "Recall that Ralph had similar opportunities to be abusive but did not succumb."

During lunch, the girls talked about the dance. None of the boys were thrilled, but all admitted it might be fun. Isaac's new senses were better than Spiderman's, and he was keenly sensitive to everything happening around him, even in classrooms down the hall. He held his body rigid, straining to focus on the conversation of his friends and tune out everyone else in the crowded cafeteria. The struggle was exhausting. But he was happy to see Stephanie smiling and looking forward to doing something enjoyable.

Nathaniel and Jack seemed to always be together now, though Isaac often found Jack's eyes on him when he thought Isaac wasn't aware. Could Jack have noticed something different about him? He wasn't wearing his hearing aids, but his mom had helped brush his hair more over the back of his ears so it wouldn't be obvious. Isaac had also made certain not to pick up anything at school he previously could not lift without help, and he hoped he wasn't obvious about taking in all the smells around him. He really wanted to tell Jack and the others the truth, but he figured Drágan was right. He'd wait until Monday after school.

"Do you think your mom could drive us all to the dance, Isaac?" Stephanie asked, interrupting his thoughts.

"Uh, yeah, sure. She won't mind." His head was hurting again.

He noticed Drágan eyeing him.

I'm okay, he thought, hoping his friend picked up the message with whatever it was they had between them. Drágan seemed to understand and visibly relaxed.

Isaac picked at his food without eating much, mainly because of all the distractions assailing him. The burger was well done and tasted fine, but his stomach rumbled for uncooked meat. Was that the latent werewolf within? He recalled Drágan eating raw bacon and decided it must be.

Drágan didn't need to feed as frequently, so he allowed Isaac to drink from Ron and Serg at their regular time. That night, they waited in the shadows for Stephanie's stepdad to return home. Drágan grabbed him first and silenced him with mesmerism, then allowed Isaac to feed. Just looking at the molester sent Isaac into a violent rage, and he would've killed the man if Drágan hadn't pulled him off.

"Let me finish him," Isaac spat, blood dribbling down his chin. "He deserves it!"

"We just talked about this today. Once you use your power to kill, you become Jourdain. Is that your desire?"

The fire burning through Isaac subsided as he pictured Jourdain's smug face, and he wiped his mouth with his sleeve. Drágan sat the stunned man down against a fence.

"He'll recover soon and return home. Come, before we're seen."

He and Drágan wandered the dark streets so Isaac could focus on blocking out the smells and sounds pummeling his finely tuned, super-enhanced senses.

"How long will it be before I don't hear and smell *everything*?" he moaned. "It's making me crazy."

"Over time, you'll learn to ignore what you don't need at the moment."

"Yeah, but how much time?" His head pounded nonstop from the influx of so many stimuli.

"I can only speak for myself. Perhaps thirty days."

"A month?" Isaac didn't think he could last that long.

"I'll be at your side," Drágan assured him. "Always."

ISAAC MADE it through Saturday needing less blood than he had the past couple of days, but he ate all the raw bacon in the fridge and had to apologize to his mom.

"We'll get through this, Isaac, as a family," she said, pulling him into a warm hug. He relished the hug because he'd been so afraid she'd no longer want to touch him. "Are you ready for the dance tonight?"

He shrugged. "I guess. I feel like everyone will see what I am."

He knew she hadn't slept well since he'd almost died. And he'd felt her eyes on him when she probably thought he was unaware. The changes in him frightened her.

She offered a wan smile. "I don't know what you're feeling, but I promise that you look cute as ever."

He smiled. His mom always knew what to say to make him feel better.

"Drágan will be there the whole time," she reminded him. "He'll help you."

"I know."

Drágan entered the kitchen. "Do you need to feed before the dance?" he asked, as though suggesting a tuna sandwich.

Isaac would have to adjust to this new normal. "I think the two deer I drank for lunch were enough."

That drew out a lovely smile from Drágan.

"The dance starts at seven, so you boys better get dressed. And don't get mad when I take tons of pictures."

"Bruh," Isaac grumbled, but tossed his mom the best smile he could muster. Her face lit up, which made him happy, and he followed Drágan from the kitchen.

The boys dressed in silence. Isaac's thoughts were too jumbled as he watched his best friend adjust his cravat in the mirror. His entire life had changed in an instant and he still wasn't sure how he felt about it, despite his affirmations to Drágan and his mom.

"Can we be killed?" he blurted after Drágan helped him adjust his clothing.

Drágan eyed him with concern. "I suppose with a stake to the heart or a silver bullet. Why do you ask?"

"I guess I was wondering if you ever thought of, I don't know, shooting a silver bullet into your heart or something because of, well, loneliness."

"The thought did cross my mind. More than once. But if I had done that, I'd never have met you."

He exited the room before the startled Isaac could reply.

True to her word, his mom took a gazillion pictures of him and Drágan in different poses, constantly telling them both to smile. "Show some teeth when you smile."

The boys looked at each other, then smiled so their fangs were visible.

"Sure that's what you want, Mom?"

He and his mom laughed, but Drágan didn't. As they headed out to the van, Isaac wondered just it would take to get that boy to laugh.

Will I be like that if I live five hundred years?

He knew he would.

Reminded by Penelope to be "gentlemen with the girls," Isaac and Drágan stepped out of the van at Mary Anne's house as the two girls came out with Mr. Givens. The girls looked even prettier than they had at the festival. Besides wearing the same dresses, both wore makeup and had done wonders with their hair. Stephanie's long tresses were wound around her head in braids that Isaac really liked. She smiled as he helped her up into the van.

Mary Anne had turned her normally curly hair into little waterfalls that dangled around her head. Drágan took her arm and helped her into the van. Both girls wore fancy heeled shoes that looked impossible to dance in.

Mr. Givens stepped in front of Drágan before the boys re-entered the van. "Protect my daughter."

Drágan clearly understood. "I will, sir."

Isaac suspected he meant from Jourdain, but there was no opportunity to ask as they settled themselves inside the van beside the girls, who prattled on about how handsome they looked. Stephanie gushed over Drágan's hair, which was styled into a long braid, courtesy of Isaac's mom.

"You have to wear it like that all the time," she insisted, and Mary Anne nodded vigorously.

"Thank you," he said with a genuine smile of appreciation.

The next stop was Nathaniel's two-story Victorian, clearly in need of a paint job, where he and Jack were waiting out front. Both looked so different in their vintage clothes, and their hair style matched, which Isaac found amusing because Nathaniel had his in cornrows, just like Jack's. He figured Jack must've done it for him. Nathaniel carried a small duffel bag, which piqued Isaac's curiosity.

Once they clambered into the rear seat of the van, Drágan properly tied their cravats. The newcomers sat back, and Nathaniel lifted the duffel onto his lap.

"What's in there?" Mary Ann asked.

Nathaniel pulled out some large and small crosses, displaying them with pride. When Drágan looked away, Nathaniel lowered them. "Sorry, man."

Isaac was grateful no one noticed that he averted his eyes too.

Nathaniel handed the small crosses to the girls. Each was attached to a thin chain. Jack pulled his own cross out from beneath his cravat, displaying it for the others with pride, letting it rest against the fabric so it was plainly visible. The girls helped each other clasp the chains around their necks. Nathaniel offered one to Isaac, who glanced down.

"No thanks. I have my own protection."

Nathaniel shrugged. "I'm not sure if the vampire can get into the dance, but if he does, we all be safe from him indoors, at least, with the small crosses. We can use the big ones outside, if we need 'em."

He set the duffel on the floor by his feet and extracted a crossbow and some arrows.

"Whoa!" Stephanie exclaimed.

"I shoot at targets in my yard," Nathaniel said.

"And he's been teaching me," Jack echoed.

"I know we can't bring it into the dance," Nathaniel went on, sounding pleased with himself, "but it'll work on that vampire if he shows up anywhere else tonight."

Drágan eyed the weapon uncertainly.

"He wasn't thinking of you, Drágan," Jack blurted, suddenly looking worried.

"I was merely thinking that your ingenuity is impressive, Nathaniel," Drágan replied.

"Thanks, man." Looking smug, Nathaniel slid the crossbow and arrows beneath his seat.

~

THE MILLWOOD HIGH gym blazed with light, and loud music poured forth as Penelope pulled into the drop-off lane. "I'll see you all inside."

"Wait, what?" Isaac said, confused.

"I signed up as a chaperone."

"Bruh," Isaac mumbled.

"I think that's awesome, Mrs. Foster," chirped Stephanie with enthusiasm. "See you inside."

The boys exited, including Jack and Nathaniel. Stephanie waited until Drágan helped her down, while Mary Anne gave Jack the eye, so he got the message too. More awkwardly than Drágan, he assisted her to the ground, noting her shoes.

"The hell you gonna dance in those?"

She wrapped her arm through his. "I'll show you."

Likewise, Stephanie draped her arm through Drágan's, and they stepped into the line at the entrance.

Isaac glanced at Nathaniel. "Guess that leaves us." He laughed and they linked their arms together, drawing a laugh out of Stephanie and Mary Anne. Jack, on the other hand, wore an expression Isaac couldn't read, but it wasn't one of amusement.

Everyone had to be cleared by showing their school ID and Homecoming ticket, but the line moved swiftly and within minutes, Isaac and his crew were inside. Normally, the gym was uninteresting, but the Homecoming decorations committee had outdone themselves. There was a massive walk-through blue and gold balloon arch just past the check-in table. Dangling from the center of the high ceiling were gold and blue streamers that hung low and stretched out to the corners of the gym.

The area near the stage was available for dancing, and a DJ dressed all in gold stood by his equipment cranking hip hop tunes. Some couples already gyrated to the pounding music, but the loudness made Isaac cover his ears. The noise was physically painful.

Maybe this wasn't such a good idea after all, he thought.

The PTA had arranged round tables in the half of the gym near the entrance, with alternating gold or blue tablecloths and centerpieces creating a bright atmosphere for groups to sit, relax, and enjoy refreshments. Food and drink could be found on a table placed against the folded bleachers, where several chaperones hovered, prepared to serve the goodies.

Stephanie made a beeline for one of the tables and dropped her purse and coat in front of a chair. Mary Anne did the same, while the boys shucked off their ankle-length coats and hung them on the backs of their chairs.

Beaming with excitement, Stephanie faced them all. "Dance time!"

She and Mary Anne fairly dragged the boys onto the dance floor and immediately started spinning and waving their hands to the beat. So close to the stage, Isaac felt the music pounding into his brain like a thousand hammers all going at once. He winced as the DJ shouted a hearty "Welcome!" into the mic.

Jack and Nathaniel were attempting to copy the girls, but Drágan stood by Isaac's side.

"If the noise is too great, perhaps you should sit."

"It's just as bad over there," Isaac said, grimacing. "Let's try to dance or Stephanie'll be mad."

He observed the other kids and the dance moves they attempted before starting to move himself. Drágan picked up the beat instantly and seemed to enjoy impressing Stephanie with wild movements of his hands and feet. Isaac was sure he'd fall flat on his face, but when he tried copying Drágan, he found he had perfect balance and rhythm. The girls looked comical gaping at him.

"You go, Isaac!" Mary Anne called out over the music.

Focusing on his goofy dance moves and on how light he felt on his feet, Isaac momentarily tuned out the cacophony of sights and smells and sounds. Still, by the second song his head began to pound. He felt light-headed and missed a step, throwing him off-balance.

Strong arms prevented him from hitting the floor. Drágan was there, practically in his face. "Perhaps you weren't ready for this."

The girls crowded in too. "You okay, Isaac?" Stephanie looked concerned as she felt his forehead. "No fever. Your head's cold, in fact."

"I think maybe it's from being sick this week," Isaac said, grimacing in pain. "I just gotta sit for a while."

"Come." Drágan guided him off the crowded dance floor, across the gym to their table, and eased him into a chair.

Penelope appeared by his side. "Are you all right, Isaac?"

Isaac hated all this attention. "I'm okay, Mom, just a headache."

"Okay. I'll be at the refreshment table if you need anything."

"Thank you, Mrs. Foster," Drágan said politely.

She crossed the gym to her station and Drágan bent close to Isaac. "Do you want me to stay with you?"

Isaac waved him off. "No. Go have fun."

"I'm here if you need me."

"I know."

Looking reluctant, Drágan crossed back into the dancing crowd to join Stephanie and Mary Anne.

Isaac lowered his head into his hands and tried to block out the din. He didn't know how long he'd been sitting still when he heard a chair move and looked up. Jack was seated beside him.

"Are you okay?"

"Yeah," Isaac replied. "It's all the noise."

"But you aren't wearing your hearing aids."

Isaac flinched. Of course, Jack of all people would notice, even with his hair different. "Yeah, I left 'em at home. Knew it would be loud."

"But you hear me fine and I'm not talking loud."

Jack suspected something.

"Yeah, you know how well I read lips."

Jack didn't look convinced. "I need to tell you something."

The change of topic caught Isaac off guard. "Sure."

Jack had his hands on the table and clasped them together tightly. "I need to tell you why I turned against you."

"Jack, you really don't."

"I do. You might hate me even more, but I do."

"I don't hate you."

"Isaac, please, just listen."

Isaac leaned in closer, placed his hands on the table, and listened. He fought to block out the music by focusing on Jack's thumping heartbeat and the blood coursing through his veins.

Jack looked down at his twisting hands. "Some time in the seventh grade, I, uh, I started to feel, uh, different...mostly about... you."

"Me?"

"Isaac, please..."

"Sorry."

"I didn't understand it at first, so I didn't know what to do or say, but I guess it was that summer before eighth grade I figured out that I, um, that I had a...a crush on you." He glanced up, his face twisted with guilt. "I tried to hint, I think, tried to figure out if, you know, maybe you liked me, too, but I was too scared to tell you 'cause I didn't wanna lose you."

Isaac's insides twisted into knots as he listened.

"That day in the school cafeteria; we were horsing around and, I guess, I was trying to get closer to you, so we had our arms around each other's necks..."

"And those guys said we looked cute," Isaac said, the memory sending shards of pain through him.

"I panicked, Isaac." Jack seemed on the verge of tears. "I was so scared they'd find out about me that I said it was you, that you were trying to kiss me." The tears came then, and Jack made no move to stop them. "I became those guys, and I wanted to stop hurting you, every day, but I was too afraid they'd find out, and then so would my mom and then...everyone. So, I made your life a living hell 'cause I didn't have the balls to do what Nat did the other day. I'm so sorry, so sorry." He lowered his head to the table and wept.

Isaac glanced around, not wanting Jack to be even more embarrassed, but everyone was dancing, and the tables were empty except for them. He scooted closer, lifted Jack's head in his hands and pressed it against his shoulder.

"I think, maybe, we cause more pain by *not* saying things than we do by saying them. I wish you told me back then."

Jack sat up, wiping his eyes with his sleeve. "Would it have mattered?"

Isaac froze. That was the big question, wasn't it? "I don't know now. But I want us to stay friends."

They hugged briefly, taking the first solid step in repairing their fractured friendship.

"This is the secret Drágan figured out?"

"Yeah."

"Have you told your mom yet?"

Jack shook his head. "I don't think she'd understand. She's not like your mom. If I told your mom she'd just give me a big hug."

"Yeah, she would," he acknowledged. He spotted Nathaniel chatting with his mom at the refreshment table. "Nathaniel's a good guy."

Jack followed his gaze. "Cute, too. I love his big ears."

Isaac laughed. "And he obviously loves your hairstyle."

Jack chuckled. "Yeah." He paused. "I guess I just wanted to clear things up with you first."

"I'm sorry I can't be what you hoped for."

"It's okay. I get it."

He was looking past Isaac when he spoke and as Isaac turned, Drágan was there, gazing down at him.

"How are you?"

"Better. Jack and me have been talking."

"Good. Now, may I have this next dance with my best friend?"

Isaac looked past him at the dancers. The DJ was playing something slow, and everyone was holding each other close. "But they're slow dancing."

"Exactly. The music is calm now."

"But we're boys. I mean, we can't..."

"Stephanie and Mary Anne are dancing together. They're best friends."

Isaac saw the two girls dancing close, Stephanie with her head on Mary Anne's shoulder.

"They're girls, it okay for them."

Drágan gave an exasperated sigh. "You Americans and your phobias about boys being close with one another."

"He's right, Isaac," Jack said as Nathaniel approached to sit down. "Hey Nat, wanna dance?"

Caught off-guard, Nathaniel removed the cookie from his mouth and eyed the dancers nervously. "Uh, but they're, you know, slow dancing."

"Exactly," said Jack, standing and holding out his hand. Grinning, Nathaniel tossed the cookie onto the table and allowed Jack to lead him onto the dance floor. Isaac watched them lean in close, arms wrapped around one another.

"You see," Drágan said, "boys do dance together." He extended his hand.

Isaac pushed away his fears, took the offered hand, and allowed Drágan to lead him among the dancers. Dragan wrapped his arms around Isaac's waist. Isaac did the same to him and their bodies pressed against each other. Isaac laid his head against Drágan's shoulder and closed his eyes.

They swayed to the soft beat of the music. At first, Isaac heard and smelled everything: clothes rustling, strong perfumes and colognes, the musky odor from some of the boys, not to mention some gossipy whispers about them dancing together. He inhaled Drágan's intoxicating aroma, felt his steady heartbeat, and focused on his stable breathing.

Slowly, as they swayed and turned, Isaac pushed out of his conscious mind everything but the boy in his arms. The DJ played three slow tunes in a row and Isaac never once opened his eyes. He now understood how to block out the world, and he knew something else too. Something he could no longer deny.

The dancers clapped for the DJ, who cranked up some heavy dance music.

Isaac stood facing Drágan. "I tuned it all out, thanks to you. Even now, that loud music doesn't bother me."

Drágan looked uneasy. "You dance well" was all he said, but Isaac was sure he wanted to say more.

Drágan broke eye contact and looked around.

Isaac followed his gaze. Mary Anne was dancing with a guy Isaac didn't know. "Where's Stephanie?"

"My question exactly."

They pushed their way through bouncing and flailing dancers to Mary Anne. Isaac got her attention.

"Where's Stephanie?"

"Ladies room," she said, turning back to her dance partner.

Drágan wore a look of dread. "I'll search for her."

He hurried through the dancers and struck out across the gym.

Isaac decided to ask his mom if she'd seen Stephanie.

"No, honey, I haven't," she said when Isaac had made his way off the dance floor and joined her at the refreshment table. "You thirsty?

He cast her a look. "That a trick question?"

She looked abashed. "Sorry. How are you handling all the noise?"

"It was hard at first, but when I danced with Drágan, I tuned everything out but him."

She smiled knowingly. "I noticed."

"Remember how whenever I'd get new hearing aids, I'd hear stuff I never did before?"

"Yeah. It drove you crazy, especially when I wasn't bothered by any of those sounds."

"Exactly," Isaac affirmed. "But once I got used to the new sounds, they didn't annoy me anymore. I think this is kind of like that, only bigger. But I'm dealing."

He glanced toward the door leading to the locker rooms and bathrooms.

"What's wrong?"

"Drágan went looking for Stephanie. He should be back by now. I'm gonna go look."

"Be careful, Isaac."

He glanced back. "Nobody can bully me now."

He jogged to the door and pushed it open. The long hallway was empty. "Drágan? Stephanie?"

There was no answer. He hurried to the door to the girls' locker room. Cracking it open, he called in, "Stephanie?"

Where could she be?

He looked to the end of the hall and noticed the door ajar. He heard voices. He was at the door in seconds and pushed it outward. There was an SUV idling in the dimly lit parking lot. Jourdain and another man were loading someone unconscious into the back seat.

Drágan!

Jourdain turned and smiled. He raised what looked like a gun.

"Look out!" came Stephanie's voice from behind him just as Jourdain fired.

Isaac reacted instinctively. He leaped into the air and twisted so the projectile whizzed past, striking the door behind him. By the time he'd landed on his feet like a gymnast, the SUV was pulling away with a screech of tires.

Isaac turned to find Stephanie attempting to stand. He grabbed her arm and helped her to her feet.

"What happened?"

"Some guy poked me with a needle when I came out of the locker room." She caught her breath. "I felt drunk or something and the guy dragged me out here. When Drágan came through the door, Jourdain fired a dart at him. It knocked him out."

"Thanks for the warning."

"How did you do that, jump into the air and everything?"

"I'll explain later. I gotta save Drágan!"

19

THE FINAL BATTLE

Isaac sat in front of the van with his mom, while the others huddled in back. Nathaniel had his crossbow locked and loaded, and Jack sat ready to hand him more arrows.

At first, Penelope didn't want him to go, but Isaac threatened to just follow the tracks on foot, even though the delay could mean serious harm to Drágan. Maybe even death. That scared her and, after hanging one of Nathaniel's large crosses around her neck, she agreed to drive.

The other kids insisted on coming, despite Penelope telling them to stay at the dance.

"What if this is just a trick to lure Isaac away," Mary Anne said, "so Jourdain can come back for us?"

Everyone turned to Isaac.

"I don't know Jourdain like Drágan does. That might be his plan."

"He used me to get Drágan," Stephanie said, "but maybe you got there before they could take me, too. I think we should go, Mrs. Foster." She held up two more large crosses for her and Mary Anne. "We have these, and we won't do anything stupid."

That's how they all ended up in Penelope's van following the tracks left by Jourdain's SUV. Despite the darkness, Isaac had seen the tracks clearly with his enhanced vision and memorized the tread pattern before they set off in pursuit. Ten miles later, he peered through the windshield, his keen eyes still able to follow the tires' imprint along the dirt road.

"Turn right here," he said, pointing to what looked like a long driveway.

His mom turned without question, and they proceeded up a dark, bumpy lane.

Isaac's blood had boiled with fury ever since they left the school. He'd destroy Jourdain one way or another!

He heard Stephanie whisper to Mary Anne, "How can Isaac see in the dark like that?"

Mary Anne shushed her.

A house came into view in the distance. One first-floor window displayed flickering light, but the house looked dilapidated and abandoned. With his newly found night vision, Isaac spotted the SUV half-hidden beneath some trees next to the house.

"We're here. Pull up next to the SUV, Mom."

"What SUV?"

"You'll see it in a minute."

Soon, the SUV appeared within the van headlights.

"Headlights off, Mom."

She turned off the lights. "Now I can't see. There's no lights around here."

"I can see," Isaac said. "Ease forward."

She followed his instructions.

"Okay, stop."

She put the van in park. Isaac turned to the others in the back.

"I'm going in. Nathaniel and Jack, you guys can stand guard outside the van with the crossbow. Everyone else, stay here and have your crosses ready."

Stephanie reached over the front seat and grabbed his arm. "You can't go in there, Isaac! He'll kill you!"

"No, he won't."

Without awaiting a response, he popped open the door and

pelted toward the house. He easily picked out the front door and slammed into it, shattering the rotted wood to splinters. Flickering candlelight at the end of the hall drew his attention. He sprinted to the end in a split-second and burst into a dirty, cobweb-infested dining room furnished only with a long beat-up table and one chair with a single candle resting on it.

Isaac needed but an instant to make out Drágan lying atop the table with Jourdain preparing a large syringe, but as important as that was, he registered the two men pointing guns at him as more crucial. He leaped into the air as both fired. He heard the darts stick into the wall behind him with a double *thud*.

Jourdain spun to face him, grinning. "You're the living proof that my plan will work."

"What plan?" Isaac crouched behind the chair, searching for an opening to attack.

"It's quite simple," Jourdain replied, picking up a dart gun from the table. "I shall use his blood, and yours, to create an army of hybrids who will follow my orders and mine alone. The human race will stand no chance against me."

He fired a dart, but Isaac wasn't there when it struck the chair. Jourdain left Drágan's table, waving his men to surround Isaac, who crouched in one darkened corner.

"Your single biggest weakness is that you're still mostly human." He fired again. The dart struck the floor by Isaac's foot. "You are susceptible to these drugs. I'm not."

"You're susceptible to this, bitch!" came Nathaniel's voice near the door as the bolt from his crossbow struck Jourdain in the arm, forcing him to drop his dart gun.

"Get out, Nathaniel!" Isaac shouted, cursing their foolishness in leaving the van.

"Get them all!" the vampire hissed to the two men, who began firing at Nathaniel as Jourdain pulled the bloody bolt from his arm.

Isaac leaped into the air, grabbing both darts before they could strike his friend, landing with a roll and crouching for the next attack.

"Another bolt!" Nathaniel shouted to Jack.

Jourdain had the syringe in hand, prepared to extract Drágan's blood. Isaac saw it all with complete clarity. A large glass container awaited his friend's coveted blood.

"Don't you touch him!" Isaac screamed as he leaped across the length of the room straight at the vampire.

Jourdain lifted a second dart gun hidden beneath Drágan's arm and fired. The dart struck Isaac in the shoulder, and he spiraled out of control, crashing onto the ground at the vampire's feet. He should have broken multiple bones, but his powerful new body was uninjured. He yanked out the dart and threw it angrily aside, but some of the drug had gotten into his system. He could almost see it working its way through his bloodstream. He tried to stand, but his legs felt wobbly.

Jourdan stood over him, pointing the gun at his chest. "You lose, baby boy."

A thunderous growl tore through the room. Isaac could make out the two men staggering back as Jourdain spun around to confront...a werewolf!

Drágan had transformed without the moon!

Screams assailed Isaac's ears. Stephanie and Mary Anne were in the room shrieking in horror. The werewolf leaped off the table and slashed its huge claws at Jourdain, raking them across his chest and tearing open his flesh. The vampire screeched as one of Nathaniel's bolts planted itself in his lacerated torso.

Jourdain stumbled back as the werewolf lunged to rip his throat out. The vampire dodged, pushed both his servants at the slavering werewolf, then leaped through the broken glass of the window as another bolt from the crossbow planted itself in his back.

The werewolf pounced on the two terrified men, ripping them to shreds.

"Let's get out of here!" Jack shouted.

Isaac watched the werewolf sink its jaws into the soft flesh of the dead men and heard the crunching of bones as the creature eviscerated them. The smell of death strengthened Isaac, and he dropped to the floor, licking up the rivulets of blood flowing his way.

"Isaac!"

"Stay out, Mom! He won't hurt me!"

Was that true?

Isaac was about to find out. Energized now as the fresh blood counteracted the tranquilizer in his system, Isaac leaped to his feet.

The werewolf spun around, muzzle red with blood, strips of flesh dangling from its teeth. Drágan as a werewolf wasn't much taller than Drágan as a boy. It stared at Isaac, emitting a low growl from deep in the pit of its stomach.

"Drágan, it's me, Isaac."

The werewolf lurched closer on its muscular legs, seeming to squint as it studied Isaac's face. It sniffed the air. Then it reached out one hairy arm toward Isaac's face. Isaac felt the back of the creature's long nails gently graze his cheek.

Isaac touched its bloody mouth. "It's just me."

The werewolf raised its head and let out an ear-splitting howl before spinning around and leaping out the shattered window.

Isaac licked the blood off his fingertips as his mom rushed forward and engulfed him in a crushing hug. He'd been so focused on Drágan that he only now realized that the candle had fallen off the chair; the old, dry wood of the house was on fire. It licked its way up the walls to the ceiling at a rapid rate.

"We have to go, Isaac!" Holding a cross in one hand, his mother grabbed his arm and pulled him through the door and down the hall.

The others were waiting outside when Isaac and his mom emerged through the shattered front entrance. The werewolf was gone. So was Jourdain. Nathaniel held his crossbow at his side, while Jack stood between Stephanie and Mary Anne, all with their crosses held out.

Isaac looked around in the dark, but neither saw nor smelled the werewolf. "What happened to Drágan?"

"He ran off into the woods," Stephanie said, her eyes wide with fear.

Isaac and Penelope stepped closer.

His friends lurched back, raising their crosses higher.

As though burned, Isaac gasped and looked down.

"How...how did you do those things in there?" Jack asked.

"And why is there blood on your mouth?" Stephanie asked, grimacing with revulsion.

Isaac wiped away the blood with his sleeve. "I have a lot to tell you, but in the van. Jourdain is still out here. And please don't point your crosses at me."

Stephanie gazed at him in horror and Jack gasped in surprise.

"You mean you're..." Stephanie couldn't continue.

"In the van," Isaac hissed, still staring at the dirt around his feet.

Lowering their crosses, they scrambled back into the van. Isaac entered last and then Penelope spun the van around to head in the direction of home. Behind them, the old house burned, lighting up the area as it crumbled in on itself.

Penelope said, "Issac, call 911 about the fire."

He complied. Not knowing the address, he told the dispatcher he could see flames over the tops of trees and smoke in the air.

Isaac fretted over Drágan while he told his friends the story of how Drágan's blood saved his life after Jourdain's attack.

"I should've known it was a trap," Isaac lamented, wanting to kick himself as he retold the story. "But I was afraid for you, Stephanie."

She nodded, absorbing his tale in silence.

"So, what, you're like Drágan now," Jack asked, "a vampire *and* a werewolf?"

"And immortal," Isaac added, the weight of his differentness really hitting him for the first time as his friends stared at him in horror.

"Oh, wow," Stephanie mumbled. She reached out and took his hand. "There's gotta be a cure, right?"

"Drágan's been looking for one for a long time. My neighbor, Doctor Wilson, is a blood specialist. He's working on it."

"So, there's hope?" Mary Anne seemed especially excited by this news.

Isaac shrugged. Was there?

"Now I get why you could hear me so good at the dance," Jack muttered, and Isaac nodded.

They rode the rest of the way in silence. Nathaniel and Jack got out at Nathaniel's house.

"You're not walking home tonight, are you, Jack?" Isaac asked.

"No. Kicking it here tonight. Don't worry, we won't let anyone in." He made eye contact with Isaac. "See you tomorrow?"

"Course."

At Stephanie's house, no lights burned and the front door stood open.

"Something's wrong," Stephanie gasped, frightened. "Mom promised to keep the door locked."

Isaac slid the van door open and dropped to the pavement. "Wait here."

He listened as he hurried up the walkway to the open front door. He heard no life signs, no heartbeats from within. Pushing open the door, his night eyes scanned the entry hall, then he moved to the living room. He'd smelled the blood from outside, so he wasn't surprised to see Stephanie's petite mother with two punctures in her throat, and her despicable stepdad lying a short distance away. His throat had been more badly damaged, as though he struggled before Jourdain drained his body of blood.

Isaac barely knew Stephanie's mom, but he did know how his friend would take this news. He exited the house with care, knowing enough not to disturb the crime scene, and returned to the van. Stephanie and Mary Anne stood outside with Penelope.

"I'm sorry, Stephanie," Isaac said, filled with sadness. "Jourdain was here tonight."

"My mother?"

Isaac shook his head.

Stephanie screamed, "Mom!" and lurched toward the house. Isaac and Penelope held her back.

"You don't wanna go in there."

Looking shellshocked, she collapsed into Mary Anne's arms, sobbing. Then Penelope drew her into a hug as the inconsolable girl wept. Fighting back his own tears, Isaac asked the stunned Mary Anne, "Can she stay with you?"

Mary Anne nodded, makeup running down her tearstained face.

Together, they managed to get Stephanie back into the van and Penelope drove to Mary Anne's house. Mr. Givens met them in the driveway, shocked to see Stephanie and Mary Anne in tears.

"The vampire," Penelope told him. "It killed her parents. Can she stay with you, Greg?"

"My God," the man said, his craggy features melting with compassion. "I'll call the police too. You'd best get home, Penny."

He led the crying girls into the house. Isaac and his mom headed for their house.

"That poor girl," Penelope lamented, her voice breaking.

"She loved her mother so much," Isaac said, having absorbed the intensity of Stephanie's grief. He pictured her stepdad's dead body and considered that Jourdain had finally done something good.

Once they were inside their house with the doors locked, Isaac faced his mom, who looked wrung out from the night's events. "What about Drágan, Mom?"

"This is his home, honey. He'll find his way back."

"I'm sleeping down here so I can let him in."

"Of course." She leaned in and kissed him on the cheek.

"Drágan didn't kill me, Mom. He was right in front of me after he transformed, but he didn't even hurt me."

She eyed him knowingly as she started up the stairs. "Of course he didn't."

Still confused by the werewolf's actions, Isaac tromped up to his room and grabbed some of Drágan's clothes. As he sat against the wall by the side door, he wondered if Drágan *would* come home. Maybe he wouldn't change back into a boy. Why had he turned in the first place? The moon wasn't full for days yet.

He kept his ears attuned for any sounds outside, but finally sleep overcame him. He was still *mostly* human, after all, he thought, as he went under.

A NOISE WOKE HIM, and he sat upright, instantly awake. The sound came from upstairs. He jumped to his feet, agile as a cat, and pelted up the stairs. Early morning sunlight filtered through the fluttering drapes as he cautiously eased open his bedroom door.

Drágan stood there, naked, and bloody. Startled, he covered his privates with his hands until he realized it was Isaac.

Isaac closed the door and approached his friend, no longer uncomfortable with Drágan's nudity. He knew that, come the next full moon, this would be him.

"I was waiting by the side door. Why didn't you knock?" Isaac asked, glancing at the open window.

"I was afraid it would be your mother who opened the door."

"Good point." Isaac studied Drágan, but Drágan would not meet his gaze, which was unusual.

"I'd better clean up" was all Drágan said.

"You go shower. I'll bring your clothes from downstairs."

Isaac left the room. When he returned with the bundle of clothes in his hands, the shower was running. He set Drágan's clothes on the bathroom counter and left.

Isaac lay on his bed, listening to the shower and focusing on the steady flow of water, hoping it would calm his pounding heart.

He had so many questions for Drágan, but first there was the matter of Stephanie's parents to deal with, which would, of course, involve the police. When Drágan entered the room, his damp hair draping the back of his shirt, pale skin aglow in the light from the window, Isaac couldn't help but stare at him, seeing him in a new light. Drágan approached the bed, and Isaac sat up so his friend could sit beside him. A long moment of awkward silence followed.

"Are you all right?" Drágan finally asked.

"Yeah. You?"

Drágan nodded. "I don't know what happened after I was drugged. I think...I heard you fighting Jourdain and...I guess I transformed to save you. I mean, I've never transformed without the moon. I don't understand."

"I was drugged too. If you hadn't changed, well, who knows what would've happened. Jourdain took a beating, though."

"I suspect he will not return for some time."

"He..."

Drágan turned and made eye contact. "He what?"

"He killed Stephanie's parents."

There was a long moment of silence, then Drágan's handsome face clouded over with self-recrimination. "Wherever I go, death follows."

"That's not true! You've been nothing but good for this town. He's the monster, not you!"

Drágan flinched at Isaac's passion, yet still looked forlorn. "And you becoming like me? That's good?"

"You saved my life. I think that's good, don't you?"

Drágan met his gaze so deeply that Isaac squirmed. "I don't know what I would've done if you had died."

Isaac saw something in Drágan's eyes he hadn't seen before, but before he could respond, his mom's voice came from down the hall.

"Isaac!" The door opened and she stuck her head in. "Any sign of —" She spotted Drágan and hurried into the room, dropping to her knees, and throwing her arms around him. "Oh, honey, I'm so happy you're safe!"

She pulled back and he smiled.

"Did you tell him about Stephanie?" she asked Isaac.

"Yeah."

"I'm going to call Greg's place and find out how she's doing." She fixed her gaze on Drágan. "I'm so glad you're home."

"Thank you."

She rose to her feet and hurried from the room.

"The police might wanna talk to me," Isaac said to Drágan, "'cause I found the bodies. We need to explain where you were."

"I understand. Let's visit Dr. Wilson first to learn whether he sent out our blood samples. Now that you're like me, I'm more anxious than ever to find a cure."

"And I'm even more anxious to see *you* cured." Isaac blushed and looked away. "Uh, I'm gonna take a quick shower. Be back in a few."

After a shorter than usual shower, Isaac dressed and then told his mom they were going next door to see Dr. Wilson.

"Don't be long," she advised. "The police want to talk to you and me."

"I know. We'll be right back."

The air was cold, with a light breeze, and the sun shone brightly in the sky as the boys tramped through the trees to Wilson's front door.

It stood open.

Exchanging a quick look of foreboding, they hurried inside.

"Dr. Wilson?" called Drágan. There was no answer and Isaac heard no movement in the entire house.

Drágan tilted his head, listening. "Faint breathing. Hurry."

They sprinted down the long hall to the open basement door, descending rapidly to Wilson's laboratory. When Isaac entered, he saw chaos. Test tubes, Bunsen burners, microscopes, all the doctor's equipment lay on the floor smashed and broken. Various liquids stained the white tile a myriad of colors. A moan came from around the long table.

Doctor Wilson lay on the floor, two nasty gashes in his throat, his white lab coat splashed dark red, and blood pooling around his head. Barely conscious, he lifted one finger, urging them to come closer. They knelt on either side. Isaac listened to the slow, uneven heartbeat and knew there was no hope.

"Jourdain," Drágan muttered in anger.

"Stole your blood samples..." the doctor wheezed. "Both...of you."

"I'll call 911," Isaac said, pulling out his phone.

"No use," Wilson whispered. Each time he spoke, more blood dribbled from the twin gashes. He opened the fist that was clenched. Isaac saw a small scrap of paper. "Breslin's number...call her...find... cure."

His breathing stopped and he was gone, just like that. Drágan used his slender fingers to gently ease the doctor's eyelids shut while Isaac extracted the slip of paper from his hand.

"What's going on here?"

Isaac leaped to his feet, ready to fight, Drágan right beside him. Mr. Givens gazed in horror at the body of Dr. Wilson.

"The vampire, I'm guessing?"

Drágan replied, "Yes."

"Why kill *him*?" Mr. Givens asked.

Isaac sniffed the air, and he knew. "You're the werewolf!"

"Yes," Mr. Givens said sadly. "Wilson was trying to help me."

"Us, as well," Dragan added.

The tall man squinted at him. "I knew you for one of us first time we met."

Drágan replied, "And I you. We can smell the wolf in others."

"Yeah, I guess." Mr. Givens looked deflated, not at all like the harsh, gruff guy who'd been in their movie. He stared at Isaac, sniffing slightly. "You too? How?"

The boys briefly explained about Jourdain and Drágan's blood and how the vampire wanted to use it to create real monsters.

Mr. Givens glanced over at the open refrigerator. Isaac looked too. It was empty.

"May I ask how it happened to you?" Isaac said, curious.

"Hunting trip in the deep south," Mr. Givens drawled, dripping recrimination. "Got bit by something in the dark. My buddies drove it off and, well, you know the rest."

"That locked door in your barn," Drágan said. "A cage, perhaps?"

"You don't miss much, do you, kid? I started out with chains. Go off in the woods, chain myself to a tree, wait out the change. Once I got control of the howling, I built the cage."

"Does Mary Anne know?" Isaac asked.

"Oh yeah. Hard to keep a thing like that secret. She's been my rock ever since her mom died. Without her, I'd have been found out years ago."

"That explains how she so calmly accepted my existence," Drágan commented.

There was a moment of silence as all three gazed at the unmoving form of the doctor.

"Now what?" Mr. Givens asked.

Isaac held out the scrap of paper. "This doctor in South Dakota. We're gonna call."

"Wilson mentioned he was consultin' with her. Lemme know what she says."

"I will."

"You boys get on home. I'll call the cops, say it was me found him. No reason for you to get involved."

"Thanks, Mr. Givens," Isaac said, relieved that he wouldn't need to see the police twice.

"We're all in this together, right?"

"Yes, sir."

He and Drágan left the lab and exited the house through the back door.

Once back home, they told Penelope about Wilson.

"My God.... Is there no end to this evil?"

"Not while Jourdain lives," Drágan said. "He must be destroyed."

She nodded, looking weak and tired, not at all like her normal self. She took the phone number from Isaac. "I'll call Dr. Breslin."

20

CONFESSIONS AND GOODBYES

Isaac phoned Stephanie to check on her. "Anything I can do?"

When she spoke, he knew she'd been crying not long before. "I can't believe my mom is gone. I keep expecting her to walk in any minute."

"I'm sure," he said. What else was there to say? Death had a way of making every word sound banal, something Drágan had told him. "We're here, my mom too, if you need anything. If you wanna just come over and watch movies or something, send a text and we'll come get you."

"Thanks, Isaac. You're my best friend besides Mary Anne."

Isaac hung up, moved by her declaration, and turned to Drágan, who'd been listening. "This isn't your fault."

Drágan said nothing.

The boys walked down the hall to Penelope's office. She was just hanging up the phone. "I just spoke with Dr. Breslin. She was devastated to hear about Dr. Wilson, but she's willing to take on your case."

She stopped there, but Isaac knew her well enough to know there was more she hadn't said. "Okay, so what's the punchline?"

"We have to go to her."

"In South Dakota?"

"Yes. If we have a blood sample sent, she can only do so much. She needs you both there for study."

Isaac's temper, more volatile than before, rose like a hurricane and he shook with anger. "We have to leave our friends? That sucks! No way!"

She rose and placed her hands on his trembling shoulders. "It won't be forever, Isaac. We'll be back. You want a cure, don't you?"

Isaac met Drágan's gaze beside him and reined in his outburst. "'Course we do. When will we have to leave?"

"We'll wait until after the funerals," she said, "Dr. Wilson's and Stephanie's parents. The police need to finish their investigation." She paused, as though afraid he might explode again. "They're coming here today, to ask questions."

"What can we say about everything that went down last night?"

"Sit and let's talk."

She had a loveseat in one corner of her office, across from the built-in bookcases. They sat down and Drágan's extreme closeness, especially his scent, forced Isaac to concentrate on his mom, which wasn't easy. She'd spoken with Mr. Givens, and they had decided on the following story: Isaac and Drágan were feeling ill at the dance. The other kids didn't want to stay if the boys left, so Penelope brought them all to her house so the boys could lie down. The other kids hung around talking with them. When it was getting late, Penelope drove the others home. Drágan chose to stay at the house and sleep. That's when they found Stephanie's parents.

"This way, in case Jourdain killed them *after* you fought him, the timeline will work. Mary Anne has already called Jack and Nathaniel and told them this story in case the police question them."

Isaac turned to Drágan, their cheeks almost touching, and asked, "That work for you?"

Drágan nodded.

WHEN THE TWO uniformed officers entered the house, they greeted Penelope and Isaac like old friends. The officers' kids were at Mill-wood High and both officers were on the PTA. They all sat in the living room.

The male officer, named Hardwick, asked Penelope to describe what happened when they left the dance, and why. She retold the story she'd shared with the boys while the female officer took notes.

"Matches the story the other kids told," Hardwick said.

The second officer, Mason, looked up from her notetaking and said to Isaac, "I know this is hard, Isaac, but tell us what happened when you arrived at Stephanie's house."

Quelling his nerves, Isaac told her exactly what happened, how they found the door open, how he went in first, worried something might have happened. He described what he saw.

"Stephanie didn't enter at that time?"

"No, ma'am," Isaac answered. "She wanted to but my mom and me, well, *I* told her it was bad, so she changed her mind."

The officers seemed satisfied, and Mason closed her notebook.

"Any idea who could have done such a horrible thing?" Penelope asked.

"Never seen the like of it, Penny, and that's the truth," Hardwick said, shaking his head, almost looking ill. "The killings were beyond brutal. Keep your doors and windows locked and admit no one you don't know."

"Don't worry."

She saw the officers to the door and Isaac finally relaxed. "Do you think they suspect anything?"

"Their vocal patterns did not indicate suspicion," Drágan said evenly.

"And their heartbeats were steady," added Isaac. "I think we're okay."

Drágan eyed him. "You forget, Isaac, that we didn't commit the crime."

"I know."

Penelope returned and hugged them both before asking Drágan, "Do you think Jourdain might still be in the area?"

"He'll seek vengeance on us for hurting him, but he got what he wanted—our blood—so I believe he will proceed with his larger plan for now and save his revenge for a later time."

~

STEPHANIE DIDN'T RETURN to school until after her parents' funeral. Dr. Wilson had already been buried in a quiet ceremony. Isaac, Drágan, Penelope, and Mr. Givens were among the few mourners to pay their respects, and Isaac's anger rose once more against the medical establishment that had ostracized such a remarkable man. At least some of Wilson's brothers were there along with their families, so that was something.

Mr. Givens told them at the funeral for Stephanie's parents that the police had compared the way they were killed with what happened to Wilson and logically attributed the murders to the same killer, motive unknown.

Those first few days back in school after the murders felt somber for the Throwback Crew. Stephanie was the life of the group. Without her, they mostly ate in silence, attended their classes, and returned home. Isaac gained more control over his craving, with Drágan's help, and managed to get through most classes without the thirst overwhelming him.

Isaac and Drágan received checks in the mail from the film festival for winning their respective categories. Drágan received five hundred dollars—an ironic number, Isaac thought—while Isaac received two checks, five hundred for best director and one thousand for best film. It turned out that, even though the others had been given awards, only Isaac received a check for winning best film, so he split his money with the rest of the group. Drágan did the same.

Isaac's first full moon was suddenly upon him. Mr. Givens had dropped off a heavy set of chains with manacles similar to those

Drágan used. Ordinarily, Isaac wouldn't be able to lift them, but his enhanced strength made that task easy.

"I wish I could be with you, as you have been with me," Drágan said, his tone mournful.

"That's not gonna work this time." Isaac didn't like the idea of having no one watching over them. They'd be in separate locations and the police were still on high alert. Anything suspicious might send them into the woods.

Looking like a wrung-out dishrag, Penelope twisted her hands together at the thought of both boys out in the woods in their other forms. "I'll stay with you."

Isaac blushed and even Drágan's pale face reddened. "Mom, we're gonna be...you know, naked."

"So? Like I haven't seen you naked before?"

Embarrassed, Isaac replied, "When I was little, and, well, what about Drágan?"

"He's my son too. I don't want you both out there alone."

"Mrs. Foster," Drágan began, his calm and soothing, "I've made this transformation every month for hundreds of years. Wild animals will not approach a werewolf, and I do not howl. If Isaac does, Mr. Givens has already been talking up the "wolf" that was heard in the woods last month so people in town won't be surprised if they hear something."

"I still want to be there." Isaac knew that tone. His mom was adamant.

As though knowing the situation, Jack and Nathaniel showed up just then, unannounced, both carrying duffel bags. "We got permission to stay here overnight," Jack said proudly.

Bewildered by their arrival, Penelope said, "I don't understand."

"Tonight's the full moon, right?" Nathaniel asked.

"Yeah," replied Isaac, confused.

"Nat and me were talking," Jack went on, "and we thought you might want somebody out there while you're both, you know, chained up. We can make sure nobody messes with you."

They reached into their duffels and pulled identical crossbows.

Jack grinned. "Got my own, now."

Isaac and Drágan exchanged a look.

Isaac said, "We, uh, we're gonna be naked."

Nathaniel's eyes blew up to the size of golf balls. "Really? I'm in for sure."

Jack elbowed him. "We didn't know that part, really. Makes sense, I guess. Don't ruin all your clothes when you, you know." His face reddened. "It's not like we go looking for naked guys or nothing but, well, you know, we just wanna help."

Drágan said, "Would their presence ease your mind, Mrs. Foster?"

Still looking surprised by the sudden turn of events, she replied, "I guess so."

Isaac faced Jack and Nathaniel. "Okay. But no pictures!"

Jack's face twisted with shock and then the three boys cracked up. Drágan didn't seem to understand why they were laughing, which made them laugh even harder.

After an early dinner for all the boys, Isaac's mom pulled him into such a tight hug that he could barely breathe. "I love you so much, Isaac."

"I know, Mom," he said, pulling away and offering a nervous smile. "I have my best friends with me. It'll be fine. I'll see you in the morning." He hugged her again. "I love you."

Embarrassed in front of his friends, he released his mom and grabbed the large duffel Mr. Givens had given him containing the chains, while Drágan carried his valise. Jack and Nathaniel wore layers of clothes and lugged the sleeping bags Isaac loaned them, along with water, flashlights, and their crossbows.

It had been decided that Jack would watch over Isaac and Nathaniel over Drágan. In silence, the four trekked out to the first tree Drágan had used which, they'd decided, would be for Isaac this time. Jack and Nathaniel hid themselves while Drágan helped Isaac prepare for what would follow.

They wrapped his chain around the tree and secured it. Mr. Givens had supplied locks and keys. Isaac glanced up; the moon was nearly at its brightest.

"I'll be right back." Drágan took a rope from his bag and vanished into the woods.

"Can we come out yet?" Nathaniel called from somewhere in the darkness.

"Not yet," Isaac called back.

Drágan returned with a young deer walking placidly by his side. He secured it to the tree.

"I'll give you privacy," Drágan said, turning his back. It was time for Isaac to strip.

Taking off his clothes in the woods at night felt so foreign to Isaac he almost decided to let the clothes get shredded. But since he hadn't brought any others, he'd need these for going home in the morning. He kicked off his shoes, pulled off his shirt, and slipped out of his pants, laying them all atop his duffle. Then his socks followed suit. Down to his boxers, he glanced around for any sign of Jack and Nathaniel. Not spotting them, he made sure Drágan still had his back turned and rapidly slipped them off.

Feeling foolish covering his privates with his hands, he said, "I'm ready."

Drágan turned and was all business, which relaxed Isaac somewhat. Without checking him out in any way, Drágan clamped on the shackles to his wrists and ankles, suggesting Isaac sit against the tree with his legs up so he'd feel less exposed.

Isaac did so, but suddenly thought back on all his years of being considered a weak loser by other kids. For some reason, Drágan suggesting he should cover himself brought back those feelings of inadequacy.

"I'm not weak, you know, Drágan, even though everyone at school thinks I am."

Drágan looked down from where he stood, and they locked eyes. "You have never been weak from the moment I met you. You are, in fact, the strongest boy I've ever known."

Without another word, he turned, grabbed his valise off the ground and called out, "Nathaniel, follow me."

Nathaniel appeared from behind a tree, Jack by his side, and stared a long moment at Isaac as though he were a stranger, then tromped through the underbrush after Drágan.

Isaac gazed at the silent Jack. His oldest friend looked back with a kind of wonder Isaac hadn't expected.

"You're not cold?"

Isaac shook his head. "You can lay out your sleeping bag there." He pointed to a spot about twelve feet away.

"What's the deer for?" Jack asked, his voice trembling.

Despite it being dark, Isaac could make out every detail of his friend's frightened face. "Food," he said. "Don't worry if you can't watch everything. I freaked the first time I saw Drágan change, threw up all my dinner. You should've seen it. It was totally gross." He offered a tiny smile he hoped might put Jack more at ease.

"Okay." Jack's deepening voice sounded so small, like when they were little boys.

Isaac waited. It didn't take long. His body temperature soared, every fiber of his being feeling scorched and raw. A spasm shuddered through him, and his body jerked so violently it flew upward an inch off the ground. More spasms followed. His legs splayed out, then his arms and he was spasming on the hard ground. He felt like he was in the center of an inferno, as if his skin were melting and his limbs were being shorn off one by one. His body twisted; his bones seemed to crack open. His shackled hands became hairy claws. He shrieked in agony.

How had Drágan endured this torment for so many years?

That was Isaac's last conscious thought.

JACK REARED back in horror as the boy he'd grown up with jerked around, his limbs twisting in what looked like impossible directions. Hair sprouted on his soft white flesh, while toes and fingers became extended claws. But the face, that's what shocked Jack the most. Isaac's cute, gentle features morphed into a rounded toothy snout, and his usually tender eyes narrowed with menace.

Jack stood frozen in place during the transformation, which lasted less than a minute, he realized afterwards. But when the werewolf pounced on the deer and tore its head off, he had to stumble away, covering his ears to block out the tearing and ripping of flesh. Thinking about Isaac's vomiting joke distracted him enough that he kept his dinner down.

When at last, the thing that had been Isaac became quieter, Jack returned to his sleeping bag and sat. The restless werewolf fought against the chains, even tried biting through them. It caught Jack's scent and spun around, snarling.

Jack trembled with fear, but fought to control it. This was Isaac, after all, his first and best friend. He gazed into the animal's baleful eyes.

"I know you won't remember any of this tomorrow, but I didn't tell you the whole truth in the gym. I didn't just have a crush on you. I love you, Isaac Foster. I'll always love you, no matter who I end up with."

As though it understood him, the werewolf raised its head and emitted a mournful howl.

~

When Isaac stirred the following morning, he found Jack bent over him, wiping away the blood from his face, just as *he'd* done for Drágan. He sat up and saw that Jack's sleeping bag lay across his waist, giving him some measure of dignity.

"Thanks."

"It looked so...painful."

Vague memories of the transformation flitted around in Isaac's mind, and he shivered. "It was, for a bit. Then I don't remember anything." He stared so intently that Jack looked down. "I feel sad right now," Isaac continued. "I think I felt sad as the wolf, too, like something made me that way. But that doesn't make sense, does it?"

"I don't know." Jack would not make eye contact.

"Could you bring the key and my clothes?" Isaac asked.

As though happy not to be so close, Jack darted for the duffel and brought it over. He helped unlock the shackles and then turned his back while Isaac stood to dress. Remnants of the gutted deer lay strewn about, and Jack looked away from the carnage.

By the time Isaac was fully clothed, Drágan and Nathaniel appeared from behind some trees with all their gear packed up. Drágan went to Isaac while Nathaniel hurried to Jack.

"You survived," Drágan said.

"Yeah. Piece of cake."

Drágan grinned.

"Jack cleaned me off before I woke up."

"I think Nathaniel was too fearful to approach me until I awoke," Drágan said, glancing at the two whispering boys.

Isaac could've listened to their conversation, but he chose not to.

~

BACK AT THE HOUSE, **Penelope** had a huge breakfast waiting for the boys, which they devoured in short order.

"I didn't watch while he took his clothes off," Jack blurted halfway through the meal, as though thinking she might suspect he had.

"Me either," Nathaniel added, glancing shyly at Drágan. "I promise."

"You're both good friends," Drágan said. "Thank you for your loyalty."

Nathaniel grinned.

Isaac watched his mom during breakfast. She seemed happy to have a tableful of loud, hungry boys scarfing her food. He suspected, now that he'd survived his first transformation unscathed, she might not stress over him as much. Which eased his mind a bit.

~

THE FOLLOWING MONDAY, Stephanie returned to school. Social

services had not found any other relatives who could take her in, so for the time being, she would stay with Mr. Givens and Mary Anne.

The Throwback Crew stood reunited in the quad, away from everyone else, with Jack and Nathaniel filling in the girls on their night in the woods.

"Were you scared?" Mary Anne asked. "I know I was, the first time I saw my dad like that."

"Scared? Of Isaac?" Jack joked. "No way." He gave Isaac a gentle shove and then shrugged. "Okay, a little."

Isaac and Mary Anne laughed.

"I was scared, I admit it," Nathaniel said quietly. "I mean, his mouth was like this big." He exaggeratedly held his hands as wide apart as he could. "And the teeth? Made Jaws look like a goldfish."

Stephanie had just listened, uncharacteristically quiet.

"We're really glad you're back, Steph," Isaac said. "This place is so boring without you."

She forced a smile. "You know it. Now that I'm here, the Throwback Crew will be even more lit."

Jack chose this moment to confess to the others what he'd already told Isaac, about his crush on Isaac and why he became a bully. He seemed more relaxed this time, perhaps because Isaac hadn't rejected him. Nathaniel seemed the most shocked, and said nothing, as though his shyness had suddenly returned.

Stephanie announced that she'd started therapy to cope with everything that had happened to her. "It's really helpful to tell all that stuff to a stranger. But no one's better than my friends."

She offered a smile, and all was well with the Throwback Crew.

Except Isaac had yet to tell them he and Drágan were leaving.

He didn't know how.

Isaac sat alone at the kitchen table after school, debating how to tell the crew about their upcoming departure, while also trying to figure out how to tell Drágan something else—something even *more* important. As though reading his mind yet again, Drágan entered, looking pensive.

"Might I join you?"

Isaac indicated the seat beside him. "Sure."

Drágan sat, and an awkward moment passed between them. Without looking up, he said, "I've not been fully honest with you."

Isaac started in surprise. "How?"

"When I first met Jourdain, I should have mistrusted such a man in my humble village," Drágan began, his voice breathy. "But I was... attracted to him and my boyish weakness led to my forever condition."

Isaac's heart began pounding. "Wait, are you saying...?"

Dragan nodded. "And that's not all. The movies have it wrong. I didn't kill you as the werewolf because...we cannot harm the ones we love the most."

Isaac's breath nearly stopped.

"I've tried my hardest to resist you," Drágan went on, his voice reeking with sadness, "for fear you'd reject me. But my feelings remain what they are." He kept his head bowed in regret.

Isaac sat stunned, unable to move for a long moment. "I uh, I guess that makes us even."

Drágan jerked up his head. "What do you mean?"

"I can't hurt you either."

Drágan gazed at him in amazement, his mouth hanging open.

"It sort of snuck up on me. I mean, I never thought of boys like that before, at least I don't think I did, not even Jack. But then you came along, all beautiful and strong and so willing to help me without asking for anything in return." He glanced down. "I finally knew I loved you when we were slow dancing in the gym. But I didn't say anything because, well, I thought *you* would reject *me*."

Drágan shook his head with wonder. "To see so much in others," he said with a heavy sigh, "but to miss the obvious in ourselves."

"Crazy, huh?"

Drágan nodded, but he smiled then, looking happier than he ever had. Isaac understood that happiness, for he felt it within himself.

"I've been wondering, you know," Isaac said, hesitantly because he was nervous, "not that it's a huge deal or anything, but, uh, you know, what it'd be like to... maybe, well, kiss you?"

Drágan's beautiful face clouded over, the smile gone in an instant. "That we cannot do. Passion, even kissing, ignites the vampire within." He paused to collect his thoughts. "Do you recall I spoke once of my most painful memory?"

Isaac nodded.

"Long ago in Paris, I met a boy my age who liked me, as I liked him. We spent much time together and Andre's love for me brought such joy. Until one night when we kissed. Overcome with bloodlust, I nearly drained him dry before I regained control."

Shocked, Isaac asked, "What happened?"

"Recovering myself, I rushed him to a medical facility. I later learned Andre had survived due to blood transfusions. I didn't know if he remembered what I'd done to him and I was too ashamed to find out. So I fled Paris, never to return."

Isaac sat in stunned silence, absorbing the reality of this story. "But, we're different, right? I mean, not quite human?"

"The bloodlust would arise no matter, and anyone in our vicinity would die."

Isaac gasped.

"Now do you understand why I couldn't kiss Stephanie, even within the confines of acting?"

Isaac nodded, disappointed he couldn't experience even that small amount of affection with Drágan. But they'd be cured one day. He had to believe that. He chose to believe it. Right now, what mattered most was that this boy he loved with all his heart, loved him in return. He reached over and took Drágan's hand in his.

"Is holding hands allowed?"

Drágan smiled. "It is."

They gazed into each other's eyes, and Isaac experienced a quiet joy he'd never felt before.

Penelope entered the kitchen and stopped short, seeing the boys holding hands. Drágan tried to pull away, but Isaac held his hand more firmly.

He looked up at his surprised mother, heart suddenly pounding with fear. "Mom, I love Drágan, which means, I guess, that I like boys, so now you know and I, uh, I hope you still love me?" He teared up, awaiting her reaction.

Her face lost its momentary surprise and broke into a beautiful smile. "You're a werewolf, and a vampire, but you think because you like boys I'll stop loving you?" She tousled his hair and bent to pull him into a warm hug. "I'll always love you, Isaac. You're the light of my life." She reached around and pulled Drágan into the hug. "So are you, Drágan. I love you both."

Isaac blinked back tears of joy.

"Thank you, Mrs. Foster," Drágan said as she stood and gazed tearfully at them both.

"Don't you think you should start calling me Mom, Drágan? Mrs. Foster sounds like we're strangers."

Drágan wiped the moisture from his eyes. "As you wish. Mom."

She studied him with love in her bright eyes. "And maybe you should stop trying to be an adult and just be a kid for once."

"I shall attempt it."

She gave him a significant look.

His face faltered, as though considering his mistake. "Bruh?" He looked hopeful.

She and Isaac laughed.

"Not quite, but you're getting there," she said.

WITH DRÁGAN convinced that Jourdain had left the area, Penelope was making plans to drive the boys to South Dakota. Isaac knew he only had a few days left with his friends, but he just couldn't bring himself to tell them.

Drágan suggested they invite everyone to the house for a party and tell them at that time. Penelope loved the idea, so Isaac agreed.

At Penelope's suggestion, the Throwback Crew members wore their vintage clothing to the party. Isaac, his mom, and Drágan had decorated the house with streamers and balloons. Penelope had ordered plenty of pizza and had soft drinks and other junk food on hand. The kids could play games or just talk and hang out.

Jack and Nathaniel arrived first and began batting balloons at each other, laughing like little boys. Mr. Givens dropped off the girls and hung out in the kitchen with Penelope.

Mary Anne whispered to Isaac, "I think my dad likes your mom."

Isaac just shrugged. *You go, Mom.*

Everyone looked so awesome in their vintage clothes, he decided to dress that way all the time. When he announced this over pizza, the others cheered.

"You know," Stephanie said, "that's a good idea. Ms. Rachel has some cute clothes."

Suddenly, they'd all decided to adopt Drágan's style of dress, to his obvious amusement.

"Okay, time for announcements," Stephanie decreed. "I'll start. That super cute guy from the film festival wants to hang out with me. It'll feel good to do something fun after all that's happened. And he's a tenth grader!"

Mary Anne squealed, "I'm next." She cleared her throat. "The hot lead in that swoony romance flick wants to hang out with *me*. Stephanie and me are gonna double date."

Everyone lustily congratulated them both.

Jack stood up and bowed until everyone threw chips at him.

"Thank you, thank you," he said, and didn't continue until the group's laughter had died down. "*My* announcement is that...you all know how I liked Isaac and that's why I treated him like garbage. Mr. Sommers would say that's irony, right? Well, I'm okay with how I am now, even though I haven't told my mom yet. Gotta work up to that. But anyway, well, Nat and me are kind of, well, officially official." He grabbed Nathaniel's hand and dragged him to his feet. "At least with this group and for doing crazy-ass stuff like holding hands." He lifted their clasped hands. "Meet Jackaniel."

They all groaned as they applauded.

"Just stick with Jack and Nat," Stephanie urged as she hugged them both.

"We would never use that cringe name," Nathaniel said as they reseated themselves on the floor. "We just wanted to hear you all groan."

That got popcorn thrown at him.

Isaac knew that now was the time, so he stood as they all clapped and cheered.

"Speech, speech!"

Isaac hesitated, unsure how to start. He glanced down at Drágan seated by his feet. Drágan's look of encouragement spurred him on.

"First of all, I want to say that you are the best friends I'll ever have."

They all cheered and whooped.

"Course we are," Stephanie said smugly, which got popcorn thrown at *her*.

"Anyway, after my mom, you're the first to know that, well, to use Jack's words, Drágan and me are officially official." He took Drágan's hand in his, and the other boy rose to stand beside him as everyone *oohed*. "And, like Jackaniel, we're acting wild by holding hands, which feels amazing, I have to say."

The kids went crazy, whooping and clapping and cheering. Both girls hugged the boys, giving them kisses on the cheek.

"I had a feeling you guys were into each other," Stephanie said after kissing Isaac's cheek.

Mary Anne nodded. "Me too."

"And you're the cutest couple ever," Stephanie concluded, earning a, "Hey, what about us?" from Nathaniel sitting on the floor.

That got *more* popcorn thrown at *him*.

When the girls reseated themselves on the floor, Jack rose to stand before Isaac. Their eyes met.

"I'm happy for you, bro," Jack said with a genuine smile that lit up his handsome face. "Really."

"And me for you," Isaac replied, returning the smile with one of his own.

They hugged as only two life-long friends can, gently and with deep affection.

Jack sat back down beside Nathaniel, but Isaac and Drágan remained standing.

"There's more?" Stephanie asked. "No, wait. One of you isn't pregnant, are you?"

Drágan's face collapsed with horror and Isaac blushed. He grabbed a couch pillow and threw it at her as everyone crumpled with laughter.

Isaac's face grew somber. "I do have news that I don't like." Everyone fell silent, realizing he was serious. "You all know that Dr. Wilson was trying to cure Drágan, and then me too, and now he's dead. But there's another doctor who might figure out how to fix our blood."

Stephanie's face lit up. "That's awesome!"

"She's in South Dakota," Isaac went on, his tongue dry. "The doctor, I mean."

"Wait," Mary Anne said, her expression uncertain, "you have to go there?"

Isaac nodded. "We leave tomorrow."

Pandemonium erupted as everyone spoke at once.

"You can't leave us," Stephanie said when the tumult died down. "I mean, you can't. We're the Throwback Crew. You started it with your movie. You're the most important one of us!"

"No, you are, Steph," Isaac said with sincerity. "You can keep the crew together till we come back."

"When will that be?" Jack asked, no longer smiling.

Isaac blinked back tears. "I don't know. Months, maybe more. We don't wanna go, but we gotta find a cure, don't you see?" Tears rolled down his cheeks. "If we don't, you'll all leave us behind. We'll have to watch you graduate, then watch you become adults, and...we'll still be...kids."

Stephanie jumped to her feet and threw her arms around him.

"That's not gonna happen, okay?" She stepped back and faced him. "You're gonna stay with us, cure or no cure. You tell the school you have some weird blood thingie that stunts your growth. But you *will* graduate with us, you hear me?"

"Stephanie…" Isaac began.

"I just lost my mom, and I won't lose you too! Promise we graduate together. Promise me!"

Isaac didn't know what to say.

From the floor, Jack said, "After everything that's happened, Isaac, we gotta stick together."

Isaac glanced at Drágan, who nodded in agreement.

"Okay, I promise." He wiped the tears from his cheeks.

Ecstatic with relief, Stephanie threw her arms around him again and kissed him on the cheek so hard he turned red. The others were on their feet hugging him and Drágan in a big circle of friendship.

Isaac's brain was overwhelmed with their scents, their competing heartbeats, and their tearful expressions. He closed his eyes and focused on only one heartbeat, that of the boy who completed him.

When Isaac and the others sat back down, Drágan remained standing, looking like he was considering what to do.

"C'mon, Drágan, sit next to me," Isaac urged, loving the gentle sound of the other's heartbeat close to his ears.

"In the spirit of learning how to be a modern teenager," Drágan began, as though he'd rehearsed what he would say, "I have a surprise that even Isaac doesn't know about."

Isaac did a double take.

The other kids shifted with anticipation.

"Don't keep us waiting," Stephanie urged.

"Yeah, out with it," Jack ordered with a grin.

"You all know that I'm a model, right?"

Everyone nodded.

"Well, we'll need money to pay Dr. Breslin in South Dakota," Drágan went on, "so I've accepted an offer to take part in a fashion show in New York City."

Isaac was surprised he didn't know, but he and the other boys took the news calmly. The girls, however, went crazy with excitement, demanding to know all the details and where they could watch it.

"According to my agent, the event will be televised," Drágan went on when the girls stopped pelting him with questions. Before they could start again, he added, "I will, of course, let you all know how you can watch it. We'll stop in New York on our way to South Dakota."

Isaac looked up at him from the floor. "Why didn't you tell me that? I think it's great."

Drágan offered a mischievous smile. "My agent asked me if I knew of another handsome boy because the fashion show was minus one model."

Isaac froze.

"Naturally, I sent her a photo of the handsomest boy I know." He proudly pulled his cell phone from one pocket, as though finally joining the ranks of teenagers the world over. "This was my agent's response." He slid open a text message and read aloud. "OMG, he's cute as hell! Yes, they will want him. I want him. With you two as a team, I can get you both so much work. Tell him he'll be rich."

Isaac's mouth hung open and his face turned beet red. The girls crowed with delight and hugged him at the same time.

"I told ya you were cute," Stephanie said with a warm smile.

"I told him first," Drágan said, grinning broadly.

"This is so exciting!" Stephanie exclaimed.

"You guys'll steal the whole show," Mary Anne gushed.

Drágan sat and handed Isaac his phone. Isaac didn't recognize the photo. It was a shot of him outside looking at something that wasn't in the picture.

"When did you take this photo?"

"When you weren't looking."

"I'm not a model, Drágan."

"All you need to do is walk and pose," Drágan said, slipping his hand into Isaac's. "Your natural charm will do the rest."

"If you don't do this, Isaac," Stephanie warned in that dangerous tone she had, "I swear I'll never speak to you again."

"You wouldn't do that and you know it," Isaac tossed back, but considered that she might.

"You're right. But please do this. I'm so excited about seeing you both on TV."

Her pleading eyes convinced him. "Okay." Then to Drágan, he added, "You really make that much money?"

Drágan nodded.

"If your agent still wants me after this show, I'll keep modeling with you. That way Mom won't have to spend all her money on doctors."

"You're a good son," Drágan replied and gave Isaac's hand a gentle squeeze.

After the hubbub about the fashion show died down, Mary Anne asked, "What will you do in South Dakota? Sounds boring."

"Well, for one thing, I'll explore more film festivals for *Wolfboy*," Isaac said.

"We can help with that," interjected Stephanie, indicating herself and the others.

"Good idea," Isaac said. "Send me what you find out. Also, I gotta choose a King story to film. Send me your suggestions." He paused, eyed the silent Drágan a moment, then added, "I'm also working on a new script for my favorite actors."

Drágan raised his eyebrows. "Really? What's the plot?"

Isaac kept a straight face. "Have you had any experience playing... a vampire?"

Drágan's eyes bulged in surprise and his mouth dropped open.

Everyone burst into laughter at the comical expression on his face.

"Gotcha," said Isaac.

Looking peeved, Drágan muttered, "Bruh."

But then he laughed.

Finally, he laughed.

THE END

ABOUT THE AUTHOR

Michael J. Bowler is the award-winning author of *A Matter of Time*, *THE LANCE CHRONICLES*, *THE HEALER CHRONICLES*, *THE FILM MILIEU THRILLER SERIES*, *THE INVICTUS CHRONICLES*, and *THE FOREVER SAGA*.

His screenplay, "The God Machine," won First Place in the 2017 Scriptapalooza competition and First Place in the 2023 Tarzana International Film Festival.

He grew up in San Rafael, California. He worked as producer, writer, and/or director on several ultra-low-budget horror films, including "Hell Spa," "Fatal Images," "Club Dead," and "Things II."

He taught high school in Hawthorne, California—both in general education and to students with learning disabilities—in subjects ranging from English and Strength Training to Algebra, Biology, and Yearbook.

He has been a volunteer Big Brother to eight different boys with the Catholic Big Brothers Big Sisters program, a decades-long volunteer within the juvenile justice system in Los Angeles and is a single father to an adopted child.

Website: michaeljbowler.com
FB: michaeljbowlerauthor
Twitter: @MichaelJBowler
Instagram: @michaeljbowler
Pinterest: http://www.pinterest.com/michaelbowler/pins/
YouTube: https://www.youtube.com/channel/ UC2NXCPry4DDgJ-ZOVDUxVtMw

To join my mailing list, go my website and sign up. I offer free books and access to preview copies of my upcoming works.

FOREVER SAGA TWO PREVIEW

FOREVER SAGA 2

If you enjoyed FOREVER BOY,
check out this excerpt from the forthcoming sequel,
FOREVER BONDS

Isaac gazed at himself in the full-length mirror while Drágan looked on, smiling. The large dressing room within the bowels of the massive Manhattan Center, a stone's throw from Madison Square Garden, provided ample space for all models to access the various outfits they'd wear for the show.

Isaac had been blown away by the sheer size and height of NYC, and Manhattan, especially the Empire State Building which he knew only from the original *King Kong*, and One World Trade Center which he'd seen on the news.

Having been to the city before, Drágan was nonplussed by the size and scale of their surroundings but relished Isaac's almost child-like wonder at all the lights and sounds and sensations that make NYC one of the most famous cities in the world.

Isaac focused on his image in the mirror. He wore a casual outfit for young men that had too much flowy material around the arms and shoulders for his taste, but it fit well and looked good on him. His hair had been professionally styled and was wavier than usual as it swept across his forehead, and a lady had put makeup on to highlight his face and eyes.

Drágan said, "You look perfect. I wouldn't be surprised if someone in the audience wants to buy you instead of the clothing."

Isaac chuckled and gave him a shove, grateful that Drágan was helping him overcome his bout of nerves. Terror was a more accurate word, but Isaac determined not to disappoint Drágan or his agent, who'd entrusted Isaac with this opportunity.

"Do you think your agent likes me?"

"She loves you. Trust me, I know. And she knows about me, at least that my blood prevents my aging."

Isaac froze. "She does? What if she tells someone?"

"She won't. If she decides to keep you on her client list, and I'm sure she will, we should consider sharing your forever status with her, as well. But for now, you must get through tonight. Are you ready?"

Isaac trembled with fear. Hundreds of people would be out in the auditorium staring at him, so he couldn't help but feel self-conscious.

"I think so. I've never been in front of so many people before."

Drágan placed his hands on Isaac's shoulders and gave a gentle squeeze. "I'll be right there with you. Just walk and turn like we rehearsed and smile a lot. You have a beautiful smile, Isaac. Use it."

His words drew out that smile and Drágan returned it with love.

A voice came over the speaker embedded high up in the call calling for all models to gather backstage in preparation for the start of the show. Isaac and Drágan would be modeling ten different outfits ranging from formal to dressy to casual during the course of the show and thus would be back and forth to the dressing room all evening.

Isaac felt panic overtake him knowing he was about to enter the lion's den.

"Remember," Drágan said, "focus on smiling and walking so you can tune out all the sounds and smells you'll encounter."

Isaac nodded.

~

Despite everyone gathering at Mary Anne's house, Stephanie was in charge, which was fine with the others. Mary Anne had a 60-inch flatscreen in the living room which, at the moment, was surrounded by her, Stephanie, Jack, and Nat. Even a bemused Mr. Givens took a seat on the sofa to watch Isaac make his debut as a fashion model. Everyone had brought over drinks or snacks and the room bubbled with excitement.

"Look at the size of that place," Stephanie exclaimed, pointing at the TV displaying a wide shot of the venue. A long walkway extended outward from the stage while, on both sides, hundreds, maybe even a thousand chairs spread outward, already occupied by fancy-dressed people chatting each other up.

Stephanie turned to the others. "Do you think Isaac's nervous?"

Jack smirked. "Is Coach Lancaster a bitch?"

They all laughed, including Mr. Givens, and Nat squeezed Jack's hand lovingly.

"Isaac will be fine," Mary Anne offered around a mouthful of popcorn. "Drágan will make sure of that."

"It's starting, everyone quiet!" admonished Stephanie as she used the remote to turn up the volume. Her therapy had been going well at helping her make sense of the abuse and to cope with the loss of her mother. But her best source of stability were Mary Anne, Jack, and Nat, who'd been inseparable since the departure of Isaac and Drágan. While they'd Facetimed with the boys, this was the first time they would see Drágan modeling and, of course, Isaac making his debut. She bubbled over with anticipation.

As the models appeared on stage and started down the runway, an announcer with a deep voice described the clothing designers by name and said something about each outfit. The ladies wore casual dresses or business attire, all of which looked ordinary to Stephanie but which, she suspected, cost a fortune because of the designers behind them.

Jack and Nat were growing restless.

"Man, this is boring," Jack lamented.

"Yeah," agreed Nat as he munched on some chips. "I want Isaac and Drágan."

Mary Anne screamed so loudly that even Stephanie jumped. "Look, there's Drágan!"

The crowd went wild when Drágan appeared wearing billowy pants and a billowy shirt that looked loose enough to be impractical but was sheer enough to show off his finely shaped physique. Stephanie held her breath. Drágan had never looked more beautiful, she thought, as he strolled down the runway like he owned it, long, flowing hair wafting from side to side, face glowing with a tantalizing smile.

"My God is he beautiful," Mary Anne exclaimed, glued to the flatscreen.

"He really is, isn't he, Jack?" Nat said, his voice breathy.

"For sure," Jack agreed, leaning forward, arms across his knees.

As Drágan walked back toward the stage, Isaac appeared in the spotlight looking almost as beautiful. His light-brown hair was styled, his smile genuine as he casually strolled down the runway to almost as many cheers as Drágan had received. Most of the audience was women and they clearly loved both boys. Isaac wore slacks and a fancy shirt that seemed to fold over itself and looked impossible to put on or take off.

"Wow," Jack said, his tone one of awe.

Seemingly to distract Jack from Isaac, Nat asked the room at large, "Who would wear this stuff?"

"Rich people," grunted Mr. Givens, who looked perplexed by the whole event.

~

Isaac quelled the butterflies in his stomach as he strode casually along the runway smiling and hoping he appeared confident. He felt anything but confident, but he absorbed Drágan's scent as they passed each other, and that comforting smell kept him visibly at ease. The lights were bright so the clapping, energized people on either side of him remained a blur, but his finely tuned ears heard such comments as, "My God he is so cute!" and "Too bad he's underage," among others.

Had he not been so focused on maintaining a pleasant, charming demeanor, he'd have gagged to hear such words coming from adults directed at a boy. No wonder Drágan had described modeling as a heartless profession.

Once he and Drágan completed two tours of the runway, alongside other handsome young men, it was back into the dressing room to change into their next outfits. Isaac had been instructed by the showrunner to make certain "the clothing is respected" and to take expert care with every item. Backstage workers assisted Isaac and Drágan in removing their outfits and then hung them up like they were the crown jewels.

The boys were helped into their second outfits by these same men and Isaac felt like he was the Prince of Wales with servants to dress him. Drágan made certain to keep eye contact with Isaac to ease his fears, for which Isaac was grateful.

"You looked beautiful out there," Drágan said as he slipped into a colorful vest. "I saw the monitor backstage as I exited the runway."

Isaac's nervousness turned to warmth at the words of this boy who meant everything to him. "So did you. You always look beautiful. You're really popular, you know."

Drágan nodded. "In a superficial way. I only want to be popular with you."

Isaac took his outstretched hand in his and gave it a gentle squeeze. "You are."

The showrunner, a hyper middle-aged man with short, cropped hair and glasses poked his head into the dressing room. "You're on in two."

"Thank you, Mr. Morris," Drágan replied as the man's head vanished like a magician's trick. Still clutching Isaac's hand, he smiled. "Shall we?"

They left the dressing room.

Jack was riveted to the screen whenever Isaac appeared on the runway. His friend looked especially dashing in his final outfit of the show, a fancy tuxedo that had turned him into a young, adorable James Bond.

The girls had been gaga over the entire fashion show, which was now drawing to a close with some gorgeous ladies in evening gowns, but Mr. Givens had left halfway through to work in the kitchen repairing the cabinet hinges.

"Can I ask you something, Jack?"

Jack turned to Nat, who looked worried, biting his lip and furrowing his brows. "Course, Nat."

Nat seemed to have retreated into himself like he'd been for so many years before becoming part of the Throwback Crew. "Are you... well, still in love with Isaac?"

Jack gasped and the girls turned to stare at them with curiosity.

"I mean, you couldn't take your eyes off him this whole night," Nat went on, sounding morose. "He's cuter than I'll ever be and I just wanna know—"

Jack grabbed his hand and pulled it to his chest. "He's not cuter than you, Nat. Yeah, he was my first crush, but I'm with you now and I couldn't be happier. We're perfect for each other. I'm loud and you're quiet."

That drew out a smile out of Nat and the girls applauded with gusto.

Jack leaned in and hugged Nat, who relaxed in his arms.

Jack knew he'd always love Isaac on some level, but Isaac was with Drágan now and that's how it would be. Besides, he and Nat *were* perfect for each other and were growing closer every day.

After changing out of his tuxedo, Isaac's regular mix of vintage and modern clothing felt heavenly. He and Drágan, with help from the support staff, hung up their fancy duds exactly where they'd found them. One of the assistants, a young man in his twenties, smiled shyly, like he wasn't supposed to talk with the models.

"For the male models today, you guys stole the show."

Drágan raised his eyebrows. "Indeed?"

"Oh, yeah, I mean didn't you hear all that screaming from the women?"

"I guess," Isaac said, watching the young man's animated expression.

Mr. Morris, the show runner entered and frowned at the assistant. "No conversing with the models, young man. Find something useful to do."

Mortified, the young man scurried from the room like a frightened rabbit.

Morris's expression turned to one of joy as he gazed at Isaac and Drágan. "You boys lit up the show tonight. Isaac, you're a natural on the runway."

Isaac indicated Drágan with a grin. "I had a good coach."

"He is the best," Morris affirmed with a grin. "I hope to see you both back here soon. Thank you, boys."

With a grin, he ducked out of the dressing room.

"I told you modelling was in your blood," Drágan said with a smile, clutching Isaac's hand.

Isaac shrugged. "It was okay. But all the stuff I heard from people out there made my skin crawl, like I was a plaything they could use anyway they wanted."

Drágan lost his smile. "I have always experienced the same, which is why I prefer photo shoots to fashion shows. However, the money *is* excellent."

Isaac nodded. "Yeah. Now we can pay Dr. Breslin to find a cure. Do you think she can?"

Drágan's handsome face clouded over. "I wish I could say I feel hope, but after five hundred years I must take a wait and see attitude."

"I guess."

"Shall we find mom?" Drágan smiled again. "I imagine she's beyond thrilled."

Isaac grinned and they left the dressing room.

There was much bustling activity backstage as the models emerged from different dressing rooms and mingled. Many chatted with fancy-dressed people Isaac didn't recognize. He searched the crowd for his mom. A middle-aged man approached. He was tall, slim, with dark hair and severe, almost pinched features, wearing a high-end suit and gloves. Isaac didn't recognize him, but Drágan did.

"Good evening, Mr. Foster-King," Drágan said deferentially. "I hope you were satisfied with how we represented your fine clothing."

Isaac was confused. "Wait, you mean..."

"Yes," Drágan affirmed. "Mr. Foster-King designed some of the outfits we wore tonight."

"Oh wow," Isaac said, extending a hand. "It's nice to meet you."

The man eyed Isaac's outstretched hand as though it were diseased.

Drágan cleared his throat and Isaac turned to him. "Mr. Foster-King is one of our employers, Isaac. As hired help, we must maintain our distance."

Humiliated, Isaac felt his face redden and lowered his hand.

"You both acquitted yourselves well this evening," Mr. Foster-King said, his voice staid and without emotion. "I hope to see numerous sales of the clothing you represented."

Isaac said nothing, leaving this to Drágan, who had the experience with people like this.

"I do hope so, sir," Drágan said. "And I hope you'll consider us for future shows."

Mr. Foster-King eyed them as though he be a real king and they mere serfs. "Perhaps."

Another man pressed his way through the crowd and stopped at Foster-King's side. "Bruce, have you seen Timmy?"

Before Foster-King could answer, Isaac gasped, his eyes fixed on the newcomer with horrified recognition. "Dad?"

Learn how Isaac reacts to his long-absent father and the shocking revelations about his family, not to mention the suspicious activities he and Drágan encounter in South Dakota.
Coming Soon: Book 2 of the Forever Saga,
FOREVER BONDS

SPINNER EXCERPT

SPINNER

Excerpt from Book One in
The Healer Chronicles,
SPINNER

Alex fidgeted as he lay in bed and listened to the wind outside. It had been an okay day at school – he'd only been called "Roller Boy" twice, which was almost a world record.

After school, he'd kicked it at Roy's house, and they cranked Hawthorne Heights tunes and chilled. Even Jane hadn't bitched at him.

So why can't I sleep?

He didn't know the answer. His eyes returned to the dancing shadows that flitted across his floor from the window. His drapes were closed, but the wind whistled through the trees, and the shadows mesmerized him. The patterns of light and dark pulled on his eyelids, dragging him sunder. A dream loomed at the edges of his consciousness. One of those dreams. Sleep overcame him, and it began....

Ms. Ashley trudged down a flight of stairs from her second-floor apartment, carrying several overflowing bags of trash. The traffic sounds were omnipresent, but otherwise the night was calm and clear.

A slight breeze ruffled her long brown hair as she slunk to the rear of the complex. Rounding the building, she passed alongside a sloping hill of ivy-covered ground toward the row of trashcans in the far corner.

Looking chilled and unsettled, Ms. Ashley lifted one lid and struggled to get all her bags in without spilling anything.

A rustling noise startled her, and she whipped her head around.

The ivy-covered hill ascended upward into darkness, but there was no movement. Only a creepy silence.

She tossed her bags into the can and dropped the lid back in place with a hollow clang.

A large cat dropped onto the top of the can from somewhere above.

She uttered a startled cry and leaped back a few steps.

The cat meowed and she chuckled, extending one trembling hand.

The animal snuggled against it, wanting to be stroked. She ran her fingers through the fur around the cat's neck and under its chin.

More rustling leaves drew her attention to the ivy.

The darkness in this corner was deep and penetrating, with the vines and leaves snaking their way up the slope barely visible. Another cat materialized from beneath the thick cover of ivy.

Then another. And another.

In seconds, the hillside seethed with cats of all shapes and sizes. Their glowing eyes shone like eerie beacons in the night. The cat beneath Ms. Ashley's fingers hissed and swiped its claws at her, raking the top of her hand and drawing copious amounts of blood.

Startled, she cried out and yanked her hand back, gazing in shock at the dark liquid spilling onto the concrete at her feet.

Her body trembled with fear as she backed away.

The cats crouched on the hillside, poised and threatening.

The one she'd been petting wailed into the night, and then they were on her, leaping and clawing at her face and hair. Hundreds of cats streamed down the hillside and flung themselves at her while the big one sat and watched like a general commanding his troops.

Ms. Ashley screamed, but loud traffic sounds drowned out her cries. Flailing, she turned and stumbled along the side of the building toward the street, crying out for help.

Claws dug into her back and raked across her neck. Teeth sunk into her arm.

She shrieked in agony as they yanked out chunks of her hair and raked at her legs, shredding her sweatpants and digging into her soft flesh.

Blood spilled from everywhere on her body.

The street loomed just ahead. She tossed one cat off in a frantic attempt to save herself, only to have three more replace it. She didn't have much time before she'd topple beneath a tidal wave of claws and fur. A large truck roared up Lincoln Boulevard as Ms. Ashley staggered toward the curb. The headlights were bright and blinding. The biggest cat flew from the retaining wall at her face and gouged a chunk of flesh out of her cheek, exposing the bone. She wailed in agony.

Her knees buckled, but Ms. Ashley managed to stay on her feet while stumbling headlong into the street at a frantic pace.

Suddenly aware that the truck was almost on her, she clutched at the nearest light post in desperation. One bloodied hand caught the post and slowed her momentum as the cats ceased their brutal attack. She gesticulated with her free hand, hoping to attract the attention of the driver. With her urgent gaze fixed on the truck, she didn't see the figure in black leap from behind the retaining wall right at her.

Strong hands pressed hard into her back and propelled her forward. The truck mowed her down in a splatter of blood and gore, flinging her broken body to the pavement and then crushing it beneath massive tires.

As the truck screeched to an ear-piercing halt near the corner, the figure in black melted into the darkness. Several cats sniffed the dead woman's remains before they, too, disappeared into the shadows. The first cat was the last to depart, watching as the horrified driver jumped from the truck cab and pelted toward Ms. Ashley's broken body.

The cat seemed to grin before vanishing into the night....

Alex screamed and bolted upright in bed, hair plastered to his sweat-sheened forehead. Heart thumping with urgent terror, he scanned his darkened room. The door leading outside was closed, but the ominous shadows still crept through the window. His desk was messy as usual, and the door to his bathroom stood ajar, but he'd left it that way. Everything looked like it had before he fell asleep.

Dropping onto his pillow, Alex fought to control his breathing and calm his pounding heart. God, he hated those dreams! Poor Ms. Ashley. He lay there, sweat making his t-shirt cling to his chest as his heart rate drew down. Could this dream be like the one about his parents? It seemed so real!

He lay in bed worrying about the morning, and what he'd find when he got to school.

Gradually, tree branches tapping against the house lulled him to sleep. The last image to assail him before he went under was that ugly- ass cat grinning at him before running off into the dark.

The following morning, Alex regarded himself in the bathroom mirror as he brushed his teeth. He'd showered and blow-dried his shoulder-length, choppy white-blond hair and it looked clean. People liked his blue eyes, when he didn't hide them behind his flowing bangs.

Alex finished pushing the brush up and down his teeth, and spat out the mint-flavored water, staring a moment at his soft, hairless cheeks and milky white skin. Sure, he seemed so innocent, a "sweet-faced boy," as his social workers had always described him to prospective foster parents. That's what made the whole thing worse.

He did look like a nice kid. But no matter how hard he tried, he always screwed everything up. He always started spinning people. He couldn't help it. And once they figured out he was doing something weird, they got scared and wanted nothing more to do with him.

He'd already been through ten foster homes, and the only reason Jane kept him at this one was because she'd figured out what he could do.

"What are you?" he asked his reflection. As always, it didn't answer.

Jane Walters stood at the door with her ear pressed against it, while two boys sat at the kitchen table watching her.

Carlos, a burly high school junior, wolfed down his cereal, while freshman Juan glared with barely contained fury. Carlos grinned at the smaller boy. Juan flinched in fear and Carlos sniggered. Juan's cereal sat untouched in front of him as he reached with trembling fingers to touch his face, wincing at the pain. The left cheek and eye were black and blue and swelling rapidly.

A motorized sound came from behind the door, like a rising elevator.

Jane stepped away and jerked her thumb at Carlos. "You, out!"

Carlos's previous bravado with Juan dropped instantly. He swallowed his final mouthful and leapt from his chair. Snatching up a backpack from the floor, he bolted out the side door, never even glancing at Jane. She regarded the sullen Juan, folding her arms across her chest.

"You know what to do." Her tone left no room for argument.

"What if he don't wanna this time? He said he wouldn't no more."

"You know what'll happen to you if he won't," she snapped.

Juan nodded.

Jane observed her reflection in the large, ornately framed mirror, obviously looking pleased with what she saw.

She turned to him, practically pinning the petrified boy to his chair. "I'll be watching."

The motorized whirring s ground to a halt as Jane darted through the door into the hallway.

The door beside the rectangular dining table popped open and Alex rolled out in his wheelchair, wearing a Hawthorne Heights band shirt, black hoodie, skinny black jeans, his black and white high-top Converse shoes, and a backpack resting on his lap. He had Roy to thank for most of these clothes since Jane never spent a dime on him unless she had to.

He popped a small wheelie and shoved the door closed with a swipe of his hand, and then turned to Juan, whose head was bent toward his cereal bowl. Alex noted the behavior and frowned. It bothered him that he frightened Juan, but he didn't blame the kid. After all, he frightened almost everyone.

"Mornin', Juan," he offered in his most upbeat tone of voice as he dropped his backpack by the door. Was that upbeat? He so seldom felt that way he really didn't know what it sounded like.

"Hi, Alex."

Juan didn't look up. Alex noted the other bowl and half-filled glass of orange juice on the table and frowned.

"Carlos must 'a heard me comin' and bailed, huh?"

Juan said nothing.

Attempting to seem nonthreatening to the younger boy, Alex added, "Left his dishes this time. Jane'll be pissed."

Juan looked up, revealing his bruised face. "You mean 'Mom', right, Alex?"

Alex ignored the correction, gazing in shock at the other boy's battered face. Furious, he wheeled over to Juan. "Did she make Carlos—-?"

Juan cut him off. "I fell, uh, hit the bed table. That's all."

He indicated the mirror on the wall with a slight head nod. Alex caught the movement and looked at Juan, blinking twice in response, his anger roiling.

Juan pleaded, "Alex, could you, you know...?"

His voice trailed off and he looked down at his cereal again. Alex scowled.

"I don't wanna go to school 'n look like this," Juan whispered, focusing his attention on the soggy corn flakes floating in his bowl like dead maggots.

Alex gazed long and hard at Juan. He was fourteen, but looked eleven or twelve, tiny and scrawny with brown skin, short hair, and big, fearful eyes. He wore baggy pants and baggy shirts, but they only highlighted how tiny he was. Had Alex ever seen the boy laugh or grin like a kid should? He didn't think so. But then, he didn't do those things either. How could they, living with a witch like Jane? He leaned in so Juan's head hid him from view of the mirror.

"You mean she don't want you to."

Juan's eyes looked round and filled with panic. "Please, Alex?"

"Aren't you afraid, like the other times?"

He reached out to touch Juan's bruised cheek, but Juan recoiled even before Alex's fingers reached him.

Alex felt that punch to the gut sensation each time someone flinched from him, which was almost everyone, except for Roy and the kids in his class.

"You are afraid. Guess I don' blame you."

Juan flushed red with embarrassment, turning his bruises a brighter shade of purple. "Alex, please?"

Alex sighed with resignation. His frown melted into a look of deep compassion as he brushed his bangs away from his eyes so Juan wouldn't be scared. At least, he didn't think he looked scary. The blue always seemed to calm people.

"Okay," Alex said, steeling himself for the pain to come. "Tell me."

Jane stood in a small closet directly behind the two-way mirror in the kitchen, smirking at the two men beside her. All the kids knew it was there, but they never knew when she might actually be on the other side. Another technique she'd developed to keep them in line. The men wore business suits, and one held a GoPro camera pointing through the glass at the two boys.

"Now watch real close," Jane admonished, though both men were already riveted to the drama playing out in the kitchen.

The younger of the two, Phil, watched intently, as though not surprised by what he was witnessing. As silver-haired Bob lifted the GoPro, his mouth dropped open in stunned disbelief.

Jane grinned as she turned from the boys to eye the two men. Shocked by what he saw, Bob lowered the camera and watched with his own eyes.

"You idiot, keep filming!" Jane snapped, her voice like a firecracker. Bob recovered from the initial surprise and whipped the camera up, continuing to record.

Phil's expression remained unreadable to Jane, but she didn't care.

These men were flunkies. The moneyman was all that mattered.

"Wish we had audio," Phil muttered.

"You'll get it from the other camera," Jane said, directing his attention to the cupboard behind the boys. The door was ajar. From this angle, through the two-way glass, she saw the blinking red light as it recorded.

Phil nodded while Jane watched, grinning at the stunned expressions of the two men beside her.

Through the mirror, she observed Alex spin his black magic, saw the pained expression on his face, and grinned when Juan, now uninjured, stared in wide-eyed fear at the freak beside him.

Yes, you're a freak, Alex, she thought, *but you're a freak who's going to make me rich.*

Alex's eyes remained closed, his features intent as his bruised face returned to normal. Several moments passed before his eyes fluttered open. "Man, Carlos—I mean that table—really hit you hard."

Juan had pulled away from Alex as far as his chair would allow.

His eyes were wide and anxious, and his voice quavered. "Yeah. Well, I… uh, thanks."

He looked down at the table again, obviously afraid to meet Alex's gaze. Alex watched him sadly, and then glanced at the mirror. He scowled at his own reflection.

She was there, probably wearing that evil smile she had. Fighting down the temptation to flip his middle finger at her, Alex turned to Juan.

"C'mon," he said with a heavy sigh. "We gonna be late for school."

He smiled as best he could manage, and Juan nodded. He rose from his chair and snatched his ratty backpack from the floor at his feet. Alex grabbed his own pack and rolled to the door, pulling it open. Juan skirted past him, making Alex feel like he had a horrible disease or something. He'd just helped the boy—for the seventh time already—and Juan was still afraid of him. But Juan's reaction was typical. Unless he spun them afterwards, everyone who saw what he could do pretty much freaked. He rolled outside and yanked the door shut behind him.

Inside the closet, Jane turned to Bob, who continued to run the GoPro even though the kitchen was empty.

"You can stop recording now," she said, folding her arms across her chest.

Bob suddenly realized there was nothing left to film and shut off the camera, staring at Jane with amazement. His face was ashen, as though he'd seen a ghost. Phil's eyes glittered with excitement, which Jane interpreted as astonishment at what he'd just seen.

"A million, remember," she insisted. "You tell him. Not a penny less."

Bob wiped his sweaty palms against his gray dress pants. "Oh, we'll definitely tell him, Ms. Walters. You can count on that."

Jane grinned.

I KNOW WHEN YOU'RE GOING TO DIE EXCERPT

I KNOW WHEN YOU'RE GOING TO DIE

Excerpt from Book One in
The Film Milieu Thriller Series,
I KNOW WHEN YOU'RE GOING TO DIE

I'm ladling out stew to ragged old men, boys in hoodies, and women clothed in layers of dirty, mismatched apparel. They've come to stay the night at one of Skid Row's rescue missions because it's better than a tent or cardboard box on San Pedro Street. I like being here more than I like being at home, so I help every weekend.

I'm chatting with a skinny boy and his mother passing through the line on their way to scarf a hot meal at one of the foldable tables when one of the mission staff taps me on the shoulder.

"Leo, there's a guy in the sleeping quarters asking for you. Said his name is Franklin."

"Thanks," I reply. I don't recognize that name, but I make my excuses to the boy and his mom and hand over my ladling duties to the girl who'd brought me the message.

To get to the sleeping quarters, I walk down a narrow, dark-paneled hall- way with the familiar smell of sweat and unwashed socks. The door to the dorm is open and I step in. It looks like a huge barn with a worn hardwood floor studded with row after row of folding cots. Since it's dinnertime, all the cots are empty except one.

An old man with surprisingly alert eyes lies atop that cot staring at me. Most of the older people who frequent the shelter have rheumy eyes, always moist and often clouded, because they've struggled for so long on the street, and maybe because they have alcohol or drug problems.

"Come here, boy." His voice is raspy and echoes faintly in the cavernous room.

At first, I don't recognize him. True, there are hundreds of homeless on the streets every day, but I've been volunteering on Skid Row since I was fourteen and after almost three years, like I said, I know most of them. I'm thinking that if this guy is a regular, he's passed under my radar.

And yet...

I have seen him, I think. Not here at the shelter. Walking to my car...? Yes! Several times over these past two or three weekends, I've noticed him. He's caught my eye because, every time, he's stared at me so intently it made me shiver. He'd be pretending to rummage through a dumpster, but his eyes would follow me until I got into my car. I confess his gaze made me uncomfortable, but I let it go. I've learned to shrug off such creepy feelings because so many of the people I meet down here have mental health issues.

I steel myself and walk between the rows of empty cots—each with its neat bedroll awaiting an occupant—and stop before the stranger with the scary eyes. Unlike most of the people, his clothes aren't especially dirty, and he doesn't smell like someone who's been on the streets for a long time. Wisps of gray hair stick out from his head at haphazard angles and his face has so many wrinkles I don't think I could count them if I tried.

I don't make eye contact, but that's because I never do. Not here, not anywhere. People tell me I'm the definition of "shy" and they're right.

"You asked to see me, sir?" I say deferentially, my gaze on his gnarled hands.

He rolls over onto his back. "I been watching you, boy. Seen you on the streets a lot."

I freeze. So, I didn't imagine it! "Yeah?"

"Yeah." The voice sounds like sandpaper scraping along a fence. "Rich boy like you helping out poor folk like me. What gives?"

I've been asked this question by all my relatives, so I'm ready with my answer. "I think people like me who are lucky to have a lot should help people who don't. And I hope I'm making the world better instead of worse. The kids I know just party and think about themselves all the time. I don't want to be like that."

A crooked smile cracks the wrinkled face. "You're the one, all right."

"The one?"

With effort, he unclasps his hands with their swollen knuckles and holds his right arm out toward me. It shakes, like he barely has enough strength to keep it aloft. "Take my hand, boy."

Unlike my best friend J.C., who never touches any of the people when he comes with me to the shelters, I usually have no worries about contact. But I hesitate this time. I mean, this guy has been watching me on the streets. But kindness makes me swallow my anxiety and I clasp his hand. He squeezes gently.

"Look into my eyes."

Ordinarily, I'd just glance into his eyes and then look away. But that commanding tone compels me. I raise my eyes and focus on his. They're brown and alert and they shimmer beneath the overhead lights. We lock gazes, and I stiffen. Something I can't quite pin down swells within me, like a surge of emotion. I suddenly feel... different.

All the tension drains from his face in an instant. Relaxed, he releases my hand, pulling his arm back with great deliberation. He rests both hands across his stomach and gazes up at me with obvious gratitude.

"Thank you, boy. Now I can die."

I shudder. "Wha-what do you mean?"

The man offers a gentle smile. "I gave you a great gift, boy. Or maybe a curse. Had it so long, I can't be sure no more. But I couldn't die till I passed it on."

I stand frozen in place, my heart thumping, my breathing on hold. A gift? A curse?

"Uh, pass what on, sir?"

He chuckles and it's a wheezy sound, like he doesn't have much air in his lungs. "Just you calling an old bum like me "sir" proves you be the one."

I feel different inside and his words scare me because I know he's done something to me. "I'm just a regular kid, sir. Nothing special."

That chuckle erupts again, wheezier this time. "Oh, you're more than a regular kid. Like you said, most kids only care about stupid crap like partying. You'll use my gift well." He lapses into a coughing fit that scares me even more.

"Want me to get some help?"

He waves away the idea with one hand. After a few moments, the hacking ceases. "No need. It's my time." He suddenly looks really pasty and gray in the face. "When you find someone worthy, boy, pass on the gift to them," he whispers, his voice very soft and almost inaudible. He closes his eyes and lies still. "Until then, make wise choices."

Then he stops breathing. Literally, just stops. One second his chest is rising and falling and then the next, there's nothing. I want to shake him back to life and ask a thousand questions, but instead I run from the room to get help.

I toss and turn all night, images of the old man's craggy face and piercing gaze filling my dreams. Each time I wake, I hear his scratchy voice repeating the same words over and over again: "I gave you a great gift, boy. Or maybe a curse."

What does that mean?

The next day, when J.C. accompanies me to the mission, he's dressed in designer jeans and a fancy shirt fit for a dance club. Maybe that's why, before we're even finished serving lunch, everyone clamors for him to perform. He's been dancing since he was little and knows so many styles I can't keep track. Dancing and fashion are the loves of his life. He cranks hip hop on his phone and launches into an awesome routine that includes some cool break dance moves, his ebony hair doing its own dance against his forehead as he spins. Everyone is clapping and cheering within minutes.

As I ladle soup into chipped white bowls and pass out fresh rolls, I keep thinking of Mr. Franklin, the old man who died. Everything about that encounter troubles me and I find my mind wandering from J.C.'s performance. To the regular mission staff, death is a common occurrence, almost a daily one. Even I've seen people die down here, but this time was different. Especially the way I felt when I locked eyes with him.

"Make wise choices."

My thoughts are interrupted by raucous applause. The song— most likely from one of those Step Up movies J.C. adores— ends and my best friend stops dancing. Staff, volunteers, and homeless alike shout and clap with gusto.

Sweat beading his forehead, J.C. looks over at me and grins. I grin back and toss him a thumbs up.

After lunch, we head to a nearby McDonald's and buy bags of hamburgers, chicken sandwiches, and fries to give out on the streets. I make momentary eye contact with each person I hand a bag to because I want them to know they're human like me. But I can't hold it for more than a second until, beneath the dim shade of the freeway overpass on Main Street, this one man grasps my arm as he takes his bag. He's a regular named Hank, an older guy with a limp who always wears a dirty Dodgers cap and mismatched clothes I'm sure he found in a dumpster.

"Thank you, Leo." Hank's voice is strained, but sincere.

I force myself to look into his grateful eyes and our gazes lock. I can't seem to look away. It's like I'm being drawn into Hank's very soul. Then I see it! Gasping, I lurch back and yank my arm away from him.

He recoils, looking stung by my action, and I want to apologize, but no words come. I'm paralyzed by what I just saw and can only offer him a silent nod.

Gripping the bag with gnarled fingers, Hank lurches down Main Street until he reaches the corner and turns out of sight.

J.C. steps around in front of me. "Hey, Leo, you okay? You look like you saw a ghost."

"I know... when he's... going to... die." I barely get the words out.

J.C. stares at me. "Huh?"

I shiver, my hand still outstretched from giving Hank the Big Mac and fries. I look down at it—my fingers are trembling. I pull them into a fist and lower my arm to my side.

"Leo?"

I face J.C., but don't meet his gaze, a chill enveloping my body and causing me to break into a cold sweat. "I-I never look people in the eye, J.C. You- you know that, right?"

He tilts his head like I'm crazy. "Duh! What are you talking about, man?" I glance again at the corner where Hank vanished. Homeless people lie on blankets and tarps or on the bare gray sidewalks. Others lounge beside colorful nylon tents or shelters made from cardboard boxes. I know many of these people by name and they know me. Several of the women stare at me with concern. I must look as scared as I feel.

"Yo, Leo, anybody home in there?"

I turn back to J.C. but focus on the lower half of his face. His brow is drawn together, and his mouth is clamped in a straight line. It's a worried look.

I clear my throat. "I looked into Hank's eyes when I handed him the food."

J.C. punches me on the shoulder and grins. "Awesome. That's progress, right?"

I shiver again. Traffic noise and passing cars distract me for a moment and derail my train of thought. I stare at the dimple in the center of J.C.'s chin and whisper, "I saw him dead, J.C."

His mouth drops open. "Huh?"

I shake my head, those horrific images fixed to the backs of my retinas like photographs. "He-he was all bloody and kind of twisted up. I-I couldn't see how he died, but I knew when he died."

He gives me one of his hard looks and then bursts out laughing. "Good one, bro. You had me going there for a sec."

"I'm not joking, J.C. He's about to die!"

I start jogging down Main, but soon I'm running, ignoring the dust I kick up from the sidewalk as I hurry in the direction Hank took. I hear J.C. curse under his breath and then his footsteps as he follows. The homeless ladies touch my shoulder in gratitude as I pass and offer their best, mostly toothless, smiles. I'm too spooked by what I've just seen to return anything but a quick nod.

"Leo, wait up."

I don't slow my stride and feel, rather than see, J.C.'s loping gait alongside me.

As I stop at the corner of Main and one of its busy cross streets, a screech of tires, followed by a loud thud and cry of human anguish, pierces my ears. I break into a sprint.

A crowd is already gathering in front of Marguerite's Place, a Mexican restaurant where I sometimes buy food for people on the streets. Traffic at the intersection has momentarily halted and people clamber out of their cars for a better look. I run to the edge of the crowd and muscle my way through.

A man's voice laments, "The light was green. He just stepped out in front of me!"

My heart rate quickens. A large pickup truck, its bed laden with gardening equipment, has stopped mid-turn onto Main, a line of cars halted behind it. A body lies in the crosswalk. Sirens assail my ears.

"Hey, kid, watch out!" a man says as I push my way past an inside ring of onlookers. I hear J.C toss out a couple of curse words in Spanish and another voice responding, "Puta madre."

I inch my way closer to the pickup so I can get a clear view of the body. I immediately recognize the ragged jeans and baggy flannel shirt. My heart pounds and I can scarcely breathe.

"Leo, what are you—"

J.C. stops in midsentence, and I feel his arm brush up against me, but I don't glance over. My gaze is fixed on Hank's bloody face. The McDonald's bag must've flown from his hand onto Main Street because it's already been crushed by a passing car. Blotches of ketchup adorn the pavement and mingle with the blood pooling from the back of Hank's head. The ratty blue Dodger's cap is splashed with ghastly streaks of red.

"Holy crap," J.C. whispers beside me. "You were right!"

My head feels light. The heat rising from the hot asphalt nearly overcomes me. I foresaw this man's death! My knees grow weak, and I grab J.C. by the arm. He wraps his arm around me, gripping my shoulder so I don't collapse. The wail of sirens gets louder.

J.C. leans into my ear, "Come on, Leo. We should jet."

I stare numbly at Hank's dead gaze and twisted limbs. I feel J.C. dragging me back and finally turn to follow him.

We escape the scene just as the police arrive and hurry back to my car, which is parked blocks away in front of the old Hotel Cecil on Main. Unlike all the other kids at La Costa High who have fancy cars, I drive a three-year- old Prius that has visible parking lot dings on the sides and "only" cloth upholstery, all of which embarrasses my mother like you wouldn't believe.

I feel J.C. slip his hand into the side pocket of my baggy cargo pants to pull out my key fob. He opens the door and eases me into the passenger seat.

"Wait," I mumble. "I'm driving."

J.C. shakes his head. "Not spooked as hell like you are. I'll drive." I nod absently and he sprints around to the driver's side.

He knows me well enough to know I don't want to talk about what happened. Not right now, anyway. We leave downtown L.A. behind us and head back via freeway and palm-lined streets to our beachfront town of La Costa in a heavy silence. He doesn't even crank the mariachi music like he usually does, for which I'm grateful.

My mind replays in an endless loop the encounter with Hank, and the one with Mr. Franklin at the shelter last night—an experience I now kind of understand, but don't really comprehend. I realize the car has stopped moving and I look around. We're already back in La Costa, parked in a space on East Hanley Street with the well-watered green expanse of Beck Park spread out before us. As I gaze through the dirty windshield, it sinks in that I completely zoned out on the ride back.

J.C. kills the engine and sighs in that very dramatic way he has. "Okay, Shy Boy, what the hell happened back there?"

I guess he thinks my town nickname will draw out a smile, but it doesn't. I'm too rattled. He must sense my fear because his tone changes. He places one hand on my arm, so I'll look at him, but I make sure not to do that. Looking at people is the problem. I get that now. I can't look someone in the eye ever again.

Okay, my thoughts are rambling. I take some deep breaths and focus on two young kids tossing around a football in the park, making sure not to look at J.C. "'Member last night I told you about the old guy that died?"

I can almost see him shrug with indifference. "Yeah? That's nothing new for that place."

I nod. "'Cept I didn't tell you what he did first." I pause, the memories flooding in and nearly drowning me under their weight. I tell him everything Mr. Franklin did and said, but J.C. just clucks his tongue in annoyance.

"So, what does that have to do with today?" He obviously hasn't made the connection.

I swallow hard and keep my eyes on that football sailing back and forth across a patch of blue sky between the two boys. "I think he gave me the power to see when people are going to die."

J.C. slaps the steering wheel. "Holy crap!"

I nod.

"We have to test this out." He's acting like I just told him I got a new video game, rather than the power to see death. "Look in my eyes."

I glance over at his eager face in horror and instantly avert my gaze. "Hell, no! I can't know when you're gonna die."

"Why not? If I died today my mom wouldn't even notice."

His voice reeks with contempt and I want to comfort him, but it's the same for me. If I vanished off the face of the earth, my mother might not realize it for months, if ever.

"I'd notice," I whisper, still looking down at the handbrake. "I don't know what I'd do without you."

Silence fills the car. Only the sound of the kids yelling as they toss the football come to my ears. I force myself to look up. J.C.'s mouth hangs open and he has this stunned look on his face. I make sure not to look into his eyes, though.

"Wow," he blurts finally, expelling a gust of air at the same time. "You really mean that?"

I nod.

He breaks into one of his genuine smiles, which he seldom uses for any- one but me, and places a hand on my shoulder. "Thanks, Leo."

Eyes still downcast, I nod again, but I'm too choked up with mixed emotions over everything that's happened and don't know what to say next.

"So, we pick a stranger." J.C. returns his hand to the wheel.

"We know everybody in La Costa."

"Then we go to a liquor store in Lawndale and buy a soda. You look into the clerk's eyes and tell me what you see."

J.C. has a way of making everything sound so easy, so simple. Ordinarily, it's one of the things I really like about him. But this is different. I just know—deep down—that there's nothing "simple" about what that man gave me, and I suspect my life will never be the same again. I want to make J.C. understand, but the feeling inside me is too intangible to put into words, so I just nod, and he starts the engine.